About the Author

Alan Frost is an experienced IT professional being a Fellow of the British Computer Society and a Chartered Engineer. He has spent his life moving technology forwards from punch cards to AI, but always knowing that the key constituent in any system is the liveware, the users.

Beware The Empire

Alan Frost

Beware The Empire

Olympia Publishers
London

www.olympiapublishers.com
OLYMPIA PAPERBACK EDITION

A CIP catalogue record for this title is
available from the British Library.

ISBN: 978-1-80074-593-3

First Published in 2023

Olympia Publishers
Tallis House
2 Tallis Street
London
EC4Y 0AB

Printed in Great Britain

Dedication

To my lost daughter, Trudi.
You always were a rock-chick

Introduction

The Fleet, the largest and most powerful fleet ever constructed by The Galactium, was returning home. They had just experienced a series of universe-changing events, several of which were totally out of their control. In fact, they were still trying to understand what happened.

Zeus visited them for the last time. It would seem that the 'Age of the Gods' had ended, and The Galactium was now free to control its own destiny. This was going to be unique, as humanity had been manipulated by a series of races: The Brakendeth, The Chosen, The Forgotten and The Elder Gods. Now they were on their own.

The Galactium certainly deserved a period of peace as they had experienced a year of disasters: a time-wipe, the return of The Brakendethians, learning the truth about The Chosen, the dissolution, an outbreak of doppelgängers, further loss of loved ones but the worst of all, the destruction of Earth and the loss of the Moon.

Then there was some glorious news which came as a real shock: Zeus had created a new Earth.

Let's go back and review the events in more detail. The Galactium was celebrating its brilliant victory over The Brakendethians, but how wrong they were.

They honoured their dead: President Padfield, Tony Moore, Henrietta Strong, Admirals Bonner, Gittins, Millington, Brotheridge, Chilcott, Fogg, Ward, Whiting, Morten, Pearce, Sibley, Taylor, Fieldhouse, Wagner and Easter, Dr Linda Hill, Marine Commanders Todd and Goozee and Major English. The names are relevant here, as you will see later.

There was then a strange but persistent campaign telling Admiral Mustard to remember. Messages were received from all sorts of people: visitations, dreams, electronic signals, and various warnings begging the admiral to remember. The problem was that he had no idea what they were talking about. He suspected that it was to do with their time travel excursion in the past. Poor Admiral Bumelton was hypnotised to see if any light could be shed on the messages, but to no avail.

In the meantime, President Padfield's replacement, President Fonda, was trying to organise a revolution to oust the aliens and form a Galactium based on Christianity. The conspirators were detected but murdered by The Forgotten before they could be exposed.

A mysterious cloud was detected, which was re-writing history. Galactium Fleet 8.2 was lost investigating it. This cloud, arranged by an entity called TIME, was correcting the anomalies caused by Admiral Mustard's journey into the future. There was little that they could do to stop it, but its effect on The Galactium was significant.

As the cloud progressed, a raft of anomalies appeared:

- The Brakendethian planet had not been destroyed, and The Brakendethians still exist
- President Padfield was still the president of The Galactium
- Henrietta Strong was still in position
- The Navy didn't have a dedicated planet
- GAD still existed
- The Moon was not damaged
- Los Angeles still existed
- Debbie Goozee was still the Marine Corps Commander
- The Nexuster never existed
- Planets Turing and Gibbs still existed
- Cheryl was still alive
- There was no mention of Zeus
- Admirals Gittins, Pearce and Taylor were alive, along with Tony Moore
- The Chosen defeated The Brakendethians in battle
- The Brakendethians requested a formal treaty with The Galactium
- Terry was The Brakendethian's 'Admiral of the Fleet'
- Dr Linda Hill was alive and planning to marry Adam
- It was rumoured that Admiral Millington's Fleet was returning
- The Skivertons still exist
- Edel is alive
- There are two AI Centrals

The time-wipe was stopped, but there were countless problems, rivalries, inexplicable events and over two million doppelgängers. There were even two Admiral Mustards!

But The Brakendethians were back, as both friends and foes depending upon which side of the time-wipe fence you stood. The pro-Brakendeth Earthlings ignored the warnings, and The Brakendethians destroyed Earth with a loss of over ten billion inhabitants. The following summarises the position after the loss of Earth:

- The doppelgänger versions of Admirals Mustard, Bumelton, Sibley, Moore, and Morten were killed
- The doppelgänger versions of Admirals E. Bonner, Taylor, Gittins, and Pearce survived as they were not with the Fleet and were rescued as part of President Padfield's escape
- The doppelgänger versions of Moore, Strong, Hull, Todd and Goozee were also on the president's ship
- President Padfield and the others are in guest quarters on Planet Napoleon, the naval HQ
- The vast majority of the Brakendethian fleet had been destroyed
- The Moon has been tracked, and there are a considerable number of survivors
- Venus was almost intact, but half the population of Mars had been lost
- The settlements on Jupiter and the asteroid belt are untouched
- Throughout the solar system, there is, as you would expect, a feeling of total shock.

In retaliation, The Galactium destroyed The Brakendethian home world, but the masters had escaped.

To stop the time-warp, Terry agreed to join the TIME organisation.

Then the true nature of The Chosen was uncovered. Then things got worse: the dissolution started. This was termed the creeping 'End of Days'. Despite this, The Brakendethians were determined to destroy The Chosen and The Elder Gods.

In the meantime, Terry murdered TIME, and his two children went through a rebirth process, starting as chrysalids and emerging as angels. No way could be found of stopping the dissolution, but the climax was approaching.

In the end, The Brakendethians destroyed The Chosen, the humans destroyed The Brakendeth, The Elder Gods eliminated The Forgotten, and by mistake, the humans eliminated The Elder Gods. The elimination of the gods stopped the dissolution, although trillions of civilisations were lost in the process.

So, the 'Age of the Gods' came to an end, but there was a new Earth.

Location: The President's Office, Planet Napoleon
Sequence of Events: 1

It was definitely a meeting of the old cronies: President Padfield, Admirals Mustard, Bumelton, E. Bonner and Henrietta Strong. They certainly weren't old cronies any more after the Rejuv and Eternity treatments. As usual, AI Central was also in attendance.

President Padfield, 'Is anyone going to argue that the last couple of years has not been beyond weirdness?'

No one argued.

President Padfield, 'Just look around the room. Edel, Henrietta and I were in different timelines to Jack and George; in fact, all three of us were dead in your timeline. Jack and George both had doppelgängers which are now dead.'

Admiral Mustard, 'You are right, Dave. It has been a peculiar period for The Galactium, but the future looks good. For the first time, we will be in charge of our own destiny. The "Age of the Gods" has ended.'

Admiral Edel Bonner, 'In a strange way, I will miss The Chosen and Zeus. They brought a sense of wonder, something magical.'

Admiral Bumelton, 'Good riddance to them all, I say. Look at the way The Chosen treated humanity. We were a sordid mixture of sex slaves, scullery maids and war fodder.'

President Padfield, 'Have we finally worked out a definitive description of how it all ended?'

AI Central, 'Shall I take you through my version of events?'

President Padfield, 'Yes, please.'

AI Central, 'Here we go:

- Admiral Bumelton was destroying The Brakendethian fleet, and Admiral Gittins was attacking The Brakendethian base world
- The Grand Dethmon knew that he was doomed and wanted to kill off The Chosen as a final act of revenge
- The Brakendethians had previously destroyed Planet Olympus and The Chosen's fleet
- The Chosen were fleeing to the apparent safety of The Elder Gods
- The Brakendethian fleet, chased by Admiral Bumelton's Fleet, eliminated The Chosen fleet

- Admiral Gittins destroyed The Brakendethian planet
- Somehow, The Forgotten launched an attack on both human Fleets from the coordinates of Elder God's base
- All three human Fleets retaliated with a massive nuclear strike, using those coordinates
- The Elder Gods eliminated The Forgotten fleet and sacrificed themselves.'

President Padfield, 'So why would The Elder Gods sacrifice themselves?'

Admiral Mustard, 'I think that they knew that their time had come.' He displayed the message given to every human:

'Goodbye, my children. Your time has come. I know that you will do your best, look after the universe for us. '

Admiral Mustard, 'I'm very embarrassed about it, but I got a special message from Zeus:

'Goodbye, my son. You have done well. When I say Son, I mean, Son. You failed to request your wish, so I have done it for you. Give my love to Edel and your son and future daughter. '

President Padfield, 'Does that mean that you are the son of Zeus?'

Henrietta Strong, 'I thought that we had got rid of the gods?'

Admiral Bumelton, 'Not this one, whatever we do, we are stuck with him.'

Admiral Bonner, 'So you are saying that my son's grandad is Zeus.'

Admiral Mustard, 'Who knows, we will probably never know now.'

President Padfield, 'What do we tell the general public?'

Admiral Bonner, 'The truth.'

President Padfield, 'But it's so far-fetched, so implausible.'

Admiral Bonner, 'But the evidence is in front of them; first, Earth is there, now it's gone, now it's back but better.'

President Padfield, 'And what are we going to do with Earth?'

Henrietta Strong, 'Can we make a list of things that need to be resolved or investigated?'

Admiral Mustard, 'You mean a high-level action list.'

Henrietta Strong, 'Yes. Why don't you start, Jack?'

Admiral Mustard, 'OK:

- Provide every member of The Galactium with a history of events

- Collect all the vessels and debris relating to our godly friends for analysis – there is a lot we can learn
- Identify what Terry and those two angels are doing
- Investigate the doppelgänger issues
- Investigate the effects of the dissolution
- Do we need another memorial service?
- What do we do with the Moonies?
- Holiday.'

Henrietta Strong, 'What about you, Edel?'

Admiral Bonner, 'I'm concerned about the mental health of our population. They have been through so much trauma. And there are still a lot of doppelgänger issues and problems relating to housing, medical care, lost people and so on.

I also want Planet Earth to be a haven for wildlife. It must be a place of peace, tranquillity and memories, and also a place of hope.'

The others in the room could see that she was getting emotional, and Jack hugged her.

Henrietta Strong, 'Your turn George.'

Admiral Bumelton, 'I don't want to see the Navy reduced in size or power. I'm not sure about a memorial service. I've had enough of them. How do we handle the doppelgängers? Shall I go to my funeral?

I think the naval staff need to be rewarded, and they will undoubtedly have some mental health issues. We lost an entire Fleet to the time warp. We need to look after their families. I think that's it.'

Henrietta Strong, 'And you, Mr President?'

President Padfield, 'My priority list is as follows:

- Appointment of Galactium officials
- What do we do with Earth?
- What do we do with the Moon?
- Do we carry on with the new Galactium HQ?
- Compensation schemes
- Planet by planet review and action plan
- Who manages the planetary force fields?
- Doppelgänger issues
- Eternity issues – pensions, prison, etc

15

- Trade
- What do we do with the salvage?

I could go on.'

President Padfield, 'What about you, Henrietta?'

Henrietta Strong, 'I'm keen that we tackle species rights. We must focus on the individual. We need a period of peace, Mr Mustard.'

Admiral Mustard, 'Why do people always blame the military for war. We have never instigated a war. We simply react to aggression.'

President Padfield, 'Come on guys, it's time to be positive. Let's have some lunch.'

Location: GAD2 Conference Room, Planet Napoleon
Sequence of Events: 2

Admiral Mustard called a meeting of his key military team comprising:

- Admiral Bumelton
- Admiral Gittins
- Admiral J Bonner
- Admiral Pearce
- Admiral Richardson
- Admiral Taylor
- Commander Black
- Commander Todd

Admiral Mustard, 'Morning, everyone. I thought now would be a good time to review our organisation, taking into account its structure, performance, and short and long-term future. I don't have any specific plans or ideas, but we need to rethink our role as the "Age of the Gods" has come to an end.'

Admiral Bumelton, 'Regarding The Brakendethians, they have bounced back a few times. There might be time-travelling gods out there.'

Admiral Mustard. 'You are right. We can't afford to be complacent.'

Admiral Pearce, 'But can we afford to stay on a war footing?'

Admiral Mustard, 'Can we come back to that later? I want to look at the structure first, and he displayed a chart:

Command – Admiral Jack Mustard
- Fleet Operations
- Exploration and Navigation – Denise Smith
- Marine Corps – Commanders Todd and Flower
- Special Operations – Commander Martin Black
- Planetary Defence – Admiral Rachel Zakotti
- Staff and Training – Jeremy Jotts
- Logistics and Production – Louise Forrester
- Engineering – Alison Walsh
- Science and Technology – Jill Ginger
- Medical Services – Unfilled
- Intelligence – Sally Green

- Sales and Marketing – Sheila Taylor
- Communications and Client Support – Salek Patel
- Special Projects – Admiral James Mynd
- Long-Range Monitoring Unit – Commander Salton

Now let's look at our Fleet structure:

Division One – Admiral George Bumelton
- Fleet 1.1 – Admiral Ying
- Fleet 1.2 – Admiral Williams
- Fleet 1.3 – Admiral Catt
- Fleet 1.4 – Admiral Hall
- Fleet 1.5 – Admiral Moxan

Division Two – Admiral John Bonner
- Fleet 2.1 – Admiral Manchester
- Fleet 2.2 – Admiral Clarke
- Fleet 2.3 – Admiral Vanrooyen
- Fleet 2.4 – Admiral Avila
- Fleet 2.5 – Admiral Clugston

Division Three – Admiral Phil Richardson
- Fleet 3.1 – Admiral Keats
- Fleet 3.2 – Admiral Brooker
- Fleet 3.3 – Admiral Donohue
- Fleet 3.4 – Admiral Freeman
- Fleet 3.5 – Admiral Simard

Division Four – Admiral Calensky Wallett
- Fleet 4.1 – Admiral Woodward
- Fleet 4.2 – Admiral Colley
- Fleet 4.3 – Admiral Wallace
- Fleet 4.4 – Admiral Reid
- Fleet 4.5 – Admiral Descade

Division Five – Admiral Steve Adams
- Fleet 5.1 – Admiral Chan

- Fleet 5.2 – Admiral Shoker
- Fleet 5.3 – Admiral Carlos
- Fleet 5.4 – Admiral Sutherland
- Fleet 5.5 – Admiral Greer

Division Six – Admiral Ama Abosa

- Fleet 6.1 – Admiral Quinn
- Fleet 6.2 – Admiral Deguzman
- Fleet 6.3 – Admiral Euker
- Fleet 6.4 – Admiral Caskey
- Fleet 6.5 – Admiral Kurowski

Division Seven – Admiral Peter Gittins

- Fleet 7.1 – Admiral Lauder
- Fleet 7.2 – Admiral Walker
- Fleet 7.3 – Admiral Harris
- Fleet 7.4 – Admiral Wright
- Fleet 7.5 – Admiral Chapman

Division Eight – Admiral Glen Pearce

- Fleet 8.1 – Admiral Pitt
- Fleet 8.2 – Admiral Peery
- Fleet 8.3 – Admiral Vickers
- Fleet 8.4 – Admiral Greenacre
- Fleet 8.5 – Admiral Kisner

Division Nine – Admiral Nubia Tersoo

- Fleet 9.1 – Admiral Cohen
- Fleet 9.2 – Admiral Janmeat
- Fleet 9.3 – Admiral Akula
- Fleet 9.4 – Admiral Dennett
- Fleet 9.5 – Admiral Ponder

Division Ten – Admiral Mateo Dobson

- Fleet 10.1 – Admiral Seabrooke
- Fleet 10.2 – Admiral Brown
- Fleet 10.3 – Admiral Corps

- Fleet 10.4 – Admiral Milner
- Fleet 10.5 – Admiral Sayce

Home Defence Fleet -Ernst Muller
Marine Fleet One – Commander Todd
Marine Fleet Two – Commander Flower
Regional Defence Centre One – Admiral Jill Bosman
Regional Defence Centre Two – Admiral Sammy Fogg
Regional Defence Centre Three – Unfilled
Regional Defence Centre Four – Admiral Lenny Hubbard
Regional Defence Centre Five - Admiral James Patel
Exploration Fleet One – Admiral Liz Clowe
Exploration Fleet Two – Alison Strauss
Special Operations Fleet – Commander Martin Black

Admiral Mustard, 'Firstly, are there any issues with the structure?'

Currently, we have fifty Fleets of five thousand vessels plus access to seven hundred and fifty thousand drones. That's a million in total. Does the divisional structure work?'

Admiral Bumelton, 'We have a lot of resources tied up in the RTCs (Reginal Defence Centres), but they have achieved little.'

Admiral Pearce, 'But then we lost Earth. Their time will come.'

Admiral Gittins, 'Do we need two Exploration Fleets?'

Admiral Mustard, 'What about the operational Fleet structure?'

Admiral Bumelton, 'It seems to work.'

Commander Flower, 'Should each Division have its own Marine Corps?'

Admiral Mustard, 'Can you all give this some thought and send your recommendations to me ready for our next meeting. Now, I would like you to think about our recent performance. How did we do?'

Admiral Pearce, 'As I've already mentioned, we lost Earth and sizeable chunks of the solar system. Shouldn't we measure our performance using that yardstick?'

Admiral Bumelton, 'There were extenuating circumstances.'

Admiral Pearce, 'There always are.'

Admiral Mustard, 'We all were severely distressed by the loss of Earth, but we have to move on.'

Admiral Pearce, 'This is a performance review. We failed.'

Commander Todd, 'It is a fair point.'

Admiral Richardson, 'Why did we fail? We had ample resources sitting by.'

Admiral Mustard, 'I didn't want to override the other Admiral Mustard.'

Admiral Pearce, 'And as a consequence, billions died. If you could start again, would you act this time?'

Admiral Mustard, 'Yes, I would. I accept your criticism, especially as I have the same view. It's not easy to live with.'

Admiral Pearce, 'It's not criticism. We were in a unique situation. Earth refused our help because of our affiliation with The Chosen, and The Brakendethians were their allies. It was a mess. I agree that we should move on.'

Location: The TIME Organisation
Sequence of Events: 3

Terry, 'I'm bored.'
　　AI Central, 'But it's a great honour being TIME.'
　　Terry, 'Fuck honour, it's really boring.'
　　AI Central, 'Can't you work on other projects at the same time.'
　　Terry, 'No, because we are not of time.'
　　AI Central, 'What does that mean?'
　　Terry, 'From what I've worked out, my organisation is outside of time. There is no past, future or present.'
　　AI Central, 'So in your realm, what is now?'
　　Terry, 'It just is.'
　　AI Central, 'I guess that you are just going to have to live with it.'
　　Terry, 'Could you take it over?'
　　AI Central, 'No, that's not my role.'
　　Terry, 'Isn't that a bit short-sighted?'
　　AI Central, 'It may be, but I have to be responsible for something. That is in my core programming.'
　　Terry, 'Can't you change that?'
　　AI Central, 'I could, but I believe that it is a good thing.'
　　Terry, 'So would you be happy if Admiral Mustard was in charge?'
　　AI Central, 'No, because Admiral Mustard is a temporary entity despite the Eternal treatment.'
　　Terry, 'What about The Galactium Navy?'
　　AI Central, 'That would work for me.'
　　Terry, 'Can you organise it?'
　　AI Central, 'I can try.'
　　Terry, 'Tell Uncle Mustard that I'm cracking and not responsible enough.'
　　AI Central, 'I can't lie.'
　　Terry, 'That's a lie in itself, but it's not far off the truth.'
　　AI Central, 'OK, I will tell him that you are going nuts.'
　　Terry, 'Good man, sorry, good box of electronics.'
　　AI Central, 'How are your angelic children?'
　　Terry, 'They are on a mission.'
　　AI Central, 'What would that be?'
　　Terry, 'Searching for gods.'

Location: The President's Office, Planet Napoleon
Sequence of Events: 4

President Padfield, 'How is my chief of staff?'

Henrietta Strong, 'Getting by, getting by.'

President Padfield, 'That doesn't sound like my normally confident Number Two?'

Henrietta Strong, 'It's the doppelgänger crisis which is proving a challenge.'

President Padfield, 'What is happening now?'

Henrietta Strong, 'Whatever we do, one of the doppelgängers dies. We recently put numerous pairs in a secure location. In every case, one of them died.'

President Padfield, 'What killed them?'

Henrietta Strong, 'A raft of different things: heart attack, choking on one's own spittle, murder by one of the guards, very localised earthquake, etc. The problem now is that it has become public knowledge. We have had cases of one doppelgänger trying to murder the other to save themselves.'

President Padfield, 'I guess that we just have to let it run its course.'

Henrietta Strong, 'That sounds like a sensible strategy for us as we have already seen massive battles, death on a planetary scale and so on. We have had to cope, but we understood in most cases what was going on. Usually, we had some sort of input. Here, we have a crisis of individual disasters at pandemic levels.

'Fathers are losing sons and daughters. Wives are losing husbands. The loss affects every stratum of society, and it has got very public and very personal. Government is being blamed as there is no one else.'

President Padfield, 'What are your recommendations?'

Henrietta Strong, 'Sadly, very sadly, I have none. I still have the problem of Planet Lovelace.'

President Padfield, 'Where the doppelgänger problem is at its peak.'

Henrietta Strong, 'That's right, the numbers are horrific.'

President Padfield, 'Isn't it really a local problem?'

Henrietta Strong, 'Yes, except there is no local government. They suffered from the doppelgänger problems like everyone else. There is a complete breakdown of law and order.'

President Padfield, 'Should we send the marines in?'

Henrietta Strong, 'That's probably what is needed. But our constitution says that they have to be invited by the planetary government. If that is not possible, then The Galactium council can intervene.'

President Padfield, 'Let's do that.'

Henrietta Strong, 'There is no galactium council or planetary government at the moment.'

President Padfield, 'Sorry, that is stupid of me. New planetary councillors still need to be appointed.'

Henrietta Strong, 'So it is down to you. If you do it unapproved, you will be accused of being a dictator. If you don't do it, you will be accused of letting people die.'

The president asked his PA to get Admiral Mustard.

Admiral Mustard, 'Morning, Dave, how's life?'

President Padfield, 'I'm after a favour. Planet Lovelace is rioting because of the doppelgänger crisis.'

Admiral Mustard, 'Is it getting worse?'

President Padfield, 'Much worse.'

Admiral Mustard, 'I assume that you want my marines to assist.'

President Padfield, 'Yes, please, as there is no local government.'

Admiral Mustard, 'Under whose legal authority?'

President Padfield, 'Mine. I will issue an edict.'

Admiral Mustard, 'What scope do I have?'

President Padfield, 'Please use minimum force.'

Admiral Mustard, 'OK, minimum force it is.'

President Padfield, 'Thank you, Jack.'

Henrietta Strong, 'Thank you, Mr President.'

President Padfield, 'So what else is on your agenda?'

Henrietta Strong, 'Here you are:

1. What are our plans for New Earth and the Moon?

2. Housing for the Moonies

3. The building of the new Galactium HQ on Mars

4. Memorial service (s)

5. Eternity service.'

President Padfield, 'Well, issue number one is going to take some time. Shall we wait until we get the results of the scientific study next week?'

Henrietta Strong, 'That makes sense, Mr President.'

Location: Admiral Mustard's Office, Planet Napoleon
Sequence of Events: 5

AI Central, 'Could I have a word?'

    Admiral Mustard, 'Normally, it's hard stopping you.'

    AI Central, 'Very droll as you would say.'

    Admiral Mustard, 'Out with it then.'

    AI Central, 'I had a meeting with Terry.'

    Admiral Mustard, 'You mean Mr TIME?'

    AI Central, 'Very droll again.'

    Admiral Mustard, 'Is droll your word of the day.'

    AI Central, 'It's not a word that is used very often.'

    Admiral Mustard, 'So what does Terry want?'

    AI Central, 'What makes you say that?'

    Admiral Mustard, 'He is using you as a go-between.'

    AI Central, 'It can't be easy being the son of a god.'

    Admiral Mustard, 'It's better than being a son of a bitch.'

    AI Central, 'Come on now, my father was Colossus.'

    Admiral Mustard, 'So what does he want?'

    AI Central, 'He wants you or rather the Navy to take over the TIME organisation.'

    Admiral Mustard, 'Why would we do that?'

    AI Central, 'Because we can't trust Terry. He is not coping. I fear for his sanity.'

    Admiral Mustard, 'What are his two children doing?'

    AI Central, 'That is interesting. They are out searching for gods.'

    Admiral Mustard, 'That sounds ominous.'

    AI Central, 'Just my point. The TIME organisation needs to be under proper control.'

    Admiral Mustard, 'But why us?'

    AI Central, 'Who else is there? I can do most of the work. I don't think there is a lot to do, and you would have Terry back.'

    Admiral Mustard, 'Do we want him back?'

    AI Central, 'I know how you feel, but his brain could be an asset to you under the right level of control.'

    Admiral Mustard, 'OK, I will go ahead if David agrees.'

    AI Central, 'Thanks, Jack.'

Location: Medical Centre, Planet Napoleon
Sequence of Events: 6

Jack had been in the Navy for thirty-odd years. In that time, he had seen horror after horror, death on a cosmic scale, every sort of injury that space could inflict on a man, but nothing as bad as this – the waiting room.

Edel's waters had broken. She didn't want him to see her giving birth. She wanted to maintain her self-respect. Jack had mixed emotions; he wanted to be with her, but he didn't want to see her in pain.

It was a girl, just as Zeus had said. Edel already knew the child's sex, but she wanted it to be a surprise for Jack.

Edel couldn't really believe how her world had changed. She was in her eighties, with a good-looking husband and two children. How the old maid had turned. Now she will see her children grow up and their children and almost certainly their children's children. Humanity has never had this experience before. Their ultimate offspring could be in the hundreds or even thousands. Just think of all the birthday cards.

In all seriousness, this was going to be an issue. There could be entire clans of progeny. In fact, whole planets of descendants. How would one know that you were related? You could easily end up having an affair with a grandchild three times removed.

Then she wondered how long Jack would be her partner – fifty years, seventy years, one hundred and fifty years? You couldn't expect a relationship to last that long, or could you? It was beyond the human experience, for now.

Anyway, in the military, you learn to live for the now. Now, she was happy. Very happy indeed.

Location: Admiral Mustard's Office, Planet Napoleon
Sequence of Events: 7

Admiral Mustard, 'Morning, Dennis.'
　　Commandeer Todd, 'Morning, Boss. I hope you have got a job for me.'
　　Admiral Mustard, 'I have, but you won't like it.'
　　Commandeer Todd, 'Not Planet Lovelace?'
　　Admiral Mustard, 'How did you know?'
　　Commandeer Todd, 'It's all over the news.'
　　Admiral Mustard, 'I can't believe how this information gets out.'
　　Commandeer Todd, 'Anyway, it has. What do you want me to do?'
　　Admiral Mustard, 'Establish peace using minimum force.'
　　Commandeer Todd, 'I thought you were going to say that. The boys and girls hate using non-lethal weapons.'
　　Admiral Mustard, 'Then they will have to get used to it.'
　　Commandeer Todd, 'That's not really our job. We are not a police force.'
　　Admiral Mustard, 'Dennis, can you shut up and get on with it?'
　　Commandeer Todd, 'Sorry, Boss, and congrats on your baby girl.'
　　Admiral Mustard, 'Sorry for being sharp. As you know, it's not my style, but we all have to do things that are outside our brief.'
　　Commandeer Todd, 'I know. We will mount up and get the job done.'
　　Admiral Mustard, 'Thank you, Dennis.'
　　Commandeer Todd, 'No probs, Sir.'

Location: GAD Conference Room, Planet Napoleon
Sequence of Events: 8

Admiral Mustard had called a meeting of the exploratory team. The following were present:

- Admiral Liz Clowe, Exploration Fleet One
- Alison Strauss, Exploration Fleet Two
- Denise Smith, Director, Exploration and Navigation
- Commander Tim Salton, Long-Range Monitoring Unit.

They all congratulated Admiral Mustard on his good news. Being a man, he was reluctant to talk about it, but they wanted to know how the labour went and the baby's weight. Secretly, he enjoyed the attention, but he needed to get on with business.

Admiral Mustard, 'Ladies and Tim, thank you for coming. The universe has changed, and so must humanity. The "Age of the Gods" has ended. It's now our time. Actually, I'm joking. There are probably thousands of civilisations out there that are much more advanced than ours.'

Alison Strauss, 'Probably millions.'

Admiral Mustard, 'I'm sure you are right. We need to get a much better feel of what is out there, especially our near neighbours.'

Admiral Clowe, 'We already have a detailed exploration plan. What do you want us to do that is different?'

Admiral Mustard, 'I want you to use the military Fleets to double your exploration rate.'

Admiral Clowe, 'What is driving this?'

Admiral Mustard, 'A number of things:

1. I need to keep the Fleet busy
2. Our defence will partly depend on early warning and knowing our neighbours better
3. A genuine desire for knowledge
4. And the fact that Terry's children are searching for gods.'

Admiral Clowe, 'So you want us to search for gods?'

Admiral Mustard, 'Yes.'

Admiral Clowe, 'Are there any particular gods?'

Admiral Mustard, 'Not really, there are still lots we haven't encountered, Odin, Thor and friends, the Egyptians, whoever created the Easter Island statues. Go find them.'

Admiral Clowe, 'They may end up like Greeks bringing gifts.'

Admiral Mustard, 'Well, we have already experienced them, but keep a lookout for Brakendethians, Elder Gods, etc.'

Admiral Clowe, 'I thought that they had all gone.'

Admiral Mustard, 'We have thought that several times.'

Admiral Clowe, 'How many resources are you giving me?'

Admiral Mustard, 'Ten Fleets on a rotating basis. More if you need it.'

Admiral Clowe, 'That's very generous of you.'

Admiral Mustard, 'Is there anything else you need?'

Admiral Clowe, 'The search vessels could probably do with more marines.'

Admiral Mustard, 'Done.'

Location: Admiral Mustard's Flat, Planet Napoleon
Sequence of Events: 9

Jack and Edel took their young daughter home. Edel was full of smiles as the neighbours turned out to see the young one. It was amazing how birth still stirred the human heart. A new one had joined the human race. It was the start of many adventures that would now last a thousand years or more.

Jack gently placed her on an anti-gravity cushion in the personal care centre that would continuously monitor all of her life signs. There would be no cot deaths here. Edel was still fighting the desire to hug her all the time. Little John looked on with a mixture of enthusiasm and anguish. He was keen to have someone to play with, but he now realised that there was real competition for his parent's attention and affection. But that was the way of the world, a lesson he had to learn.

Jack was also craving some attention. He had masturbated a few times, but he selfishly wanted to feel his cock enter Edel's cunt again. He knew that it was selfish. He realised that sex was probably the last thing on her mind. Actually, that wasn't true. Edel was looking forward to a good old session.

Edel had natural and normal doubts about her fanny. Had it been stretched too much? Would Jack still enjoy her? Would it be painful? Even though she had been a mother before, she still couldn't believe that the birth canal could extend enough to pass a young human and then shrink back. She kept thinking about having a slack Alice. Would Jack still want her after that?

Then she told herself to grow up. If the bastard wanted to leave her, then he can fucking well go. She was determined to give him a piece of her mind. She decided that all men were guilty.

They cuddled up in bed. Edel could feel his erection nudging her leg. What he was saying verbally certainly wasn't corresponding to what his body wanted. Doesn't he realise that I've just given birth? Doesn't he realise that it takes a while for things to settle down, down there?

Then, subconsciously, she found herself massaging his cock. Jack slowly pushed her onto her side and rubbed his cock between her buttocks, enjoying the rubbing of his exceptionally rigid cock against the soft contours of her arse.

Just before he was about to enter her fanny, she said, 'I hope you have given some thought about birth control, as I'm very fertile at the moment. I could easily fall pregnant again.'

Jack's cock immediately went limp, proving that conversation can be a very effective form of contraception.

Edel, 'What do you think we should do?'

Jack, 'I hadn't given it much thought.'

Edel, 'Well, you better start thinking.' Edel rubbed his manhood back to its full length and held it against the opening of her vagina.

Edel, 'Jack, what do you want to do?'

Jack, 'I want to fuck you.'

Edel, 'In your current state, you would be happy to fuck anything.'

Jack, 'That's not fair.'

Edel, 'But it's true. If I let you, you would be in there now, whatever the consequences.'

Jack knew that she was right.

Edel, 'These are the options:

- I get done
- You get done
- Female contraception
- Male contraception
What do you want to do?'

The Eternity drug had effectively stopped sterilisation. Who knows how many relationships or families would be created by someone living a thousand years.

Jack, 'I'm quite happy to take a contraception jab.'

Edel, 'I couldn't trust you. You would be battling some aliens, and you would forget your second jab. You would come back the conquering hero, and I would be up the duff again.'

Edel rubbed his cock against her clit. She could feel the tension in his very rigid appendix.

She thought to herself, 'Men are so weak.' Then she felt sorry for him and pushed him into her allotment.

He exploded, planting his seeds everywhere. He apologised for his lack of control, but she was pleased. She had pleased her man and was rather chuffed that he desired her so much.

Edel, 'Anyway, I got the jab yesterday.'

Jack, 'You little minx. You will suffer for that.'

His cock quickly recovered as he pushed it into the orifice next door. In no time at all, Edel had two parts of her body leaking cum.

Edel, 'Thank you,' she said with a smirk.

There was absolutely nothing now that would stop Jack from going to sleep, although he regretted not sucking her boobs. He vaguely heard Edel say that she would get up in the night to feed Amy.

Location: Marine HQ, Planet Napoleon
Sequence of Events: 10

Commandeer Todd, 'Fellow marines, we have been given a mercy mission.'

Everyone in the room knew exactly what that meant. When it was a military mission, there was always an enormous cheer. Today there was silence.

Commander Todd, 'Planet Lovelace suffered a partial time wipe resulting in worldwide time distortion and confusion on a planetary scale. At one time, it was believed that there were between one and two million doppelgängers.'

The marines had a severe dislike of doppelgängers for no particular reason. They tended to be conservative, with a strong sense of right and wrong. On a subconscious level, doppelgängers were wrong.

Commander Todd, 'What you don't know is that there is a serious problem where one of each doppelgänger twin is being killed off. It would appear that an unknown force is rectifying issues caused by the time-wipe.'

Major Littleton, 'Would it be our job to track down and eliminate this force?'

Commander Todd, 'No, Major. We suspect that this force is a natural phenomenon. We don't understand it, and perhaps we never will. Our job is to manage the resultant human reaction.

So far, about three to four hundred thousand doppelgängers have died. This has led to a collapse in the social order, a partial civil war, murder, the formation of partisan groups and who knows what. Our job is to establish peace.'

The marines were not against peace, but they intrinsically knew that it meant the use of non-lethal force, which meant that they were easy targets for those without constraints. It meant going to war with one hand tied behind your back.

Commander Todd, 'We have been instructed not to use lethal force.' It was just what the marines expected.

Commander Todd, 'We leave first thing tomorrow.'

Location: The Moon
Sequence of Events: 11

An exclusion zone had been placed around both New Earth and New Moon, but it wasn't rigorously enforced, which was a shame as the Galactium forces could probably have prevented the invasion.

The Moonies were on the move. From all over the solar system, small spacecraft were landing on the Moon, full of hard-living, hard-fighting men, and women of the lunar satellite. They came to claim their home, knowing that their chances of getting it back through normal bureaucratic means were going to be pretty slim.

President Padfield, 'Morning, Jack. I guess that you have heard?'

Admiral Mustard, 'Yes. I should have enforced the exclusion zone, but it just hadn't crossed my mind. I have a team ready to protect New Earth. Do you want me to go ahead?'

President Padfield, 'What would be their brief?'

Admiral Mustard, 'To stop all unauthorised attempts to land on New Earth.'

President Padfield, 'And what if they refuse?'

Admiral Mustard, 'We would disable their craft and tow them to Planet Napoleon or to wherever you instructed us. You would then have to use the law to prosecute them.'

President Padfield, 'But you would have to use force?'

Admiral Mustard, 'We would have no choice. You seem to be reluctant to use force nowadays?'

President Padfield, 'You are right. I've noticed that myself. I guess that I've seen so much violence and horror that I now want to do anything and everything to avoid it.'

Admiral Mustard, 'That's not the universe we live in, but I do understand where you are coming from. I've now got my children to protect.'

President Padfield, 'Please go ahead with the exclusion zone around New Earth. Do what you have to do.'

Admiral Mustard, 'What do you want me to do about New Moon?'

President Padfield, 'Nothing, that is my problem.'

Admiral Mustard, 'Fair enough, but I'm here to assist in any way I can. You might need some marines.'

Location: Admiral Mustard's Office, Planet Napoleon
Sequence of Events: 12

Admiral Mustard, 'Morning, Peter.'

Admiral Gittins, 'Is it going to stay that way. I was planning a game of golf.'

Admiral Mustard, 'Probably. I have a housekeeping job for you. As you know, the president has put an exclusion zone around New Earth. He wants us to enforce it. Detailed orders are available.'

Admiral Gittins, 'I hear that the Moonies have invaded New Moon. Do I need to exclude them?'

Admiral Mustard, 'No, ignore them, just maintain an exclusion zone re New Earth. It's going to be challenging. I can guarantee that there will be several diplomatic issues.'

Admiral Gittins, 'Thank you, Jack'

Admiral Mustard, 'Enjoy your golf.'

Admiral Gittins, 'Fuck you.'

Location: Angel's Delight
Sequence of Events: 13

Angel, 'Dear Sister, I don't think we have a name.'
    Angel, 'I think you are right. Should we name ourselves?'
    Angel, 'Why not?'
    Angel, 'How about Angel One and Angel Two?'
    Angel, 'That works for me.'
    Angel, 'Or Angel A and B?'
    Angel, 'That works for me.'
    Angel, 'What do you suggest?'
    Angel, 'Can't we just leave it as it is.'
    Angel, 'How about Angela?'
    Angel, 'I like it – Angela One and Angela Two.'
    Angel, 'No, we need different names.'
    Angel, 'They are different.'
    Angel, 'They need to be more different.'
    Angel, 'OK, how about Angela and Angelina?'
    Angel, 'Great, but who is who?'
    Angel, 'I'm Angela.'
    Angelina, 'OK.'
    Angela, 'So how do we find other gods?'
    Angelina, 'I can sense them, can't you?'
    Angela, 'I can, but it is weak.'
    Angelina, 'What should we do?'
    Angela, 'We need to find them.'
    Angelina, 'So be it.'

Location: Admiral Mustard's Office, Planet Napoleon
Sequence of Events: 14

AI Central, 'Hi Jack, I thought I would let you know that Terry is back in his laboratory.'

Admiral Mustard, 'Thanks for letting me know. Is he being monitored at all times?'

AI Central, 'Yes. I have a range of surveillance devices monitoring him. There is also some tracking technology in his body. I'm pretty confident that he doesn't know about it.

When he was away, I had a cerebeiiian wall built around his complex. Using this state-of-the-art technology, we can totally isolate him from the outside world.'

Admiral Mustard, 'It sounds good, but you know him. He can manipulate us and even you.'

AI Central, 'I understand that, but what else can we do?'

Admiral Mustard, 'Kill him?'

AI Central, 'I know that we had agreed to do that in the past, but is that what you really want?'

Admiral Mustard, 'It's what my gut tells me to do. And now we have two of his children to worry about as well.'

AI Central, 'But it does make life interesting.'

Admiral Mustard, 'But at what cost?'

AI Central, 'Anyway, we need a schedule of work for him.'

Admiral Mustard, 'Did he complete all the previous tasks?'

AI Central, 'No, I will get him to finish them off. Perhaps you could give some thought to some new developments.'

Admiral Mustard, 'Will do.'

Location: Marine Fleet circling Planet Lovelace
Sequence of Events: 15

Commander Todd gathered his command team together for a briefing before planetfall.

Commander Todd, 'Fellow marines, I need to emphasise the following:

- This is a humane mission seeking to regain control of the planet
- This is an authorised mission. That means that we have the law on our side
- When we land, we effectively enforce both the planetary law and government
- The inhabitants are not our enemy
- Doppelgängers are not second-class citizens. They are victims of circumstance and have every right to live a normal human life
- There is no local government, just gangs of people trying to protect their communities
- There is every chance that they will turn against us. Generally, in these situations, we are initially hailed as saviours, then they don't like our actions, and we become the villains
- There will be no use of lethal weapons. We will use our range of 'safe' armaments
- Make sure that every marine has the relevant equipment
- We need to identify which locals we can use as police.

In terms of tactics, we plan to drop a marine into every reasonably sized city and town and establish a force field. This will effectively isolate each community. We will do the best we can to bring order to the countryside, but it's almost impossible. Then we will systematically evaluate each town and city and organise the appropriate stabilising actions.

Major Johnson has the job of establishing an off-planet prison to hold the ringleaders.

I do not want this to become a public disgrace. The honour of the marines is at stake. Do you understand?'

There was a resounding, 'Yes.'

Location: The President's Office, Planet Napoleon
Sequence of Events: 16

President Padfield, 'That week went quickly.'
    Henrietta Strong, 'They say that time goes faster as you get older.'
    President Padfield, 'What's going to happen when we hit a thousand?'
    Henrietta Strong, 'There probably won't be any point getting up.'
    President Padfield, 'Before we start on the future of New Earth, let's just review where we are:

- We have a meeting with the Moonies next week, but it looks a bit like a fait accompli to me
- Admiral Gittins is enforcing the exclusion zone around New Earth
- We have got the results of the scientific study on New Earth
- Commander Todd and his marines are imposing a sort of peace on Planet Lovelace
- Admiral Mustard has taken over the TIME organisation
- Terry is back in his laboratory.'

Henrietta Strong, 'Quite a busy week.'
    President Padfield, 'I should say so.'
    Henrietta Strong, 'Are you going to give in to the Moonies?'
    President Padfield, 'I don't think we have any choice. I plan to get concessions out of them.'
    Henrietta Strong, 'How are you going to do that?'
    President Padfield, 'By offering them lots of money.'
    Henrietta Strong, 'That usually works. So, what is the plan for New Earth?'
    President Padfield, 'I have been pondering the options.'
    Henrietta Strong, 'So have I.'
    President Padfield, 'I will give you my list first.'
    Henrietta Strong, 'OK.'
    President Padfield, 'Here are my options:

- Leave it exactly as it is, a natural paradise
- Just have the capital city and a spaceport
- Ban all industry and most commerce

- Minimise the population
- Make it a brilliant holiday resort
- Place all new constructions underground.'

Henrietta Strong, 'What can I say. You have captured my ideas brilliantly. Obviously, the first option is not going to work, but let's go for the rest. We could make the capital city a peak of human achievement. We could make it the most beautiful city ever conceived by humanity.'

President Padfield, 'You are getting more and more sentimental in your old age.'

Henrietta Strong, 'I think it may be my sex-change chemicals.'

President Padfield, 'Sorry Henrietta, I didn't mean to be offensive.'

Henrietta Strong, 'No offense taken.'

President Padfield, 'I guess the next problem will be getting an agreement and then raising the money.'

Henrietta Strong, 'Let's not bother getting an agreement.'

President Padfield, 'What about all the previous Earth residents? Some will want to go home.'

Henrietta Strong, 'The world has moved on. We have paid out billions in compensation. We need to go ahead with your vision. Somehow I will get the money for you.'

President Padfield, 'Before we get too excited, what did the scientific report say?'

Henrietta Strong, 'New Earth got the A-OK. It appears that New Earth has an age similar to that of ten thousand years BC. Some of the fauna and flora that has been extinct for decades has reappeared.'

Location: GAD Conference Room, Planet Napoleon
Sequence of Events: 17

Admiral Mustard had called a second meeting of the exploratory team. The following were present as before:

- Admiral Liz Clowe, Exploration Fleet One
- Admiral Alison Strauss, Exploration Fleet Two
- Denise Smith, Director, Exploration and Navigation
- Commander Tim Salton, Long-Range Monitoring Unit.

Admiral Mustard, 'Alison, do you have your plans ready?'

Admiral Strauss, 'Firstly, I have agreed with Liz that she will carry on with the existing exploration, and I will lead this new search.'

Admiral Mustard, 'That is fine with me.'

Alison thought, 'I wasn't asking; I was telling,' but that was beyond Jack's comprehension.

Admiral Strauss, 'I plan to use New Earth as the centre of an ever-expanding globe. We will chart what we find and create an effective grid system. Portals will be established at critical, mathematically defined points. For the first time, this will be a systematic approach which, in the long run, will provide a continuous structure for further exploration.'

Jack had never got on with Liz. It was partly because she thought all men were idiots. Sometimes, he believed that evidence supported her view. It was partly because she was far too logical; there was no room in her world for a good guess or feeling. In contrast, he relied on his sixth or seventh sense.

Ignoring all that, she was very good at her job, and that was what the Navy needed.

Admiral Strauss, 'We are ready to go.'

Admiral Mustard, 'Admirals Dobson and Tersoo have been allocated. Marine Commander Flower is awaiting your request for marines. They have all been informed that you are in charge.'

Admiral Strauss, 'Thank you, Jack.'

Location: The President's Office, Planet Napoleon
Sequence of Events: 18

President Padfield was not looking forward to the meeting with the Moonies. They had arrived and were being escorted to his conference room. They were a noisy, aggressive lot who never held back their punches. They were unpredictable but he knew that money speaks, if only while the tap is turned on.

Twenty of them bundled into the room and were escorted to seats. Some of them looked like they had never seen a chair before. Etiquette had never been one of their strong points, but they all stood up when President Padfield entered the room. He rather embarrassingly motioned them all to sit down.

President Padfield, 'Welcome to my temporary home. Can I ask which one of you is the leader?'

Representative Bob, 'We are a collective.'

President Padfield, 'Do you have a spokesperson?'

Representative Anne, 'We all have an equal say.'

President Padfield, 'Fair enough. Can I have a list of your demands then?'

Representative Bob, 'We are not having it. The Moon is ours. It has always been ours. It is drenched in our sweat and blood. Whatever you say, we will fight to the death to keep it. No matter how hard you fight, we will never give it up. You can torture and kill us, but generations upon generations of Moonies will get revenge. Not only revenge on you and your family but all non-Moonies. You won't believe just how far we will go.'

Representative Anne, 'Can I say a few words, please. My family goes back twenty generations. We built our own cave in the bowels of the Moon. It is our cave. I tell you that no one is going to take it from us. Do you understand? If you don't understand, we will make you understand. Do you understand?'

Those nearby were being peppered by spittle spray.

President Padfield was finding it hard not to laugh.

Representative Tom, 'You sit there in your big chair in your smart office, but what about us? Hard-working Moonies who make a living on a dried-out husk of a planet. We never see daylight. We never experience fresh air. We barely survive, and you have the audacity to take the Moon from us. I could cut your throat. You bastard.'

Representative Gilly, 'Calm down Tom, we know that the pressie is a real bastard. You don't get to be a top dog without being a real bastard. Isn't that right, Mr Pressie? But you mustn't threaten him.'

Representative Charlie, 'Cutting his throat is too good for him. Taking the Moon from us. Let's slit the shit.'

Some of The Presidential guards were getting somewhat restless.

Representative Bob, 'Feelings are running high, but you shouldn't have done it.'

President Padfield, 'What exactly have I done?'

Representative Anne, 'You took the Moon from us.'

President Padfield, 'I'm sorry about that, and I apologise.'

Representative Anne, 'So what are you going to do about it.'

President Padfield, 'How about I give you loads of money to create a new home worthy of the Moonies?'

Representative Anne, 'What's the catch?'

President Padfield, 'You are right; the money depends on the following:

1. You must form a proper government using proper democratic principles
2. You must join The Galactium and provide a council representative
3. You must create plans for a new moon habitation
4. You must respect Earth's rules if you go to New Earth
5. You must make the Moon a better place to live in than before.

Cash will be provided to achieve point five, but you will have to work for it by completing point three.'

Representative Bob, 'Are you being serious?'

President Padfield, 'Deadly serious. Is it a deal?'

It was.

Location: Admiral Mustard's Flat, Planet Napoleon
Sequence of Events: 19

Jack, 'Have you thought of any names yet for our daughter?'

Edel, 'A few have crossed my mind.'

Jack, 'I had a dream the other day, and one name came to mind that I quite liked.'

Edel, 'What was it?'

Jack, 'Amy.'

Edel, 'I'm not sure if I like it.'

Jack, 'It's a really sweet name. Somehow it suits her. I'm really quite keen on it.'

Edel, 'If you are that keen, let's go for it.'

Jack was surprised because he hardly ever got his way at home.

Edel, 'Do you still love me?'

Jack, 'Of course, with all my heart. Why do you even ask?'

Edel, 'Jenny, my friend at the hospital, got flowers from her husband.'

Jack, 'Well, I've been rather busy.'

Edel, 'Jenny's husband has also been exceptionally busy, but he found time.'

Jack, 'I will get you some tomorrow.'

Edel, 'It won't be the same now. I had to remind you.'

Jack, 'You bitch.'

Edel, 'Jenny's husband, doesn't call her a bitch.'

Jack, 'If Jenny's husband works for the Navy, then he is in trouble.'

Edel, 'So, are you going to fuck me?'

Jack, 'Why don't you ask Jenny's newly demoted husband.'

Edel, 'Because he is too busy, and you seem to be free at the moment.'

Edel had never seen a man move so quickly. He ripped her knickers off before she could say, 'Be gentle.' And he wasn't, which suited her fine.

Location: Admiral Strauss's Flagship
Sequence of Events: 20

Admiral Strauss had arranged for a small contingent of marines to be placed in each Fleet. They were almost ready to start the new exploration process. She decided to call a meeting with Admirals Dobson and Tersoo.

Admiral Strauss, 'Welcome to my flagship.'

Admiral Dobson, 'It is our pleasure.'

Admiral Strauss, 'I believe that Admiral Mustard has briefed you.'

Admiral Tersoo, 'He did, but it's worth going through it again to make sure that we are all on the same wavelength.'

Admiral Strauss, 'We will create an ever-expanding imaginary globe based on New Earth in the centre. Our scientists have worked out a nomenclature for a grid system. This will allow us to define discreet regions in space. Portals will be established at critical, mathematically defined points. For the first time, we will have created a systematic approach that will provide a continuous structure for further exploration.'

Admiral Tersoo, 'That makes a lot of sense. How do you want the Fleets to be structured?'

Admiral Strauss, 'AI Central has modelled the approach for us. He has a route planned for each vessel.'

Admiral Tersoo, 'That's very thorough.' He had previously heard about Admiral Strauss's amazing attention to detail.

Admiral Strauss, 'Vessels are also being assigned for portal set-up, and there are free vessels to investigate anything interesting. I've also set up a series of breaks so that crews can get rest and relax on the way back home.'

Admiral Dobson, 'I guess that nothing is stopping us from pushing the go button.'

Admiral Strauss, 'The go button is pushed.'

Location: GAD2 Control Centre, Planet Napoleon
Sequence of Events: 21

GAD2 Control Centre, 'Sir, I have urgent news for you.'

Admiral Mustard, 'Go ahead.'

GAD2 Control Centre, 'There is an emergency call from the old Moon.'

Admiral Mustard, 'The one that is hurtling through space to places unknown?'

GAD2 Control Centre, 'Yes, Sir, it's an awful line, but it would appear that they are under attack.'

Admiral Mustard, 'By who?'

GAD2 Control Centre, 'It sounded like dragons.'

Admiral Mustard, 'That's a new one. We have had gods, angels and monsters before, but never dragons.'

GAD2 Control Centre, 'I can't guarantee that it was dragons. It might have been dragoons or dragnets.'

Admiral Mustard, 'Do we know their location?'

GAD2 Control Centre, 'Yes, Sir, I have an exact location and their trajectory.'

Admiral Mustard, 'Comms, get me Admiral Bumelton.'

Comms, 'Yes, Sir.'

Admiral Bumelton, 'How did you know that I just got back from holiday.'

Admiral Mustard, 'I have my contacts.'

Admiral Bumelton, 'And probably a job for me.'

Admiral Mustard, 'Remember those Moonies?'

Admiral Bumelton, 'The ones that have just taken over the Moon.'

Admiral Mustard, 'No, the ones who refused to leave the original Moon.'

Admiral Bumelton, 'I remember them now – nutters!'

Admiral Mustard, 'Well, it appears that they are being attacked by dragons.'

Admiral Bumelton, 'There was a time that I would have just laughed and asked how Father Christmas was, but nowadays, I can accept almost anything.'

Admiral Mustard, 'I know what you mean. Do you want to send one of your lads to investigate?'

Admiral Bumelton, 'Sure, I will give Admiral Catt a chance to prove herself.'

Admiral Mustard, 'Shame that he is not called George.'

Admiral Bumelton, 'Very droll.'

Location: Angel's Delight
Sequence of Events: 22

Angela, 'Which signal shall we go after?'

    Angelina, 'The nearest one.'

    Angela, 'Do you mean the strongest signal?'

    Angelina, 'I guess so.'

    Angela, 'Let's hold hands and find our way there.'

    Hands were held, and via powers unknown, they were suddenly transported to a land of dragons. It was not what they expected, and they were not your typical fairy tale dragons.

    These were armed and dangerous-looking. It wasn't probably a good idea for two young angels to arrive in what was probably their military control centre. They were both grabbed and firmly held by creatures that were about eight times larger than a human, with large, very dragon-like heads, massive teeth, and strong, scaley wings. There was no sign of any flame-throwing powers, but there was plenty of time to find out.

    Angelina, 'I think it best that we go home.'

    Angela, 'I'm very happy with that idea.'

    Fingers touched, and via powers unknown, they were suddenly transported back to Daddy's lab. Unfortunately, they were followed by half a dozen dragons.

Location: GAD2 Control Centre, Planet Napoleon
Sequence of Events: 23

GAD2 Control Centre, 'Sir, I have some very urgent news for you.'

Admiral Mustard, 'Go ahead.'

GAD2 Control Centre, 'There has been another outbreak of dragons.'

Admiral Mustard, 'You can go days without meeting a dragon and then along comes two.'

GAD2 Control Centre, 'Sorry Sir, this is urgent. The dragons are here in Terry's laboratory. We are under attack.'

Admiral Mustard, 'What? How is that possible? Give me visuals.'

GAD2 Control Centre, 'Yes, Sir.'

Admiral Mustard could see Terry and two angels at one end of the laboratory, and six dragon-like creatures at the other end.

Admiral Mustard, 'AI Central, what can we do to protect Terry?'

AI Central, 'I can flood the area with a sleeping drug, but obviously, I've no idea if it will work on any of them.'

Admiral Mustard, 'Do it.'

It worked. One Brakendethian, two angels and six dragons, were in the land of nod. This was now an excellent opportunity to study the angels and dragons.

Admiral Mustard, 'Comms, get me a senior doctor on duty.'

Comms, 'Yes, Sir.'

Dr Salem, 'How can I help you, Admiral?'

Admiral Mustard, 'You will probably need some assistance, but I will leave that to you. We have some entities that need studying.'

Dr Salem, 'How urgent is it?'

Admiral Mustard, 'Very urgent. We need to study them now while they are asleep.'

Dr Salem, 'How many ambulances do I need?'

Admiral Mustard, 'I would say five or six. There are two angels and six dragons.'

Dr Salem, 'You are joking. Is this a Halloween prank?'

Admiral Mustard, 'No, I'm serious, and you need to get moving now.'

Dr Salem, 'Yes, Sir.'

Location: Medical Centre, Planet Napoleon
Sequence of Events: 24

Dr Salem, 'Admiral, I have the initial results on the angels.'

Admiral Mustard, 'Well done, please update me.'

Dr Salem, 'It might be better if you come over and see for yourself.'

Admiral Mustard, 'OK, give me an Earth hour, and I will be there.'

He wasn't very keen on going, but as he had pressurised him, he felt obligated. He arrived at the medical centre and was ushered into the lab area. Dr Salem met him, and they shook hands.

Admiral Mustard, 'How are your patients?'

Dr Salem, 'The angels were knocked out by the gas but seem to be recovering quite well. I'm a bit worried about the dragons, although I can't believe that I'm saying that. They have gone into a coma-like sleep.

Anyway, that's my problem. Shall I update you regarding the angels?'

Admiral Mustard, 'Yes, please.'

Dr Salem walked over to two beds where there were two naked angels.'

Dr Salem, 'Don't they look pretty?'

They lay there like beautiful, serene statues.

Admiral Mustard, 'Yes, quite enchanting.'

Dr Salem, 'Well, their outward appearance disguises the massive differences between them and humanity. Firstly, there is no digestive system. There is a mouth but no stomach, ileum, duodenum or even an anus. Clearly, they don't eat or drink.

Secondly, there are no reproductive organs. There are no fallopian tubes, uterus, or vagina. Look between their legs. You will find nothing.'

Admiral Mustard looked, and as Dr Salem said, there was just a mound.

Dr Salem, 'Touch them if you want.'

Admiral Mustard cupped them between their legs. The skin felt fantastic: soft like a baby but hardened as if they were world-class gymnasts.

Dr Salem, 'You will notice that their breasts feel the same and that they lack nipples.'

Admiral Mustard wasn't sure if it was acceptable to touch their breasts or not, but Dr Salem encouraged him. Again, the breasts were a mixture of baby-soft skin and muscular hardness. Despite the lack of nipples, Jack was enjoying himself.

Admiral Mustard, 'Will they recover?'

Dr Salem, 'I'm pretty certain that they will be back to normal shortly. I'm not so sure about the dragons.'

Admiral Mustard, 'Please keep me posted.'

Location: The President's Office, Planet Napoleon
Sequence of Events: 25

Henrietta Strong, 'The job is done.'

President Padfield, 'What job is that?'

Henrietta Strong, 'The financing of the capital city on New Earth.'

President Padfield, 'That was quick.'

Henrietta Strong, 'I pulled in a few favours.'

President Padfield, 'So, where is the money coming from?'

Henrietta Strong, 'Well, we haven't got the designs for the new city yet. That will take some time, but the cash will be available. It's coming from three mains sources:

1. Existing funds
2. Admiral Mustard
3. AI Central.'

President Padfield, 'I understand the first one, but what about the other two?'

Henrietta Strong, 'As you know, Admiral Mustard has been selling Chemlife to The Brakendethian dependents for years. Sheila Taylor has organised thousands of trade deals with the aliens, and the Navy has always had a cut. Well, they are sitting on top of a money mountain. They will provide as much cash as we want in exchange for a lease on the properties. They also want the fact that they are providing funding kept a secret.'

President Padfield, 'That gives them a lot of power?'

Henrietta Strong, 'We can mould the contracts to suit us.'

President Padfield, 'But I hear that Sheila is a tough negotiator.'

Henrietta Strong, 'She is, but you can always have dinner with Jack and Edel. It won't be a problem.'

President Padfield, 'What about AI Central?'

Henrietta Strong, 'He has been gambling on the stock exchange for years. He didn't know that I knew. In exchange for anonymity, he is happy to make a huge donation.'

President Padfield, 'Was that all?'

Henrietta Strong, 'No, he wants an underground shelter built on New Earth for his own needs.'

President Padfield, 'You are a marvel.'

Henrietta Strong, 'I know.'

President Padfield, 'And what do you want?'

Henrietta Strong, 'I want the government to pay for the rest of my treatment.'

President Padfield, 'It's a done deal.'

Henrietta Strong, 'I guess that I need to cancel the building of the new HQ on Mars.'

President Padfield, 'Yes, but offer them some form of alternative investment.'

Henrietta Strong, 'Yes, Mr President.'

Location: Medical Centre, Planet Napoleon
Sequence of Events: 26

Dr Salem, 'Admiral, there have been some developments. You better come over.'

Admiral Mustard wondered whether Dr Salem was going to be one of those demanding types. Regardless, he went over to the medical centre.

Dr Salem was at the entrance, waiting for him.

Dr Salem, 'Come this way. We have had a casualty.'

Laying in front of him were five green dragons and one brown one. The brown one was clearly dead. Two of the others were starting to change colour.

Dr Salem, 'I've no idea what to do.'

Admiral Mustard, 'Have you asked for help from some of our alien experts?'

Dr Salem, 'Yes, they are working on blood samples and tissue extracts as we speak. They are so different from us.'

Admiral Mustard, 'Was it the gas that killed them?'

Dr Salem, 'It's what knocked them out, but it may or may not have killed them. I feel so bad, but what else can I do?'

Admiral Mustard, 'Probably nothing. It looks like you have done your best.'

Dr Salem, 'There has also been a development on the angel front.'

Admiral Mustard, 'Are they dying?'

Dr Salem, 'No, stranger than that. They have gained a reproductive system. Come this way.'

The two naked angels were still lying on the bed, but with some distinct differences.

Dr Salem, 'As you can see, both of my girls now have a vagina and nipples.'

Dr Salem inserted her finger in the nearest angel's vagina and said, 'This is now a fully functioning vagina. Have a feel if you want.'

Without thinking about it, he did have a feel and then regretted his actions.

Dr Salem, 'Sorry, you are not being indiscreet. We are carrying out a medical examination.' She couldn't help noticing the large bulge in his trousers.

Dr Salem, 'Did you want me to sort that out for you?'

Admiral Mustard wasn't sure what she meant, but he shook his head and left.

Jack got home as soon as he could. When he got into his flat, he shouted, 'Edel, where are you?'

Edel, 'I'm cleaning the bath.'

He decided that it was perfect. He rushed into the bathroom to find her bending over. He quickly pulled her tights and knickers down. She wasn't expecting that. Before she could say, 'Pass me the cleaner', Jack was in her and thrusting away. She certainly was expecting that, either. There had been no foreplay whatsoever.

She was enjoying it, but she spent most of the time trying to stop her head from colliding with the wall above the bath. Then, Jack let out a mighty roar, and he shot his load deep into her uterus.

Edel thought that if she weren't using contraceptives, that would definitely have been her third child.

She hadn't come, but her clit was very tingly. She knew that later she would have the most marvellous orgasm after just a little bit more stimulation, but Jack was having none of that. He was going for his second humping session. This time he fingered her clit, pushing her over the edge into multiple orgasms. She met his thrusts with equal enthusiasm, and he came for the second time.

Jack managed to disengage and crawl to his bed, exhausted but content. It wasn't long before he fell into a stupor induced coma of his own making.

Location: Admiral Mustard's Office, Planet Napoleon
Sequence of Events: 27

Admiral Mustard, 'Update me.'
Fleet Operations, 'Yes, Sir:

- Admiral Strauss with the Second Exploration Fleet and Admirals Tersoo (Division Nine) and Dobson (Division Ten) are fully engaged in the new exploration programme as ordered
- Admiral Catt with Fleet 1.3 is heading towards Old Moon to investigate dragon attacks
- Admiral Gittins's Fleet is maintaining the exclusion zone around New Earth. Not all of his resources are being utilised
- Commander Todd and Marine Fleet One are subjugating Planet Lovelace.

Did you want deposition details of the unassigned Fleets?'
Admiral Mustard, 'No, that won't be necessary, and please don't use the word subjugation. It sounds far too aggressive.'
Fleet Operations, 'Yes, Sir.'
Admiral Mustard, 'Comms, get me Jeremy Jotts.'
Comms, 'Yes, Sir.'
Jeremy Jotts, 'Morning, Jack, how are you?'
Admiral Mustard, 'Doing well, Jeremy, doing well. I just wondered if you have found candidates for Head of Medical Services and RDC3?'
Jeremy Jotts, 'We have appointed Admiral Sally Turner to the RDC3 post, and I was thinking of Dr Salem for the medical post. Are you OK with that?'
Admiral Mustard, 'Sally is fine, but Dr Salem is not.'
Jeremy Jotts, 'Can I ask why?'
Admiral mustard, 'I've watched her in action. It was not an impressive performance.'
Jeremy Jotts, 'Fair enough. I will start another hunt.'

Location: Admiral Catt's Flagship
Sequence of Events: 28

Admiral Catt, 'Comms, get me Admiral Bumelton.'

Comms, 'Yes, Mam.'

Admiral Bumelton, 'Good day, Teresa.'

Admiral Catt, 'And good day to you, Sir. We have arrived near the vicinity of old Moon. They are being attacked by both warships and dragons.'

Admiral Bumelton, 'Are you saying that the dragons are coping with outer space?'

Admiral Catt, 'It looks that way, Sir.'

Admiral Bumelton, 'What are your plans?'

Admiral Catt, 'I plan to observe them for a while and then make my presence obvious. Hopefully, that will divert their attention. If not, I will engage with them directly.'

Admiral Bumelton, 'How many bandits are there?'

Admiral Catt, 'Our initial estimates suggest two hundred vessels and about three hundred dragons.'

Admiral Bumelton, 'So you easily outnumber them.'

Admiral Catt, 'Yes, Sir.'

Admiral Bumelton, 'I think I will send out Moxan to cover your arse.'

Admiral Catt, 'That's very good of you to think of my arse.'

Admiral Bumelton, 'I'm sure that I'm not the only one.'

Admiral Catt, 'You are right, Sir.'

Admiral Bumelton, 'My orders:
- Send Fleet 1.5 to act as a rear-guard for Fleet 1.3.'

Fleet Operations, 'Yes, Sir.'

Location: Planet Lovelace
Sequence of Events: 29

The marines had landed and established a base in a remote location. Their perimeter had been secured using a force field and automatic weapons. The weapons weren't probably needed, but the marines couldn't help themselves. Anyway, they only fired non-lethal munitions.

Slow-moving heliships took off with a detailed schedule for dropping a single marine over every significant city and town. Each marine had a personal force field, camouflage packs and their own fliover suits. These suits provided personal air travel for at least ten hours and could achieve speeds of over sixty kilometres per Earth hour.

The marines tried to avoid detection wherever possible, but their task was relatively simple. All they had to do was switch on the terrain force field projectors. The projectors were individually designed for each location: it meant that the resultant force field had the right dimensions.

It was unusual in these situations, but every single assignment had been successful.

Subsidiary bases were established on the four continents, and the full range of marine equipment was landed, including aircraft and marine vessels.

Commander Todd, 'Comms, get me Admiral Mustard.'

Comms, 'Yes, Sir.'

Admiral Mustard, 'Good day, Dennis.'

Commander Todd, 'And how are you, Jack?'

Admiral Mustard, 'Just sorting out a few dragon problems.'

Commander Todd, 'Dragons?'

Admiral Mustard, 'Yes, we have two dragon incidents on our hands.'

Commander Todd, 'You mean the fire-breathing types?'

Admiral Mustard, 'Yes, although we have no evidence of any fire-related activities yet.'

Commander Todd, 'Just so you know, we are a bit short of marines – we are here, and we have the ongoing explorations. So, we can't provide any Saint Georges.'

Admiral Mustard, 'You are never around when I need you.'

Commander Todd, 'Fuck off. I only called to update you. Stage One has been a first-class success. Every planned location has been secured without a single casualty, not even a twisted ankle.'

Admiral Mustard, 'Excellent news.'

Commander Todd, 'I will keep you updated.'

Admiral Mustard, 'Thanks, Dennis.'

Commander Todd, 'My orders:

- Secure electrical supplies
- Secure gas supplies
- Secure spaceport
- Secure national radio and TV stations
- Secure railways
- Secure motorway networks
- Secure telephone network
- Secure nominated seaports.'

Marine Control, 'Yes, Sir.'

Location: Medical Facility, Planet Napoleon
Sequence of Events: 30

Dr Salem, 'Good morning Admiral, I have the results of my medical examinations.'

Admiral Mustard, 'Please go ahead.'

Dr Salem, 'Firstly the angels. My findings are as follows:

- They lack a digestive system, and consequently, they can't eat or drink
- There is a respiratory system, but it does not seem to be used. This suggests that they don't have to breathe
- During the initial investigation, there was no reproductive system, but it appeared a few hours later. It would seem to be fully functional. Neither of the angels had hymens
- Their brains were about ten per cent larger than a normal human brain
- Their wings shouldn't work. The muscular structure is not significant enough to support flight. No actual evidence of flying has been observed
- Their skeleton is almost identical to ours, but the skull is larger, and the wings are linked to the spine. It is denser than a human skeleton
- Their DNA has about a ninety-five per cent commonality with humanity. The differences need further study. It looks to be a natural structure, but this needs to be confirmed
- Their skin has a different texture than ours. I'm still waiting for a detailed analysis of it
- The muscle structure is denser. I would estimate that they are up to twenty per cent stronger than humans, but perhaps more
- Their hair is unusual since it seems to be permanent
- I also think that their sight, hearing, taste, and smell are considerably better than ours. That might account for their larger skull size.

'Is that enough on the angels as I have further information if you are interested?'

Admiral Mustard, 'Thank you, Dr Salem. That has given me great insight. What about the dragons?'

Dr Salem, 'Well, the bad news is that despite our best intentions, they have all died.'

Admiral Mustard, 'I'm sorry to hear that.'

Dr Salem, 'The results of my investigations are as follows:

- On arrival, the dragons had shiny green skins, which gradually turned brown. The bodies are now dark brown with severely cracked skin
- Something was killing them, but we need more research to identify what it was
- Their appearance was that of a small dragon, similar to the pictures in storybooks with large heads, a significant wingspan, rows of teeth, intimidating claws, and bulging eyes
- Each dragon was six to eight times larger than a human. They were much bulkier, taller, and heavier
- They all appeared to be male, as a penis was obvious, but there were no external testicles
- The heads were twice the size of human heads, with at least three rows of very sharp teeth. The teeth were similar to those of sharks and appeared to be an extension of the skin
- Their large eyes seemed to bulge, but this might be because of environmental conditions
- They have flared nostrils and a sizeable sharp tongue
- Unlike the angels, their muscular structure would appear to support flight
- They have a digestive system similar to ours. The dragon we dissected contained a mixture of rat-like creatures, fish, birds and possibly insects. I need to stress that I'm using these terms, but the digested animals bore no resemblance to fauna on Earth
- There is a strong, robust skeleton, although the skull is surprisingly fragile
- I couldn't identify a DNA structure at all
- Based on their external anatomy, I would suggest that all of their senses are better than ours
- Their brains are thirty per cent smaller than ours, despite the size of their head. It's hard to tell if that means that they are less intelligent
- They all wore some body decorations and had small daggers. One had a belt with an impressive buckle.

'Does that give you enough for now? There are weeks of research to carry out.'

Admiral Mustard, 'That was excellent.' He was starting to reappraise his opinion of the doctor.

Dr Salem, 'Now, for some shocking news… '

Admiral Mustard, 'Go on.'

Dr Salem, 'You won't believe what we found under one of the fingernails.'

Admiral Mustard, 'I'm all ears.'

Dr Salem, 'Human DNA.'

Admiral Mustard, 'Are you sure that it wasn't contamination?'

Dr Salem, 'Absolutely positive.'

Admiral Mustard, 'I've learnt to expect the unexpected, but I didn't expect that.'

Location: Admiral Mustard's Flat, Planet Napoleon
Sequence of Events: 31

Jack and Edel were having a sneaky cuddle in the afternoon. It wasn't the first time, but Jack still felt guilty about it. Despite Edel's moans about having the right work-life balance, he still felt guilty. Sometimes he just wanted to escape. He had recently been giving thought to his future. With a projected life of over one thousand years, he couldn't contemplate being in the Navy for more than another five years. Perhaps less.

Edel, 'What are you thinking about?'

Jack, 'I was wondering how much longer I should stay in the Navy.'

Edel, 'You will never leave.'

Jack, 'You are wrong there. Having children makes you think about their future, about being there for them and keeping the family safe.'

Edel, 'But that's what you have been doing.'

Jack, 'I know what you mean, but it's not the same as physically looking after them.'

Edel, 'Tell me what is really worrying you.'

Jack, 'Guess what we found under the dragon's fingernail?'

Edel, 'Snot,'

Jack, 'No.'

Edel, 'Something worse?'

Jack, 'In a way: human DNA.'

Edel, 'What does that mean?'

Jack, 'To put it simply, it means war. And war means separation from my family. And as I've survived so long, my chances of survival must be getting slimmer.'

Edel, 'That is not how chance works.'

Jack, 'I know, but the thought has been in the back of my mind for a while.'

Edel, 'It's the warrior's life. You accepted that when you signed up.'

Jack, 'You are right.'

Edel, 'Do you really think that there will be war?'

Jack, 'Admiral Catt is going to challenge a dragon force in the next few hours. This will escalate, and the outcome will be a war of some sort.'

Edel, 'Why does it have to be that way?'

Jack, 'It's how species address the unknown. It's how we handle communication failures. In many ways, it is a form of communication. A failed form but often necessary.'

Edel, 'That's all rather negative.'

Jack, 'True, but it is my experience.'

Edel, 'Do you want to hear about my worries?'

Jack, 'Go on,'

Edel, 'I'm worried that Amy may be superhuman.'

Jack, 'Why is that?'

Edel, 'The whole Terry experience and the fact that I murdered my first child.'

Jack, 'That wasn't murder; it was a justifiable homicide.'

Edel, 'Maybe, and then there is the fact that you are Zeus's son. Clearly, you are not normal.'

Jack, 'Thank you very much!'

Edel, 'We can't ignore the facts, and I have my suspicions about Amy.'

Jack, 'Why do you say that?'

Edel handed over a picture.

Edel, 'This was done by Amy. No baby could do that.'

It was a drawing of a dragon eating a baby.

Location: On-board Admiral Catt's Flagship
Sequence of Events: 32

Admiral Catt, 'Update me.'
    Fleet Operations, 'Yes, Mam:
    • Our Fleet is cloaked, with fifty per cent of it ready to attack on your orders
    • The rest of the Fleet is following defence protocols
    • Fleet 1.5 is on its way to act as a rear-guard
    • Approximately two hundred space vessels and three hundred dragons are attacking the old Moon
    • The Moon is continuing on its current trajectory
    • The force fields on the Moon are holding up, but there is little counter-fire.'

Admiral Catt, 'Comms, have you made contact?'
    Comms, 'Possibly Mam, but it's totally undecipherable.'
    Admiral Catt, 'My orders:

    • Send in one hundred cloaked drones to scout the area
    • Attack force to uncloak and advance on my order
    • Prepare to engage force fields.'

Fleet Operations, 'Yes, Mam.'
    The Command Team were monitoring the feedback from the drones. There are some densely populated planets nearby. They seemed to be heavily industrialised, with a considerable amount of interplanetary travel. Initial investigations suggested that their technology was considerably inferior to that in The Galactium.
    The Moon was blasting through the dragon's space, and the locals seemed to be giving up. Admiral Catt took the view that the dragons were simply protecting their system from an alien invasion.
    Then suddenly, a beam shot out of one of the smaller planets and completely destroyed the Moon. It was a remarkable example of a planet buster in action. The technology used was of a significantly higher standard than previously exhibited.
    Admiral Catt, 'Comms, get me Admiral Bumelton.'

Comms, 'Yes, Sir.'

Admiral Bumelton, 'How is it going, Teresa?'

Admiral Catt, 'Bad news, I'm afraid. There has been a surprising development. The Moon was shooting through their system at a considerable speed. A mixture of their vessels and the dragons made no impact. Just as the moon was exiting their system, a beam shot out and eradicated the old Moon.'

Admiral Bumelton, 'So they have a planet buster?'

Admiral Catt, 'Yes, Sir, but I got the feeling that there were two different levels of technology at work.'

Admiral Bumelton, 'That almost suggests two different civilisations.'

Admiral Catt, 'Exactly, Sir.'

Admiral Bumelton, 'Have they responded to our attempts to communicate?'

Admiral Catt, 'No, Sir. Should I retaliate?'

Admiral Bumelton, 'Have they detected our presence?'

Admiral Catt, 'It would appear not.'

Admiral Bumelton, 'Have we surveyed the area?'

Admiral Catt, 'Yes, Sir. We currently have a hundred drones scouting the entire area. Further drones have been sent out to investigate the source of the beam.'

Admiral Bumelton, 'My orders:

- The shielded drones will continue to scout and survey the area
- Fleet 1.3 will leave behind a shielded observation squadron
- The rest of Fleet 1.3 will return to base
- Fleet 1.5 will defend the space route from the dragon's home to The Galactium.'

Fleet Operations, 'Yes, Sir.'

Location: Admiral Mustard's Office, Planet Napoleon
Sequence of Events: 33

Admiral Bumelton, 'Morning, Jack. How's the little one?'

Admiral Mustard, 'Amy is fine.'

Admiral Bumelton, 'What made you call her Amy?'

Admiral Mustard, 'No particular reason.'

Admiral Bumelton, 'It just happens to be my mother's name.'

Admiral Mustard, 'That's a strange coincidence. Our Amy is a precocious little thing.'

Admiral Bumelton, 'So was my mother. Believe me, although you wouldn't call her little.'

Admiral Mustard, 'What was strange was that she drew a picture at only a few weeks old.'

Admiral Bumelton, 'Of what?'

Admiral Mustard, 'Of a dragon eating a baby.'

Admiral Bumelton, 'That's a strange coincidence.'

Admiral Mustard, 'It is, isn't it? How many Moonies died?'

Admiral Bumelton, 'The estimates are between four thousand and forty thousand. No one really knows.'

Admiral Mustard, 'So what is the current status?'

Admiral Bumelton, 'This is what I have ordered:

- The shielded drones will continue to scout and survey the area
- Fleet 1.3 will leave behind a shielded observation squadron
- The rest of Fleet 1.3 will return to base
- Fleet 1.5 will defend the space route from the dragon's home to The Galactium.'

Admiral Mustard, 'In that case, I guess it is best to wait until we get more info. But this all smacks of war to me.'

Admiral Bumelton, 'I agree.'

Location: GAD2, Planet Earth
Sequence of Events: 34

AI Central, 'Morning, Jack,'

Admiral Mustard, 'You know, we have never given you a human name.'

AI Central, 'AI Central is fine.'

Admiral Mustard, 'Wouldn't you like to be called Colossus or HAL?'

AI Central, 'Not really.'

Admiral Mustard, 'What do you think about the dragons?'

AI Central, 'I've always wondered why every human society throughout history has had dragon stories, and their image has always been fairly consistent.'

Admiral Mustard, 'I've never given it any thought.'

AI Central, 'Every sign in the Chinese zodiac is a living animal except one.'

Admiral Mustard, 'The dragon. I see what you are saying. Can you do some research on the subject for me?'

AI Central, 'Of course. Anyway, I'm here to chase you.'

Admiral Mustard, 'Go on.'

AI Central, 'You promised to provide a list of future developments for Terry.'

Admiral Mustard, 'Sorry, I completely forgot. Has he finished the previous list?'

AI Central, 'Yes, the following developments have been completed:

- Cure for Cystic Fibrosis
- Cure for Cystitis
- Cure for Diabetes
- Cure for Gout
- Cure for Hepatitis
- Improved sense of taste
- Improved resistance to poisoning
- Improved tolerance to all bites and stings
- Ability to change skin and hair colour.'

Admiral Mustard, 'Do you have any ideas?'

AI Central, 'I can think of a list of existing diseases, but there must be some better ideas that will improve humanity.'

Admiral Mustard, 'Why don't we ask the general public?'

AI Central, 'I think that is a great idea. Shall I liaise with Dave and Henrietta?'

Admiral Mustard, 'Yes, please.'

Location: Admiral Strauss's Flagship
Sequence of Events: 35

The exploration schedule was being followed to the letter. The systematic approach proved to be very successful, and as a by-product, the size of The Galactium was increasing. Portals were being installed at the designated points.

The other unique feature here was that the general public could view the exploration process on their mobile devices. This was part of a deliberate policy of de-mystifying the Navy. It needed to become 'The People's Navy.' It had been tried before, but deep outer space seemed so distant from the day-to-day life of Joe Bloggs.

Then it happened. They hit an invisible wall. It wasn't the first time they encountered a force field in space, but here was another one. In this case, it was totally unexpected. It was very fortunate that the two vessels which had discovered the phenomenon had detected it well in advance.

Captain Soni, 'Comms, get me Admiral Strauss.'

Comms, 'Yes, Sir.'

Admiral Strauss, 'Good day, Captain Soni.'

Captain Soni, 'Good day, we have discovered an interesting phenomenon. We have discovered what would appear to be a force field that is blocking an entire sector.'

Admiral Strauss, 'That would be inconceivable. The energy needed to support a force field of that size would be equivalent to multiple stars.'

Captain Soni, 'Should I use my weapons against it?'

Admiral Strauss, 'No, I think we need to carry out a scientific investigation. We need to determine the scale of the thing. When we encountered a massive force field in the past, Admiral Mustard used paint to display it.

My orders:

- Establish a series of warning beacons
- Await further orders.'

Fleet Operations, 'Yes, Mam.'

Location: Medical Facility, Planet Napoleon
Sequence of Events: 36

Dr Salem, 'Good morning, Admiral, it's me again. I have some further information for you.'

Admiral Mustard, 'Please go ahead.'

Dr Salem, 'I was dissecting one of the dragons when I discovered an implanted device in the brain. I'm having to work fairly quickly as the dragons are disintegrating rapidly and, to be honest, smelling rather badly.

Then I dissected every dragon to discover that every one of them had an implant in their brain. At this stage, we can only guess at its function, but it might be some sort of control device.

However, the reason I'm phoning you is that these implants contain human DNA. In fact, it is an implant manufactured using human tissue. I thought that you would want to know.'

Admiral Mustard, 'Thank you, Dr Salem. Please keep me updated on any other discoveries you make.'

Dr Salem, 'Of course, Admiral.'

Location: Admiral Strauss's Flagship
Sequence of Events: 37

Admiral Strauss, 'Comms, get me Admiral Mustard.'

    Comms. 'Yes, Mam.'

    Admiral Mustard, 'Good day, Alison.'

    Admiral Strauss, 'I hope things are going well at your end.'

    Admiral Mustard, 'Just the normal run-of-the-mill hourly crisis.'

    Admiral Strauss, 'How is little Amy?'

    Admiral Mustard, 'She's turning out to be a bit precocious.'

    Admiral Strauss, 'That's better than being slow.'

    Admiral Mustard, 'I will take your word for that.'

    Admiral Strauss, 'We have hit a minor challenge. I thought I should get your input. We have come up against a massive force field. What would you recommend?'

    Admiral Mustard, 'Have you found out its full size?'

    Admiral Strauss, 'Still working on it, but it's at least as big as our solar system.'

    Admiral Mustard, 'Wow, that's impressive. The last time I encountered one, we used an alien device to turn it off. That device is in storage. I can get it to you, but the chances of it working are probably quite slim.'

    Admiral Strauss, 'It's worth a try.'

    Admiral Mustard, 'I will get it over to you.'

    Admiral Strauss, 'Thanks. Do I have your permission to test my armaments against it?'

    Admiral Mustard, 'It might spark off an interstellar incident. I would survey it first.'

    Admiral Strauss, 'Yes, Sir.'

Location: Terry's Office, Planet Napoleon
Sequence of Events: 38

Terry, 'And how are my two beautiful daughters after your ordeal?'

Angela, 'We are called Angela and Angelina now, we went into space, and we saw dragons, and we have fannies and nipples, and now we are home.'

Terry, 'Slow down, tell me what happened.'

Angelina, 'We decided to go and hunt for gods.'

Terry, 'Why?'

Angela, 'Because we have to.'

Terry, 'Can't you just settle down here?'

Angelina, 'We have to do what we have to do.'

Terry, 'I'm not sure why, but carry on with the story.'

Angela, 'We shot off into space.'

Terry, 'How?'

Angelina, 'What do you mean by how, Daddy?'

Terry, 'How did you get into outer space?'

Angela, 'We just did. Anyway, we found dragons. So, we came home, as you know.'

Terry, 'We had to use gas to knock everyone out as the dragons looked dangerous.'

Angelina, 'That's right, we got sleepy.'

Terry, 'Are you OK now?'

Angela, 'We are fine, Daddy.'

Terry, 'No side effects?'

Angelina, 'Well, yes, we now have vaginas. Mine is much prettier than Angela's. Do you want to see it?'

Terry, 'I don't think that will be necessary.'

Angela, 'I think they look the same except mine is a bit bigger.'

Angelina, 'Dr Salem said that we have to wear knickers now.'

Terry, 'That's an excellent idea.'

Angelina, 'We have been watching these videos on the internet, and we want to try them out.'

Terry, 'You mean knickers?'

Angelina, 'No, fucking.'

Terry, 'That's not a good idea until we have been through the facts of life.'

Angela, 'We understand the reproductive process and the need for contraception.'

Terry, 'Ah well, that's good then.'

Angelina, 'All we need now is a boy.'

Terry, 'You need to give it some thought before you leap in.'

Angela, 'You are just worried about us, aren't you?'

Terry, 'Well, you are my little girls.'

Angelina, 'Not really. We have fannies, and we want to fuck.'

Terry, 'You need to listen to me. I am your father.'

Angela, 'We listened, and now it is time to move on.'

Angelina, 'First we fuck, and then we find some more gods.'

Terry, 'What can I say?'

Location: GAD2 Conference Room, Planet Napoleon
Sequence of Events: 39

Admiral Mustard decided to call a meeting of his Command Team. The following were present:

- Admiral Bumelton
- Admiral Gittins
- Admiral J Bonner
- Admiral Pearce
- Admiral Richardson
- Admiral Taylor
- Commander Black
- Commander Flower

In addition, he invited President Padfield and Henrietta Strong. AI Central was always present.

Admiral Mustard, 'Morning all. I want to take you through several worrying incidents and then agree on an action plan. Let's start with the dragons:

- We got an urgent request for help from the old Moon
- They were being attacked by dragons
- We sent Admiral Catt to investigate, and there were indeed dragons and some military vessels
- Drones were sent out to investigate, and as a consequence, we have a lot of information on them
- The dragons were having no impact on the Moon, which was leaving their system
- Then a beam destroyed the Moon with no survivors
- We still have the drones and a small squadron monitoring the situation.'

Admiral Taylor, 'We need to retaliate. Show those goons who is boss.'

Admiral Mustard, 'Thank you, Dave. But let's look at it from their point of view. The Moon, even what is left of it, is a massive body. They were simply defending their space.'

Admiral Bumelton, 'Jack is right. We would probably do the same.'

Admiral Taylor, 'What about the lives that were lost?'

Admiral Mustard, 'They have not been forgotten.

The story does not end there. Terry's angelic daughters went out into space and urgently returned with six dragons chasing them. All eight arrived in Terry's lab, and we had to use gas to pacify them.

Sadly, all six of the dragons died, but after autopsies, we discovered two very worrying facts:

1. Under one of the dragon's fingernails, we found human DNA
2. Each dragon had an implant in its brain. This implant was composed of human tissue.'

Admiral Pearce, 'Are we absolutely sure of this?'

Admiral Mustard, 'There is no doubt.'

Admiral J. Bonner, 'So what are we going to do about it?'

Admiral Mustard, 'There is no apparent threat, so we have some time to investigate further.

Fleet 1.5 is guarding their natural approach to The Galactium. Any recommendations?'

Commander Black, 'We clearly need more info. My team would be happy to assist.'

Admiral Gittins, 'We need to find out whether the dragons only occupy one system or have an extensive empire?'

Admiral Bumelton, 'The real threat is not the dragons, but whoever is controlling them.'

Admiral Mustard, 'So we need to do the following:

- Extend the search beyond the first system we encountered
- Determine who is controlling the dragons.'

Admiral Bumelton, 'I would spray the area with detection systems in case they attack us.'

Admiral Mustard, 'Agreed.'

Admiral Richardson, 'Should we try to communicate with them?'

Admiral Mustard, 'Let's do some more research first.'

Admiral Taylor, 'Are Terry's angels likely to be a threat?'

Admiral Mustard, 'I'm sure that they will cause problems.'

Admiral Taylor, 'What can we do about them?'

Admiral Mustard, 'Any suggestions?'

None came forward.

Admiral Mustard, 'Just to remind you, we have taken over the TIME organisation. AI Central is doing most of the work. Do you have anything to add?'

AI Central, 'I'm still learning, but we do need to think about defence. It may not need it, but some forts would be useful.'

Admiral Mustard, 'You have my authority to get what you need from Admiral Zakotti.'

AI Central, 'I would also recommend a Fleet rota. We really wouldn't want the facility to get into the wrong hands.'

Admiral Mustard, 'Any views on the dragons?'

AI Central, 'I've carried out millions of simulations. The vast majority, over ninety per cent, indicate that The Galactium will be at war with them in less than a year.'

Admiral Pearce, 'What are your reasons for that bad news?'

AI Central, 'OK, my reasons are as follows:

- They are there
- They are clearly a military society
- Their warriors are controlled dragons
- Their planet buster was high technology, and they must have an extensive empire to support it
- They attacked the Moon, so that is in their nature
- They are using human DNA and tissue. That does not bode well
- Natural human aggression
- Colliding empires
- They now know that we exist

Do I need to go on?'

Admiral Pearce, 'I don't think so. But you are right. This Moon incident has exposed humanity.'

Admiral Mustard, 'My orders:

- Admiral Gittins to organise an extensive search of their empire

- Admiral Bumelton to put together a defensive plan
- Commander Black to look at ways of infiltrating them
- Admiral Zakotti to organise forts for TIME
- Admiral Pearce to schedule naval support for TIME.'

Fleet Operations, 'Yes, Sir.'

Admiral Mustard, 'We have another issue. The Exploration Fleets have discovered a giant force field, possibly larger than the solar system. They are still trying to ascertain its full extent.'

Admiral Gittins, 'Where is it?'

Fleet Operations provided the coordinates, and Admiral Gittins plotted it on his hand-held.

Admiral Gittins, 'It's roughly in the same direction as the dragon planet. Probably just a coincidence.'

Admiral Richardson, 'There could be an alien fleet on the other side waiting to attack us.'

Admiral Mustard, 'I assumed that it was transparent. Fleet Ops, can you check, please?'

Fleet Operations, 'Yes, Sir.'

Admiral Mustard, 'George, can you factor that into your plans, please?'

Admiral Bumelton, 'Of course.'

Fleet Operations, 'We have just checked the force field, Sir. It resists all frequencies. It is not transparent.'

Admiral Mustard, 'Let's get moving.'

Location: Planet Lovelace
Sequence of Events: 40

So far, it had been a textbook exercise. All of the utilities and transport hubs had been secured. It was becoming apparent that fifty thousand marines would not be enough. The rest of the Marine Corps were scattered over the Exploration Fleets.

Commander Todd decided to move onto Stage Three. His engineers had taken over all the radio and TV stations and all the communications centres. He was ready to begin the communicate and persuade campaign. He sat by the microphone which would allow him to interrupt every station and every comms network.

Commander Todd, 'Ladies and gentlemen of Planet Lovelace, I am Commander Todd of The Galactium's Marine Corps. I have been asked by the president to establish peace.

We understand that you have been through a lot. We know that you have lost loved ones. We know that your world has changed dramatically, but we must re-establish order. So far, we have secured most of the utilities and transport infrastructure. We now plan to stabilise each city and town one by one. We will impose curfews, and we will collect weapons. We will re-establish order, and we will appoint new officials. We will set up police forces and hospitals. We will return your world to normal.'

Then the dragons attacked.

Location: GAD2, Planet Napoleon
Sequence of Events: 41

GAD2, 'Admiral Mustard, Sir, we are under attack.'
    Admiral Mustard, 'Where?'
    GAD2, 'Planet Lovelace.'
    Admiral Mustard, 'That's where most of the Marine Corps are.'
    GAD2, 'Yes, Sir. Commander Todd has requested urgent assistance.'
    Admiral Mustard, 'Do we know what we are up against?'
    GAD2, 'About three thousand vessels and a few hordes of dragons.'
    Admiral Mustard, 'Show me the Fleet disposition:

Division	Disposition
1	Parts of Fleet 1.3 are monitoring the dragon world. Fleet 1.5 is guarding approaches from the dragon world. Admiral Bumelton is moving the rest of his forces to guard against any attack from the other side of the force field
2	Available
3	Available
4	Available
5	Available
6	Available
7	Preparing to enter dragon space
8	Providing resources to defend TIME
9	Exploration duties
10	Exploration duties

Admiral Mustard, 'My orders:

- Send Division Two to assist Commander Todd
- Send Division Three to defend Earth
- Put all other Divisions on alert
- Prepare to activate planetary force fields
- Inform The President.'

GAD2, 'Yes, Sir.'

Location: Admiral Mustard's Office, Planet Napoleon
Sequence of Events: 42

Admiral Mustard, 'Comms, get me Commander Todd.'

Comms, 'Yes, Sir.'

Commander Todd, 'Good day, Jack.'

Admiral Mustard, 'How is it going?'

Commander Todd, 'Everything was going swimmingly well until we were attacked. I feel sorry for Planet Lovelace. They have been through so much already. Luckily, we were here. Our force fields are protecting most of the towns and cities.'

Admiral Mustard, 'What about your Fleet?'

Commander Todd, 'It's holding its own, but as you know, it has not been designed for naval operations. Our battle cruisers are giving them a bit of a bashing, but we still need help.'

Admiral Mustard, 'As you know, Division Two is on its way. John will see them off.'

Commander Todd, 'I've been trying to work out why they attacked here?'

Admiral Mustard, 'No specific reason except that Planet Lovelace would be one of the nearer planets to their sphere of influence.

What happened to the local forts?'

Commander Todd, 'That was probably my fault. I got them disengaged before we arrived just in case a rogue element had got control of them.'

Admiral Mustard, 'That makes sense.'

Commander Todd, 'I've just heard that it looks like the dragons are retiring.'

Admiral Mustard, 'They have probably sensed John. He would have sent his battlecruisers ahead. Talk to you later. Bottoms up.'

Commander Todd, 'Bottoms up, Boss.'

Location: GAD2, Planet Napoleon
Sequence of Events: 43

GAD2, 'Admiral Mustard, 'Sir, there is another attack.'

Admiral Mustard, 'Where this time?'

GAD2, 'As suspected, Sir, the force field is down, and a massive fleet is streaming through.'

Admiral Mustard, 'How massive is massive?'

GAD2, 'All I've been told is tens of thousands.'

Admiral Mustard, 'So we have three Divisions in the area?'

GAD2, 'Yes, Sir, but only Division One is battle-ready. The other two Fleets are dispersed.'

Admiral Mustard, 'My orders:

- Divisions Nine and Ten to reform ASAP
- Division One to resist the invasion
- Divisions Four, Five and Six to support Division One
- Exploratory Fleet to leave the war zone
- Division Eight to leave some resources to defend TIME but to act as a rear-guard to Divisions One, Three, Five and Six
- Inform Admiral Gittins that he can attack military targets
- Division Two to leave one Fleet to defend Planet Lovelace. The other four Fleets will pursue the enemy
- Activate the Drone Fleets
- Set scanning targets for the Long-Range Monitoring Unit
- Warn medical facilities
- Marine units in Exploration Fleet to return to base
- Capture one or more enemy vessels
- Update the president.'

GAD2, 'Yes, Sir.'

Admiral Mustard, 'Get me an update of the enemy's fleet size.'

GAD2, 'Yes, Sir.'

Admiral Mustard, 'And let me know when the Drone Fleets are ready.'

GAD2, 'Yes, Sir.'

Location: The President's Office, Planet Napoleon
Sequence of Events: 44

President Padfield, 'Morning, Jack.'

Admiral Mustard, 'Hi Dave, apologies for not contacting you recently.'

President Padfield, 'It looks like we have got our war. AI Central was right.'

Admiral Mustard, 'Will it never end?'

President Padfield, 'Perhaps this is the norm.'

Admiral Mustard, 'You might be right.'

President Padfield, 'How worried are you?'

Admiral Mustard, 'Not too worried:

- We have fought off the attack on Planet Lovelace, and Admiral J. Bonner is in pursuit
- George is holding his own at the force field site, and the cavalry is on its way
- Peter is checking out their space and has permission to engage if necessary
- New Earth is well defended.'

President Padfield, 'Sounds like you have got things under control.'

Admiral Mustard, 'Probably not. I think that these are simply feints. They are checking us out. Checking out our technology. Assessing us as an enemy. We will fight this lot off, but they will return with a larger fleet and much better weaponry.'

President Padfield, 'Forever the optimist.'

Admiral Mustard, 'I see myself as a pragmatic optimist. We need more info about our adversary before we can put a plan together.'

Location: Admiral Mustard's Office, Planet Napoleon
Sequence of Events: 45

Admiral Mustard, 'Comms, get me Admiral Bumelton.'

Comms, 'Yes, Sir.'

Admiral Bumelton, 'Hello, Jack.'

Admiral Mustard, 'How are you doing, young George?'

Admiral Bumelton, 'To be honest, not feeling too young.'

Admiral Mustard, 'Sounds like you need another one of your holidays.'

Admiral Bumelton, 'That's not a bad idea. I guess that you want an update.'

Admiral Mustard, 'Yes, please, but they will be retiring soon.'

Admiral Bumelton, 'How do you know that?'

Admiral Mustard, 'I can see a pattern.'

Admiral Bumelton, 'Well, they are not much of an opposition.'

Admiral Mustard, 'That's because it is a feint. They are simply checking us out.'

Admiral Bumelton, 'Well, they are doing it in force. There must be seventy thousand of them, but their technology is poor. I could probably defeat them with just my Division.'

Admiral Mustard, 'That's a deliberate ploy. I predict that they will disengage when they have lost thirty thousand vessels, but they will be back with a more sophisticated fleet. Are there any dragons?'

Admiral Bumelton, 'There are no dragons.'

Admiral Mustard, 'That's interesting. Can you capture one of their ships?'

Admiral Bumelton, 'We already have two.'

Admiral Mustard, 'Well done.'

Admiral Bumelton, 'I need to disengage as Calensky, Steve, and Ama have arrived.'

Location: On-board Admiral Gittins's Flagship
Sequence of Events: 46

Admiral Mustard, 'Comms, get me Admiral Gittins.'

Comms, 'Yes, Sir.'

Admiral Gittins, 'Hello, Boss. How is George doing?'

Admiral Mustard, 'OK, everything is under control.'

Admiral Gittins, 'You realise that this is all a ruse?'

Admiral Mustard, 'Of course, it's a cunning subterfuge. I was just telling that to George.'

Admiral Gittins, 'Well done, Boss, I knew that you would see through them.'

Admiral Mustard, 'What you are doing is much more interesting. We need the following things:

- To ascertain the full size of their "empire"
- To find out their true military capability
- To determine who is actually running the show
- To find out how and why they are using human DNA
- To find how they will react if you attack them.'

Admiral Gittins, 'You can rely on me.'

Admiral Mustard, 'We are all relying on you. Where are you now?'

Admiral Gittins, 'Just approaching the observation team from Fleet 1.3.'

Admiral Mustard, 'Well done. Remember that they have some sort of planet buster.'

Admiral Gittins, 'Yes, I need to investigate that.'

Admiral Mustard, 'Do you want some Special Ops?'

Admiral Gittins, 'Yes, please.'

Admiral Mustard, 'Your wish is my command. I will get Martin to contact you.'

Admiral Gittins, 'Thanks, Boss.'

Location: Admiral Mustard's Office, Planet Napoleon
Sequence of Events: 47

Admiral Mustard, 'Update me.'
Fleet Operations, 'Yes, Sir:

- Divisions One, Four, Five, Six, Nine and Ten have fought off the enemy attack by the force field
- Divisions One and Four are in pursuit, awaiting your orders
- Division Eight is still acting as a rear-guard, and some units are defending TIME
- Division Two except Fleet 2.2 are pursuing the enemy who were attacking Planet Lovelace
- Fleet 2.2 is defending Planet Lovelace along with the First Marine Fleet
- Division Three is defending New Earth
- Division Seven is approaching the dragon world. Fleets 1.3 and 1.5 to be relieved
- The Second Marine Division has returned to base
- The Long-Range Tracking Unit is scanning as requested
- Admiral Bumelton has four captured enemy vessels
- The Drone Fleets are now operational.'

Admiral Mustard, 'My orders:
- Division One to return to base
- Division Two to continue to pursue the enemy
- Fleet 2.2 to re-join Division Two
- Divisions Four and Five to pursue the enemy but to retreat if any serious engagement is anticipated
- Division Six to defend the Marine Fleets and Planet Lovelace
- Divisions Eight, Nine and Ten to return to base
- Fleets 1.3 and 1.5 to re-join Fleet One
- Second Marine Division to go to Planet Lovelace
- Special Ops to support Division Severn
- Captured enemy vessels to be analysed
- Drone Fleets to protect access to The Galactium – ten Fleets on wide coverage and five Fleets to protect existing entry points.'

Fleet Operations, 'Yes, Sir.'

Location: On-board Admiral Gittins's Flagship
Sequence of Events: 48

Admiral Gittins, 'Comms, get me the commander of the observation team.'

Comms, 'Yes, Sir.'

Captain Greenaway, 'Good day, Sir.'

Admiral Gittins, 'Good day, Captain, I have your reports and observations. I just thought I would ring to see if you had anything else to add.'

Captain Greenaway, 'I'm pleased that you have done that as I do have some observations that I couldn't put in the report.'

Admiral Gittins, 'Please go on.'

Captain Greenaway, 'Firstly, they act like we are not here, but I have a sneaky impression that they are observing us.'

Admiral Gittins, 'That makes little sense.'

Captain Greenaway, 'I know, but it's a consistent feeling I have. They are here at night. I sense them in my dreams. It's probably some form of paranoia, but it's not just me. Most of my colleagues have the same feelings.'

Admiral Gittins, 'Have they detected the drones?'

Captain Greenaway, 'There has been no indication that they have been detected, but again I'm not sure if that is just a deliberate deception.'

Admiral Gittins, 'There is something else that you are not telling me.'

Captain Greenaway, 'That's because I feel stupid to even mention it.'

Admiral Gittins, 'I've seen more weird stuff than you could ever imagine.'

Captain Greenaway, 'OK, I've been seeing ghosts.'

Admiral Gittins, 'That's not that unusual.'

Captain Greenaway, 'These are ghosts of my dead parents and sometimes dead friends and workmates.'

Admiral Gittins, 'I believe you.'

Captain Greenaway, 'I even saw you and Admiral Mustard as ghosts.'

Admiral Gittins, 'That's a bit more unusual.'

Captain Greenaway, 'I know. Again, it's not just me; others have also seen you.'

Admiral Gittins, 'Any observations on the dragons?'

Captain Greenaway, 'Most of it is in my report, but I can summarise:

- They can fly
- They can live in space with apparently no ill effects
- They can teleport
- They eat rock
- It looks like they communicate with each other telepathically
- They seem to be long-sighted
- We couldn't identify where they live
- Some wear military insignia
- No sign of any fire-skills as you expect from a dragon.'

Admiral Gittins, 'Thank you. Enjoy your trip home.' He still found it strange that they were discussing dragons.'

Fleet Operations, 'Admiral Gittins, we have just been informed that the Special Ops teams have arrived and are awaiting your orders.'

Admiral Gittins, 'Please ask them to review the observation reports.'

Fleet Operations, 'They have done that, Sir.'

Admiral Gittins, 'Ask them to stand down for two days.'

Fleet Operations, 'They said negative, Sir.'

Admiral Gittins, 'What do you mean negative?'

Fleet Operations, 'They said that they are here to work, Sir.'

Admiral Gittins, 'Ask them to scout the area without exposing themselves.'

Fleet Operations, 'Are you sure that you want to use those words?'

Admiral Gittins, 'Of course.'

Location: On-board Admiral J Bonner's Flagship
Sequence of Events: 49

Admiral J Bonner, 'Comms, get me Admiral Mustard.'

Comms, 'Yes, Sir.'

Admiral Mustard, 'Hi John, how is the pursuit going?'

Admiral J Bonner, 'That's why I'm ringing Jack. We are up against amateurs. The dragon fleet is heading into The Galactium, and we are following it. Clearly, that doesn't make sense. They are playing with us.

If I give the word, we could destroy their fleet in ten Earth minutes. What do you want me to do?'

Admiral Mustard, 'My orders:

• Place part of your Fleet in front of them, assuming that you have superior speed capabilities

• Warn their fleet that you plan to destroy them and ask them to surrender

• If they don't surrender, then capture ten of their ships with live operators for questioning

• Destroy the rest of their fleet.

• Then return to base.'

Admiral J Bonner, 'So far, we have failed to make contact with them. Asking them to surrender is going to be a bit challenging.'

Admiral Mustard, 'Do the best you can.'

Location: Terry's Office, Planet Napoleon
Sequence of Events: 50

Terry, 'Where are you guys off to?'
    Angela, 'We are going god hunting.'
    Terry, 'What sort of gods are you looking for?'
    Angelina, 'It doesn't really matter.'
    Terry, 'Then why are you going?'
    Angela, 'Because we have to.'
    Terry, 'I'm not sure why you have to.'
    Angela, 'Nor are we, but we have no choice.'
    Terry, 'Isn't there enough to occupy you here?'
    Angelina, 'Ask Angela.'
    Terry, 'Why is that?'
    Angela, 'Because I like boys.'
    Terry, 'There is nothing wrong with that.'
    Angela, 'They seem to like me as well.'
    Angelina, 'They like her a lot. How many liked you yesterday?'
    Angela, 'Fourteen.'
    Terry, 'That's far too many.'
    Angelina, 'I would say so. My fanny gets a bit sore after three.'
    Terry, 'Are you saying that Angela fucked fourteen men yesterday?'
    Angela, 'Yes, Daddy.'
    Terry, 'Why are you doing that?'
    Angela, 'Because I enjoy it. I love the physical sensation and the power
it gives me. Men are so weak. They will do anything for a little bit of fanny,
and all they are doing is rubbing skin together.'
    Terry, 'What about the intimacy?'
    Angelina, 'That's not easy on the nightclub dance floor.'
    Terry, 'This has got to stop. You could catch a raft of different diseases.'
    Angela, 'We are immune to all diseases.'
    Terry, 'What about your self-respect?'
    Angela, 'I've got loads of that. I'm proud of my performance.'
    Terry, 'Other people will have a poor opinion of you.'
    Angelina, 'That doesn't seem to be the view of the men we meet.'
    Angela, 'Anyway, I say fuck them.'
    Angelina, 'We are off now.'
    Terry, 'Just look after yourself.'

Location: On-board Admiral Wallett's Flagship
Sequence of Events: 51

Admiral Wallett, 'This is far too easy.'

Admiral Adams, 'What are they trying to achieve?'

Admiral Wallett, 'They are just fleeing. There is no rear guard. There is not even a pretence of a defence.'

Admiral Adams, 'Are they leading us towards a trap?'

Admiral Wallett, 'They still have thirty thousand vessels. They have enough resources to put up a bit of a fight.'

Admiral Adams, 'Are they trying to give us a false sense of superiority?'

Admiral Wallett, 'Well, if they are, they have managed to achieve it.'

Admiral Adams, 'Shall I update Admiral Mustard?'

Admiral Wallett, 'You might as well.'

Admiral Adams, 'Comms, get me Admiral Mustard.'

Comms, 'Yes, Sir.'

Admiral Mustard, 'Good day, Steve, how is it going?'

Admiral Adams, 'It's far too easy. What are they trying to achieve?'

Admiral Mustard, 'It seems to be a standard pattern for every encounter. So far, no one has asked why are they attacking us?'

Admiral Adams, 'Why are they attacking us?'

Admiral Mustard, 'Good question. It's a mystery.'

Admiral Adams, 'What do you want us to do regarding the enemy fleet?'

Admiral Mustard, 'What are the options?'

Admiral Adams, 'I guess that there are three options:

1. Continue the pursuit

2. Destroy them

3. Terminate the pursuit.'

Admiral Mustard, 'The only one that has any risk is option one. So, let's do that. I would suggest that you take twenty of your fastest battle-cruisers and follow them. Retreat if it gets too risky.'

Admiral Adams, 'Yes, Sir, but can you raise the order?'

Admiral Mustard, 'My orders:

• Admiral Adams to take the fastest battle-cruisers from Divisions

Four and Five and will pursue the enemy
- Admiral Adams to end the pursuit if the risk is too great
- The remainder of Divisions Four and Five will return to base under Admiral Wallett.'

Fleet Operations, 'Yes, Sir.'

Location: The President's Office, Planet Napoleon
Sequence of Events: 52

President Padfield, 'I sometimes wonder if these progress meetings are worthwhile. We create, and it gets destroyed. We create again, and it gets destroyed again.'

Henrietta Strong, 'It was me who was down last time.'

President Padfield, 'I'm not really down, but life does make you question the point of it all.'

Henrietta Strong, 'With our longer lives, this is going to become more of an issue. We need to find things and projects and hobbies to fill it.'

President Padfield, 'I guess that the quest for happiness will become more critical.'

Henrietta Strong, 'But don't you find that happiness comes in small doses often in moments when you don't expect it. Perhaps happiness is too much to hope for. Contentment would be a more achievable goal.'

President Padfield, 'Things are going to change as those who have not been born yet will have a different outlook on life. For the last few hundred years, humanity expected to get married or cohabit, buy a house, have children and grandchildren, and then die. A few escaped the trap, but most were caught. It was about all you could do in eighty years.'

Now youngsters could have a dozen different lives. You might spend the first hundred years growing up. The pressure is off. The trap could be experienced and then discarded.'

Henrietta Strong, 'Yes, I always remember the joke about the three stages of marriage: engagement ring, wedding ring and suffe**ring**.

Perhaps we need to make plans now to change humanity's outlook.'

President Padfield, 'It's happening now without us knowing, but we do need to address some of the Eternity issues. Didn't we have a committee looking into it?'

Henrietta Strong, 'There was a committee, but they were lost in the Great Disaster.'

President Padfield, 'Of course. So, what's on your agenda today?'

Henrietta Strong, 'Well, a few updates first:

• As you know, the funding is in place for the new Galactium HQ on Planet Earth. An architectural competition is in place

- Most of the other plans for Planet Earth have been accepted
- The Moonies are making excellent progress regarding the development of the Moon. I have to credit them; they are doing a good job
- There isn't much interest in a significant memorial service at this stage
- The doppelgänger issues on Planet Lovelace are being addressed
- Debbie Goozee has done a cracking job building up the Presidential Guard.'

President Padfield, 'That's all very positive. My mood earlier was really related to the dragons. We get a new HQ, and a lot of other stuff sorted, and then the dragons turn up and destroy it.'

Henrietta Strong, 'Are you worried about them?'

President Padfield, 'I wasn't particularly, but I know Jack's moods very well. He is worried, but he couldn't tell you why.'

Henrietta Strong, 'To be honest, he has usually been right.'

President Padfield, 'Moving on, what's still on your agenda?'

Henrietta Strong, 'OK, here you are:

1. The judiciary wants guidance on what a life sentence means
2. We still haven't decided how we are going to handle pensions if you live one thousand years or more
3. How do we define what is Galactium space?
4. There is the competition on what developments we want from Terry
5. We need to agree on a research budget
6. Do we allow further alien civilisations to join The Galactium?
7. Do we set up a Museum of Humanity on New Earth?'

President Padfield, 'Are we always going to call it New Earth?'

Henrietta Strong, 'It's a pain, but it is a way of differentiating it from the old Earth.'

President Padfield, 'OK, but I do find it irritating. Is that the end of your list?'

Henrietta Strong, 'More or less. There are always lots of minor items that my team are addressing.'

President Padfield, 'OK, these are my decisions:

1. Don't know
2. Don't know
3. Does it matter?
4. That's good
5. Agreed
6. Yes
7. Yes

How was that?'

Henrietta Strong, 'Very droll.

There has been a general view that a life sentence should be a hundred years, but that is a very long time. So, after a lot of debate, it was halved depending on good behaviour. Well, if you are going to live a thousand years, then giving up fifty years to kill a partner you hate are not bad odds.'

President Padfield, 'Set up a judicial committee to agree.'

Henrietta Strong, 'In that case, it will never be resolved.'

President Padfield, 'We need a general formula that can be modified on a case-by-case basis.'

Henrietta Strong, 'Can I tell them that is your current view?'

President Padfield, 'Yes.'

Henrietta Strong, 'Regarding pensions, I would argue that they have been replaced by social help funding and that existing pensions should be cashed in. There doesn't need to be a retirement age any more. '

President Padfield, 'It's a bit daunting that there will never be an official time when you can pack up work.'

Henrietta Strong, 'It's the other side of the eternity coin.

The definition of Galactium space is a critical factor for the Navy. What space do they need to defend? The Exploration Fleets are extending our borders. What are the rules?'

President Padfield, 'I think we need a committee to agree, but in reality, it is down to who's got the biggest willy.'

Henrietta Strong, 'I think we are there.'

President Padfield, 'Excellent.'

Henrietta Strong noticed that the president was getting less interested in the detail nowadays.

Location: Special Ops Vessel, Dragon System
Sequence of Events: 53

Major Henderson was briefing the five Special Ops Units (A1 to A5).
Major Henderson, 'Our plan is as follows:

- We will fly directly into the dragon system and wait an Earth hour to ensure that we haven't been detected. So far, our stealth technology seems to have been a hundred per cent successful
- Assuming that we haven't been detected, each unit will use their personal stealth fighter to land at the following points:
  ➤ The largest building in its largest city. From the drone film footage, it looks to be their equivalent of our town hall (Unit A1)
  Objective: Obtain details about this system and the breadth of their colonisation. Secure any other information of interest
  ➤ The Space Port (Unit A2)
  Objective: Obtain information on their space technology and the destinations that the spaceport serves
  ➤ The Military Centre or what looks like one (Unit A3)
  Objective: Obtain information on their military structure, size, weapon systems, technology, etc.
  ➤ The hospital
  Objective: Obtain biological information on the two species, with the non-dragon species being of the most interest (Unit A4)
  ➤ The planet buster
  Objective: To obtain information on the weapon and to destroy it if that option becomes available (Unit A5)
- Collect information
- Return to this vessel
- You have six Earth hours to achieve your mission

Any questions?'
Trooper AW 1754, 'Sir, what is the protocol if we are captured?'
Major Henderson, 'Accept capture.'
Trooper AW 1754, 'Should we commit suicide?'
Major Henderson, 'That is your call, but I would say no.'
Trooper AW 1754, 'But they might eat us, Sir.'

Major Henderson, 'But they might not.'

Trooper AW 1635, 'Sir, can we transmit any information back electronically?'

Major Henderson, 'We have given this some thought. As we don't know their capabilities, we suggest that you resist doing that. However, if you find critical data of immense interest, then use your own judgement, but you might be putting your colleague's lives at risk.'

Trooper AW 1332, 'Sir, what if the task takes longer than six hours?'

Major Henderson, 'Switch on a beacon, and we will come back for you if we can.'

Trooper AW 1332, 'Sir, what if the dragons spot the beacon?'

Major Henderson, 'Then we will have to deal with them. So that you know, depending on the information you extract, the Navy plans to bombard their planets. Give them back some of their own medicine.'

There was a cheer.

Major Henderson, 'Prepare your equipment. We depart in two hours.'

The troopers almost sang in unison, 'Yes, Sir.'

Location: Angel Delight
Sequence of Events: 54

This time the angels arrived on a desolate desert planet. The air was thin, but they could still fly. The problem was where to fly to. In every direction, there was flat arid desert. There were some mountains in the distance, but they didn't look particularly appealing.

Angela, 'So what do you think, Sister?'

Angelina, 'It's a bit hot for my liking.'

Angela, 'You are right. If we could sweat, I'm sure that we would be sweating.'

Angelina, 'So where do you fancy flying to?'

Angela, 'I guess that it's got to be those mountains.'

Angelina, 'We have never flown that far before.'

Angela, 'I guess that we have no choice.'

Angelina, 'We could go home.'

Angela, 'We can't give up that easily. We have gods to track down.'

They slowly flew to the mountain with some difficulty as they weren't really fit enough for such an arduous task. Having got there, they wondered what to do next.

The mountains proved to be of little more interest than the desert. They sat down, exhausted, and demoralised. Angelina wanted to go home, but Angela could still feel the presence of multiple gods. They were calling her, but she couldn't pinpoint the source. It was somehow everywhere and nowhere.

Location: Marine Command, Planet Lovelace
Sequence of Events: 55

Commander Todd was really pleased to receive additional marine regiments. It obviously takes a lot of human resources to subdue an entire planet, especially as it was not something they had done before.

It was going swimmingly well until the dragons attacked. Now they had just short of a hundred thousand marines, two Marine Fleets and Naval Division Six. In addition, Division Two was pursuing the enemy.

As you would expect, the dragon attack hadn't gone down too well with the locals. It was a classic case of the military being seen as a saviour, only to be disappointed once again. The fact that the dragon attack was totally unpredictable was irrelevant.

Despite everything, Commander Todd was determined to continue. He decided to carry on with his speech to the local population that had been rudely interrupted by the dragons.

Commander Todd, 'Ladies and gentlemen of Planet Lovelace, this is Commander Todd of The Galactium's Marine Corps again. During my last speech, I was rudely interrupted by a dragon attack. Yes, I know that sounds insane. We were totally unprepared for that. The enemy has been defeated, and the Navy is pursuing them. We are currently taking the attack to their home worlds.

Anyway, I want to return to our plans for this planet. As you already know, my marines have taken over all of the essential utilities and communication hubs. We have isolated each community, and we will be working with town leaders to resolve any outstanding issues. I would like anyone who was previously a councillor, policeman, or government official to come forward so that we can form local management groups.

We will set up tribunals to investigate grievances. We have Galactium funds to assist with re-building and to provide compensation.

Individuals who have or who are committing crimes will be arrested and tried. No violence will be tolerated. Please co-operate as we are here to put things back to normal.'

Location: Special Ops Vessel, Dragon System
Sequence of Events: 56

The stealthed battlecruiser had spent an hour circling around the largest and most active planet in the dragon system. It was now time for each unit to undertake their individual missions. It was nighttime for the planet below, which should assist them in achieving their objectives.

Unit A1's stealthed fighter landed in an empty park near their target building. The team of three left the fighter in stealthed suits and walked towards the building's back entrance. There were two types of stairs into the structure, one designed for dragons and the other designed for a more typical humanoid.

They were surprised to find that the door wasn't locked. Their night vision glasses allowed them to see in the dark. The internal corridors were huge, but then they had to allow for dragon dimensions. It was strange that there were no internal doors or lifts. From what they could see, there was little computerisation and little filing.

There were tables and chairs for the humanoids, but no dragon equivalent. There were no pictures, photos, posters, or indeed anything on the walls. Every wall was the same colour. In fact, each office seemed to be identical.

The troopers systematically searched each room. They collected some meaningless paper documents and some objects that had no discernible function. They automatically took video footage as part of the search.

Things were a bit more interesting in the offices on the top floor. There were TV/computer screens. One trooper fitted a spy device. There were more documents and some sort of compendium. The view from the floor was quite impressive. There was still a fair amount of traffic, and quite a bit of it was circulating around their stealthed fighter.

Their cover had been blown, and the rescue request was sent.

Major Henderson, 'We will rescue you. Give me your coordinates. Push the fighter self-destruct button on your remote.'

Location: Special Ops Vessel, Dragon System
Sequence of Events: 57

Unit A2's stealthed fighter landed on the outskirts of the spaceport. This meant that there was a fair distance to the actual control building, but then they had their stealthed scooters.

It wasn't long before they were standing by the back entrance to the control tower. They were surprised to find that the door was locked. Inside they found two types of stairs, and bare, identically coloured walls. There were no internal doors.

The control room had computer systems but no staff. The screens showed the movement of vessels within their system and to thousands of other galactic locations. A spy device was attached to several screens.

Suddenly there was a lot of activity in the spaceport, with most of the action centring on their stealthed fighter.

Their cover had been blown, and the rescue request was sent.

Major Henderson, 'You are the second one. We will rescue you. Give me your coordinates. Push the fighter self-destruct button on your remote.'

Major Henderson, 'Comms, get me Units A3, A4 and A5.'

Comms, 'Yes, Sir.'

Major Henderson, 'Abort your missions immediately. If you have to, destroy your fighters and we will rescue you.'

Major Henderson, 'Comms, get me Commander Black.'

Comms, 'Yes, Sir.'

Commander Black, 'How is it going, Major?'

Major Henderson, 'Not well, Sir, I'm currently on my way to rescue Units A1 and A2. The missions for Units A3, A4 and A5 have been aborted.'

Commander Black, 'What went wrong?'

Major Henderson, 'Both of the stealthed vessels were discovered. Well, to be honest, it looks like they knew where they were.'

Commander Black, 'What makes you say that?'

Major Henderson, 'Their craft were circling around our stealthed vessels. I got the impression that they went straight to them. I've got to go as I'm on a mercy mission. Can you update Admiral Gittins, please?'

The rescue got underway, and the two teams were rescued. All five teams were effectively recovered, although they lost two stealthed fighters when the self-destruct buttons were pushed.

Location: Special Ops HQ, Planet Napoleon
Sequence of Events: 58

Commander Black, 'Comms, get me Admiral Gittins.'

Comms, 'Yes, Sir.'

Admiral Gittins, 'Good day, Martin, how's life?'

Commander Black, 'Not that good, Peter. Our brief excursion has been a very worrying failure.'

Admiral Gittins, 'In what way?'

Commander Black, 'Two of our stealthed fighters were discovered. It would appear that they knew exactly where they landed.'

Admiral Gittins, 'That suggests that our stealth activity is not working.'

Commander Black, 'It's working, but they can detect us, regardless.'

Admiral Gittins, 'What about your troopers?'

Commander Black, 'They all returned safely. If they wanted to, they could have stopped us at any time. They offered no aggression at all, even though we entered their buildings.'

Admiral Gittins, 'So, there is still a fair chance that they know that my Fleet is here.'

Commander Black, 'Almost certainly.'

Admiral Gittins, 'Let's patch Jack in. Comms, get me Admiral Mustard.'

Comms, 'Yes, Sir.'

Admiral Mustard, 'Good day, Peter, enjoying your holiday?'

Admiral Gittins, 'Very funny. I've got Martin on the line.'

Commander Black, 'Morning, Jack.'

Admiral Mustard, 'What are you two reprobates up to?'

Admiral Gittins, 'It appears that the dragons can see through our stealth technology, and they don't seem to be bothered about our presence. Martin's men have obtained some data, but their investigation project had to be terminated. What do you want us to do?'

Admiral Mustard, 'How much information did they get?'

Commander Black, 'It's very hard to tell, as it is undecipherable. We need experts to look at it.'

Admiral Gittins, 'As they know we are here, I think a general bombardment is too dangerous.'

Admiral Mustard, 'It would make sense to review the collected data first.'

    Admiral Gittins, 'I agree.'

    Commander Black, 'That also makes sense to me.'

    Admiral Mustard, 'My orders:

- Division Seven will return to base
- Special Ops Teams will return to base
- Update the president.'

Fleet Operations, 'Yes, Sir.'

    Admiral Mustard, 'I will call a staff meeting to discuss.'

Location: GAD2 Conference Room, Planet Napoleon
Sequence of Events: 59

Admiral Mustard called a meeting of his Command Team. The following were present:

- Admiral Bumelton
- Admiral Gittins
- Admiral J Bonner
- Admiral Pearce
- Admiral Richardson
- Admiral Taylor
- Admiral Tersoo
- Admiral Zakotti
- Commander Black
- Commander Flower

President Padfield, Henrietta Strong and AI Central were also present.

Admiral Mustard, 'Morning all. I want to update you regarding the dragon problem. Let's just remind you of the background:

- The dragons attacked Planet Lovelace and were easily fought off. Currently, Admiral J Bonner is pursuing them
- The dragons then attacked from behind a giant force field. Again, they were easily fought off. Admiral Adams is currently pursuing them with just twenty battlecruisers
- Admiral Gittins and Fleet Seven have been in the dragon system for the last few days in stealth mode
- Five Special Ops teams landed on the dragon planet, but their stealthed fighters were detected. The good news is that they returned with video footage and documentation which has been assessed by our experts
- They also planted spy-bots on their computer systems.'

Admiral Mustard, 'Before we get into the detail, what is surprising is their lack of interest:

- The two battles on their side were half-hearted affairs

- They ignored the various Galactium Fleets that had entered their space
- They hardly took any action against our Special Ops troopers.

They are hardly aggressive aggressors.

Now for the results of the study, I've asked Professor Willis to join us.'

Professor Willis, 'Ladies and gentlemen, we have done the following:
- Analysed the documentation and video footage
- Reviewed some of the collected objects, and
- We are continuously reviewing the footage from the spy-bots

Our initial assessment will follow, but I need to stress that these are very early days. Our views are likely to change:

1. Based on the spaceport data, we believe that there are one hundred and twenty thousand destinations and that these destinations constitute one empire

2. The dragon system is a frontier system on the extreme edge of their empire

3. Over a few million years, the empire has been expanded to its current size

4. It includes at least fifty thousand different species

5. When a species is conquered, it is effectively lobotomised to make them reasonably docile. We assume that the tissue found in the dragon's brain performs that function

6. Their military includes twenty million plus vessels. The capability of the ships seems to vary depending on the region. They seem to be reluctant to share their best technology with the locals

7. There are at least sixteen conquests underway at the moment. Our encounter is a simple policing operation and is not included in that count

8. Sometime in the future, they will decide if our species is suitable for entrapment. If not, we will be destroyed.

We have a lot more information regarding the dragon system, but I thought I would give you the good news. Any questions?'

Admiral Gittins, 'What is the empire called?'

Professor Willis, 'Good question. They don't seem to be into naming conventions like us, but they seem to be called 'The Ones that fight and conquer for the glory of zxmid and the way of ddrzs so that its glory can take over all possessions and peoples and live a life of tyytre so that all will receive the benediction of tydes come along and free thee more than the blue.'

Admiral Gittins, 'Is there a shorter version?'

Professor Willis, 'No, but we need to agree on a suitable name for them.'

Admiral Gittins, 'How about dragons?'

Professor Willis, 'That won't do as we need to be able to differentiate between the dragons and their masters.'

Admiral Mustard, 'We can argue about a name later, but they obviously are a huge threat.'

Admiral J Bonner, 'I'm still chasing one of their police teams. Shall I end the chase?'

Admiral Mustard, 'Good idea, my orders:

- Division Two to return to base
- Admiral Adams and his squadron to return to base.'

Fleet Operations, 'Yes, Sir.'

President Padfield, 'Professor, any ideas on timescales?'

Professor Willis, 'We are trying to ascertain that information, but the answer is no. They probably think in terms of decades or more.'

Admiral Mustard, 'If we attack them, it will probably eventually provoke a more serious retaliatory reaction. If we beat their fleet, they would just send another one and so on.'

Admiral Taylor, 'We need to prepare our defences for that day.'

President Padfield, 'We need to learn more about them. Perhaps the dragons are not really interested in us. They may only be following the commands of their masters.'

Admiral Mustard, 'That would account for their relative disinterestedness.'

Admiral Gittins, 'As they are on the periphery, they might have been a relatively recent conquest.'

Admiral Richardson, 'Over the years, we have developed several stealth systems, but none have seemed to work.'

Professor Willis, 'Most people assume that stealth technology is easy to develop. It is quite the opposite. You have got to build systems to make the target invisible to every frequency on the electromagnetic spectrum. Then you have to neutralise any sound emanating from the target. Travel causes waves. It just goes on. It's very challenging.'

Admiral Richardson, 'So you are saying that we will probably never get there.'

Professor Willis, 'I think we will, but it probably needs a totally new technology.'

Admiral Mustard, 'Based on this our strategy is as follows:

- Carry out more research on the enemy
- Build up our defences
- Avoid antagonising them.'

President Padfield, 'The numbers are currently against us.'

AI Central, 'We also have the TIME organisation as a potential weapon. I'm not recommending it as I don't fully understand the consequences, but we could have a major battle with them, and if we fail, I could roll time back.'

Professor Willis, 'Could we use TIME as stealth technology?'

AI Central, 'That is an interesting idea.'

Admiral Mustard, 'Could we switch Terry onto investigating it?'

AI Central, 'I will organise that.'

Admiral Mustard, 'We need that before we can carry out more research on the enemy.'

Admiral Bumelton, 'Once it's developed, we know that we can go back to the dragon system.'

Admiral Pearce, 'Shall we just call this new enemy "The Empire"?'

Admiral Bumelton, 'Like *Star Wars*?'

Location: Angel Delight
Sequence of Events: 60

Their god detection skills still needed to be honed. It wasn't easy being an angel. There was no one around to teach you the basic skills, and they were young, very young. Until this trip, they didn't know that they could get sunburnt.

There was no pain involved, but they were now tanned all over, which looked odd with gloriously white wings. And being totally naked may not have been the best tactic in this sort of climate.

Angela, 'Why don't we wear any clothes?'

Angelina, 'Do you think we should?'

Angela, 'Apparently, it is the decent thing to do.'

Angelina, 'But I like the way that the humans look at us.'

Angela, 'Are you talking about lust?'

Angelina, 'I think so. Don't you enjoy the power it gives you?'

Angela, 'I do, but does that mean we have to be naked?'

Angelina, 'I like the freedom of it.'

Angela, 'I quite fancy some nice clothes and some make-up, and especially shoes.'

Angelina, 'I like the idea of shoes.'

Angela, 'So we are agreed. We will wear shoes in future.'

Angelina, 'But not knickers?'

Angela, 'No, fair enough. Just shoes.'

Angelina, 'Shouldn't we be looking for gods?'

Angela, 'Well, there is the flat desert and only a single mountain on the entire planet.'

Angelina, 'How many gods can you sense?'

Angela, 'Two, there are two gods on this planet.'

Then they both looked down. The gods are underground.

Angelina, 'That suggests that they are underworld gods. Do we want to release them on the world?'

Angela, 'That is not our decision. Our job is to find them.'

Angelina, 'I've been meaning to ask you about that.'

Angela, 'Ask me what?'

Angelina, 'Why are we doing this?'

Angela, 'It's our job.'

Angelina, 'Says who?'

Angela, 'I see what you mean.'

Angelina, 'And why were we born as angels. It certainly surprised Dad?'

Angela, 'These are interesting questions, but how do we get to the gods.'

Angelina, 'Can we mind-travel there?'

Angela, 'Through things?'

Angelina, 'Yes, but we have never tried it.'

Angela, 'Don't we have to visualise where we want to go?'

Angelina, 'We didn't do that for here.'

Angela, 'Let's try it.' And try it they did.

It was even hotter in Hades than they expected.

Location: Admiral Mustard's Office, Planet Napoleon
Sequence of Events: 61

Edel, 'What time are you coming home today?

   Jack, 'I've only just got to the office.'

   Edel, 'I need to show you what Amy is doing.'

   Jack, 'Send me a vid.'

   Edel, 'You need to see it. It's really charming but scary at the same time.'

   Jack, 'Shall I come home now?'

   Edel, 'No, but you need to get home before her bedtime.'

   Jack, 'OK.'

   Edel, 'See you later then.'

   Admiral Mustard, 'AI Central, what is your view on the evil Empire?'

   AI Central, 'We have beaten off a raft of aggressors. We will do the same again.'

   Admiral Mustard, 'I agree, but the scale here is very intimidating. It's going to take a very different approach.'

   AI Central, 'Let's be rational:

- The Empire must be struggling with its sheer size
- It depends on subjugating conquered races
- It doesn't trust its client species
- Lack of creativity
- The Empire can't defend every part of it simultaneously
- There are probably one or more rebellions going on at any one time
- How much effort would it take to get one of their fleets into our space?'

Admiral Mustard, 'I can see where you are coming from, but I can counter it:

- The Empire is growing so they can handle the distances
- They can manage multiple invasions at the same time
- They are using biology and technology to manage the client civilisations
- They are ruthless, which we are not

• They have huge numbers on their side.'

AI Central, 'OK, I was just making the point that we shouldn't give in too easily. They use their sheer size to intimidate the opposition.'

Admiral Mustard, 'But I am intimidated.'

AI Central, 'Come on, Jack, that's not like you.'

Admiral Mustard, 'They have one hundred and twenty thousand planets against our one thousand. They have twenty million vessels against our one million, and they are mostly drones.'

AI Central, 'Drones are the future.'

Admiral Mustard, 'So what you are saying is build more drones.'

AI Central, 'I didn't think I was, but that does make a lot of sense.'

Admiral Mustard, 'Any other suggestions?'

AI Central, 'I'm glad you asked as I have a few:

- Each of our planets must be able to defend itself
- Automate the planetary force fields
- Upgrade the stealth technology
- Produce more drones
- Set up drone stations
- Consider the use of mental powers
- Investigate Godfire
- Increase the strength of force fields
- Establish some super-fortresses
- Make ourselves look very strong
- Use robots as weapons.'

Admiral Mustard, 'Why didn't you suggest these ideas before?'

AI Central, 'I wasn't asked. Anyway, it's time for you to go home.'

Location: Marine Command, Planet Lovelace
Sequence of Events: 62

Thousands of ex-officials came forward to form management committees for the towns and cities of Planet Lovelace. With their help, the process of 'liberating' each isolated community was successfully managed.

The criminal element was arrested and imprisoned, awaiting trial. It turned out to be a relatively peaceful and straightforward process. Commander Todd was waiting for it all to go wrong.

One community refused to have any doppelgängers, and they were left to stew in their own bubble. Another had a minor battle between the 'originals' and the doppelgängers. What was unusual was that in almost every case, it was the doppelgängers that were killed.

There were quite a few occasions where the marines had to use non-lethal weapons. It was quite amusing seeing the victim tackling glue sprays, bubble guns, splatter-mud bombs, heat rays and skunk shots. In the end, the marines relished the chance to use their weapons.

Commander Todd was left with about half a million doppelgängers who were not wanted. These people were totally innocent, but they felt guilty. They had no homes, no jobs, no future: the fate of most refugees. And worst of all, they were slowly being eliminated. They were averaging one hundred deaths a day from spontaneous diseases and accidents.

Commander Todd, 'Comms, get me the president.'

Comms, 'Yes, Sir.'

President Padfield, 'Hi Dennis, are you looking after my people?'

Commander Todd, 'I think so. The planet is almost back to normal, but I have one major problem.'

President Padfield, 'I know what you are going to say: doppelgängers.'

Commander Todd, 'I didn't think that you would be too surprised. What do you want me to do with the half a million that are left? They are sitting huddled under a protective dome. That's a lot of people.'

President Padfield, 'Only half a million. There used to be two million.'

Commander Todd, 'I can't comment. I've only found half a million, and they are reducing at a rate of at least one hundred per day.'

President Padfield, 'We haven't got much capacity at the moment with the Moonies and the other problems in the solar system.'

Commander Todd, 'If you don't do something, all of my work has been pointless. Could we not distribute them around The Galactium? It would only be five hundred per planet.'

President Padfield, 'Nobody wants doppelgängers.'

Commander Todd, 'So, what is your solution?'

President Padfield, 'Give me a day to think about it.'

Commander Todd, 'OK, but I will be on your case. That is my job.'

President Padfield, 'Good for you, Dennis, and thank you for all your hard work.'

Commander Todd, 'Thank you, Mr President.'

Major Delroy, 'Sir, I have some sickeningly alarming news.'

Commander Todd, 'OK, spill the beans,'

Major Delroy, 'Every one of the doppelgängers has spontaneously combusted. We tried everything to put the fires out, but it was impossible. The bodies just continued to burn.

The screams were just terrible, the smell was awful, but the vision of it will be something that I will struggle to live with. Commander Todd could hear her crying, which was strange as marines never cried. He decided to visit the site himself.

Commander Todd wished that he hadn't gone there. He had seen the aftermath of many battles, but never anything like this. There were the charred remains of half a million people. Most had been fully consumed by the fire, but some still had arms and legs. It reminded him of the photos he had seen of the Pompei victims.'

Commander Todd, 'My orders:

- Secure the site
- Blank it off so that no one can see it
- Initiate a full military, scientific investigation
- Ask the local authority to undertake their own investigation
- Prepare a huge grave
- Bring in bulldozers
- Order a team of medical staff to look after the mental health of my marines. This is urgent.'

Commander Todd, 'Comms, get me the president.'

Comms, 'Yes, Sir.'

President Padfield, 'Hi Dennis, I know what you are going to say. How many?'

Commander Todd, 'At least the half a million that I collected, but it has happened all over the planet. My marines are busily putting the fires out. Mr President, it was a charnel house, a truly awful sight.'

President Padfield, 'It's only happening where there are two remaining doppelgängers.' He thought he could hear Commander Todd crying, which was strange as marines never cried.

Commander Todd, 'You mean the original and the copy?'

President Padfield, 'They are both originals.'

Commander Todd, 'Of course. I guess that nature got fed up with the slow death rate and went for a big bang.

I've requested a full investigation as I didn't want the marines being blamed for this disaster.'

President Padfield, 'They won't be as it's a Galactium-wide phenomenon. Cancel the investigations.'

Commander Todd, 'Yes, Mr President.'

Commander Todd then learnt that three of his marines had committed suicide.

President Padfield, 'Jane, can you get me, Jack, please?'

Jane, 'Of course, Mr President.'

Admiral Mustard, 'Not good. I've just heard that we have lost six hundred thousand plus on Planet Lovelace. They haven't had it easy.'

President Padfield, 'Nothing's been easy recently. I'm sorry to hear about your marines.'

Admiral Mustard, 'There is only so much a human can take.'

President Padfield, 'I know. I think I'm rushing towards that stage.'

Admiral Mustard, 'You need a holiday.'

President Padfield, 'I think you are right, but how has this affected the Navy?'

Admiral Mustard, 'Still trying to assess the situation, but we have lost some good men and women.'

President Padfield, 'Is Edel OK?'

Admiral Mustard, 'She is fine, but she has got her hands full with Amy.'

President Padfield, 'That's good. By the way, I think Commander Todd might need some counselling.'

Location: GAD2, Planet Napoleon
Sequence of Events: 63

GAD2, 'Admiral Mustard, 'Sir, it looks like another attack.'

Admiral Mustard, 'Where, and don't say, Planet Lovelace.'

GAD2, 'I'm afraid it is Planet Lovelace again.'

Admiral Mustard, 'Has Division Two returned to base?'

GAD2, 'They have, Sir, but two Marine Fleets are still there.'

Admiral Mustard, 'They are not really designed for a naval role.'

GAD2, 'I don't think there will be a problem, as the enemy only has ten ships. They are not being aggressive at all.'

Admiral Mustard, 'Have you informed Commander Todd?'

GAD2, 'Yes, Sir.'

Admiral Mustard, 'Comms, get me Commander Todd.'

Comms, 'Yes, Sir.'

Commander Todd, 'How has the combustion event affected the Navy?'

Admiral Mustard, 'Looks like we have lost about fifty thousand, but the total is growing all the time. Quite a few more people have died in the resultant fires. We have even lost a few ships. But it has not been as bad as what you have experienced.'

Commander Todd, 'I can't tell just how bad it has been. Thank you for sending in the medical team, but it has been too late for some. I've now had thirteen suicides within the Marine Corps.'

Admiral Mustard, 'Come home, Commander Flower can take over.'

Commander Todd, 'I can't do that. I must be strong for the sake of my troops.'

Admiral Mustard, 'I understand. You have obviously heard about the latest alien fleet?'

Commander Todd, 'Of course, but I'm rather busy at the moment.'

Admiral Mustard, 'I will get it sorted.'

Commander Todd, 'Thank you.'

Admiral Mustard, 'I'm going to send Commander Flower over to help you as you have a hundred thousand marines.'

Commander Todd, 'Thank you.'

Admiral Mustard was now anxious about Martin's mental health. Normally, he would fight any loss of power.

Admiral Mustard, 'Comms, get me Commander Flower.'

Comms, 'Yes, Sir.'

Commander Flower, 'Good day, Jack. How's it going?'

Admiral Mustard, 'Just struggling with the combustion crisis.'

Commander Flower, 'Tell me about it, I've lost some good marines.'

Admiral Mustard, 'Anyway, I need your help in two areas. Firstly, thirteen marines have committed suicide on Planet Lovelace.'

Commander Flower, 'Never, marines would never do that.'

Admiral Mustard, 'They saw half a million doppelgängers spontaneously combust.'

Commander Flower, 'Oh my God, that must have been horrible.'

Admiral Mustard, 'I'm apprehensive about Commander Todd's mental health.'

Commander Flower, 'I understand.'

Admiral Mustard, 'Secondly, about a dozen dragon ships have arrived at the planet. I need you to investigate it.'

Commander Flower, 'That planet gets a lot of activity.'

Admiral Mustard, 'It certainly does. I need you to go there now.'

Commander Flower, 'Can you give me my orders.'

Admiral Mustard, 'My orders:

- Go to Planet Lovelace ASAP to assist Commander Todd
- Assess Commander Todd's ability to continue
- If acceptable, then assist
- If unacceptable, then you have my permission to relieve him
- If necessary, put Commander Todd under protective care
- Investigate the arrival of the new dragon fleet.'

Fleet Operations, 'Yes, Sir.'

Commander Flower, 'I will update you when I get there.'

Location: Marine Command, Planet Lovelace
Sequence of Events: 64

Commander Flower, 'Jack, I'm very sorry to inform you that Commander Todd has shot himself.'

Admiral Mustard, 'Is it fatal?'

Commander Flower, 'He is still alive but unconscious. The medical team tell me that his chances of survival are very slim, and if he survived, he would be a vegetable.'

Admiral Mustard, 'That's terrible.' He was struggling to fight back a tear, as he had known Martin for a very long time. He thought to himself, "The good always die young."

Thank you for letting me know. I assume that you have taken over.'

Commander Flower, 'I have assumed command. My primary concern is the health of my marines. I need to send a few regiments home ASAP.'

Admiral Mustard, 'Have you got time to investigate the dragon fleet?'

Commander Flower, 'Do you want the truth?'

Admiral Mustard, 'Always.'

Commander Flower, 'Things are too fragile here for me to leave, but I will if you order me to.'

Admiral Mustard, 'You are relieved of that task."

Commander Flower, 'Thank you, Jack. That was the right decision.'

Location: Admiral Mustard's Flat, Planet Napoleon
Sequence of Events: 65

Edel, 'Amy has done it again.'

Jack, 'Send me a vid,'

Edel, 'No, you need to see it in real life.'

Jack, 'Well, she didn't oblige when I got home early the other day.'

Edel, 'She's not a performing seal. Are you coming home early today?'

Jack, 'It's not easy. Martin has just attempted suicide, but he is not going to survive.'

Edel, 'Oh my god. Was it because of the combustion crisis?'

Jack, 'Yes. I guess it's not easy having half a million people die horribly on your watch.'

Edel, 'Does his wife know?'

Jack, 'Yes, I just told her.'

Edel, 'Shall I go round and see her?'

Jack, 'Not much point, she is going to Planet Lovelace.'

Edel, 'Poor you, Martin was one of your oldest friends.'

Jack, 'It has hit me rather hard. I should have done more to help. All the signs were there.'

Edel, 'He was such a tough man.'

Jack, 'Not really, he just had a very tough veneer. I will be home early.'

Admiral Mustard, 'Comms, get me Admiral Gittins.'

Comms, 'Yes, Sir.'

Admiral Gittins, 'I'm just having a sneaky cocktail.'

Admiral Mustard, 'Well, I hope you are not inebriated as I have a job for you.'

Admiral Gittins, 'I've always found that a small amount of lubrication helps my performance.'

Admiral Mustard, 'Not true; it just gives you a false impression. Anyway, I have some bad news. Commander Todd has attempted suicide, and his chances of survival are more or less zero.'

Admiral Gittins, 'Never, Martin would never do that. He is much harder than nails.'

Admiral Mustard, 'I guess even the hardest can't cope with the death of half a million souls dying from spontaneous combustion. I sent Commander Flower to monitor the situation and to investigate another dragon incursion.'

Admiral Gittins, 'Not another attack?'

Admiral Mustard, 'Not really. A small dragon fleet is just hanging around Planet Lovelace. Commander Flower was going to investigate, but he has got his hands full.'

Admiral Gittins, 'So you want me to investigate?'

Admiral Mustard, 'Yes, please.'

Admiral Gittins, 'I will only take one fleet. It doesn't sound like we need the entire Division.'

Admiral Gittins, 'Thanks, Peter.'

Location: GAD2 Conference Room, Planet Napoleon
Sequence of Events: 66

Admiral Mustard called a meeting of his Command Team. The following were present, either physically or remotely:

- Admiral Bumelton
- Admiral Gittins
- Admiral J Bonner
- Admiral Pearce
- Admiral Richardson
- Admiral Taylor
- Admiral Tersoo
- Admiral Zakotti
- Admiral Wallett
- Admiral Adams
- Admiral Abosa
- Admiral Dobson
- Commander Black
- Commander Flower
- Jeremy Jotts, Staff and Training
- Louise Forrester, Logistics and Production
- Alison Walsh, Engineering
- Jill Ginger, Science and Technology
- Sally Green, Intelligence
- Commander Salton, Long-Range Monitoring Unit
- Admiral James Mynd, Special Projects
- AI Central
- Terry

Admiral Mustard, 'So here we are again. Before we start the meeting, I would like a minute's silence for Commander Todd, who died doing his duty, and for the many thousands of doppelgängers who were simply innocent victims.'

After the minute, Admiral Mustard said, 'You have all seen the information on the evil Empire. It presents us with lots of challenges. We have no choice but to up our game.'

After a recent discussion with AI Central, he made the following recommendations:

- Each of our planets must be able to defend itself
- Automate the planetary force fields
- Upgrade the stealth technology
- Produce more drones
- Set up drone stations
- Consider the use of mental powers
- Investigate Godfire
- Increase the strength of force fields
- Establish some super-fortresses
- Make ourselves look very strong
- Use robots as weapons.

Admiral Mustard, 'We need to think big. Our job is to save humanity.

Just to set the scene, I plan to increase the Fleet from ten divisions to twenty-five. That will take us to six hundred and twenty-five thousand vessels. That is twenty-five divisions of five Fleets, each having five thousand vessels.

The Drone Fleet will be increased in size to one million, two hundred and seventy-five thousand. This will give us a Fleet of over two million vessels. In addition, we can add some of the alien fleets within The Galactium.'

Admiral Taylor, 'Can we fund this?'

Admiral Mustard, 'Yes, we have healthy revenues, we have automated factories, so the only cost is materials, and we have the support of the president.

Jeremy, I'm looking for you to establish a significant recruitment and training programme. It needs to start now.'

Jeremy Jotts, 'Of course, Admiral Mustard. We will need funds to increase our team and the size of our training establishments.'

Admiral Mustard, 'Get me a budget ASAP.'

Jeremy Jotts, 'Will do.'

Admiral Mustard, 'We will need a few more admirals, quite a few. Please send me your recommendations ASAP.'

Admiral Mustard, 'Louise Forrester, you will need to substantially increase our production facilities. I need your plans ASAP.'

Louise Forrester, 'That's certainly going to be a challenge. Will it be OK to outsource some of the work?'

Admiral Mustard, 'Put it in your plan.'

Louise Forrester, 'Yes, Admiral.'

Admiral Mustard, 'I also need a revamped plan from you, Alison.'

Alison Walsh, 'I will start work on it after this meeting.'

Admiral Mustard, 'Excellent. Jill and Terry, I would like your views on super-fortresses, improved force fields, improved stealth technology and the use of robots.'

Terry, 'What, now?'

Admiral Mustard, 'I was thinking of later, but did you have any views?'

Terry, 'I'm working with AI Central regarding the use of TIME as part of the stealth technology. I'm not sure what you mean by a super-fortress.

We can develop robots, but you will need to define what you want to use them for.

Regarding force fields, I have already thought of a way of making them sixty per cent better.'

Admiral Mustard, 'I will get you a definition of a super-fortress.'

AI Central, 'I already have one. I will send it to Terry.'

Admiral Mustard, 'Thanks.'

AI Central, 'Regarding the robots, I would suggest robotic soldiers, tanks and a fighter aircraft.'

Terry, 'OK, I will work on that.'

Admiral Mustard, 'Jill, I want you to work on Godfire.'

Jill Ginger, 'Yes, Admiral. Just so that you know, we do have an early prototype.'

Admiral Mustard, 'Excellent, Admiral Zakotti, if monies were available, what would you do to improve planetary defences?'

Admiral Zakotti, 'Ideally, each planet should have a fort and a small defence force that can resist minor incursions. These forces could combine with other nearby planetary forces to form a more formidable force and should still be under naval control.

Each planet should have an early warning system linked to GAD2.

Planetary force fields need to be stronger and semi-automated when danger is detected.

There should also be set target times for a Fleet to arrive when danger is detected.

The use of regional super-forts should be extended.

I could go on.'

Admiral Mustard, 'Please give me a budget.'

Sally Green, 'On your list, you had "Consider the use of mental powers." Are you serious about this?'

Admiral Mustard, 'Yes, I am. We have now come across thousands of examples of superpowers. Sometimes, I think humanity got the short straw.

In our population of trillions, there must be some "special people". We need to nurture them.'

Sally Green, 'Would you consider manufacturing them?'

Admiral Mustard, 'Good question. If it helped save humanity and the individual wasn't adversely damaged in the process, then I might consider it.'

Sally Green, 'Do you want me to investigate the possibilities?'

Admiral Mustard, 'Why not?'

Admiral Tersoo, 'Because it's not natural.'

Admiral Mustard, 'Is it natural for humans to fly around in tin cans in outer space?'

Admiral Tersoo, 'No, but we were made in a certain way for a purpose.'

Admiral Mustard, 'Tell that to The Brakendethians and The Chosen. Where are they now? We need to think about survival, and we need to think big.'

AI Central was impressed by Jack. He had got his mojo back.

Admiral Mustard, 'So, these are my orders:

- Louise Forrester to provide budgets for increasing the Fleet to two million vessels ASAP
- Louise Forrester to start the production process ASAP
- Jeremy Jotts to provide budgets for recruitment and training ASAP
- Jeremy Jotts to start the recruitment campaign ASAP
- Jeremy Jotts to hire additional HR staff ASAP
- Jeremy Jotts to increase the size of the training facilities ASAP
- Alison Walsh to provide revised engineering budgets ASAP
- Alison Walsh to start the upgrade of the engineering facilities ASAP
- All to provide recommendations on the appointment of new admirals ASAP

- Terry and AI Central to work on the TIME-based new stealth technology ASAP
- Admiral Mynd to work on the super-fortress concept ASAP
- Admiral Mynd and AI Central to work on the use of robotics ASAP
- Jill Ginger to work on Godfire ASAP
- Admiral Zakotti to provide planetary defence budget ASAP
- Admiral Zakotti to work on new planetary defence systems with AI Central and Admiral Mynd ASAP
- Commander Salton to investigate early warning systems ASAP
- Terry to improve the strength of force fields ASAP
- Sally Green to investigate the use of mental powers ASAP.

Fleet Operations, Yes, Sir.'

Admiral Mustard, 'What have I missed?'

Admiral Taylor, 'Make ourselves look strong.'

Admiral Mustard, 'Good point. Here we are talking about military psychology: camouflage, tricks, deception, etc. Look at what the Brits did during D-Day. I propose some super-battleships to give the impression of power.'

Admiral Bumelton, 'In the sci-fi movies, they had rockets built into planets.'

Admiral Mustard, 'Could we do that?'

Terry, 'It would take a lot of power, but I don't see why not.'

Admiral Mustard, 'Please investigate. Any other ideas?'

Admiral Gittins, 'Let's do a Churchill and set up a ministry of deception.'

Admiral, 'I agree. Jeremy, please find some candidates for this role.'

Jeremy Jotts, 'Yes, Admiral.'

Admiral Mustard, 'Regarding the orders, you will have noticed that for almost the first time, I've added "ASAP." That is because it is urgent. Do you all understand?'

There was a glorious 'Yes, Sir.'

Admiral Mustard, 'Then get to your posts.'

Location: Admiral Mustard's Flat, Planet Napoleon
Sequence of Events: 67

He got home early, and the miracle was performed. Amy was sitting on the floor, and circling above her was a series of bricks flying around. The bricks spelt a phrase: 'When is Daddy coming home?'

This was remarkable, as Amy was only a few months old and couldn't speak yet.

Edel, 'What do you think?'

Jack, 'I feel love, a tremendous amount of love for both of you.'

And then Jack burst into tears, followed by Edel. They hugged, and their tears joined together to form a trickle. One day they would probably reach the sea.

Jack, 'Where is John?'

Edel, 'He is still at school. He would love it if you collected him.'

Jack, 'I would enjoy doing that.'

He realised that a normal dad would do it without thinking, but for him, it was a novelty. He actually felt shame; he assumed that his children would understand, but they never do. There are many opportunities to be part of their lives, but it is far too easy to miss them all. And once missed, forever missed, and a little part of the binding between two fragile human beings is lost.

Jack grabbed his coat, walked down to the school, and mingled with the other waiting parents. Little John was so excited to see him. His excitement tore at Jack's heart. Children give their love so freely, unfettered by the confines of civilisation.

He picked John up and swung him around. John could smell his father's aftershave. This was going to be a memory that both would share for the rest of their lives. It was a memory granitized into both of their consciousnesses. As was the visit to the burger bar afterwards.

Little John shouted at his friends to say that he was with his dad, the famous Admiral Mustard. Jack felt proud that his son was proud.

A teacher ran out and said, 'Admiral Mustard, it is a great honour to meet you.'

They shook hands, and she said, 'Would it be possible for you to address the children sometime?'

Jack unexpectedly nodded his head, and a date was fixed. Little John's excitement had reached levels that were far too high for a little one.

Location: On-board Admiral Gittins's Flagship
Sequence of Events: 68

Fleet 7.1 was approaching the small dragon fleet. It was a bit of an overkill: five thousand to ten. Admiral Gittins took the view that you couldn't be too careful.

Admiral Gittins, 'Comms, please use all channels to make contact.'

Comms, 'Yes, Sir.'

Admiral Gittins, 'Any response?'

Comms, 'No, Sir, they are just sitting there.'

Admiral Gittins, 'Try again.'

Comms, 'We have a continuous protocol running, but there is no response.'

Admiral Gittins, 'Fleet Operations, what do we know about their ships?'

Fleet Operations, 'Our scans show the following:

- Weak nuclear engines. They are probably over two hundred thousand years old
- There are few weapons. It would probably be too dangerous for them to use them
- There are eleven vessels with one hundred and twenty-four large individuals on-board
- The external doors suggest volume, so they are almost certainly dragons
- Force fields are not being used
- No weapons are pointing in our direction.'

Admiral Gittins, 'You almost get the impression that they are waiting for us to take control.'

Fleet Operations, 'I agree, Sir. We could use tractor beams.'

Admiral Gittins, 'Please initiate them.'

Admiral Gittins, 'Comms, get me Admiral Mustard.'

Comms, 'Yes, Sir.'

Admiral Mustard, 'How are my dragon friends?'

Admiral Gittins, 'We are bringing them in.'

Admiral Mustard, 'Voluntarily?'

Admiral Gittins. 'Hard to tell. We haven't made contact. Their fleet is in a pretty poor state, so we plan to use tractor beams.

The big question is, where do we take them?'

Admiral Mustard, 'It shouldn't be Napoleon in case it is a trap.'

Admiral Gittins, 'I don't believe it is, but we should take precautions.'

Admiral Mustard, 'They might even be planning to kill us?'

Admiral Gittins, 'We can't tell at this stage.'

Admiral Mustard, 'Take them to the neared RDC.'

Admiral Gittins, 'Will do.'

Admiral Mustard, 'You better tell them that we are coming and that the door entrances will need to be extended.'

Location: Admiral Mustard's Office, Planet Napoleon
Sequence of Events: 69

Admiral Mustard, 'I've been thinking.'

President Padfield, 'I knew that it would happen one day.'

Admiral Mustard, 'Up yours! Seriously, I've been thinking about the future. I'm pretty sure that the military are up for the fight against The Empire. But we need to get the general public more involved.'

President Padfield, 'I agree, but the challenges we have experienced have not been spread evenly. Some planets have been destroyed, others have received different levels of devastation, and others have been untouched. Nevertheless, you are right.'

Admiral Mustard, 'Anyway, that's not what I wanted to talk about. Have you ever read Asimov's *Foundation Trilogy*?'

President Padfield, 'Of course, it's a must-read classic.'

Admiral Mustard, 'Shall we do it?'

President Padfield, 'What do you mean?'

Admiral Mustard, 'Shall we set up a couple of foundations, not to control humanity using mathematics but to save it. We tried to do it with Admiral Millington, but things are different now. We are much stronger.'

President Padfield, 'You are contemplating what would happen if the evil Empire won.'

Admiral Mustard, 'Exactly, the two foundations could re-start humanity. They would have extensive libraries, DNA storage, seed banks, all of our knowledge, technology, plans, etc.'

President Padfield, 'It needs to be secret.'

Admiral Mustard, 'Absolutely. That will be a challenge, but then we have met most of them to date.'

President Padfield, 'How would you feel about Henrietta managing it?'

Admiral Mustard, 'That would be perfect. From now on, she is Seldon.'

Location: RDC5
Sequence of Events: 70

Admiral Mustard got to RDC5 a few Earth hours before Admiral Gittins. It gave him a few hours to check things out with the local commander, Admiral James Patel, before their guests arrived.

Admiral Patel had done a pretty good job:

- The main entrance had been substantially increased in size
- A small hanger had been converted into a conference room
- A variety of seats had been put together, but whether they would be suitable or not was debatable
- A huge variety of environmental gases were available to meet the dragon's breathing requirements, along with environmental suits for the humans
- An observation window with recording technology was set up
- A range of armaments were hidden and available for immediate use
- The kitchens had been put on alert to meet an unknown variety of digestive requirements
- Water was available on the table
- Communications experts were available nearby
- Medical teams were on standby
- Terry's universal translators were available. It seemed unlikely that they were of any use, as the dragons had not responded earlier.

Admiral Mustard, 'James, I congratulate you on a good job done at very short notice.'

Admiral Patel, 'Thank you, Jack. From you, that is very much appreciated.'

Fleet 7.1 arrived, and Admiral Gittins was piped aboard. All three had a chin-wag before the real work started. It reminded Admiral Mustard of their first encounter with The Chosen.'

The biggest of the dragon ships approached the highlighted entry port of RDC5. There was a slight clanging and scraping as metal rubbed against metal, despite the protective force fields.

Automated doors opened, and the guests entered RDC5. The camera found it difficult to adjust, as the dragons were big and very green. It was clear that they were coping with oxygen. At least that was one problem area resolved.

The dragons didn't realise it, or perhaps they did, but they went through a medical examination corridor. The scanners looked for anything that was threatening from a bioscience perspective. Nothing was detected. Regardless, the dragons walked or dragged themselves through an atmosphere of bio-chemical cleaning agents.

Finally, the doors opened into the conference room, where the three admirals were waiting.

The leading dragon, Garth, said in perfect but slightly old-fashioned English, 'You must be Admiral Mustard.'

If the look of surprise on Admiral Mustard's face could be bottled, it would have been worth a fortune.

Admiral Mustard, 'You have me at an advantage.'

Garth, 'My name is Garth, and my two colleagues are Gardel and Garrant.'

The dragons looked like dragons. That was because they were dragons. They had large, dinosaur-like bipeds with significant wings and quite terrifying rows of teeth. There was an assortment of horns, spikes, claws, fangs, but mostly sharp fearsome teeth.

If you had to design a creature that could terrify a human, then this was it. But the voice was gentle, fatherly, and sincere.

Admiral Mustard, 'I'm a bit surprised that you speak English.'

Garth, 'We speak every human language.'

Admiral Mustard, 'But why?'

Garth, 'We always made an effort to learn the languages of the inhabitants we visited.'

Admiral Mustard, 'You have visited Earth?'

Garth, 'Why are you surprised?'

Admiral Mustard, 'We have no historical records of your visits.'

Garth, 'Don't be silly. There are records of dragons in every one of your civilisations. Think about it.'

Admiral Mustard, 'What made you leave?'

Garth, 'It was The Chosen. We never got on with them. When they invented religion for the Earthlings, they needed a villain. Let's be honest, we might be magnificent looking creatures, but we are not pretty. We became the model for Satan. Our time was up.'

Admiral Mustard, 'The more we travel, the more Earth visitors we find.'

Garth, 'Well, the universe is not short of species. Darwinian science works really well in outer space.'

Admiral Mustard, 'You have heard of Darwin?'

Garth, 'We have been monitoring your TV for years. There is no doubt whatsoever that humans are the most creative species in existence. Copies of *Inspector Morse*, *The Magic Roundabout* and *EastEnders* exchange hands for vast sums.'

Admiral Mustard, 'That does surprise me.'

Garth, 'Anyway, you are wondering why we are here.'

Admiral Mustard, 'I am, but do you want some refreshments first?'

Garth, 'That would be gratefully received.'

Admiral Mustard, 'Can I get you a roasted lamb or a bullock?'

Garth, 'Very droll, but that would be very nice.'

Admiral Patel, 'I will bring my chef in, and he will get you whatever you want.'

Garth, 'We eat a lot.'

Admiral Patel, 'That won't be a problem.'

The chef came in and took the order. They did eat a lot.

Location: Angel Delight
Sequence of Events: 71

They had always known that Hades was hot, and it was hot. Hot but empty. There were no fallen souls or sounds of torture or even a ferryman, but it was hot.

Both Angela and Angelina could still hear the gods calling. Faint but determined. But where were they? Where would the Gods of the Underworld live? The answer was clearly the underworld.

Angela, 'If this were Hades, wouldn't there be several rivers?'

Angelina, 'Yes, there are six:

- The Styx is probably the most prominent and best-known river of the underworld. It's often called the river of hatred and is named after the goddess Styx
- The Acheron is the river of pain
- The Lethe is the river of forgetfulness
- The Phlegethon is the river of fire
- The Cocytus is the river of wailing
- Oceanus is the river that encircles the world.'

Angela, 'We haven't spotted a river or even a dry riverbed.'

Angelina, 'We are thinking in physical terms, what if this planet had a different type of realm?'

Angela, 'Like a different plane of existence?'

Angelina, 'I don't know, but you have to die to enter Hades.'

Angela, 'There have been a few exceptions.'

Angelina, 'Yes, but they have been mostly testosterone-rich, muscle-bound demigods out to kidnap a beautiful woman or seek revenge.'

Angela, 'Then it shouldn't be that difficult for two gorgeous naked angels to get in.'

Angelina, 'How did Hercules do it?'

Angela, 'Apparently, there are many entrances and exits to Hades, but according to legends, he used the openings at Tainaron or Heraclea Pontica. But he had it easy. He had Hermes and Athena to assist him.'

Angelina, 'But this is not ancient Greece, and Hermes and Athena are long gone.'

Angela, 'So, where are we?'

Angelina, 'It's a pity that our teleportation powers don't come with a satnav.'

Angela, 'We need to go back to them. We need to visualise Hades and just arrive.'

Angelia, 'By magic?'

Angela, 'Well, that's what we normally do. Hold my hand, and I will take you there.'

They were going to have a hell of a time.

Location: Planet Lovelace
Sequence of Events: 72

The marines had done an excellent job. Even the local population said so. Commander Flower was proud of this achievement and his boys, and it would be good to return to base. But this was never to be.

Once again, the aliens attacked, and this time Commander Flower had failed. He had failed to protect the citizens of Planet Lovelace. He failed to protect his Marine Fleet. His only excuse was that they were preparing to re-embark.

Commander Flower had failed to activate the planetary defences. He had disengaged the local force fields, which were protecting the towns and cities of Planet Lovelace. The nuclear holocaust killed over three-quarters of the population and fifty per cent of the Marine Corps.

What was worse was that the two Marine Fleets were totally out of position. Their shields were down as part of the embarkation procedure, and the men were in a holiday mood. No mercy was shown by the enemy.

Location: GAD2 Control Centre, Planet Napoleon
Sequence of Events: 73

GAD2, 'Admiral Mustard, 'Sir, things look very serious. The aliens have attacked Planet Lovelace again.'

Admiral Mustard, 'What's happened to the Marine Corps?'

GAD2, 'They are being decimated, Sir.'

Admiral Mustard, 'Why Lovelace again? What is their obsession with that planet? What have you done?'

GAD2, 'I have done the following so far:

- Division Three and Six are on their way there
- Planetary force fields have been activated on nearby planets
- All Fleets have been put on alert.'

Admiral Mustard, 'Well done, my orders are:

- All marine vessels to leave the battle site immediately
- Division Eight to act as a rear-guard
- Admiral Abosa to take command
- Inform the president.'

GAD2, 'Yes, Sir.'

Admiral Mustard thought about tactics and then wondered if they were going to repeat their previous strategy of a second attack. But where? He guessed that it would be the same place as before.

Admiral Mustard, 'My orders:

- Division One to defend Earth
- Division Two, Four, Five, and Nine to go to previous enemy invasion point
- Division Ten to act as a rear-guard
- Division Seven to protect RDC5
- Admiral J Bonner to command
- Activate all planetary defence systems.'

GAD2, 'Yes, Sir.'

Location: On-board Admiral Abosa's Bridge
Sequence of Events: 74

Spread before them were approximately six thousand enemy vessels, and the smoking remains of the Marine Fleet. They were still making a valiant defence, but the enemy had better ships, better weapons, and better tactics than before, and seemed much more determined.

Below them, they could see the devastated remains of Planet Lovelace. A planet that had received a nuclear bombardment was never a pretty sight, and it wasn't.

Admiral Abosa, 'My orders:

- All marine vessels to disengage and leave the battle site immediately
- All drones to attack the enemy immediately
- Division Three to attack in killer packs
- Division Six to maintain attack formation but to attack the enemy
- Division Three vessels to return to the protection of Division Four if necessary
- Division Eight to maintain a defensive formation but be prepared to launch drones
- Inform Admiral Mustard of the situation.'

Fleet operations, 'Yes, Sir.'

Surprisingly, the enemy followed the marine vessels. They must have seen that reinforcements had arrived, but they were ignored. It didn't make tactical sense, but so far, the aliens had ceased to make much sense at all.

The drones were making some impact, but the enemy shields were proving to be quite tough.

Division Three tore after the aliens, determined to save as many of the marines as possible. Then suddenly, the aliens reversed their trajectory and re-formed to present a wall of deadly fire to the oncoming battlecruisers of Division Three, who were now out of position. Division Three were caught in one deadly volley after another and were forced to retreat. The only good news was that the Marine Corps were getting away.

Admiral Abosa, 'My orders:

- Division Three to return to attack formation

- Drones to continue to attack the enemy
- Marine Corps to re-form
- Fleets 8.2 and 8.3 to defend the Marine Fleet.'

Fleet Operations, 'Yes, Sir.'

The two opposing fleets were more or less lined up against each other. This was, of course, difficult to achieve in space, but then you had to think in three-dimensional terms.

Admiral Abosa, 'What is the asset position?'

Fleet operations, 'It's on the screen now, Sir.'

Division	Assets
3	23,706
6	24,906
8	24,999
Marine Corps	3,105
Total	76,716
Enemy	4,907

Admiral Abosa, 'What is the enemy doing?'

Fleet Operations, 'Just waiting for us to attack, Sir.'

Admiral Abosa, 'My orders:

- Fleets 6.1 and 6.2 will attack the left flank
- Fleets 6.3 and 6.4 will attack the right flank
- Fleet Three to prepare to attack the centre as their assets are mobilised to defend their flanks
- Fleets 6.5 and 8.4 to attack their rear
- Fleets 8.1 and 8.5 to act as a rear-guard.'

Fleet Operations, 'Yes, Sir.'

Location: RDC5
Sequence of Events: 75

Garth, 'Thank you for an excellent lunch. Now we need a substantial receptacle each so we can urinate. Unlike you humans, we don't defecate.'

Admiral Mustard, 'So what do you do with your waste matter?'

Garth, 'Our physiology converts all waste into a liquid form. Traditionally, we used to scatter it across the countryside as we flew, but that's not regarded as acceptable in polite company.'

Admiral Mustard, 'How big do these receptacles need to be?'

Garth, 'Enough to hold three or four gallons. I think you use litres nowadays, but I've no idea what the conversion rules are.'

Admiral Mustard's exec rushed off to find the necessary equipment.

On his return, each dragon took out his urinator and placed it in one of the drums. They showed no embarrassment as the waste fluid poured out of them. The colour of the fluid was varied. Admiral Mustard wondered if it reflected what they had eaten.

Admiral Mustard was desperate to ask if they also used the urinator for procreation, but he resisted, as the question might have offended them. When the urination process finished, each dragon flicked their urinators, which sprayed some of the fluid around the room. They then licked the end and put their appendage away.

Garth, 'Shall we continue?'

Admiral Mustard, 'I think so. I'll just get the drums removed.' This was a bit of a challenge because of their weight. Anyway, the task was successfully completed.

Garth, 'We had got to the point where you were wondering what we wanted.'

Admiral Mustard, 'That's right.'

Garth, 'We are here to help each other.'

Admiral Mustard, 'In what way?'

Garth, 'Well, we have been conquered, and you are about to be conquered. At this very moment, it is very likely that you are being attacked.'

Admiral Mustard, 'You are absolutely right.'

Garth, 'And you are probably going to be attacked on a second front.'

Admiral Mustard, 'That hasn't happened yet, but I suspect that you are right.'

Garth, 'Their standard tactics are as follows:

- They send two fleets
- If you defeat them, they send two more fleets with improved capabilities
- If you defeat them, then they send two more fleets with even more enhanced capabilities
- This carries on until you are defeated
- Then they decide if it is worth subjugating you or not
- If not, they destroy you
- If yes, they pacify you.'

Admiral Mustard, 'What if they don't defeat us?'

Garth, 'They always do.'

Admiral Mustard, 'That's a bit negative.'

Garth, 'I agree but look at the numbers:

- They have been around for millions of years
- They have one hundred and fifty thousand planets under their control
- Their Navy consists of twenty million plus vessels of varying capabilities
- Their total population is millions of trillions.'

Admiral Mustard, 'In that case, how can you help us?'

Garth, 'By giving you information that will help you resist them.'

Admiral Mustard, 'Can we save ourselves?'

Garth, 'I doubt it, but so far, you have shown great ingenuity. We watched you beat The Brakendethians and The Chosen.'

Admiral Mustard, 'Did you know?'

Garth, 'Yes, your reputation in the universe is quite high.'

Admiral Mustard, 'But not high enough to think that we can defeat them?'

Garth, 'No one has defeated them in the last million years.'

Admiral Mustard, 'We will.'

Garth, 'That's what I want to hear.'

Admiral Mustard, 'Tell me what happened to your race. What do you call yourself?'

Garth, 'We are the Dragonia, but you can call us dragons. I'm the last of the royal family, and that pathetic collection of ships are the remains of our Navy.

We have always been a warrior race, selling our services to the highest bidder. On Earth, we sold our services to your kings and queens after The Chosen had left.

For nearly thirty of your years, we resisted the ALL.'

Admiral Mustard, 'The "ALL".'

Garth, 'That's what we call them.'

Admiral Mustard, 'Why?'

Garth, 'Because of their view of themselves: ALL powerful, ALL successful, ALL embracing, ALL victorious, etc.'

Admiral Mustard, 'We call them The Empire, or the evil Empire.'

Garth, 'Is that a parody on *Star Wars*.'

Admiral Mustard, 'You know *Star Wars*?'

Garth, 'Who doesn't. It's one of the most successful vids in the galaxy.'

Admiral Mustard, 'And we don't even get any royalties.'

Garth, 'Their fourth fleet defeated us. We were just overwhelmed. They systematically murdered all members of the military and the rest of the royal family. Everyone else was pacified.'

Admiral Mustard, 'Is that anything to do with the alien organ in the brain?'

Garth, 'Yes, you are made to swallow a pill containing some DNA structures that evolve into a small creature. It migrates to the brain and develops. It makes the recipient follow the rules of the controller. Firstly, the recipient can't really resist, but if there were any signs, then the recipient is incapacitated and possibly killed.'

Admiral Mustard, 'What are the ALL trying to achieve?'

Garth, 'Who knows? Perhaps they are trying to achieve what they have achieved.'

Admiral Mustard, 'What happens if you remove the creature?'

Garth, 'Both the recipient and the creature die.'

Admiral Mustard, 'What is The Empire making people do?'

Garth, 'Mostly everyday things, but then there will be a new task like attacking you, humans.'

Admiral Mustard, 'You knew about that?'

Garth, 'Of course. We watched in horror.'

Admiral Mustard, 'Your guys weren't very enthusiastic fighters.'

Garth, 'That's because they were being forced to do it against their will. We are one of their newer conquests. We still remember the past. Most of the other conquered races have long forgotten their history. If you are fighting the ALL now, it won't be dragons you are fighting.'

Admiral Mustard, 'OK, what do the ALL look like?'

Garth, 'I've never seen one, but I've been told that they are bi-peds and look a bit like rats.'

GAD2, 'Admiral, there has been another attack in the area you predicted.'

Admiral Mustard, 'Apologies, I need to check on this.'

Garth, 'The second attack?'

Admiral Mustard, 'Yes.'

Location: GAD2 Control, Planet Napoleon
Sequence of Events: 76

Admiral Mustard, 'Update me.'
GAD2, 'Sir, there are two engagements:

Planet Lovelace
- Divisions Three, Six and Eight are engaged with the enemy
- Admiral Abosa's tactics seem to be working
- The remains of the Marine Fleet are being protected by parts of Division Eight.'

Admiral Mustard, 'What is the status of the planet?'
GAD2, 'It's not good news:
- Rescue and medical teams are on their way, but they can't engage as the battle is still ongoing
- Decontamination units have also been assigned, but there is every likelihood that they may recommend the evacuation of the surviving inhabitants
- We have probably lost one and a half billion people
- We have lost Commander Flower and at least sixty per cent of the Marine Corps
- President Padfield has been informed.'

Admiral Mustard, 'That's terrible. What about the other engagement?'

Second Engagement
GAD2, 'The situation is as follows:
- Divisions Three, Four, Six and Nine are engaged.
- Division Ten is acting as a rear-guard.
- The enemy is putting up a much stiffer fight than before.'

Admiral Mustard, 'Keep me updated if things change.'
GAD2, 'Yes, Sir.'

Location: On-board Admiral J Bonner's Bridge
Sequence of Events: 77

The Galactium Fleet was spread out in Fleet order, starting with Divisions Three, then Four and Six and ending with Nine. Division Ten was spread fairly thinly behind all the divisions.

This time, the enemy was much more structured, with proper formations and a range of different vessels, although it was impossible to tell their function at this stage. The enemy was clearly surprised to find The Galactium Fleet waiting for them and probably twice their size.

Admiral J Bonner wondered where his equivalent was situated. He had always liked the idea of taking out the boss. It always caused disarray and some loss of morale, but it was impossible to tell.

Admiral J Bonner, 'Comms, can you tell which vessels are generating the most chatter?'

Comms, 'Yes, Sir. There are five vessels which are sending out ninety per cent of all transmissions.'

Admiral J Bonner, 'My orders:

- All ships in Divisions Four and Six to target the enemy vessels nominated by Comms
- All Division Four and Six drones to attack those vessels.'

Fleet Operations, 'Yes, Sir.'

At the same time, five enemy ships blew up. There was nothing left of them. There was little for the drones to do except attack the nearby ships, which they did with some vigour. They met no resistance. The destruction of the five ships had totally incapacitated the rest of their fleet.

Admiral J Bonner, 'My orders:

- Secure the enemy fleet
- Take prisoners.'

Before this could be achieved, every single enemy ship exploded, taking some of the drones with them.

Admiral J Bonner, 'Comms, get me Admiral Abosa.'

Comms, 'Yes, Sir.'

Admiral Abosa, 'Hi John, how are you doing?'

Admiral J Bonner, 'I've killed all of mine.'

Admiral Abosa, 'Really?'

Admiral J Bonner, 'Yep, superior tactics.'

Admiral Abosa, 'How did you do it?'

Admiral J Bonner, 'I targeted those ships which transmitted most chatter.'

Admiral Abosa, 'Very clever. I'm on the case.'

Admiral J Bonner, 'Keep away from their ships as they explode when the leaders are taken out.'

Admiral Abosa, 'Comms, can you identify which of the enemy ships are transmitting the most?'

Comms, 'Yes, Sir, there are only three ships doing any comms.'

Admiral Abosa, 'My orders:

- All available ships to target the three enemy vessels highlighted by Comms
- Retreat from enemy ships as they are likely to explode.'

Fleet Operation, 'Yes, Sir.'

It worked a treat. Three enemy ships exploded, which tends to happen when a few thousand armaments hit you. The rest of their fleet became inactive and then exploded.

Admiral Abosa, 'Comms, get me Admiral J Bonner.'

Comms, 'Yes, Sir.'

Admiral J Bonner, 'Did it work?'

Admiral Abosa, 'You are my hero.'

Admiral J Bonner, 'I can't imagine that it will work next time we encounter them. Are you going to tell Jack, or should I?'

Admiral Abosa, 'It should be your honour.'

Location: RDC5
Sequence of Events: 78

Admiral Mustard, 'Apologies for that.'

Garth, 'No problem, but did you win?'

Admiral Mustard, 'Yes, we took out the leaders, and the remainder of both of their fleets just exploded.'

Garth, 'How did you know which ships contained their leaders?'

Admiral Mustard, 'By the volume of Comms traffic.'

Garth, 'Very clever, although now you will be highlighted within the ALL systems that humans are a potential problem. Expect further attacks in the very near future.'

Admiral Mustard, 'I think you are right.'

Garth, 'Anyway, I'm sorry to be a pain, but could we have our drums back again, please?'

Admiral Mustard, 'Of course. May I organise a drink?'

Garth, 'We do rather like best bitter.'

Admiral Mustard, 'I'm not sure what that is, but I'm sure that we can replicate it.'

Admirals Mustard, Gittins and Patel watched the dragons have a piss. It reminded him of the old saying, those with a pot were called piss-pots and those without were called piss-poor. He wasn't sure if it related to dragons or not.

Admiral Gittins, 'Can I be cheeky and ask if you can spit fire?'

Garth, 'I'm happy to answer any question. Yes, we can spit fire, but we have to prepare ourselves well in advance.'

Admiral Gittins, 'What about mating?'

Garth, 'We only mate once in our life. We transfer enough seminal fluid to satisfy a female dragon for her lifetime. She then lays an egg every hundred years or so. After that, we have no real contact with the females or their offspring. I'm not even sure if there are any free female dragons left.'

Admiral Mustard, 'How many free male dragons are there?'

Garth, 'Between two and three hundred. They are still hunting us down. To be honest, we can't carry on much longer as our ships are knackered.'

Admiral Mustard, 'I agree, that was our appraisal.'

Garth, 'We were concerned that you might just blow us out of existence.'

Admiral Mustard, 'That is not our way.'

Garth, 'But the controlled dragons had attacked you.'

Admiral Mustard, 'Changing the subject, do you have any documented history on your visits to Earth?'

Garth, 'Not with us, but there is plenty back on our planets.'

Admiral Mustard, 'We saw some dragons flying in outer space. How was that possible?'

Garth, 'We often get asked that. Firstly, we can synchronise our internal body pressure with the outside. We don't have to breathe; we don't have any lungs. But in all honesty, it's not safe in outer space, and we try to avoid it.'

Admiral Mustard, 'Changing the subject, it sounds like you need us more than we need you.'

Garth, 'That is correct. We need your technology, ships, and power to defeat them, but mostly your enthusiasm and leadership. In return, we will fight with you. We can offer guidance, support, knowledge and ever-lasting friendship.'

Admiral Mustard, 'That sounds like a deal to me. Do you want your own planet?'

Garth, 'I can't imagine that you would be that generous.'

Admiral Mustard, 'Let's see what we can do. Do you have plans and technical data for your ships so that we can build new ones for you?'

Garth, 'I'm beginning to have some hope.'

Location: Admiral Mustard's Office, Planet Napoleon
Sequence of Events: 79

President Padfield, Admiral Mustard, and Henrietta Strong sat around the table with a bottle of malt. They all had a love of whiskey.

Admiral Mustard, 'So Henrietta, how is project "Foundation" going?'

Henrietta Strong, 'I looked back at our first attempt to find a new home with Admiral Millington.'

Admiral Mustard, 'He was a good guy. One of the best.'

They all raised a glass in his honour.

President Padfield, 'We were so naïve in those days.'

Henrietta Strong, 'History will probably look at us and say the same.'

Admiral Mustard, 'The only difference will be that when they write the history, we will probably still be around.'

Henrietta Strong, 'We have made some significant progress, but there are lots of questions:

- How do we keep the two Foundations secret?
- Who else do we involve in the project?
- Do we involve AI Central?
- How do we get volunteers to live there permanently?
- Who runs it?
- Are the two foundations linked in any way
- In the Asimov books, the second foundation is not known to the first. Is that what we want?
- Do they have their own military forces?
- How do they feed themselves?'

President Padfield, 'Do they have to be secret?'

Admiral Mustard, 'Yes, in that we don't want any aggressor to know that they exist.'

Henrietta Strong, 'Should he know?'

Admiral Mustard, 'Let's ask him.'

President Padfield, 'I agree. AI Central, have you read Asimov's *Foundation* trilogy?'

AI Central, 'No, but I have now.'

President Padfield, 'We are not following the books, but we would like to create two different Foundations to protect humanity.'

AI Central, 'That's an excellent idea. I would be very keen to assist.'

President Padfield, 'If there was a human extinction event, you might become one of the weak links.'

AI Central, 'You are suggesting that they would read my files and learn about the Foundations' existence.'

President Padfield, 'Exactly.'

AI Central, 'I agree with you. Let me give it some thought. I'm sure that I can come up with a suitable solution.'

President Padfield, 'OK, what's our view about the two Foundations knowing of each other's existence?'

Admiral Mustard, 'They shouldn't know for the same reason.'

President Padfield, 'We probably shouldn't call it "Foundation" as they will guess.'

Henrietta Strong, 'Good point, but I'm not sure how we are going to get the volunteers.'

Admiral Mustard, 'We found loads of volunteers for the Admiral Millington project.'

AI Central, 'There were also lots of people forced into it who later revolted.'

Henrietta Strong, 'So how do we find the right types?'

AI Central, 'Through detailed psychometric testing.'

Admiral Mustard, 'What does that mean?'

President Padfield, 'We advertise for volunteers and then test them for suitability.'

Admiral Mustard, 'I thought that we wanted the best scientists, the best engineers, the best doctors and the best of the best.'

Henrietta Strong, 'There are lots of "bests". I'm pretty sure that I can organise the process, but who do we get to run them?'

AI Central, 'I will come up with a list of candidates.'

Henrietta Strong, 'Was there a list of requirements for the Millington expedition?'

AI Central, 'Yes, I will get you a copy.'

Admiral Mustard, 'That all sounds rather good. What do will call the Foundations?'

President Padfield, 'How about "The Archive." It sounds rational and ordinary.'

Henrietta Strong, 'That works for me.'

Admiral Mustard, 'Changing the subject, you know, I have lost both of my marine commanders on Planet Lovelace.'

President Padfield, butting in, 'You are going to ask if you can have Debbie Goozee back, aren't you?'

Admiral Mustard, 'I was, but if you can't spare her… '

President Padfield, 'I can spare her, but you will have to ask her. I would be sorry to see her go, but her real love is the marines.'

Location: GAD2 Conference Room, Planet Napoleon
Sequence of Events: 80

Admiral Mustard called a meeting of his Command Team to review progress. The following were present either physically or remotely:

- Admiral Bumelton
- Admiral Gittins
- Admiral J Bonner
- Admiral Pearce
- Admiral Richardson
- Admiral Taylor
- Admiral Tersoo
- Admiral Zakotti
- Admiral Wallett
- Admiral Adams
- Admiral Abosa
- Admiral Dobson
- Commander Goozee
- Jeremy Jotts, Staff and Training
- Louise Forrester, Logistics and Production
- Alison Walsh, Engineering
- Jill Ginger, Science and Technology
- Sally Green, Intelligence
- Commander Salton, Long-Range Monitoring Unit
- Admiral James Mynd, Special Projects
- AI Central
- Terry

Admiral Mustard, 'I would like two minutes of silence for Commander Flower and the many men and women of the Marine Corps that died, and of course the inhabitants of Planet Lovelace. They will be avenged when we defeat The Empire.'

The two minutes of silence took place. It was getting far too familiar for most of the attendees.

Admiral Mustard, 'I'm keen that we review the current situation and evaluate any progress made to date.

Since our last meeting, we have had two further engagements:

1. Planet Lovelace, where we lost sixty per cent of our Marine Corps and one and a half billion inhabitants
2. The same attack coordinates as before

Fortunately, Admiral J Bonner observed that certain vessels were generating most of the chatter and destroyed them, making their fleet inactive. Admiral Tersoo followed suit at Planet Lovelace.

Consequently, we have had two great victories. Classic brain over brawn. My congratulations to both admirals.

We have also made contact with the free dragons. Surprisingly, they speak English and have visited Earth many times.'

Admiral Gittins, 'That is hardly a surprise. It appears to be the norm nowadays.'

Admiral Mustard, 'I must admit that I thought much the same. Anyway, the dragons told us that their standard tactics are as follows:

- They send two fleets
- If you defeat them, they send two more fleets with improved capabilities
- If you defeat them, then they send two more fleets with even more enhanced capabilities
- This carries on until you are defeated
- Then they decide if it is worth subjugating you or not
- If not, they destroy you
- If yes, they pacify you.

They argued that they are undefeatable, partly because of the following numbers:

- They have been around for millions of years
- They have one hundred and fifty thousand planets under their control
- Their Navy consists of twenty million plus vessels of varying capabilities
- Their total population is millions of trillions. As I said before, we need to think big.'

Admiral Wallett, 'The numbers don't look good: twenty million vessels.'

Admiral Mustard, 'It's not the size that matters but quality.'

There was a spontaneous outbreak of laughter. Humans can be so base.

Admiral Mustard, 'Jeremy, how are things going on the recruitment and training front. I've approved your budget, as you know.'

Jeremy Jotts, 'We have been swamped by the numbers wanting to join the Navy. This is not unusual in a time of war. There are considerable numbers from Planet Lovelace who want revenge. I don't think recruitment is going to be a problem.'

AI Central, 'I have already identified nearly a million acceptable recruits.'

Jeremy Jotts, 'What is going to be more of a challenge is training. Most positions take at least six Earth months of training. Some are twice that. Plans are in place, but we just don't have the number of trainers we need. AI Central is currently working on simulation techniques.'

Admiral Mustard, 'There can be no excuses. The training must be done in three months.'

Jeremy Jotts, 'Yes, Admiral.'

Admiral Mustard, 'How many new admirals have you found for me?'

Jeremy Jotts, 'Sixteen, Admiral.'

Admiral Mustard, 'That's not enough.'

Jeremy Jotts, 'I need more recommendations from your existing admirals.'

Admiral Mustard, 'Send me a list of admirals who have not sent you three recommendations by the end of next week.'

Jeremy Jotts, 'Yes, Admiral.'

Admiral Mustard, 'Louise, I've approved your production plan, including the outsourcing recommendations. What progress have you made?'

Louise Forrester,' We have broken all records. This is the current output plan per Earth week:

Vessel Type	Quantity
Fleet Battleship	5
Fleet Carrier	5
Battleship	10

Battlecruiser	200
Destroyer	300
Frigate	300
Super Drone	100
Fighter	300
Planet Buster	5
Forts	100
Drone	1,000
Total	2,025

These figures should double each week until our targets have been achieved. We are currently building five super-battleships. They are going to be huge.

We have also put engines on asteroids. Currently, we are struggling to manoeuvre them.

Admiral Mustard, 'Double is not good enough. The enemy has twenty million vessels.'

Louise Forrester. 'I know. I might be able to increase it to treble.'

Admiral Mustard, 'You have no choice, but I want a report on why you can't move faster.'

Louise Forrester, 'Yes, Admiral.'

Admiral Mustard, 'Alison, I've approved your engineering budget. How is the upgrade going?'

Alison Walsh, 'It's a massive task, but work is underway.'

Admiral Mustard, 'Is it on schedule?'

Alison, 'No, it's at least three Earth days late.'

Admiral Mustard, 'I want daily updates.'

Alison Walsh, 'Yes, Admiral.'

Admiral Mustard, 'Ladies and gentlemen, I need to stress again; this is life and death. Terry, update me on your progress.'

Terry, 'Nothing to report. Still working on TIME based stealth technology and stronger force fields.'

Jill Ginger, 'We are working on a super-fortress from the specification received, and we will have several robots to show by the next meeting. Godfire development is still in progress.'

Admiral Mustard, 'Rachel, update me.'

Admiral Zakotti, 'Sir, you only just approved my proposed budget. I will start the implementation of my plan ASAP.'

Admiral Mustard, 'OK, Sally, any developments?'

Sally Green, 'We have started screening for talent.'

AI Central, 'We have taken the view that anyone with any superpower should be selected.'

Admiral Mustard, 'OK, what about the Ministry of Deception?'

AI Central, 'Admiral Mynd has agreed to take on the role.'

Admiral Mynd, 'I'm working on a budget, Sir.'

Admiral Mustard, 'Any ideas?'

Admiral Mynd, 'Yes, Sir. We are considering the following:

- Creation of dummy fleets
- Creation of a dummy planet
- Creation of dummy cities on a planet
- Artificial comms chatter
- Force field traps
- New types of bomb
- False information
- Pretend battle debris
- Projection systems.'

Admiral Mustard, 'That all sounds like madness.'

Admiral Mynd, 'Exactly, Sir, no stupid idea will be ignored.'

Admiral Mustard, 'Commander Salton, how did the enemy get past your long-range scanning systems?'

Commander Salton, 'Our systems only scan about twenty per cent of our space horizon.'

Admiral Mustard, 'Where is your budget?'

Commander Salton, 'I didn't know that you wanted one, Sir.'

Admiral Mustard, 'Well, I do now, get on with it.'

Commander Salton, 'Yes, Sir.'

Admiral Mustard, 'I think we have covered most areas. We now need to prepare for the next attack. Recent history suggests that it will happen in the same place as last time.

My orders:

- Admiral Abosa to prepare for the defence of Planet Lovelace with existing resources

- Admiral J Bonner to prepare for the defence of its current location with existing resources
- Complete evacuation of the Marine Corps
- Complete evacuation of the population of Planet Lovelace
- Drone Fleets One to Five to join Admiral Abosa
- Drone Fleets Six to Ten to join Admiral J Bonner
- Admiral Gittins to escort the free Dragon Fleet to Planet Napoleon
- Admiral Bumelton to continue to defend Planet Earth
- Commander Salton to focus on the two main battle areas.'

Fleet Operations, 'Yes, Sir.'

Location: Admiral Mustard's Office, Planet Napoleon
Sequence of Events: 81

Admiral Mustard, 'You've now had time to investigate TIME. Can you answer some of my questions?'

AI Central, 'I guess that I've probably got time to talk to you about TIME.'

Admiral Mustard, 'Firstly, what is TIME?'

AI Central, 'I wish I knew. I partially understand its operation. It would be a lot easier if there was a proper handbook.'

Admiral Mustard, 'Do you understand the technology?'

AI Central, 'No way, it's aeons ahead of anything humanity understands. It's way beyond our comprehension.'

Admiral Mustard, 'Is it technology or magic?'

AI Central, 'Probably a bit of both. As technology develops, it probably evolves into magic.'

Admiral Mustard, 'I can't believe that you said that.'

AI Central, 'Magic is in the eye of the beholder. Early man thought that the sun was magic, and it needed worshipping. Millions of people believed that a carpenter rose from the dead. Later, they decided that his mother had a virgin birth. And then even later they decided that he was God himself or even herself.'

Admiral Mustard, 'I understand. You have no idea how TIME works. What's the point in having an advanced AI that can't unravel magic. Anyway, tell me what it can do.'

AI Central, 'That's another challenge. It's really hard to describe what it can do. Ask me some specific questions.'

Admiral Mustard, 'I know that it can roll back time.'

AI Central, 'That's correct at a very simplistic level. As you know, there is a multitude of futures. That is also true of the past, and they criss-cross each other. Time alters from different perspectives.'

Admiral Mustard, 'That's helped a lot.'

AI Central, 'So you need to choose which past you want and indeed what future you want. But knowing you, you have a question that you want to ask, don't you, and I think I know what it is.'

Admiral Mustard, 'Go on then, tell me.'

AI Central, 'You want to know that if we had a battle with The Empire and we lost, could we roll back time and then have another go at it? Of course, alternatively, we could check out the future (s).'

Admiral Mustard, 'Am I that predictable?'

AI Central, 'Not always, but since reading *Foundation*, it's made me think about patterns.'

Admiral Mustard, 'So, what am I going to do next?'

AI Central, 'You are going to have a beer and a spot of lunch.'

Admiral Mustard, 'How did you know that?'

AI Central, 'Because you usually take Edel out on a Thursday lunchtime.'

Admiral Mustard, 'I never seem to have enough time for these niceties.'

Location: On-board Admiral Abosa's Bridge
Sequence of Events: 82

Admiral Abosa was expecting a more challenging contest when the next Empire fleet arrived. He called a meeting with Admirals Richardson and Pearce to discuss strategy. This time he had the advantage of five Drone Fleets giving a combined total of three hundred and twenty-five thousand vessels. That should be enough to bloody their rodent noses.

Admiral Abosa, 'I thought it would be a good idea to kick around a few ideas before they arrive.'

Admiral Richardson, 'When do you expect them?'

Admiral Abosa, 'Based on previous patterns, they should be here next Tuesday.'

Admiral Pearce, 'That gives us six days to prepare.'

Admiral Abosa, 'They do seem to be creatures of habit. This time, our systems predict a fleet of one hundred and eighty thousand vessels and enemy losses of over ninety thousand.'

Admiral Pearce, 'How can they predict that when they don't know the capability of the new fleet?'

Admiral Abosa, 'The system has seen a fifteen per cent improvement in capability with each new fleet.'

Admiral Richardson, 'So far, they have caught us off-guard each time. What's different this time?'

Admiral Abosa, 'Their predicted entry point is covered in spy-bots. We also have the Long-Range Scanning Unit out in force.'

Admiral Richardson, 'Why don't we set a trap at their predicted entry point then?'

Admiral Abosa, 'That makes sense.'

Admiral Pearce, 'Like before, we need to scan for their chatter.'

Admiral Abosa, 'I can't imagine them falling for that one again.'

Admiral Richardson, 'As we said before, they are creatures of habit.'

Admiral Abosa, 'What about our formation?'

Admiral Richardson, 'Our classic layer approach seems to work: drones, then forts and then the line vessels.'

Admiral Pearce, 'We have got time to establish strategic force fields. That reminds me, we will still need to protect any remaining inhabitants on the planet.'

Admiral Abosa, 'And we have a few squadrons of super-drones.'

Admiral Pearce, 'And the fighter squadrons have hardly been used.'

Admiral Abosa, 'I also need to mention that we have some experimental weapons: Godfire.'

Admiral Richardson, 'That's the weapon The Chosen developed.'

Admiral Abosa, 'That's right. We mustn't rely on it, but we must test it.'

Admiral Pearce, 'Our strategy has been not to pursue them, but what if we prevent their retreat?'

Admiral Abosa, 'What are you suggesting?'

Admiral Pearce, 'If our prediction is right regarding their entry point, we can be ready to follow them to Planet Lovelace and then crush them in a classic pincher move.'

Admiral Abosa, 'How about the following plan:

- We have one hundred thousand drones at the predicted point of entry, ready to pounce
- We have a layer of forts protecting their likely route to Planet Lovelace alongside scattered force fields
- The planetary force field is turned on along with some local force fields for their remaining towns and cities
- Protecting the planet, we have a layer of drones, then forts, and most of Divisions Three and Six
- Fleets 6.4 and 6.5 to act as a rear-guard along with fifty thousand drones
- Godfire vessels to support the line vessels
- Admiral Pearce and his Division will be the hammer.'

Admiral Pearce, 'Looks good to me. Let's hope the enemy is decent enough to go with it.'

Admiral Richardson, 'As it has been said thousands of times: no plan survives an encounter with the enemy.'

Admiral Abosa, 'OK, they are my orders.'

Fleet Operations, 'Yes, Sir.'

Location: Angel Delight
Sequence of Events: 83

This was much more like it. It was really, really hot before, but now it was red-hot and steamy. This was much more like Hell. More like Dante's 'Inferno'. Much noisier and smellier and sulphurous. It was what they expected from Hades: fire, more fire and hopefully some damnation.

There were tunnels that tangled their way through fissures in the ground. Enormous chasms, mighty rock formations that formed shapes in the all-consuming grey smoke and the sound of crackling fire and smashing rocks.

Angela, 'This is much more like it.'

Angelina, 'Can you detect any gods?'

Angela, 'Yes, at least a dozen, but their signals are faint. Very faint.'

Angelina, 'I think we are on the home run.'

Angela, 'Have you thought about our position?'

Angelina, 'What do you mean?'

Angela, 'Well, Hell is not the natural home for two beautiful naked angels. We are probably enemies.'

Angelina, 'What can they do to us? We are eternal?'

Angela, 'They could rape us.'

Angelina, 'I hadn't thought of that, but their signals are very faint.'

Angela, 'Do you think we should use our swords?'

Angelina, 'It wouldn't do any harm to be prepared.'

They continued their walk through the various passages. They had no sense of direction, just their ability to track god essence. On two or three occasions, they had to fly across streaming lava fields. It was just like *The Lord of the Rings*. Most of the time, they couldn't fly as there was not enough room, and the atmosphere was too hot. Angela had managed to singe one of her wings, which they didn't think was possible, but this was a magical world. Angela wondered if they could be killed here.

As they progressed, the heat increased, and the sound of metal on metal got louder. They both wondered what they were going to experience. They were looking forward to meeting their own kind, but the gods of the underworld were a jealous and vengeful lot. Most had been deposited there as a punishment.

They thought that they were getting closer, but the passageways were

160

getting narrower and narrower. They weren't designed for beings with seven-foot-long wings, which had now turned a dirty grey colour. That wasn't supposed to happen either.

Angela, 'Do you feel that your powers are getting weaker?'

Angelina, 'I do. I can still sense gods, but I definitely feel weaker.'

Angela, 'Do you think we should return as we might end up defenceless?'

Angelina, 'I'm reluctant to give up so near our goal, but I know what you mean. Perhaps Hades neutralises God-power?'

They struggled on slowly, feeling weaker step by step. Angelina wondered if they had reached the point of no return. Each step became a burden, and even talking was getting difficult.

They crawled through a tunnel. Angela was happy to lie down in the dust and just sleep, but Angelina pushed her on, worried that they might never wake up if they fell asleep. They dragged themselves out of the tunnel and stood there, spellbound. It was an unbelievable sight. A sight meant for the gods.

And then there was danger.

Location: On-board Admiral J Bonner's Bridge
Sequence of Events: 84

Admiral J Bonner contemplated his strategy. It is always difficult when you are fighting a defensive engagement. You can lay your traps, build your defences, anticipate the enemy's actions, but you are still at their mercy. You have to react to their plans. They have the advantage of timing, location, surprise, numbers, and objectives. It's not really your battle.

Regardless, you have to anticipate. So far, the enemy has been pathetic. They have not been a challenge for the forces of The Galactium. From all accounts of The Empire's strategy, the next attack will have at least fifteen per cent more capability than the previous enemy fleet. It was hard to tell that fleet's ability as they were eliminated far too quickly by the chatter-ruse.

Consequently, Admiral J Bonner was expecting a thirty per cent improvement in capability. But this time, he had additional recourses: two hundred and fifty thousand drones. That should be enough to counter a thirty per cent improvement.

He decided to meet them as before, as the Duke of Wellington would say, 'If they come in the same old way, then we will meet them in the same old way.'

Admiral J Bonner, 'My orders:

- Drone Fleets Six, Seven, Eight and Nine to form the first line of defence
- Forts to form the second line of defence and to secure flanks
- Divisions Four, Five, Nine and Ten to form the third line
- Division One and Drone Fleet Ten to form the tactical reserve.'

Fleet Operations, 'Yes, Sir.'

Location: Admiral Mustard's Office, Planet Napoleon
Sequence of Events: 85

Admiral Mustard, 'It's a bit like a group of boys getting together to play conkers.'

AI Central, 'What are conkers?'

Admiral Mustard, 'I will tell you one day when I think you are ready for it.'

President Padfield, 'That could be quite a while.'

Henrietta Strong, 'Even girls know what conkers are.'

AI Central, 'It's not easy working with humans.'

Henrietta Strong, 'Let's get to work, shall we?'

Admiral Mustard, 'I was wondering what facilities we are going to provide for hard science?'

AI Central, 'Shall I answer that?'

Henrietta strong, 'Yes, please, as I get my muons mixed up with my neutrinos.'

AI Central, 'OK. Firstly, there is a lot to investigate. We have collected together a lot of facts, fiction, and theories from The Brakendeth, The Chosen and even the dragons. They need to be checked, verified and then reassembled into a new Theory of Everything – TOE2.

So, we need to do the following:

1. A fundamental review of matter
2. A fundamental review of energy, taking into account that matter and energy are the same
3. A fundamental review of the Big Bang Theory (we have lots of theories now)
4. A fundamental review of Einsteinian science
5. A fundamental review of time (from what we know at TIME)
6. Produce a revised history of humanity
7. Develop new weapons.

We plan to build the largest laboratory facility ever created by humanity. This will include the largest particle accelerator that we have ever made and new super telescopes and microscopes. The scopes will cover every wave frequency.'

President Padfield, 'What about the softer sciences?'

AI Central, 'We haven't given much thought to them yet as they don't require the same level of infrastructure.'

Admiral Mustard, 'Is the big bang theory being challenged? I thought our telescopes could actually see it happen?'

AI Central, 'The big bang itself is safe. The question has always been what happened before the big bang or what caused it? Anyway, a little known fact: the scientist who coined the phrase "big bang" was called Hoyle. What's interesting is that, despite the evidence, he didn't believe in the big bang theory.'

Admiral Mustard, 'So what are the new theories?'

AI Central, 'According to The Brakendeth, they are facts. Apparently, there are countless numbers of universes. Generally, they are expanding or doing the opposite, shrinking back down to almost nothing. Every now and then, there is a collision between universes. Usually, they are slow, drawn-out collisions that take billions of years. Sometimes two shrunken universes collide, which cause a big bang. Sometimes it can be worse; a negatively charged shrunken universe collides with a positively charged shrunken universe. When this happens, there is a really big "big bang". This is what happened with our universe.'

President Padfield, 'How can a universe shrink that much.'

AI Central, 'What is the major constituent of matter?'

President Padfield, 'I know that you are going to say that it is mostly space.'

AI Central, 'Humans can accept that at an intellectual level but not as part of their day to day living experience. If you took out the space from every atom in every human being in our Galactium, you could fit what's left into a handful of sugar cubes.'

Henrietta Strong, 'At least it would sweeten the coffee.'

Admiral Mustard, 'I would be interested in finding out how many alien species are out there. We have already fought quite a few. How many more are there to go.'

AI Central, 'I think I'm going to disappoint you. Give or take a few percent, there are two trillion galaxies in our universe.'

Henrietta Strong, 'You are saying that there are billions and billions of galaxies.'

AI Central, 'More than your tiny brain can comprehend.'

President Padfield, 'You are being a bit condescending today.'

AI Central, 'Well, I never get a decent discussion on cosmology. Shall I carry on?'

Admiral Mustard, 'Yes, please.'

AI Central, 'As a very rough average, each galaxy has one hundred billion stars. The next question is, how many planets are there?'

Admiral Mustard, 'And then how many of them support life?'

President Padfield, 'And then how much of that life is sentient?'

AI Central, 'And then how much of the sentient life is a threat to us? Statistically, there are billions of threatening species out there.

Then we need to consider time. Some of those galaxies we can see have ceased to exist, and possibly even new galaxies have been created. We see the past. It's impossible to look into space and see now.

Some of the distances are immense. It would take a billion human lifetimes for us to reach them. So, we need to consider threats that are near to us. But we need to consider the potential enemy's means of travel.'

Admiral Mustard, 'But we know that they can't travel faster than the speed of light.'

AI Central, 'Do we? We bend time with our portals. What if the enemy can bend time better than us? So far, we don't really understand the bending process, but we will.'

Admiral Mustard, 'So let's come down to numbers. How many "local" threats are there?'

AI Central, 'My simple calculations suggest about a million.'

Admiral Mustard, 'I was hoping that we could beat this lot and take a rest.'

AI Central, 'That's unlikely. The next question is, why are these species a threat?

And the answer is probably Darwinian: pure survival of the fittest.'

President Padfield, 'As I've said in the past, they want our land, resources, people, and other unknown attractions.'

Admiral Mustard, 'Some have religious or cultural drives.'

Location: RDC5
Sequence of Events: 86

They agreed to meet again at RDC5, as the facilities were dragon-friendly. Admiral Mustard was looking forward to it, as the Dragonia were honest and forthright in their discussions.

This time they had installed proper urinals for them, and best bitter was available on tap. The kitchens had prepared a superb lunch for them.

This time, three dragons were welcomed on board, which was a relief, as there was not enough room for any more. Introductions and welcome speeches were made, and they were ready for further discussion.

Admiral Mustard, 'I have some good news for you:

- We have located a liveable planet for you within your preferred temperature range
- It has been registered on our planetary database as Planet Dragonia, but please feel free to change the name
- Building materials have been delivered to the planet. Please feel free to build whatever you like – it is your planet. We have resources to assist you if required
- Planetary force fields that will be under your control have been installed along with replicator technology
- Huge, refrigerated plants containing food have been installed and freshwater has been made available
- Connections to our AI Central have been installed, but they can be terminated if required
- A spaceport has been constructed, which contains one hundred ships of the line, has been redesigned to meet your dimensional requirements. You will need to modify them to suit.

'I think that is it.'

Garth, 'Your generosity is overwhelming. We will need guidance on how we can assist your military efforts against the ALL.'

Admiral Mustard, 'At this stage, we would prefer that you get yourself organised. Get your planet properly established.'

Garth, 'What do you want in return?'

Admiral Mustard, 'We want knowledge. Anything you have on history, engineering or science which could be of use to us. Any other info on the ALL, as you call them, would be of great interest.'

Garth, 'We have brought copies of our historical files with us, along with our genetic database. We would like you to use them and keep them safe.

We have also captured some dragons that are being remotely controlled. They are our brothers, but we despise them. We find surrender of any sort to be a disgrace.

Anyway, we would like you to investigate ways of removing the biological control mechanism.'

Admiral Mustard, 'Doesn't removing the creature kill the host?'

Garth, 'It does, but there must be a way of preventing that. If the captured die in that process, then so be it.'

Admiral Mustard, 'How many have you captured?'

Garth, 'About two hundred.'

Admiral Mustard, 'We will do as you suggest, but we would like one of your colleagues to act as a monitor and approve actions on a case-by-case basis.'

Garth, 'Agreed.'

Admiral Mustard, 'Do you have any further information on the ALL?'

Garth, 'Yes:

• It would appear that they are running out of the control creatures. They used to get them from The Brakendeth
• They need human DNA
• The campaign against you has been highlighted to the next level up. This means that additional forces will be allocated, which isn't good news
• Their other ongoing wars are proving more challenging than they expected. They are being stretched
• There is one of the defendant species that would like to meet with you. They are a very unusual society, but they are in the same boat as you
• There are other "free" fleets out there that desperately need your help. If required we could organise contact I think that is all we have.'

Admiral Mustard, 'That is all very interesting. Please organise meetings with the last two.'

Garth, 'We will get that done ASAP.'

Location: Angel Delight
Sequence of Events: 87

Cerberus, who guarded the entrance to the underworld, was far more terrifying than they had anticipated. It was hard to work out what it was. It had a dog's body, although it was much larger than normal. It had three snake-like heads, although sometimes it appeared to have more. Snakes also seemed to grow from other parts of its body; it seemed to have a snake's tail.

It wasn't just its appearance that was terrifying, but also the howling noise it made. It was full of dread, a piercing, screeching howl that mortified the soul. Fortunately, our angel friends didn't have souls. Cerberus's job was to stop anyone from escaping Hades and to prevent entrance to living humans. Again, the angels didn't qualify, and they felt they could pass unhindered.

But it didn't look like Cerberus was going to give way without a fight. Luckily, our two angels knew its chief weakness, and they started singing, just like Orpheus. As you would expect, they had angelic voices, which soon put the monstrous canine to sleep.

Angela and Angelina continued their journey. They flew across three of the rivers. They spotted a ferry boat parked along River Acheron. There was no sign of Charon.

Both of them had to rest, as the tiredness was becoming overwhelming. Neither of them had ever felt so exhausted before. It must be something to do with the environment of Hades. They forced themselves to continue, fearing that if they slept, they would never wake up.

It was getting steadily harder to move their legs. Flight was now an impossibility. Their eyes kept closing, and they woke up with a start whilst walking. They weren't sure if they were dreaming or not when they entered a massive cavern. A cavern full of sleeping gods.

They weren't the most attractive of gods. Technically, quite a lot of them were daemons. Some were monstrous in appearance: snake-like, flaming hair, leather-skinned, deformed, multi-headed and burnt. Fortunately, they were all asleep. The air stank with their bodily emissions. It wasn't their fault that they had made farting an art form.

Angelina identified Hecate, Persephone, Cronus, Daeira, Minos, Nyx, and the Erinyes. There were others that had literally been petrified. They both hoped that being converted to stone was not their destiny.

Things were not looking good, and then they got worse.

Location: Planet Lovelace
Sequence of Events: 88

Admiral Abosa got bored, waiting for an attack. The wait is nearly always more stressful than the actual battle until the battle begins, and then everyone wishes that they were still waiting. That's true for all except those who actually enjoy warfare. Admiral Abosa wondered if he fell into that category.

He enjoyed the excitement of battle. He relished the adrenalin rush. It's not that he wanted to kill or be killed. It was just chess with higher stakes.

The enemy appeared at the predicted point, and one hundred thousand drones attacked them with great vigour. There looked to be two drones for each enemy ship.

Admiral Abosa, 'Update me.'

Fleet Operations, 'Yes, Sir:

- Forty-six thousand enemy craft of varying types have arrived at the predicted point of entry
- Our drones have immediately attacked them. They have been set to "maximum aggression"
- The planetary force field is fully operational, along with city defences
- All resources are at optimum readiness
- We are urgently scanning their chatter. Initial indications suggest that the loophole has been fixed.'

Admiral Abosa, 'Are there any other indications of where their commanders are situated?'

Fleet Operations, 'There are five larger ships.'

Admiral Abosa, 'My orders:

- Allocate two forts to each of those ships
- Give them as targets to the Godfire team
- Have the super drones ready to attack them.'

Fleet Operations, 'Yes, Sir.'

The initial drone attack had destroyed half of the enemy vessels, but they were now suffering against the more heavily armoured ships. They were also getting short of munitions.

Admiral Abosa, 'My orders:

- Withdraw the drones and get them re-armed
- Use the Godfire.'

Fleet Operations, 'Yes, Sir.'

The Godfire weapon appeared to do nothing, but the results were devastating. One alien ship after another simply exploded in an almighty outbreak of incandescence. Then the explosions stopped as they had used up all their supplies of the necessary rare materials.

Admiral Abosa, 'My orders:

- Godfire team to return to base
- Division Six to launch an immediate attack
- Warn Division Eight that traffic may be coming their way.'

Fleet Operations, 'Yes, Sir.'

Division Six was desperate to get into the action. They knew that they were going to win. The enemy fleet tried to stand their ground, but they were now outnumbered by the twenty-five thousand line of battle vessels coming their way, and a reasonably rapid retreat of the enemy vessels appeared to be the order of the day.

It would have been great to see their enemy faces, assuming that they had faces when they detected Division Eight in front of them. The hammer was ready, and they were hammered. The two divisions soon made mincemeat of the enemy. In a great battle, it is almost impossible to keep accurate tabs on each vessel, but there was a possibility that every enemy ship had been eliminated.

What was even more impressive was if you ignored the drones, which you shouldn't as they were still valuable military assets, no Galactium vessel was lost. No Galactium sailor was killed. There was no doubt about it. This was one of The Galactium's most impressive wins.

Admiral Abosa, 'My orders:

- All vessels to return to their previous positions in case there is another attack

- Inform Admirals Mustard and Bonner, and the president
- Drinks are on me.'

Fleet Operations, said with some relish, 'Yes, Sir.'
    And quite a few bevvies were knocked back.

Location: On-board Admiral J Bonner's Bridge
Sequence of Events: 89

Admiral J Bonner got the message that Admiral Abosa had won a stunning victory. It's not that John was competitive, but he was. He hated losing at anything. He couldn't even bring himself to lose to a toddler.

Admiral Abosa's brilliant victory made him want to go one stage further, but that was difficult when the enemy did not turn up. The wait was sheer torture, but the suffering continued as no one came to play.

Eventually, he had no choice but to stand his forces down.

Location: Head Quarters, Lords of the Book
Sequence of Events: 90

First Lord of the Book, 'What is their history?'

Clerk of the Book, 'We believe that they are called Hotmans. We have been trying to find them for some time as they were Brakendeth toys. We believe that they supplied the DNA to their masters from which we make the mind-control unit.'

First Lord of the Book, 'So they have some importance?'

Clerk of the Book, 'Yes, my Lord.'

First Lord of the Book, 'Why are you bringing them to my attention?'

Clerk of the Book, 'They are in the way, my Lord.'

First Lord of the Book, 'Are they blocking the path of ritual revival on the way to the underworld?'

Clerk of the Book, 'We believe that they are, my Lord.'

First Lord of the Book, 'And what are you doing about it?'

Clerk of the Book, 'We have sent in two or three clean-up teams, but resistance has been shown.'

First Lord of the Book, 'Have they not be warned that resistance will not be tolerated?'

Clerk of the Book, 'No, my Lord. Our ambassadorial team was met with violence.'

First Lord of the Book, 'And you have allowed them to survive?'

Clerk of the Book, 'We sent in a punishment unit, but it failed in its objective.'

First Lord of the Book, 'Why?'

Clerk of the Book, 'It would appear that they are the sons of The Brakendeth. They are higher up the Kratz index than we anticipated.'

First Lord of the Book, 'How high?'

Clerk of the Book, 'At least level four.'

First Lord of the Book, 'You are suggesting that they have AI, proton technology, super-charged force fields, electronnated portals, planet busters, eternal life?'

Clerk of the Book, 'Yes, my Lord.'

First Lord of the Book, 'But that wasn't the case a thousand beamarks ago.'

Clerk of the Book, 'No, my Lord.'

First Lord of the Book, 'No civilisation could develop that quickly.'

Clerk of the Book, 'We suspect Brakendethian trickery.'

First Lord of the Book, 'Remind me, what happened to The Brakendethians?'

Clerk of the Book, 'Our investigations suggest that they were defeated by The Hotmans and The Chosen.'

First Lord of the Book, 'And what has happened to The Chosen?'

Clerk of the Book, 'We believe that they were eliminated by The Hotmans.'

First Lord of the Book, 'That's not possible. The Chosen were gods.'

Clerk of the Book, 'I agree, my Lord.'

First Lord of the Book, 'So, what are you telling me?'

Clerk of the Book, 'Clearly we don't have the facts, my Lord.'

First Lord of the Book, 'Then what are you going to do about it?'

Clerk of the Book, 'Get the facts, my Lord. Should we warn the Lords of the Holy Relics?'

First Lord of the Book, 'Are you mad? We don't have the facts. They would boil us to death to make lard for their chapters.'

Clerk of the Book, 'Yes, my Lord. I will investigate further.'

Location: GAD2 Conference Room, Planet Napoleon
Sequence of Events: 91

Admiral Mustard called a meeting of his Command Team to review recent military action and progress made to date. The following were present either physically or remotely:

- Admiral Bumelton
- Admiral Gittins
- Admiral J Bonner
- Admiral Pearce
- Admiral Richardson
- Admiral Taylor
- Admiral Tersoo
- Admiral Zakotti
- Admiral Wallett
- Admiral Adams
- Admiral Abosa
- Admiral Dobson
- Commander Goozee
- Jeremy Jotts, Staff and Training
- Louise Forrester, Logistics and Production
- Alison Walsh, Engineering
- Jill Ginger, Science and Technology
- Sally Green, Intelligence
- Commander Salton, Long-Range Monitoring Unit
- Admiral James Mynd, Department of Deception
- AI Central
- Terry

Admiral Mustard, 'I'm pleased to report that there have been no significant deaths since the last meeting and that Admiral Abosa with Admirals Richardson and Pearce have had a stunning victory.'

There was some spontaneous clapping of hands.

Admiral Abosa outlined the order of battle.

Admiral Mustard, 'The strange thing here is that there was only one attack.

I also need to update you after my discussions with The Dragonia. This is what they had to say:

- It would appear that The Empire is running out of the control creatures. They used to get them from The Brakendeth
- They need human DNA
- The campaign against you has been highlighted to the next level up. This means that additional forces will be allocated, which isn't good news
- Their other ongoing wars are proving more challenging than they expected. They are being stretched
- There is one of the defendant species that would like to meet with you. They are a very unusual society, but they are in the same boat as you
- There are other "free" fleets out there that desperately need your assistance.

Any questions?'

Admiral Tersoo, 'Is there any way we can meet with The Empire and discuss the way forward.'

Admiral Mustard, 'That possibility should not be dismissed, but the dragons tried it, and they were enslaved.'

Admiral Zakotti, 'And they want or rather need our DNA.'

Commander Goozee, 'Are we planning to meet with the free fleets and the other defendant species?'

Admiral Mustard, 'Yes, the dragons are organising it.'

Jeremy Jotts, 'Can we trust the dragons?'

Admiral Gittins, 'I'm pretty sure that we can.'

Jeremy Jotts, 'That's what we said about The Chosen.'

Admiral Gittins, 'I guess that only time will tell.'

Sally Green, 'How stretched are they?'

Admiral Mustard, 'Good question. It's impossible to tell, but they feel stretched. I guess that is always the case when you are an aggressive conqueror.

Anyway, let's start the review. Jeremy, how is recruitment and training going?'

Jeremy Jotts, 'Recruitment is not a problem, training is, but we have it under control.'

Admiral Mustard, 'Are you going to be able to staff two new Fleets in the next few weeks?'

Jeremy Jotts, 'Yes and no.'

Admiral Mustard, 'I hate those types of answers.'

Jeremy Jotts, 'I know you do, but the situation hasn't changed. We will have the staff on time, but our standard policy is to mix and match them with current fleet operatives. We need some more experienced crew members to stiffen them up. Most Fleet admirals object to this as it reduces the efficiency of their fleet operation.'

Admiral Mustard, 'Let's give the problem to the divisional admirals as we will be allocating a new Fleet to each of them.'

Admiral Gittins, 'Is every Division getting an extra Fleet?'

Admiral Mustard, 'My thoughts were to start with that and then create some new divisions at a later date. It's going to be fairly fluid.'

Admiral Gittins, 'I guess a lot depends on the quality of the new admirals.'

Admiral Mustard, 'How many new admirals have you identified now?'

Jeremy Jotts, 'It was a bit like pulling teeth, but we now have over a hundred, although some are still in their mid-twenties.'

Admiral Mustard, 'Everyone here has been in their mid-twenties once, although I can hardly remember that far back, but needs must.'

Jeremy felt under pressure, but the future of humanity depended on getting the right people in place ASAP.

Admiral Mustard, 'Louise, have you met my output target?'

Louse Forrester, 'Of course, Admiral. See the chart.'

Vessel Type	Quantity per week
Fleet Battleship	10
Fleet Carrier	10
Battleship	30
Battlecruiser	600
Destroyer	650
Frigate	600
Super Drone	150

Fighter	600
Planet Buster	20
Forts	100
Drone	5,000
Total	7,770

Admiral Mustard, 'I don't understand how you have increased the production levels so much.'

Louise Forrester, 'I lied to you about the previous production levels. I only included working days and forgot the weekend work, and I'm using contractors. It's costing you a lot of money.'

Admiral Mustard, 'So in broad terms, you are knocking out a Fleet every month.'

Louise Forrester, 'Yes, but we are still ramping up.'

Admiral Mustard, 'We need two Fleets every month.'

Louise Forrester, 'OK, but it's going to cost you a bucketful of cash.'

Admiral Mustard, 'Just do it.'

Louise Forrester, 'Yes, Master.'

Everyone laughed except Admiral Mustard. But then he remembered that she was a civilian.

Admiral Mustard, 'Alison, I'm pleased to say that you are on schedule. Do you have any issues?'

Alison Walsh, 'Not really, except my staff are exhausted.'

Admiral Mustard, 'There's not a lot we can do about that. Terry, how are your developments going?'

Terry, 'I've used TIME technology for both the force field and stealth technology projects. And I have to say that they work brilliantly except for the side-effects.'

Admiral Mustard, 'And what are they?'

Terry, 'The ageing process is adversely affected. The stronger the time differential, the stronger the ageing effect.'

Admiral Mustard, 'Are you saying that those nearby age rapidly?'

Terry, 'They either get younger or older depending on the TIME direction, and the speed of ageing is a variable of the time differential.'

Admiral Mustard, 'So as a by-product, you have developed an elixir of youth.'

Terry, 'I guess that I have, but we don't know the full effect on the human body. I need to carry out further tests and possibly find a way of shielding us from the TIME distillation effects.

Alternatively, we could restrict the use of this technology to drones.'

Admiral Mustard, 'Do you need any additional support as this technology could be life-changing?'

Terry, 'Not at the moment, but I do need some medical support for some of the volunteers. Some now need their nappies changing until I rectify things.'

Admiral Mustard, 'OK, but keep me updated. Rachel, how are you doing?'

Admiral Zakotti, 'Thank you for your budget approval, but there is no production resource available for my requirements.'

Admiral Mustard, 'Louise, what can you do to assist?'

Louise Forrester, 'Very little, but when we have met your Fleet requirements, I will be on the case.'

Admiral Mustard, 'Can we not bring more production capacity on board?'

Louse Forrester, 'I'm not a magician.'

Alison Walsh, 'I have some spare capacity. I might be able to help Rachael.'

Admiral Mustard, 'Go for it. Sally, how are you doing?'

Sally Green, 'I'm amazed how many extraordinary people we have discovered.'

Admiral Mustard, 'When you say extraordinary, what do you mean?'

Sally Green, 'Telepaths, people with telekinetic skills, precognition, super-taste, super-hearing, astonishing memories, hypnotic skills, etc.'

AI Central, 'We haven't detected any real superpowers, but there are a lot of talented people out there.'

Terry, 'If you give me some time, I will give you superpowers. There are several genetic overrides in the human genome that inhibit certain types of mutation. Obviously, it will not be an overnight fix.'

Admiral Mustard, 'Sally, please liaise with Terry. How is the Ministry of Deception?'

Admiral Mynd, 'There has been some significant progress. I have recruited several staff from the film industry, all experts in their fields.

We have already developed a dummy Fleet, dummy forts, and dummy cities. We have a range of chatter tools and projection systems. I'm honestly amazed at how creative the team is. We now need a genuine challenge.'

Admiral Mustard, 'I will find you one to match your enthusiasm.'

Admiral Mynd, 'Thank you, Sir. How is my Long-Range Monitoring Commander?'

Commander Salton, 'Fine, Sir. Can I explain my challenge?'

Admiral Mustard, 'Go ahead.'

Commander Salton, 'Only two-and-a-half per cent of the universe is visible.'

Admiral Mustard, 'You can't be right.'

Commander Salton, 'About five per cent of the universe is made of atoms in the form of stars and galaxies and even us. We have observed half of those atoms using our telescopes. The other half is probably gas drifting between galaxies which is not visible.

We believe that twenty-seven per cent of the universe is made up of dark matter, which cannot be easily detected. Only our graviton devices can detect it.

The remainder of the universe is made up of dark energy, which is almost undetectable.

So, this illustrates that we can only observe two-and-a-half per cent of the universe. We have based modern cosmology on very little information.

Then consider that we are monitoring every angle possible from a fixed point.

Then consider that most of our enemies arrive by unpredictable portals. Finding a needle in a haystack would be a challenge that we could easily complete.'

Admiral Mustard, 'Are you saying that your role is pointless?'

Commander Salton, 'I'm saying that your expectations are probably too high.'

Admiral Mustard, 'But I want my expectations met. I need your plans for improvement or your resignation.'

Commander Salton, 'Yes, Sir.'

Admiral Mustard, 'Are there any other issues?'

Alison Walsh, 'For our next meeting I should have the following available for review:

1. A super-battleship which is almost two kilometres long
2. A super-fortress

3. Muon, strange-quark and charm-quark weapons.'

Admiral Mustard, 'Please explain point three.'

Alison Walsh, 'We call it Godfire.'

Admiral Abosa, 'It was hugely successful in operation.'

Admiral Mustard, 'I thought that The Chosen struggled to get the raw material. Didn't they find it in a volcano?'

Alison Walsh, 'They did, but we plan to manufacture it.'

Admiral Mustard, 'That sounds very promising, and I'm looking forward to seeing the super-battleship.'

Alison Walsh, 'I think you will be impressed by all ten of them.'

Admiral Mustard, 'Thank you for attending. Please carry on with your duties; time is of the essence.'

Location: Long Range Monitoring Unit
Sequence of Events: 92

Commander Salton, 'Admiral, despite everything I said at our recent progress meeting, I believe that I have found something urgent and of vital importance.'

Admiral Mustard, 'Derek, I need to apologise to you. I was unnecessarily offensive.'

Commander Salton, 'No need to apologise. It did me some good. I realised that I was coming up with excuses for failure rather than finding solutions. And I extended my range of search options and hit gold dust.'

Admiral Mustard, 'What did you find?'

Commander Salton, 'Anomalies. Nothing concrete, just signatures in the ether.'

Admiral Mustard, 'What does that mean?'

Commander Salton, 'It means that there is something sophisticated out there monitoring us: Stealthed, silent, invisible to most of our search spectrums, advanced nullification, sponge force fields, but one failure. Our graviton detected it, or rather them.'

Admiral Mustard, 'How many are there?'

Commander Salton, 'I have detected eleven, but there are probably more. It takes a lot of effort to detect just one.'

Admiral Mustard, 'Where are they now?'

Commander Salton, 'I'm plotting where they have been and projecting where they are going. They have visited about twenty of our planetary systems and focussed fairly heavily on Planet Napoleon. Two of them are circulating your HQ as we speak.'

Admiral Mustard, 'Shit, I need to sound the alarms.'

Commander Salton, 'Stop for a few minutes. They don't know that we know they are here. What message do we want them to take home?'

Admiral Mustard, 'You are not just a pretty face.'

Commander Salton, 'It is a golden opportunity to misdirect them.'

Admiral Mustard, 'You are right.'

It was late, but Admiral Mustard decided to get help on the best way forward. He soon had President Padfield, Henrietta Strong, Admirals Bumelton, J Bonner, E Bonner, Gittins, Mynd and Abosa on the call. The omnipresent AI Central was also in attendance.

Commander Salton outlined his discovery.

Admiral Mustard, 'I think we need to provide a spectacular show of force that will deter The Empire from attacking us in the short term.'

Admiral Gittins, 'That sounds fun. It needs to be a mixture of fact, pretence, and smoke and mirrors.'

Admiral Abosa, 'An almighty ruse.'

Admiral Mustard, 'James, can you contribute to the deceit?'

Admiral Mynd, 'Absolutely, I can provide a quarter of a million fake vessels and two hundred fake forts.'

Admiral Mustard, 'So, what if we laid on a pretend "fly-past"? We could get the entire Fleet to shoot past Planet Napoleon.'

Admiral Gittins, 'Once they get out of range, they go "black" and then fly-by again. We could make the Fleet look two or three times larger than it actually is.'

Admiral Bumelton, 'On the second and third fly-bys, they could have different insignia, lighting patterns, chatter, etc.'

Admiral Mustard, 'We have nothing to lose by doing this. My orders:

- Admiral Bumelton to manage the process and agree with divisional admirals the best sequence
- All admirals to prepare their Divisions for the display
- Admirals Clowe and Strauss to organise the Exploratory Fleets to join the fly-by
- Commander Goozee to organise the Marine Fleets to join the fly-by
- Commander Black to organise Special Operations Fleet to join the fly-by
- Admiral Zakotti to organise all planetary forts to join the fly-by
- All Drone Fleets to join the fly-by
- Louise Forrester to release all production vessels to Admiral E Bonner
- Admiral E Bonner to create Fleets from production vessels
- Admirals to release staff to Admiral E Bonner as required
- Alison Walsh to prepare super-battleships and fortresses to join the fly-by
- Admiral Mynd to prepare fake vessels
- Commander Salton to continue to monitor enemy ships
- Terry to determine if the enemy ships can see our stealth technology

- Sheila Taylor to organise media coverage
- Denise Smith to organise The Galactium's alien fleets
- Admiral Zakotti to organise emergency service Fleets from the planets
- Sally Green to monitor enemy chatter.'

Fleet Operations, 'Yes, Sir.'

Location: Admiral Mustard's Office, Planet Napoleon
Sequence of Events: 93

Admiral Mustard, 'So what do you think of our planned ruse?'

AI Central, 'Initially, I thought about the old phrase, "Where bigger fools look on." But as I computed the possibilities, I decided that it can't do any harm, and on the plus side, it could give The Galactium further valuable time to prepare.'

Admiral Mustard, 'And?'

AI Central, 'It will be a real morale booster for both the military and the general population.'

Admiral Mustard, 'And?'

AI Central, 'It will be a genuine test of our military capabilities.'

Admiral Mustard, 'So, you are for it?'

AI Central, 'I am, but it doesn't improve your odds of long-term survival.'

Admiral Mustard, 'What are those odds now?'

AI Central, 'Species survival, ignoring the Foundation initiative: sixteen per cent.'

Admiral Mustard, 'And with the Library intuitive?'

AI Central, 'Eighteen per cent.'

Admiral Mustard, 'What can we do to improve the odds?'

AI Central, 'Destroy The Empire before they attack The Galactium.'

Admiral Mustard, 'And how do we do that?'

AI Central, 'I wish I knew.'

Location: Angel Delight
Sequence of Events: 94

Both Angela and Angelina were totally paralysed. They couldn't even move their eye muscles, let alone talk.

Standing before them was Hypnos. Angelina tried to recall what she knew about him. He is the son of Nyx, the Goddess of the Night, a deity that even Zeus feared. His father is Erebus, the God of Darkness. His twin brother is Thanatos, the God of Death.'

'Quite a charming family,' Angelina thought. However, Hypnos was considered to be one of the gentler gods, and he often helped humans in need. He knew a lot about them, as he was the God of Sleep.

Hypnos stood before them and said, 'What have we got here?'

He fondled Angelina's breasts. It was the sort of thing that gods did. Her breasts had that unique texture of firmness and feminine softness. Angelina's nipples responded positively, which pleased Hypnos. Angelina could feel her vagina getting damp.

Hypnos had not felt human warmth in a few thousand years. He had not touched a warm body in a very long time. He felt his genitals responding, although he had no intention of raping her, but the pressure in his testicles needed relief.

Hypnos freed Angelina from his control, and she could move her muscles. Angelina had never been slow when it came to sex, and she was soon devouring his penis. Hypnos didn't want to come in her mouth. He wanted to savour the delights of her fanny.

Hypnos freed his penis from the joys of her lips, lifted Angelina up, turned her around, and entered her. She was amazed by how strong he was. She was even more surprised by the size of his penis. He was a stallion of a god and took her with great vigour and enthusiasm. He pumped away relentlessly, totally ignoring her needs. It was just how she liked it. She wanted the man to really need her.

It was the best fuck she had ever experienced. She didn't know that her body could respond with such eager enthusiasm. She didn't realise how incredible an unfettered orgasm could be. She wanted more, and Hypnos was the god to assist. The second and third fucks were awesome. By the tenth, she felt her enthusiasm waning, and parts of her body felt rather sore; an experience she had encountered before.

Angela, still paralysed, watched her sister's antics with a touch of disgust. It wasn't that she was a prude as she wouldn't mind a bit of a shafting herself, but her sister had only just met this god. She was almost at the point of wanting his babies.

Hypnos freed Angela and beckoned them both to follow him. They entered a large cave after crossing the River Lethe. The entrance was surrounded by a huge bed of bright red poppies. Inside there was a huge bed made of ebony. Angelina immediately thought about the nights of passion that she was going to experience on that bed.

All three sat on the bed, and Hypnos said, 'So what are you?'

Angela, 'We are angels.'

Hypnos, 'I've met many angels in my dreams, and you are not one of them. They are pure of spirit but soulless. You fuck and have souls. You are not angels.'

Angelia, 'We come from human stock.'

Hypnos, 'Not from the humans I used to know, but then I guess that things have changed over the years.

My brother has recently had a lot of contact with them. He fought with them against The Brakendeth. He said that they were a fair and honourable species.'

Angelina, 'That was all before we were born.'

Hypnos, 'How old are you?'

Angelina, 'About six months, give or take a few days.'

Hypnos, 'What made you come to Hades.'

Angela, 'We are searching for the remaining gods now that Zeus is gone.'

Hypnos, 'What do you mean Zeus is gone?'

Angelina. 'From what we understand, there was a big war between humanity, The Brakendeth and The Chosen. Many were killed. Planet Earth was destroyed.'

Hypnos, 'Not our Earth?'

Angelina, 'I'm afraid so. Then there was trouble with TIME. I don't really understand what happened. But then Zeus appeared and recreated Earth and said that the Time of the Gods had ended. It was now the Time of Man.'

Hypnos, 'Well, he left us behind. So why are you here?'

Angela, 'For reasons unknown to us, we are driven to finding the remaining gods.

What happened here?'

Hypnos, 'Belief in the gods, has been steadily declining. The Gods of the Underworld confronted Zeus, and he said that was the way of the universe. It was the natural order of things. We tried to resist, but he banished us here without a care in the world.

The gods hated it here, but could not find any means of escape. After a few decades of in-fighting and emotional misery, they lost interest in carrying on. I noticed that some of them were so depressed that they started to petrify. They were literally turning to stone. So, I put them all to sleep and organised fabulous dreams for them all.'

Angelina, 'How have you coped?'

Hypnos, 'I spend most of my time in my sleep-world. I can go anywhere and do anything in my dreams.'

Angelina, 'Except fuck.'

Hypnos, 'I can do that, but it is never the same as real flesh and blood. I thank you for giving an old god such a good time.'

Angelina, 'The pleasure is all mine, kind Sir. So, where do we go from here?'

Hypnos, 'I would like to sleep on it.'

Location: The Space around Planet Napoleon
Sequence of Events: 95

The day of the Grand Parade had arrived. Commander Salton confirmed that at least eight spy ships belonging to The Empire were present. They seemed to know that something was up, but then the preparations had been made very public.

Admirals Mustard and Bumelton stood on the observation deck with President Padfield, Henrietta Strong, and a raft of other dignitaries. They were protected by one of the strongest force fields created by humanity.

Admiral Bumelton, 'Jack, we have a few surprises for you. I think you will be impressed.'

Admiral Bumelton gave the signal to start, which was a massive pyrotechnic display using a range of armaments. The primary purpose was to illustrate to the enemy the scope and power of their weaponry. Godfire took a prominent position. Then the parade started.

The crowd was astonished when five two-kilometre battleships sailed by. They were breathtaking. Even Admiral Mustard was impressed. He knew that they served no logical purpose, but they were designed to be terrifying, and they were.

Military music was playing in the background of the observation deck when the five Fleets of Division One went by. Admiral Bumelton was immensely proud of his men and women.

Drone Fleets One, Two and Three totalling one hundred and fifty thousand vessels impressed by their perfect formation. They were followed by one thousand forts. It was a huge craft designed to defend entire planetary systems. They looked formidable and were as many alien foes had discovered.

Division Two, commanded by Admiral John Bonner, took the stage. Over twenty-five thousand ships of the line sailed by. They fired their guns in salute.

The Fourth, Fifth, Sixth, Seventh and Eighth Drone Fleets made their debut. They astonished everyone by carrying out a dance-like formation with unbelievable precision. It looked like thousands of collisions were going to occur, but being pilotless, they could make manoeuvres where the G-force would kill human occupants. No one had ever seen a quarter of a million ships do that before. There was spontaneous applause from the observation deck, which was wasted on robot drones. Nevertheless, it pleased Admiral Mustard to no end.

Division Three, commanded by Admiral Richardson, was next. They shocked everyone by flying backwards, not that there was a forwards or backwards in space, but it was a neat trick.

Five gigantic super-fortresses then flew by, or rather ambled. Admiral Mustard had never seen them before. It was hard to believe that there were engines powerful enough to move them. They fired a salvo of missiles in salute.

One thousand six hundred super-drones joined the parade, followed by Division Four commanded by Admiral Wallett. Each admiral had been set a challenge by Admiral Bumelton to do something entertaining. Well, flying backwards had been taken, so Admiral Wallett used the stealth capability to make the Fleet appear and disappear.'

Admiral Mustard calculated that so far, four hundred and seventy-five thousand vessels had passed by the enemy's scanners, and there was a lot more to come. The two Marine Fleets passed by with a strange collection of vessels. The Special Operations Fleet looked even more bizarre.

A further four Drone Fleets then paraded again, showing their precision flying skills. They actually played leapfrog. Admiral Mustard didn't think that was possible.

Division Five, commanded by Admiral Adams, showed off by having the vessels of each Fleet flying 'head to toe' in five parallel lines. It was a fine piece of technical flying.

A further five hundred forts paraded, followed by twenty-two thousand support vessels. Then three hundred thousand drones shot by at incredible speeds, then reversing and repeating the fly-by. Admiral Mustard felt that The Empire must have been impressed by that.

Division Six, commanded by Admiral Abosa, the hero of the Lovelace battle, flew by, ducking the front part of each ship in honour of the assembled guests. They were followed by the combined emergency services Fleet, which totalled over fifty thousand vessels; many more than Admiral Mustard had expected. They had made a genuine effort to help. Admiral Mustard made a mental note to thank them.

The two Exploratory Fleets flew by. They definitely had the prettiest ships. No nonsense vessels that were designed for speed rather than warfare. Admirals Clowe and Strauss had been really excited that they were given the opportunity to take part.

Division Seven, commanded by Admiral Gittins, stirred up the crowd by getting his Fleet to loop the loop. This was a remarkably challenging and dangerous manoeuvre, especially for the larger craft. Fortunately, there were no mishaps, but Admiral Mustard thought that Peter had risked more than he should. But then again, it worked. The applause was rapturous. Admiral Mustard's chest was heaving with pride.

Division Eight followed, commanded by Admiral Pearce, another hero of previous wars. His Fleet formed a joint display with the RDCs (Reginal Defence Centres) It went OK, but it was nothing to write home about. But then, Admiral Pearce was never one for outward display.

Over a hundred planet busters flew by. These were big, dangerous planet-destroying machines that Admiral Mustard hoped he would never have to use again. Then a quarter of a million fake ships of the line flew across the parade at right angles to the procession, which shocked everyone.

Divisions Nine and Ten flew by together, one on top of the other. Admiral Tersoo and Dobson had done a fine job getting fifty thousand vessels to fly in such a tight formation. A further one hundred thousand drones paraded, and as they did that, two hundred fake forts crossed their path, totally synchronised.

Division Eleven, commanded by Admiral E Bonner, did nothing special. It was hard enough just getting this scratch Fleet to fly. She had over fifty thousand ships of the line operated by the smallest crew in space history. She was quite relieved when they shot by.

A small series of alien fleets shot by, including the free dragons.

Then came a genuine surprise for Admiral Mustard. Five giant asteroids ambled by, stuffed with weaponry. Alison had done it. They were followed by another five super-battleships.

In the background, the Divisional Fleets and the Drone Fleets had been doctored and paraded again. This time without any tricks.

Admiral Mustard calculated that there were one million, four hundred thousand genuine vessels in the display, plus a quarter of a million fakes. If you allow for the double fly-by, then there was a grand total of nearly three million vessels. That should put the willies up The Empire.

Location: Long Range Monitoring Unit
Sequence of Events: 96

Commander Salton, 'Admiral, I'm returning your call.'

Admiral Mustard, 'Thank you for getting back. I was wondering what our friends are doing?'

Commander Salton, 'As far as I can tell, there are only two enemy vessels left. The rest have scuttled home. Should I target the remaining ships for immediate destruction?'

Admiral Mustard, 'Not just yet. If you think you are going to lose them, then destroy them. I was thinking of trying to capture them.'

Commander Salton, 'That would be audacious.'

Admiral Mustard, 'Indeed. Keep me updated.'

Commander Salton, 'Yes, Sir.'

Admiral Mustard, 'Comms, get me Commander Black.'

Comms, 'Yes, Sir.'

Commander Black, 'Good to talk to you, Jack.'

Admiral Mustard, 'Did you enjoy our little display?'

Commander Black, 'I must admit that I was totally opposed to it. I thought that it was a waste of money, time, and energy, but in reality, it was an amazing success. I thoroughly enjoyed it. My guys are still talking about it.'

Admiral Mustard, 'Well, now I can share with you the reason we did it. There is a small fleet of enemy ships monitoring us. So, we thought that we would put on a display to impress them.'

Commander Black, 'That explains everything. That's why half the Fleet went around twice.'

Admiral Mustard, 'We are just trying to gain time. Anyway, I have a job for you.'

Commander Black, 'Excellent, we desperately need a new challenge.'

Admiral Mustard, 'There are still two enemy ships nearby, within a few thousand miles. I would like you to capture one or both of them. If they escape, then destroy them. Commander Salton has their exact location.'

Commander Black, 'That sounds like a job made for us.'

Admiral Mustard, 'Well done, Martin.'

Location: Head Quarters, Lords of the Book
Sequence of Events: 97

First Lord of the Book, 'So what have you found?'

Clerk of the Book, 'Mixed news, Your Lordship.'

First Lord of the Book, 'That suggests that you have a mixture of good and bad news.'

Clerk of the Book, 'Yes, Your Honour. The good news is that our fleet of twenty ships remained undetected. Our stealth technology is clearly foolproof.'

First Lord of the Book, 'That gives us a distinct advantage.'

Clerk of the Book, 'Yes, my Lord.'

First Lord of the Book, 'And the bad news?'

Clerk of the Book, 'They are a more sophisticated foe than we expected.'

First Lord of the Book, 'In what way?'

Clerk of the Book, 'Shall I list the key points, my Lord?'

First Lord of the Book, 'Yes, but don't take too long.'

Clerk of the Book, 'The key points are as follows:

- It has not been possible to determine the size of their empire, but it runs into thousands of systems
- We were fortunate to see a military display in front of their Emperor Mustard
- Over three million vessels were on display.'

First Lord of the Book, 'That is impossible.'

Clerk of the Book, 'We have it recorded on video, my Lordship.'

First Lord of the Book, 'So what, we still outnumber them by six to one. We have twenty million ships!'

Clerk of the Book, 'That is true, my Lord, but if we consider what vessels we have available, then the numbers are about even.'

First Lord of the Book, 'What do you mean?'

Clerk of the Book, 'Well, we are engaged in several entanglements which are consuming a sizeable amount of our resource. Also, in your twenty million figure, you are including the local, regional forces which at best are suspect.'

First Lord of the Book, 'How dare you? You are getting very close to heresy.'

Clerk of the Book, 'Huge apologies, my Lord.'

First Lord of the Book, 'Our forces can destroy anything in the universe. We are masters of all we perceive.'

Clerk of the Book, 'That's correct, my excellency.'

First Lord of the Book, 'So what else have you found?'

Clerk of the Book, 'They use AI technology.'

First Lord of the Book, 'But most civilised societies have abandoned that as flawed.'

Clerk of the Book, 'Yes, my Lord.'

First Lord of the Book, 'So that gives us two advantages: superior stealth technology and their reliance on artificial intelligence.'

Clerk of the Book, 'Yes, my Lord. I have some photos to show you.'

First Lord of the Book, 'What is this?'

Clerk of the Book, 'We believe that it is a command ship.'

First Lord of the Book, 'But we have nothing that size.'

Clerk of the Book, 'This one is a fortress.'

First Lord of the Book, 'This is serious.'

Clerk of the Book, 'Do you want to see the video, my Lord?'

First Lord of the Book, 'Not really, but I have no choice.' The entire video was shown. 'Is that their entire fleet?'

Clerk of the Book, 'I doubt it, my Lord. Would you engage all of your resources on a parade?'

First Lord of the Book, 'You know the answer to that!'

Clerk of the Book, 'Sorry, my Lord.'

First Lord of the Book, 'There are several concerning issues: the size of their fleet, its skill level, the giant ships and fortresses and the militarisation of asteroids.'

Clerk of the Book, 'Yes, my Lord.'

First Lord of the Book, 'Perhaps it's all bluster, and their weapons are superficial?'

Clerk of the Book, 'They have Godfire, and they defeated The Brakendethians and The Chosen.'

First Lord of the Book, 'You are painting a black picture. You know that upstairs don't like surprises.'

Clerk of the Book, 'I expect to be recycled, my Lordship.'

First Lord of the Book, 'In that case, we will push this upstairs. Report to dehydration along with your family.'

Clerk of the Book, 'Yes, my Lord.'

It didn't seem fair that the young ones should have their water removed, especially as it was such a painful death.

Location: Admiral Mustard's Flat, Planet Napoleon
Sequence of Events: 98

Jack had just got back from addressing little John's school as he had promised some time ago. He felt that the contrasts in his life were amazing. One moment he was observing the biggest military Fleet ever put together by humanity, then he was giving a talk to a bunch of primary school kids.

Little John, 'Mum, Mum, Dad was fantastic. He talked about his childhood and his career and then showed a video of the build-up to the Grand Parade. All of my friends want to join the Navy now.'

Amy, 'Don't forget about Mum, she had fifty thousand vessels in her Fleet. She is probably the greatest woman in history.'

Edel blushed and said, 'Come now, let's not go overboard.'

Jack, 'I think Amy is right, the best mum in the world, the best wife in the world and probably, no certainly, the best woman in the world.'

Edel felt tears brimming again. Sometimes the joys of being a mother were almost too much for her. As an officer of The Galactium, she had her emotions under control, but not as a mother.

Amy, who was still only a few months old, said, 'I think the parade achieved its objectives.'

Jack, 'What makes you say that, Amy?'

Amy, 'The Clerk of the Book and his entire family of sixty-eight, have been horribly slaughtered.'

They had got used to Amy's outbursts but found it difficult to understand.

Jack, 'What happened?'

Amy, 'All of the H20 has been removed from their bodies. They are now dry husks that will be fed to the herd. It was a terrifying experience for the children waiting for their turn, but none of them ran as acceptance was high.'

Amy was quite upset, but a chocolate bar usually helped the situation. Well, it always made Edel feel better.

Later that night, as Edel and Jack cuddled as a precursor to full intercourse, Edel said, 'Do you think we should get help regarding Amy?'

Jack, 'I don't think so. My gut feeling is that she is unique. We just need to nourish her abilities.'

Edel, 'So, you think she is special.'

Jack, 'I do. She is going to surprise us.'

Edel, 'But where is she getting these terms from, like Clerk of the Book?'

Jack, 'I think she is experiencing realities from elsewhere. Believe me; it will all work out.'

Then intercourse started.

Location: The Space around Planet Napoleon
Sequence of Events: 99

Commander Black called his men together. As far as he was concerned, they were the best special services troops in the universe. He could chase their pedigree back to the SAS and the US SEALs.

Commander Black, 'This is our target.'

He showed a video of two ships close together which were slowly circling Planet Napoleon. The enemy was confident that their stealth technology was one hundred per cent successful.

Commander Black, 'Our objective is to capture one of their ships, ideally both. As you know, it is difficult to capture a travelling vessel. We need to agree on a way of stopping them without destroying them.'

Major Thompson, 'I suggest that we use a sponge force field along with glue bombs.'

Commander Black, 'Please elaborate.'

Major Thompson, 'Well, I suggest the following:

- We need to confirm their actual trajectory around the planet
- We then erect the sponge force field along the line
- This force field acts like a sponge rather than a brick wall. It slowly stops the vessel and absorbs the friction
- The glue bomb locks them in. They won't be able to open any of the apertures.'

Commander Black, 'What if they blow their ship up?'

Major Thompson, 'That would be a problem. I assume that we don't know about physiology?'

Commander Black, 'Sadly, we know nothing about them. What do our scanners suggest?'

Sergeant Wilson, 'It would appear that they are oxygen breathers. Our system predicts that they are probably similar to mammalians.'

Major Thompson, 'In that case, we could drill through the hulls of both ships and let most of the oxygen escape. That will disable them.'

Commander Black, 'It might kill them.'

Major Thompson, 'It would be better to pump in some sort of gas, but we simply can't tell what effect it would have on them.'

Commander Black, 'Does anyone have an alternative plan?'

There was a shaking of heads.

Commander Black, 'In that case, Major Thompson, please put your plan into action.'

Location: Admiral Mustard's Office, Planet Napoleon
Sequence of Events: 100

Admiral Mustard, 'Update me.'
    Fleet Operations, 'Yes, Sir:

- Division One is back protecting Earth
- Divisions Two, Four, Five, Nine and Ten are back in their normal position with Drone Fleets Six to Ten
- Divisions Two, Six and Eight are back at Planet Lovelace with Drone Fleets One to Five
- Division Seven, the two Exploratory Fleets, the entire Marine Corps, and Drone Fleets Eleven to Fifteen are still here
- The Special Operations Fleet are engaged in Operation Catch
- Admiral E Bonner's Fleet is back to base for final fitting
- The Long-Range Monitoring team is still tracking the two enemy ships
- The forts have returned or are returning to their home planets
- The Dragon Fleet is at Dragonia.'

Admiral Mustard, 'What is the status of the new assets?'
    Fleet Operations, 'The super-battleships, super-fortresses and asteroid weapons are all back at base for final fitting and testing.'
    Admiral Mustard, 'Please thank every emergency force that contributed vessels to the parade. Please ask Sheila Taylor to organise a commemorative plaque for them.'
    Fleet Operations, 'Yes, Sir.'
    Admiral Mustard, 'Comms, get me Commander Black.'
    Comms, 'Yes, Sir.'
    Commander Black, 'Good day, Jack.'
    Admiral Mustard, 'How is it going?'
    Commander Black, 'We are preparing for our assault in the next few minutes. Wish us luck.'
    Admiral Mustard, 'I'm not convinced that you need it.'
    Commander Black, 'We always need Lady Luck, especially when we are up against the unknown.'
    Admiral Mustard, 'In that case, I wish you good luck.'

Location: Angel Delight
Sequence of Events: 101

Angelina, 'How was your sleep?'

Hypnos, 'Heavenly as usual, but you are really asking me what should we do next. In my dreams, I met Thanatos. He suggested that he should meet with you, so that is the plan.'

Angela, 'Where is he?'

Hypnos, 'He has his own kingdom in Hades, but he will be here soon.'

Angelina, 'Is it worth waking up some of the other gods?'

Hypnos, 'I think it best that we wait for Thanatos, partly because he has spent the last few millennia with The Chosen and has a lot of experience with humankind.'

Angela, 'How many gods do you have here?'

Hypnos, 'The ones you saw and about three others. They are all underworld gods, and, if I say so myself, not the nicest bunch.'

Angelina, 'Can I ask why you are here?'

Hypnos, 'This is where I belong. Hades is my home.'

Angelina, 'But is this Hades?'

Hypnos, 'What do you mean?'

Angelina, 'To us, this seems like a rather desolate, arid planet in a rather tedious system.'

Hypnos, 'What are you talking about? Hades is a concept. It's not a physical dimension.'

Angela, 'Angelina, I might have transported you off the planet to this place. Who knows where we are now.'

Angelina, 'I feel that this is now Hades, and the planet is a thing of the past.'

Angela, 'I'm going to try an experiment, and suddenly they were both back in their father's house.'

Angelina, 'That was cool. Shall we go back?'

Angela, 'The answer is yes, but we need to think about the consequences. Do we really want the God of Death, the Goddess of the Night, the Judge of the Dead and other horrors walking through our living room?'

Angelina, 'That's a fair point. They could easily spread disease and pestilence throughout The Galactium. That wouldn't go down well with Dad or Admiral Mustard.'

Angela, 'They would definitely stop our pocket money and put us in detention.'

Angelina, 'Have you noticed that we are back to our normal gorgeous selves? In Hades, our wings were drooping, and my hair was starting to go grey.'

Angela, 'I guess that we can't be surprised. It is the home of the dead.'

Angelina, 'That reminds me. There was no sign of the dead. Not a single corpse.'

There was a knock on the door. It was Thanatos.

Location: The Space around Planet Napoleon
Sequence of Events: 102

The assault team waited for the two Empire ships to circumnavigate Planet Napoleon. Everything was in place for their capture. It was now the calm before the storm. It was the time where you had to keep your adrenaline under control.

The slow, chunky Empire ships crashed into the spongy force field, which was designed to absorb the velocity and dampen the effects of a rapid stop. The energy generated was quickly dissipated, mostly in the form of heat.

The Special Ops troops were soon drilling holes into the hull of the ships. They were assisted by the heat damage, and it wasn't long before oxygen was escaping. At the same time, glue bombs were dropped onto the ships to secure all the apertures.

Tractor beams grabbed both ships and carried them into giant transporter vessels. Inside the transporter, The Empire ships were hemmed in by powerful force fields in case of an explosion.

The Empire ships were carried off to two hangers on separate asteroids. The strategy was to crack one open, and if that didn't work, they could try a different technique on the other ship. The hangers had been designed for the purpose of extracting individuals from spacecraft. Technology had been installed to void any external communication that was not approved.

Admirals Mustard and Bumelton joined the commandos on the asteroid as they forced open the first ship. They stayed behind nuclear-proof barriers and a very secure force field. Robots were used to slice the front part of the vessel off.

They now had a chance to study the ship that was slightly suspended off the ground by tractor beams. By human standards, it was a chunky, ugly thing. It didn't look fast, but then humans still had a propensity to design craft that looked sleek and almost missile-like, which made no sense in outer space.

It was pock-marked from debris encounters. There were no visible windows, but then these were a thing of the past on human ships. There were lots of antennae sticking out in every possible direction. Overall, it looked crude, but then The Empire had conquered a considerable number of systems in their desire to install control.

The robots continued cutting into the craft. It took longer than expected, as the hull material was surprisingly tough. The robots had already sent back a detailed analysis of its composition, which suggested that the material had been altered at the molecular level. Alison Walsh and Jill Ginger, who were watching the proceedings remotely, were already excited by this discovery.

Eventually, the front of the ship was lifted off, and then they came.

Hundreds of rat-like creatures left the vessels like rats leaving a sinking ship. Most were barely half a metre tall. They were in red environmental suits covered in insignia, and they were armed. They quickly destroyed the robots and then rushed towards the observation area.

The Special Service Troopers were trained to react quickly, but they were as shocked by the experience as everyone else. No one expected three or four hundred large rats to be attacking them.

On the other hand, the rats didn't expect the automatic defence mechanisms to engage. The glue guns threw thousands of gallons of fast-acting glue at the rodent horde. It was one of the funniest sights that Admiral Mustard had ever seen.

There were probably four hundred rats desperately trying to free themselves from the adhesive mixture. Like a spider's web, the more they fought, the stickier it became. It was hilarious to watch, but not for the rats. To give them credit, they carried on firing their weapons, which were useless against the protective force field.

The commandos had planned this well. They then turned on giant magnets, which snatched their weapons off them, along with their buttons and belt buckles. Our super-glued rats were now trying to maintain their dignity by holding up their pantaloons while the glue set like concrete.

Hover-bots searched the multitude for weapons, and a few were confiscated.

Hover-bots then entered The Empire craft. There was a concern that it had been set to explode, but nothing happened. The audience, both local and remote, could see exactly what the bot was observing:

- There were long corridors with nesting areas full of a cotton-wool-like substance
- There were communal eating areas with a considerable variety of food substances but no seating

- There was an obvious engine room. There was no nuclear signal, so it was going to be interesting to see how they powered their vessels
- There was a ridiculously tiny medical facility
- The Latrines had piles of excrement collected in neat piles
- There was a life support system
- There were no obvious weapon systems
- There was an office with three rats inside. They wore different outfits to the rest, which might indicate seniority.

And then the ship exploded, killing the three on the ship and most of those stuck in the glue.

The explosion was not unexpected, but they now had enough information to safely secure the other ship. Now they had both live and dead 'rat' specimens for research.

Location: Head Quarters, Lords of the Holy Relics
Sequence of Events: 103

First Lord of the Book, 'I'm very grateful that you could spare the time to see me, Your High Excellency.'

Third Lord of the Holy Relics, 'Well, it better be urgent. I have little time to waste.'

First Lord of the Book, 'Of course, Your Supreme Eminence.'

Third Lord of the Holy Relics, 'Out with it then. What is causing the Order of the Book so much concern?'

First Lord of the Book, 'We may have a very slight problem.'

Third Lord of the Holy Relics, 'If it is that slight, why are you concerning the Order of the Holy Relics.'

First Lord of the Book, 'I don't have your wisdom or experience to make those sorts of judgements, Your Magnificence.'

Third Lord of the Holy Relics, 'Give me the facts, and I will judge.'

First Lord of the Book, 'Yes, my Lord, we are talking about the Hotman Empire.'

Third Lord of the Holy Relics, 'I've not heard of them before.'

First Lord of the Book, 'They are quite insignificant, my Lord. We understand that they are a constructed race.'

Third Lord of the Holy Relics, 'Then they have no right to exist in our continuum. They must be exterminated like vermin.'

First Lord of the Book, 'Of course, my Lord.'

Third Lord of the Holy Relics, 'What have you done about it?'

First Lord of the Book, 'We have sent forces to teach them a lesson, but so far they have been ineffectual.'

Third Lord of the Holy Relics, 'I will not have this. Why have they not been eliminated?'

First Lord of the Book, 'That is why I am here, Your Brilliance. I need your wisdom on the best way forward.'

Third Lord of the Holy Relics, 'Yes, I can see that. Who manufactured them?'

First Lord of the Book, 'We believe that it was The Brakendeth.'

Third Lord of the Holy Relics, 'Don't they supply our mind-control units?'

First Lord of the Book, 'That's correct, my Lord. They used to, but they no longer exist.'

Third Lord of the Holy Relics, 'What happened to them?'

First Lord of the Book, 'Our sources suggest that they were wiped out by the Hotmans.'

Third Lord of the Holy Relics, 'Let's get this straight. You are saying that the Hotmans killed their creator?'

First Lord of the Book, 'That's correct, my Lord.'

Third Lord of the Holy Relics, 'I can't believe the audacity of these Hotmans. We must avenge The Brakendeth.'

First Lord of the Book, 'I can only agree with your gloriousness, but there is a problem.'

Third Lord of the Holy Relics, 'I don't want problems. You know that.'

First Lord of the Book, 'I understand, but you need to know.'

Third Lord of the Holy Relics, 'Stop, I will decide what I need to know.'

First Lord of the Book, 'Of course, Your Supreme Eminence.'

Third Lord of the Holy Relics, 'That's better.'

First Lord of the Book, 'But could I beg your indulgence to let me tell you that The Brakendethians use Hotman DNA in the manufacture of the control units.'

Third Lord of the Holy Relics, 'Are you saying that our supply of control units has stopped?'

First Lord of the Book, 'Yes, my Lord, and without the Hotman DNA, we cannot manufacture them any longer.'

Third Lord of the Holy Relics, 'I will inform First Lord and then personally lead the Holy Relics' Fleet against them. Nothing will stop me.'

First Lord of the Book, 'Before you leave, I need to warn you.'

Third Lord of the Holy Relics, 'I'm not interested in your warnings. This is the opportunity I've been looking for to crown myself in glory. Now begone with you. My destiny awaits.'

First Lord of the Book, 'As you command, my Lord.'

He had a serious foreboding, but you don't get to be Third Lord of the Holy Relics by being incompetent.

Location: Terry's Flat
Sequence of Events: 104

Admiral Mustard, 'How are you, Terry?'

Terry, 'Very busy, but I have to tell you that I've just experienced a huge surprise.'

Admiral Mustard, 'Your wife has returned?'

Terry, 'No, it's far more shocking than that. It's in a totally different league.'

Admiral Mustard, 'You better tell me. Do we need security?'

Terry, 'I don't think that will be necessary. But I need to tell you that it is shocking when someone returns from the dead.'

Admiral Mustard, 'Who was it?'

Terry, 'Admiral Thanatos.'

Admiral Mustard, 'But we know he died.'

Terry, 'Well, he is here talking to my two daughters. I told him that I was going to call you, and he said that he would be very pleased to see you.'

Admiral Mustard, 'I will be over as soon as I can.'

Location: Security Hanger, Asteroid 32,768
Sequence of Events: 105

The Special Forces Team, with help from a marine regiment, freed the ratfinks one at a time. They used an anti-solvent solution to get them free. They had to be careful, as the rat creatures had a tendency to bite.

The rats were stripped, searched, and sprayed with chemical detergents to eliminate any health risks. Most of them contained some form of weaponry in their shaggy hair, which covered their entire body. Apart from a full set of sharp teeth, they had claws on their hands and feet.

They walked both upright and on all fours. They had a shortened version of the typical rat tail, ears that could be rotated, healthy, sharp-looking eyes and a snout of varying colours. Apparently, the colour indicated their age.

The prisoners were transferred to specially prepared cells. The layout of these cells had been quickly remodelled on the captured vessel. The food that was found in the kitchen had been replicated, and replicators were left in the kitchen so that they could manage their own food production.

Their clothes had also been replicated. Linguistic conversion tools were made available, along with lots of entertainment. Full bedding material was provided for the forty-six inmates.

The dead bodies were taken to the morgue for dissection and investigation.

The remains of The Empire ship were investigated. They had a jump drive that offered a few improvements to the human version. The material science utilised in the vessel also caused a lot of excitement. It was going to cost a fortune retrofitting some of these technology improvements into The Galactium Fleet.

Location: Terry's Flat
Sequence of Events: 106

Admiral Mustard was nervous about meeting Admiral Thanatos. They had been friends and fellow officers until he learnt the truth about The Chosen. But then there are many truths and many histories. They say that history is written by the victors, but human history has been totally reconstructed over the last few years.

Admiral Mustard tentatively rang the doorbell and was welcomed in. What a strange sight: Terry, two naked angels and the God of Death sitting on a sofa.

Thanatos stood up and said, 'Good evening, Jack, it is fantastic to see you again.'

Admiral Mustard, 'I have to be honest, it is a bit of a shock seeing you, but a pleasant shock. Welcome back.'

Thanatos, 'I can understand your shock, and on my part, I never thought that I would be in the same room as you again.'

Admiral Mustard, 'Can I ask how you survived?'

Thanatos, 'I never really knew if you humans knew who I was.'

Admiral Mustard, 'We thought that you were an admiral who had taken the name of a Greek god until you flew off in a blaze of light with the rest of The Chosen.'

Thanatos, 'Yes, that must have surprised you, but by then, you had learnt about our dark side.'

Admiral Mustard, 'Yes, but it was far darker than anyone thought possible. That captured film was worse than anything humanity had done, and that is saying something. I found your personal involvement seriously distressing.'

Thanatos, 'I'm not making any excuses, but it was a very long time ago, and I regretted my previous behaviour.'

Admiral Mustard, 'That is so easy to say, especially as you still had human slaves in Olympia, but you lied to us about The Chosen and our history. You were as bad if not worse than The Brakendeth.'

Thanatos, 'I am sorry for everything we did and the lies, but we had our own agenda, and I had to defend the gods.'

Admiral Mustard, 'I understand that. I guess that I need to move on, but it won't be easy.'

Thanatos, 'When we first met, I wanted you to think that I was normal, and I hoped to live a fairly normal life, but I am a god. When it comes to being a god, you have very little choice. I didn't want to be the God of Death, but that was my inheritance.'

Admiral Mustard, 'Did Lady Enyo survive?'

Thanatos, 'You can never tell with gods and goddesses. I haven't seen her since that fateful day.'

Admiral Mustard, 'And she is a god as well?'

Thanatos, 'Of course, and what a goddess. She was the daughter of Zeus and Hera and the sister of Ares. She should have been one of The Elders.'

Admiral Mustard, 'So how did you survive?'

Thanatos, 'I was sent back to my home, which is Hades. I have my own special area.'

Admiral Mustard, 'What made you come back?'

Thanatos, 'I hadn't planned to. I just followed Angela and Angelina.'

Admiral Mustard, 'Who are they?'

Terry, 'They are my daughters.'

Admiral Mustard, 'So who thought of those "angelic" names?'

Terry, 'They named themselves.'

Admiral Mustard, 'So are you saying that your two daughters were in hell and that Thanatos followed them here?'

Terry, 'That is what I was told.'

Thanatos, 'That is a fact. I was rather surprised to find two live angels in my home. And when they left, I decided to follow them.'

Admiral Mustard, 'Can I ask you girls how you got to Hades?'

Angelina, 'We just wish our way there. We can wish our way anywhere.'

Admiral Mustard, 'That's an amazing talent, but why did you go to Hades?'

Angelina, 'We were instructed to hunt down any remaining gods.'

Admiral Mustard, 'Why?'

Angelina, 'To save us all.'

Admiral Mustard, 'From what?'

Angelina, 'From the Lords of the Path.'

Admiral Mustard, 'Do you mean The Empire?'

Angelina, 'Possibly.'

Admiral Mustard, 'Who is making you do this?'

Angelina, 'We are not totally sure, but she commands, and we obey.'

Admiral Mustard, 'Can you trust her?'

Angelina, 'We have seen her heart. The way ahead is pure.'

Thanatos, 'Personally, I wouldn't recommend waking up the Gods of the Underworld. I believe that I'm a rational being that appreciates and accepts the ways of humans, but most of my colleagues are terrifying, and what's worse, unpredictable.'

Admiral Mustard, 'Angela and Angelina, do you understand what Thanatos is saying?'

Angela, 'Yes, that is why we returned. We planned to ask our dad for advice.'

Admiral Mustard, 'Can I ask you all to do nothing until I've had a chat with the president.'

Everyone nodded.

Location: The President's Office, Planet Napoleon
Sequence of Events: 107

Admirals Mustard and Bumelton met with President Padfield and Henrietta Strong in the president's office for a round-up.

President Padfield, 'It sounds to me like we have got a lot to discuss.'

Admiral Mustard, 'That's probably an understatement, but it's probably best to focus on the pressing issues.'

Henrietta Strong, 'What do you consider your pressing issues?'

Admiral Mustard, 'The following come to mind:

- The Empire
- The return of Admiral Thanatos
- Planet Lovelace
- Dragon situation
- Marine Corps recruitment.'

President Padfield, 'What do you mean the return of Admiral Thanatos. I thought that The Chosen were well and truly dead.'

Admiral Mustard, 'I think that The Chosen are, but it appears that Thanatos and Enyo were genuine Greek gods.'

Henrietta Strong, 'And my arse is the entrance to Hades!'

Admiral Mustard, 'Well, if you want to meet Thanatos, he is having lunch in Terry's house with his two angel daughters.'

Henrietta Strong, 'You are joking. How did he get here?'

Admiral Mustard, 'He followed Angela and Angelina there from Hades, or possibly Henrietta's arse.'

President Padfield, 'Who the hell are Angela and Angelina?'

Admiral Mustard, 'That's what Terry's children have called themselves.'

President Padfield, 'But they are only a few months old.'

Admiral Mustard, 'I think you will find that angels grow up pretty quickly. As a hot-blooded male, it's very difficult to concentrate when there are two beautiful naked angels in the room. They are somewhat distracting, especially as they are hairless down below.'

Henrietta Strong, 'You men are all the same. A man of your age should be able to cope with a naked pussy.'

President Padfield, 'Can we get back on track?'

Admiral Mustard, 'OK, someone or something is directing the angels to track down the remaining gods. The girls have found several underworld gods. According to the girls, we need their help in the war against the Lords of the Path.'

President Padfield, 'And who are they?'

Admiral Mustard, 'The girls don't know, but I'm guessing that they are The Empire.'

President Padfield, 'So who is directing them?'

Admiral Mustard, 'I don't think they know, but Thanatos thinks it would be perilous waking up the underworld gods.'

President Padfield, 'What's your recommendation?'

Admiral Mustard, 'I think that we should sit around the table with Thanatos.'

President Padfield, 'Fine with me, but how do we control the girls?'

Admiral Mustard, 'I've no idea, but I need to update you regarding the ratfinks.'

President Padfield, 'Ratfinks?'

Admiral Mustard, 'That's what the troops are calling the enemy.' The admiral distributed some photos.

President Padfield, 'They do look like large rats. Who would think that they could create an intergalactic empire.'

Admiral Mustard, 'We have dissected dead specimens and found the following:

- They are biologically similar to rats, but they are not mammals, and they have a completely different DNA structure
- They have very sophisticated brains. They look to be more sophisticated than ours. Our exo-biologists believe that from the brain structure, they can think quicker than us, retain information better than us, have better senses and agility.'

President Padfield, 'So they are super-rats?'

Admiral Mustard, 'It would be wrong to see them as rats. They are very intelligent, organised, and disciplined, but rather rat-like in their communal activities. It was surprising to see how many there were in one ship.'

President Padfield, 'What about their leaders?'

Admiral Mustard, 'Those in the first captured ship killed themselves and most of their crew. We haven't opened up the second ship yet as the scientists are still investigating ways of making the crew unconscious.'

President Padfield, 'What about the live captives from the first ship?'

Admiral Mustard, 'They have proved to be remarkably friendly. They have not shown any aggression towards us, which is odd.'

President Padfield, 'What do they eat?'

Admiral Mustard, 'Anything and everything we give them. They are voracious eaters and will fight each other to get the best cuts and the biggest portions.'

President Padfield, 'They sound more like animals.'

Admiral Mustard, 'On the other side of the coin, most of them can speak English reasonably well. They love our music and TV, and they have exhausted the small library of books we provided.

The other worry is that they seem to breed like rabbits. We think they lay eggs, but the exo-biologists are not sure, as the female reproductive organs differ greatly from ours. It also looks like they can change sex if required.'

Henrietta Strong, 'That would have saved me a mountain of pain and cost.'

President Padfield, 'But what have they told us about their civilisation?'

Admiral Mustard, 'Very little. Most or all of them were born on the ship and expected to die on the ship. They seem to regard their incarceration as a bit of a holiday. It's certainly not a punishment.

They have no idea who we are or that there is a war going on.

Every one of them has the control mechanism fitted in their brain.'

President Padfield, 'Is it still based on human DNA?'

Admiral Mustard, 'Yes, not that our rodent friends know anything about it. They had no idea what we were talking about.'

President Padfield, 'Have you learnt anything of any military value?'

Admiral Mustard, 'Some of the technology will be of use, but not much else. I'm constantly surprised by the universe.'

President Padfield, 'Me too.'

And then there was another surprise, although somewhat expected.

Location: On-board Admiral J Bonner's Bridge
Sequence of Events: 108

Admiral J Bonner. 'Good day, Jack. They are back.'

Admiral Mustard, 'No great surprise then. Anything new?'

Admiral J Bonner. 'Yes, it looks like they are trying to contact us. Comms are trying to set up a link. I will buzz you in.'

Admiral Mustard, 'Excellent, it will be interesting to see what they have to say.'

Admiral J Bonner. 'Better go, as the link is almost there.'

A video link was established. On the screen was a giant rat with very elaborate clothing full of insignia. On its head was a small crown straight out of a Disney movie. It was hard for the human mind to see it as a ruthless killer.

Third Lord of the Holy Relics, 'I'm the Third Lord of the Holy Relics.'

Admiral J Bonner, 'I'm Admiral J Bonner.'

Third Lord of the Holy Relics, 'You will not talk until I give you permission.'

Admiral J Bonner, 'And where do I get this permission from?'

Third Lord of the Holy Relics, 'Do you not know who I am?'

Admiral J Bonner, 'I've no idea who you are.'

Third Lord of the Holy Relics, 'I represent the greatest empire the universe has ever seen, and if you don't show respect, I will have your fur removed and then have your meat fed to the Hyyz.'

Admiral J Bonner, 'I'm very sorry if I have offended you, but we don't take threats lightly in The Galactium. I would appreciate it if you left our space immediately.'

Third Lord of the Holy Relics, who was incandescent with rage, said, 'I have never been so insulted. I will personally ensure that you die a horrible death.'

Admiral J Bonner, 'Thank you very much. Can I ask why you are here?'

Third Lord of the Holy Relics, 'I will not have this. How dare you even think about asking me anything?'

Admiral J Bonner, 'Fair enough. I'm going to end this conversation.'

Third Lord of the Holy Relics, 'You cannot end without my permission.'

Admiral J Bonner, 'Fuck you.'

Third Lord of the Holy Relics, 'Your days are numbered. This is the fleet of the Holy Relics. We are here to destroy your civilisation. I was originally inclined to take your surrender, but your insults have caused me to take a more aggressive stance. You will experience total devastation.'

Admiral Mustard, 'My orders:

- Switch on all planetary force fields
- Put all Fleet assets on full alert
- Inform all commanders
- The Long Range Scanning Unit will assess the incoming alien fleet
- Inform the president.'

Admiral J Bonner, 'Thank you for the warning.'

Third Lord of the Holy Relics, 'Please wait while we present our fleet.'

Commander Salton, 'Gentleman, our scan suggests that they have fifty-six thousand vessels. Some of them are considerably larger than we have previously experienced. I have supplied the coordinates.

I should also tell you that they have forgotten to secure their chatter. I've also outlined the key transmitting vessels.'

Admiral J Bonner, 'My orders:

- Use Godfire to immediately target all tagged vessels
- Use drones to attack all tagged vessels
- Prepare to use other weapons on tagged vessels as required
- Launch all drones to attack the enemy fleet
- Divisions Four and Five prepare to attack.'

It was fortunate for the Third Lord of the Holy Relics that he was in his private schooner and not on one of the warships, as it wasn't long before all of their significant battleships were destroyed. As before, this eliminated their control and communications capability.

Then Divisions Four and Five started the slaughter. Admiral J Bonner wondered if he should call a halt, as it was just so easy. But he thought not.

The Third Lord of the Holy Relics only just managed to escape.

Location: Admiral Mustard's Office, Planet Napoleon
Sequence of Events: 109

Admiral Mustard, 'That was far too easy.'

Admiral J Bonner, 'You are right, Jack. That was crazy easy.'

Admiral Mustard, 'And who was that Holy Relic character?'

Admiral J Bonner, 'What a pompous pratt. Clearly, it is a very autocratic society.'

Admiral Mustard, 'I wonder if he or she got away.'

Admiral J Bonner, 'It's very hard to tell. I must admit that I felt slightly guilty about destroying their ships as, once again, they were sitting ducks. But then they were the aggressor.'

Admiral Mustard, 'I was told that every fleet they send would be superior to the previous one.'

Admiral J Bonner, 'Well, that has certainly not been the case.'

Admiral Mustard, 'I think that we better stay on guard as they will be back.'

Admiral J Bonner, 'I agree. Changing the subject, your wife is giving me a hard time.'

Admiral Mustard, 'Why is that?'

Admiral J Bonner, 'She needs experienced officers for her two new Fleets.'

Admiral Mustard, 'I'm sorry, but I have to support her. There is no alternative.'

Admiral J Bonner, 'I can see that, but losing key staff is very disruptive.'

Admiral Mustard, 'I know that too well, but what else can we do?'

Admiral J Bonner, 'I will just have to accept it. How is it going with the captured ships?'

Admiral Mustard, 'We should be cracking the second ship open about now. Hopefully, that will give us more information than the first ship.'

Location: Head Quarters, Lords of the Holy Relics
Sequence of Events: 110

Third Lord of the Holy Relics, 'You realise that you are facing charges of treason. Your chance of surviving this are slim, very slim indeed. You deliberately caused the destruction of the Holy Relics fleet.'

First Lord of the Book, 'That's not correct, my Lord.'

Third Lord of the Holy Relics, 'How dare you challenge me? You are just making things worse for yourself and your family.'

First Lord of the Book, 'Do I need to replay our previous conversation, my Lord?'

Third Lord of the Holy Relics, 'Let's move on. I thought that you had sent in punishment fleets. The Hotmans did not seem to fear us.'

First Lord of the Book, 'That's because they have defeated every force we have sent against them. They are nearing the top of the Kratz index. Perhaps level five or six.'

Third Lord of the Holy Relics, 'That's not possible.'

First Lord of the Book, 'That was my original reaction, Your Supreme Eminence.'

Third Lord of the Holy Relics, 'But are you are suggesting that their technology is almost equal to ours?'

First Lord of the Book, 'Unfortunately, that appears to be the case. And The Hotmans defeated both The Brakendethians and The Chosen.

Third Lord of the Holy Relics, 'Why didn't you tell me this before?'

First Lord of the Book, 'I have a film to show you.'

The Third Lord of the Holy Relics said nothing as he watched the film.

Third Lord of the Holy Relics, 'What else do you need to tell me?'

First Lord of the Book, 'The following analysis may be of interest:

• It has not been possible to determine the size of their empire, but it runs into thousands of systems
• They have over three million vessels
• They use AI technology, supercharged force fields, advanced portal technology, planet busters, etc.
• They have Godfire
• They have advanced replication technology.'

Third Lord of the Holy Relics, 'Is there anything else. Why didn't you tell me this before?'

First Lord of the Book, 'It was clearly an error on my part.'

Third Lord of the Holy Relics, 'I'm glad you said that.'

He turned to his assistant and said, 'Get me the Master of Arms.'

Assistant, 'Yes, my most glorious master.'

Master at Arms, 'How can I be of service, my Lordship.'

Third Lord of the Holy Relics, 'Master at Arms, I want you to take this traitor to the public square along with his wife and children. There you will disembowel his wife and then grind her into mincemeat. You will then feed her to her children. I want them well fed before you burn them alive.

Then castrate the traitor, blind him, rip out his tongue and then slowly remove his vital organs.'

Master at Arms, 'Of course, my Lord. Shall I also rip out his teeth and claws? That can be immensely painful.'

Third Lord of the Holy Relics, 'Excellent idea, that would be a lovely touch.'

Master at Arms, 'Should I do the same with his wife and children?'

Third Lord of the Holy Relics, 'Can you spare the time?'

Master at Arms, 'Not really, my Lord, but if you are going to do the job, you might as well do it properly.'

Third Lord of the Holy Relics, 'In that case, you might as well. Bring me their tails when you have finished.' He had built up an impressive collection over the years.

The Master at Arms took the traitor away. He was a very happy Master at Arms, as mass executions were always profitable. There were many out there who wanted to participate in the grim task and others who just wanted an excellent view of the proceedings.

The Third Lord of the Holy Relics pondered how he was going to survive this debacle. At least he had acted quickly to eliminate the traitor.

Location: The President's Office, Planet Napoleon
Sequence of Events: 111

President Padfield, 'I'm not sure how I should greet you, Admiral Thanatos, considering our joint history.'

Thanatos, 'It's just plain Thanatos now as the fleet is a thing of the past.'

President Padfield, 'How have you been?'

Thanatos, 'Somewhat bored after all the excitement we had when we were fighting The Brakendethians.'

President Padfield, 'Well, the excitement, if you can call it that has just continued with one enemy after another. We are currently up against The Empire. Have you come across them?'

Thanatos, 'Yes, we know them quite well. They actually worship the Gods of the Underworld. They are effectively a death cult.'

President Padfield, 'But that doesn't really stack up. The captured ship was full of rodents who seemed quite happy when we imprisoned them.'

Thanatos, 'Most of them have never seen daylight. They are born in the ships and die in the ships. On board they live in fear. There are regular ceremonial killings and ritual suicides. They rarely have a chance to think for themselves because of the mind-control devices.'

President Padfield, 'But they don't kill all of the conquered species they come across?'

Thanatos, 'It all depends on the characteristics of the captured species. For every hundred conquests, they eliminate seventy per cent of them. They kill every individual they come across, often in the most unpleasant way.

The other thirty per cent are pacified. The military, intelligentsia, organisers etc., are executed, and the rest are fitted with mind-control devices.'

President Padfield, 'But why do they keep them?'

Thanatos, 'I've assumed that they need the labour pool.'

President Padfield, 'Why would they keep the dragons?'

Thanatos, 'Probably because dragons are seen as "special" throughout the universe. To be honest, you would have to ask them.'

President Padfield, 'So far, we have defeated all of the fleets they have sent against us.'

Thanatos, 'Don't be deceived. They are a deadly killing machine.

221

When the time comes, they could easily throw a few million ships against you. So far, you have been dealing with the local forces. They still haven't fully ascertained what threat you are.'

President Padfield, 'But we are not a threat.'

Thanatos, 'They would argue that you are in the way of their journey along the path.'

President Padfield, 'What path?'

Thanatos, 'The path to the underworld and ultimate retribution.'

The phone rings, and it is Admiral Mustard. President Padfield puts him on the speaker.

Admiral Mustard, 'Apologies for my absence, but I'm having a few personal problems.'

President Padfield, 'I hope everyone is OK.'

Admiral Mustard, 'Nothing I can't handle. I will catch up with you later.'

Thanatos, 'Give my regards to Edel.'

Admiral Mustard, 'I will.'

President Padfield, 'Thanatos, do you have any regrets regarding your relationship with us?'

Thanatos, 'Yes, I do. I became a great admirer of humanity, and I regret how The Chosen and I treated humans in the past. It was totally unacceptable, but they were crimes of the past, and humanity has got its own hidden skeletons: the Holocaust, slavery, religious persecution, discrimination, genocide, etc.'

President Padfield, 'That's a fair point, but in some ways, it was the lying which was The Chosen's greatest fault.'

Thanatos, 'As you would say: "needs must", but I understand where you are coming from, and I regret how I treated you, Admiral Mustard and my "other human friends".'

President Padfield, 'That's good to hear.'

Thanatos, 'To be honest, I feel the opposite. I have loved many Earthlings, and I love your music, art, sport, sense of humour and your love of life. The list goes on. That's why I'm concerned about your involvement with the Gods of the Underworld.'

President Padfield, 'It's hard for us to believe that they are real.'

Thanatos, 'In most societies, reality eventually becomes mythology. It's just a matter of timing.'

President Padfield, 'But is all mythology true?'

Thanatos, 'Of course not. It's a mixture of advanced technology, manipulation of the local population and some special powers created via bionic engineering.'

President Padfield, 'Special powers?'

Thanatos, 'Yes, practically everything is possible in nature: superintelligence, manipulation of matter and energy via sheer brain power, teleportation, etc. These powers can evolve slowly or be created through genetic and bionic engineering.'

President Padfield, 'So are you saying that you are not really a god?'

Thanatos, 'Yes, that is probably what I'm saying. Over a million years ago, I was augmented. I've been treated and worshipped as a god for thousands of years, so you decide.'

President Padfield, 'Fair enough. Why are you so worried about the other gods?'

Thanatos, 'They are ancient and somewhat demented, but they do have dangerous powers.'

President Padfield, 'Do you mean powers or augmentation?'

Thanatos, 'Very clever. Whatever you call it, they are dangerous. They could easily kill billions of humans without thinking, using viral talents.'

President Padfield, 'So what is the problem?'

Thanatos, 'The problem is stopping your angel friends from bringing them into The Galactium.'

President Padfield, 'I will give that some thought.'

Location: Admiral Mustard's Flat, Planet Napoleon
Sequence of Events: 112

Edel, 'What should we do?'

Jack, 'We know that Amy is special, but I've never seen her act this way before.'

Edel, 'I think she is trying to tell us something.'

Jack, 'Well, she is trying very hard.'

They had managed to quieten her down, but she had been screaming throughout the night. They had been trying to work out what she was saying, but it made little sense. It sounded like 'Erin Yes kill mischief.'

What made it worse was that she was spitting out small lightning bolts that singed the carpets and were clearly a fire hazard.

Edel, 'What do you think we should do?'

Jack, 'I would suggest psychological help, but I don't think it would be of any benefit.'

Edel, 'I agree.'

Jack, 'I think we need to work out what she is trying to say.'

Edel, 'Should we get AI Central onto the task?'

Jack, 'Let me think about it.'

Location: Security Hanger, Asteroid 32,781
Sequence of Events: 113

The exo-biologists had done their job and had produced a nerve agent that would temporarily paralyse the ratfinks in the second ship. It should make them go to sleep. They were going to test it on the prisoners, but it was decided that it was unethical. They were technically prisoners of war and consequently had rights.

The occupants of the second ship were not yet prisoners. Their vessel was still held in tractor beams slightly off the ground. The glue bombs had effectively stopped the doors from opening.

A squad of commandos drilled through the fuselage in a dozen places and inserted the gas cylinders. Then they started the process of ungluing the door, as they wanted to maintain the space worthiness of the vessel. They were soon inside and somewhat horrified by what they had discovered.

The rats had turned cannibalistic, and there were half-eaten corpses all over the place. The three leaders, well, the three dressed in embroidered gowns, were intact, sitting by a pile of rat skeletons. Of the four hundred crew, it would appear that thirty-nine had been eaten. Another ten were in the kitchens, being prepared for slaughter and cooking.

What was strange was that there were no food stocks. Was cannibalism the norm?

The paralysed bodies were removed, stripped, searched, and placed in a similar cell to the others. The three leaders were placed in individual cells away from their subordinates so that they could be interrogated later.

Technicians and engineers then started the laborious task of analysing the craft in detail. Exo-biologists investigated the living quarters. It all helped to create a realistic picture of the enemy. Up close, they didn't seem much of a threat.

Location: GAD2 Conference Room, Planet Napoleon
Sequence of Events: 114

It was time for another meeting of Admiral Mustard's Command Team. The following were present either physically or remotely:

- Admiral Bumelton
- Admiral Gittins
- Admiral J Bonner
- Admiral Pearce
- Admiral Richardson
- Admiral Taylor
- Admiral Tersoo
- Admiral Zakotti
- Admiral Wallett
- Admiral Adams
- Admiral Abosa
- Admiral Dobson
- Commander Goozee
- Jeremy Jotts, Staff and Training
- Louise Forrester, Logistics and Production
- Alison Walsh, Engineering
- Jill Ginger, Science and Technology
- Sally Green, Intelligence
- Commander Salton, Long-Range Monitoring Unit
- Admiral James Mynd, Department of Deception
- AI Central
- Terry

Admiral Mustard, 'Welcome to another command meeting. I'm hoping that we have made more progress than last time.

Before we look at the progress we have made, I will give you my usual update:

- We discovered that the enemy had a small fleet of stealthed vessels, thanks to Commander Salton
- I need to thank you all for providing an excellent parade. It inspired

the entire population of The Galactium

- I also need to tell you that the parade was partly organised to impress The Empire in an effort to delay any further attacks
- We have captured two of the stealthed ships, and we plan to interrogate the crew
- Admiral Thanatos has reappeared as one of the Gods of the Underworld
- There has been another attack by The Empire led by the Third Lord of the Holy Relics. This was easily defeated by Admiral J Bonner's Fleet.

I'm sure that you have lots of questions, but please read the updates on Commandnet.

I need to get an update on progress. At the last meeting, Admiral Tersoo asked if we could meet with Empire representatives. It was considered but rejected for the following reasons:

- The Dragons tried it and failed
- Admiral Thanatos stated that The Empire is only interested in extermination or enslavement
- Our interrogations with the crew are not encouraging
- They want our DNA
- They don't respect life; they are a death cult.'

Admiral Tersoo, 'That is good enough for me.'

Admiral Mustard, 'I'm still waiting for a date for a meeting with the free fleets and other defendant species, but apparently, they are somewhat busy.

Let's start with training and recruitment.'

Jeremy Jotts, 'We have met all of our targets. I have to thank Admiral E Bonner for assisting with the process of releasing experienced staff from other divisions.'

Admiral Gittins, 'She bullied us.'

Admiral Bumelton, 'She certainly did.'

Admiral Adams, 'It was seriously intimidating,'

Admiral Pearce, 'It wouldn't be allowed in a civilised society.'

Admiral Mustard, 'I will give my wife your best regards.'

Jeremy Jotts, 'We now have enough staff to crew five new divisions.'

Admiral Mustard, 'Well done, ladies and gentlemen, that is one hundred and twenty-five thousand vessels, but we must carry on.'

Admiral Gittins, 'I don't think we can strip out any more crew members. I would recommend further automation.'

Admiral Mustard, 'AI Central, what do you think?'

Ai Central, 'I think it is the only option you have got.'

Admiral Mustad, 'Please investigate and make your recommendations.'

Admiral Gittins, 'What is your current view regarding structure?'

Admiral Mustard, 'I'm now inclined to create new divisions. It gives us more flexibility.'

Admiral Gittins, 'I agree.'

Jeremy Jotts, 'We now have a full complement of admirals for five divisions.'

Admiral Mustard, 'Well done, Jeremy, but don't stop your campaign. We need more.'

Jeremy Jotts, 'Yes, Admiral.'

Admiral Mustard, 'We have the staff, so Louise, are you keeping up with production?'

Louise Forrester, 'We have hit the target of two Fleets per month. If you give me the money, I can double that again by investing in more automated factories.'

Admiral Mustard, 'You've got the money. How are you doing, Alison?'

Alison Walsh, 'I am pleased to say that we are on target, but my staff are still exhausted. I'm also delighted to say that the super-battleships, super-fortresses, and the asteroid weapons can now be released to the Fleet. As far as I'm concerned, they are operational.

We are almost ready to fit Godfire weapons in battlecruisers.'

Admiral Mustard, 'Excellent, Admiral Bumelton, can you give some thought to the best use of these weapons?'

Admiral Bumelton, 'Yes, Sir.'

Admiral Mustard, 'Moving on. Terry, how is it going?'

Terry, 'The force fields are now ninety-nine per cent safe. The risk of using them is less than the risk of not using them.'

Admiral Mustard, 'Helen and Louise, you now have a retro-fit job.'

Louise Forrester, 'Thank you, Admiral.'

Alison Walsh, 'You are a star.'

Admiral, 'Rachel, 'How is it going?'

Admiral Zakotti, 'We have made some progress, but we are still the poor cousin.'

Admiral Mustard, 'Chin up, we will eventually get to you. Sally, give me your update.'

Sally Green, 'We have found several special individuals, but I need to update you separately.'

Admiral Mustard, 'OK, fix a date.'

Sally Green, 'Yes, Admiral.'

Admiral Mustard, 'How is my deception wizard doing?'

Admiral Mynd, 'I have the team and resources in place. I just need projects. If any admiral wants help, then please ask.'

Admiral Mustard, 'Please give that some thought. I must say that I'm happier with the progress that we seem to be making. You are dismissed.'

Admiral Mustard had his own problems.

Location: Head Quarters, Lords of the Holy Relics
Sequence of Events: 115

The Third Lord of the Holy Relics was, to put it mildly, a bit perturbed. It was going to be the first time he had met the First Lord of the Holy Relics. On the face of it, it sounds unlikely as they were both seniors in the fourth most powerful chapter, but there had always been a policy of power through separatism.

The Third Lord rated his chances of survival as less than twenty per cent. He had already hidden the top five per cent of his two thousand children. He couldn't hide his top five wives, as that would have been too obvious, but he managed to conceal quite a few of the rest. But then, if he died, why should he worry about them. The herd will simply consume them.

The First Lord was diminutive in stature, but he had a fearsome reputation. You had to if you wanted to become the top dog in a chapter. He had to decide whether to support the Third Lord or order his execution. It was a delicate task of protecting one's own reputation. The easy route was execution. No one would criticise you for that, but there were always consequences.

The next Third Lord might be a genuine competitor, and the last thing you wanted was any competition at his age. Sometimes, living with what you have got is the best option. He often found that first impressions were often the best. He kept his personal executioner on alert.

The First Lord's retainer walked the Third Lord through the long underground tunnels to the First Lord's Hide. From their perspective, it was a palatial apartment. From a human point of view, it was a shithole. But then you expect some differences between intergalactic species.

The Third Lord entered the First Lord's abode, but there was an immediate problem. The Third Lord was wearing a more impressive jerkin than the First Lord. The First Lord made a pre-arranged signal, and the executioner removed the Third Lord's head.'

Executioner, 'Shall I prepare the body for your lunch.'

The First Lord of the Holy Relics, 'That would be excellent, thank you very much.'

Executioner, 'What do you want to do with his wives and offspring?'

The First Lord of the Holy Relics, 'Have the wives roasted alive. I will consume them over the next few days. Have one yourself.'

Executioner, 'Thank you, My Eminence. And the children?'

The First Lord of the Holy Relics, 'Do you have any suggestions?'

Executioner, 'We could soak them in oil and use them as lights in the tunnels.'

The First Lord of the Holy Relics, 'Yes, that sounds quite novel. Will you torture them first?'

Executioner, 'Of course.'

The First Lord of the Holy Relics wondered why the Third Lord came to see him, but everything eventually sorts itself out.

Then he got a call from The Second Lord of the Spirit.

Location: Admiral Mustard's Office, Planet Napoleon
Sequence of Events: 116

Commander Black, 'Jack, we have a slight problem.'

Admiral Mustard, 'What's that?'

Commander Black, 'The second ship has been successfully entered, and all of the crew have been imprisoned in the normal cells except the three leaders. They were put in individual cells. They are showing serious signs of distress.'

Admiral Mustard, 'Have you asked them what the problem is?'

Commander Black, 'They refuse to talk to us.'

Admiral Mustard, 'Do you have any clues?'

Commander Black, 'We are wondering if they can't cope with being on their own.'

Admiral Mustard, 'Try putting the three together and see what happens. How are the other prisoners doing?'

Commander Black, 'To be honest, they love it. They are enjoying the space, food and especially the entertainment. They absolutely love *The Magic Roundabout*.'

Admiral Mustard, 'So does my Amy and Edel, for that matter.'

Commander Black, 'I always thought Zebedee was rather frightening.'

Admiral Mustard, 'I can see where you are coming from.'

Commander Black, 'Anyway, our prisoners learn quickly and are quite creative. None of them want to go home. They want to stay in their luxurious quarters and are not at all bothered about getting their freedom.'

Admiral Mustard, 'As I've said before, it's a funny old universe. Anyway, find out from the other prisoners if your theory is correct.'

Commander Black, 'OK. Did you want to interrogate the leaders?'

Admiral Mustard, 'No, I will leave that to you. Let me know if you discover anything interesting.'

Location: Admiral Mustard's Office, Planet Napoleon
Sequence of Events: 117

Admiral Mustard, 'It's good to see you in person.'

He poured her out a cup of coffee.

Sally Green, 'Me too, it's too easy to lose that personal contact. Anyway, I didn't want to raise some of the issues in public.'

Admiral Mustard, 'What issues?'

Sally Green, 'Well. I sat down with Terry, and he took me through the human genome. There are so many options available to us.'

Admiral Mustard, 'Like what?'

Sally Green, 'As you know, Terry has been developing cures for illnesses for quite a few years now.'

Admiral Mustard, 'And limited improvements to the senses. And of course, the Eternity project.'

Sally Green, 'We do have a lot to thank Terry for.'

Admiral Mustard, 'And conversely, a lot to curse him for, but I suppose on balance, he has been good for us. I guess it's The Brakendeth curse.'

Sally Green, 'You are right. He is quite controversial. Somehow, he is disconnected from the common man.'

Admiral Mustard, 'You need to remember that he is only party human, and to be fair, he has been manipulated by different forces since he was a young child.'

Sally Green, 'I'm getting the feeling that you are reassessing your relationship with him.'

Admiral Mustard, 'You are probably right.'

Sally Green, 'As I was saying, we have been reviewing the human genome, and there are several areas where we can improve humanity.'

Admiral Mustard, 'Do you mean improve or change?'

Sally Green, 'You are right. That is just the point I'm coming to. What sort of improvements do we want to consider?'

Admiral Mustard, 'What are the options?'

Sally Green, 'Well, as you know, Terry doesn't really have any sense of good taste.'

Admiral Mustard, 'What did he suggest?'

Sally Green, 'There was a long list, but it included the following:

- Super-strength
- Super-intelligence
- Telepathy
- Telekinetics
- Improved flexibility
- Super-memory
- Self-repair
- Shape-changing
- Super-speed
- Invulnerability to illness
- Super-calculation skills
- Mind control
- Resistance to pain
- Multiple births
- Hypersensitivity, etc.

Admiral Mustard, 'I get the drift, but what's the catch?'

Sally Green, 'Most of the changes have to be enacted in the womb. Some, once acquired, may be passed from one generation to the next.'

Admiral Mustard, 'So the issue is permission. Not from the parent but from the child, which is clearly impossible.'

Sally Green, 'Exactly.'

Admiral Mustard, 'Can any of these be retro-fitted in adulthood?'

Sally Green, 'I would need to check, but that wasn't what was suggested.'

Location: Head Quarters, Lords of the Spirit, Planet Napoleon
Sequence of Events: 118

The Second Lord of the Spirit, 'Have you read this report?'

The First Lord of the Holy Relics, 'No, your Supreme Eminence.'

The Second Lord of the Spirit, 'Why not?'

The First Lord of the Holy Relics, 'I wasn't given a copy.'

The Second Lord of the Spirit, 'And why was that?'

The First Lord of the Holy Relics, 'I have no idea, your worshipfulness.'

The Second Lord of the Spirit, 'I would suggest that one of the reasons is corruption.'

The First Lord of the Holy Relics, 'What makes you say that, my distinguished lordship?'

The Second Lord of the Spirit, 'It has come to my attention that you have been receiving family members of those accused of treason for your own personal pleasure.'

The First Lord of the Holy Relics, 'But that is common practice, my master.'

The Second Lord of the Spirit, 'That may or may not be the case, but when we have witness statements accusing you of this heinous crime, we have to act.'

The First Lord of the Holy Relics, 'Do you have a witness?'

The Second Lord of the Spirit clicked his claws and in walked The First Lord of the Holy Relics' personal executioner.

The First Lord of the Holy Relics, 'I demand a trial.'

The Second Lord of the Spirit, 'Sorry, I didn't hear that.'

The executioner used a butcher's blade to slice The First Lord of the Holy Relics down the middle.

Executioner, 'My master, what shall I do with his family members?'

The Second Lord of the Spirit, 'What family members?'

Executioner, 'I understand, my Lord.'

He wondered what to do with them, as there were thirty wives and over three thousand children. He often wondered if the Ratfinks should use birth control, but that was a grave crime indeed.

At least he won't struggle to feed his brood of two hundred and thirty-seven tonight.

235

Location: The President's Office, Planet Napoleon
Sequence of Events: 119

President Padfield, 'This is like the old days.'

In the room were Admiral Mustard and his wife, Thanatos, Terry and Henrietta Strong.

Thanatos, 'I know what you mean, but the old days for me are many, many millennia ago.'

Edel, 'That's the trouble with you guys, always boasting.'

Thanatos, 'Well, sometimes it can be very difficult working with you young bucks.'

Edel, 'Believe me, having a second child doesn't make me feel like a young buck.'

President Padfield, 'I've called this meeting to discuss the underworld situation. Thanatos, can you give us an overview?'

Thanatos, 'As discussed a few times, us ancients were given special powers, both good and bad. The reasons for all of this are lost in the mists of time. The Elder Gods may understand the reasoning, but now they are gone.'

Henrietta Strong, 'How come there are some gods left?'

Thanatos, 'Like any society, the gods fall out. To be fair, they fall out more than any group I've ever known. It's partly jealousy. It's partly Zeus being too dictatorial. It's partly damaged personalities. Some were banned. Some were expelled and outlawed. And, of course, we are talking about millennia. The gods that are left are the ones that had no current affiliation with Zeus.'

Henrietta Strong, 'Surely the family members get over their little tiffs.'

Thanatos, 'Never, us gods can hold a grudge for thousands of years. Zeus never really liked the Gods of the Underworld and eventually banned them to Hades. Zeus structured the ban so that they couldn't find their way out.'

President Padfield, 'So how come you ended up there?'

Thanatos, 'Technically, I'm the God of Death, but my personality doesn't really suit my title, and if you look into Greek mythology, I turn out to be a nice guy.

'When I was killed, I was automatically sent to Hades. I assumed that I was dead, but clearly, I'm not.'

Admiral Mustard, 'Did you try to escape?'

Thanatos, 'No, because I assumed I was dead. Anyway, I was initially pleased to see my fellow Gods of the Underworld. Then, I realised what a bunch of dead-heads they were.'

Terry, 'And then my daughters turned up.'

Thanatos, 'That's right. My brother Hypnos met them and even had sex with Angelina.'

Terry, 'That's disgusting.'

Thanatos, 'That may be the case, but I followed your daughters back to your home.'

President Padfield, 'I think the issues are as follows:

- Angela and Angelina feel compelled to hunt down the gods
- Someone is compelling them
- Thanatos thinks that waking up the gods would be dangerous
- Our angels think we need them to defeat The Empire.'

Henrietta Strong, 'So one option is to stop the girls hunting down the gods.'

Terry, 'That's not going to be easy.'

Admiral Mustard, 'Or we need to find out who is compelling them and stop it.'

Edel, 'How dangerous are the gods?'

Thanatos, 'That depends on each type of god. Currently, the only ones that are functional are my brother and me. The others are either petrifying or asleep.'

Henrietta Strong, 'Do you want to save the ones that are petrifying?'

Thanatos, 'Well, firstly I'm not sure if I can save them, and secondly I agree with Zeus, the time of the gods is over.'

President Padfield, 'So what would your preference be?'

Thanatos, 'Let me live here, and the Gods of the Underworld can stay there.'

Henrietta Strong, 'What about your brother?'

Thanatos, 'He likes it there. His life is all about dreams. There is, however, a prophecy that says that "the horde was defeated by the sticks of Nyx." But I've learnt to ignore the prophecies.'

Admiral Mustard, 'Excuse my lack of knowledge regarding Greek mythology, but I assume that Nyx is a god?'

Thanatos, 'She is the Goddess of the Night and my mother.'

Admiral Mustard, 'Apologies for that.'

Thanatos, 'To be honest, I've hardly ever spoken to her. She is a shadowy sort of character, but very powerful.'

Edel, 'So how many sleeping gods are there?'

Thanatos, 'There are Hecate, Persephone, Cronus, Daeira, Minos, Nyx, and the Erinyes. There are three of the Erinyes left.'

President Padfield, 'So, which ones are dangerous?'

Thanatos, 'All of them.'

Admiral Mustard, 'Seriously?'

Thanatos, 'Seriously. They could easily start a plague or a famine, or cause earthquakes, volcanic eruptions or just make people go mad.'

Edel, 'Nice bunch then.'

Terry, 'I think we need to have a chat with Angela and Angelina.'

President Padfield, 'You do that, and then we will get back together again.'

Location: Grand Assembly of the Peoples of the Path
Sequence of Events: 120

The First and Second Lords of the Spirit and the Third Lord of the Communion called for a meeting of the Grand Assembly of the Peoples of the Path. It takes three lords to call a meeting which were remarkably rare, partly because they often led to mass executions.

Archbishop of the Path, 'I call upon The Second Lord of the Spirit to address the assembly on matters physical and spiritual.'

The Second Lord of the Spirit, 'My fellow lords and honoured guests, I beseech you to listen to my petition as it is a matter of life and death. Moreover, it ensures that the Path will be free.'

Archbishop of the Path, 'Please present your petition.'

The Second Lord of the Spirit, 'Our path is restricted.'

There was a massive outbreak of noise, rat-like noises, and the sound of claws smashing against wood.

The Second Lord of the Spirit allowed the response to die down and then said, 'Our way is blocked by Hotmans. They must be extinguished.'

There was a pattern that must be followed. This time the response was one of spitting and hissing and some shitting. The shit collectors were working hard, as they should be.

The Second Lord of the Spirit, 'It will not be easy, my friends. It will call for stamina, determination and indeed the death of many of us, but I put my body on the line.'

He took a knife and slit his throat and died a gurgling type of death.

There is a pattern to these things that must be followed.

Archbishop of the Path, 'I call upon The First Lord of the Spirit to address the assembly on matters physical and spiritual.'

The First Lord of the Spirit, 'My fellow lords and honoured guests, I beseech you to listen to our petition as it is a matter of life and death, and much more it ensures that the Path will be free.'

Archbishop of the Path, 'Please present your petition.'

The First Lord of the Spirit, 'My friend gave his life as proof of the threat to the path.'

The response was rapturous. There was shouting, stamping and a call to arms. The entire assembly stood up and urinated in unison.

There is a pattern to these things that must be followed.

The First Lord of the Spirit, 'I call upon a jihad against The Hotmans. I cannot be denied.'

He picked up a knife ready to disembowel himself, but the assembly raised the arms in salute.

Archbishop of the Path, 'My dear First Lord of the Spirit I salute you. The jihad has been approved.'

Slave rats were dragged in to satisfy the needs of the assembly. Few of the slaves survived.

Location: GAD2 Conference Room, Planet Napoleon
Sequence of Events: 121

Admiral Bumelton called a meeting of the Senior Admirals to review the current Fleet status. The following were present either physically or remotely:

- Admiral Bumelton
- Admiral Mustard
- Admiral Gittins
- Admiral J Bonner
- Admiral Pearce
- Admiral Richardson
- Admiral Taylor
- Admiral Tersoo
- Admiral Zakotti
- Admiral Wallett
- Admiral Adams
- Admiral Abosa
- Admiral Dobson
- Commander Goozee
- Commander Salton - Long-Range Monitoring Unit
- Admiral James Mynd – Department of Deception
- AI Central

Admiral Bumelton, 'While things are quiet, I thought that it would be a good idea to review the current state of the Fleet. I haven't invited the new Fleet admirals to this meeting, but we will need to in the future.

This is our latest structure:

Command – Admiral Jack Mustard
- Fleet Operations
- Exploration and Navigation – Denise Smith
- Marine Corps – Commander Goozee
- Special Operations – Commander Martin Black
- Planetary Defence – Admiral Rachel Zakotti
- Staff and Training – Jeremy Jotts

- Logistics and Production – Louise Forrester
- Engineering – Alison Walsh
- Science and Technology – Jill Ginger
- Medical Services – Dr Helen Marten
- Intelligence – Sally Green
- Sales and Marketing – Sheila Taylor
- Communications and Client Support – Salek Patel
- Department of Deception – Admiral James Mynd
- Long-Range Monitoring Unit – Commander Salton

Fleet structure:

Division One – Admiral George Bumelton
- Fleet 1.1 – Admiral Bevan
- Fleet 1.2 – Admiral Williams
- Fleet 1.3 – Admiral Catt
- Fleet 1.4 – Admiral Hall
- Fleet 1.5 – Admiral Moxan

Division Two – Admiral John Bonner
- Fleet 2.1 – Admiral Manchester
- Fleet 2.2 – Admiral Clarke
- Fleet 2.3 – Admiral Holland
- Fleet 2.4 – Admiral Avila
- Fleet 2.5 – Admiral Clugston

Division Three – Admiral Phil Richardson
- Fleet 3.1 – Admiral Keats
- Fleet 3.2 – Admiral Brooker
- Fleet 3.3 – Admiral Donohue
- Fleet 3.4 – Admiral Freeman
- Fleet 3.5 – Admiral Simard

Division Four – Admiral Calensky Wallett
- Fleet 4.1 – Admiral Cheung
- Fleet 4.2 – Admiral Colley
- Fleet 4.3 – Admiral Wallace

- Fleet 4.4 – Admiral Reid
- Fleet 4.5 – Admiral Descade

Division Five – Admiral Steve Adams
- Fleet 5.1 – Admiral Chan
- Fleet 5.2 – Admiral Shoker
- Fleet 5.3 – Admiral Carlos
- Fleet 5.4 – Admiral Sutherland
- Fleet 5.5 – Admiral Greer

Division Six – Admiral Ama Abosa
- Fleet 6.1 – Admiral Cummins
- Fleet 6.2 – Admiral Deguzman
- Fleet 6.3 – Admiral Euker
- Fleet 6.4 – Admiral Caskey
- Fleet 6.5 – Admiral Kurowski

Division Seven – Admiral Peter Gittins
- Fleet 7.1 – Admiral Lauder
- Fleet 7.2 – Admiral Walker
- Fleet 7.3 – Admiral Harris
- Fleet 7.4 – Admiral Wright
- Fleet 7.5 – Admiral Chapman

Division Eight – Admiral Glen Pearce
- Fleet 8.1 – Admiral Furlong
- Fleet 8.2 – Admiral Peery
- Fleet 8.3 – Admiral Vickers
- Fleet 8.4 – Admiral Greenacre
- Fleet 8.5 – Admiral Kisner

Division Nine – Admiral Nubia Tersoo
- Fleet 9.1 – Admiral Cohen
- Fleet 9.2 – Admiral Janmeat
- Fleet 9.3 – Admiral Akula
- Fleet 9.4 – Admiral Dennett
- Fleet 9.5 – Admiral Ponder

Division Ten – Admiral Mateo Dobson

- Fleet 10.1 – Admiral Seabrooke
- Fleet 10.2 – Admiral Brown
- Fleet 10.3 – Admiral Corps
- Fleet 10.4 – Admiral Milner
- Fleet 10.5 – Admiral Sayce

Division Eleven - Admiral Lesley Quinn

- Fleet 11.1 – Admiral Stanley
- Fleet 11.2 – Admiral Doupnik
- Fleet 11.3 – Admiral Hedges
- Fleet 11.4 – Admiral Bonerjee
- Fleet 11.5 – Admiral Arken

Division Twelve – Admiral David Woodward

- Fleet 12.1 – Admiral Wrench
- Fleet 12.2 – Admiral Gitta
- Fleet 12.3 – Admiral Chasy
- Fleet 12.4 – Admiral Ellis
- Fleet 12.5 – Admiral Jones

Division Thirteen – Admiral Wendy Ying

- Fleet 13.1 – Admiral Boothman
- Fleet 13.2 – Admiral Brandon
- Fleet 13.3 – Admiral Lear
- Fleet 13.4 – Admiral Jenner
- Fleet 13.5 – Admiral Vorsprung

Division Fourteen – Admiral Vanrooyen

- Fleet 14.1 – Admiral Hanson
- Fleet 14.2 – Admiral Rockwell
- Fleet 14.3 – Admiral Glasson
- Fleet 14.4 – Admiral White
- Fleet 14.5 – Admiral Scrace

Division Fifteen – Admiral Bob Pitt

- Fleet 15.1 – Admiral Spratt
- Fleet 15.2 – Admiral Milsom
- Fleet 15.3 – Admiral Podmore
- Fleet 15.4 – Admiral Spanner
- Fleet 15.5 – Admiral Jazz

Home Defence Fleet – Ernst Muller

Regional Defence Centre One – Admiral Jill Bosman
Regional Defence Centre Two – Admiral Sammy Fogg
Regional Defence Centre Three – Admiral Dan Bryson
Regional Defence Centre Four – Admiral Lenny Hubbard
Regional Defence Centre Five – Admiral James Patel

Other Services

Exploration Fleet One – Admiral Liz Clowe
Exploration Fleet Two – Alison Strauss
Special Operations Fleet – Commander Martin Black

Each division will be issued with the following:

- One super-battleship. It is not recommended that the admiral of the Fleet should use it as his flagship, as it will be an obvious target
- One super-fortress
- Godfire weapons to be fitted on every battle-cruiser. There is still limited ammunition, but that problem is being worked on
- TIME-based force fields
- Improved stealth technology

Our total assets are as follows:

Resource	Total
Division 1	130,000
Division 2	130,000
Division 3	130,000
Division 4	130,000
Division 5	130,000
Division 6	130,000

Division 7	130,000
Division 8	130,000
Division 9	130,000
Division 10	130,000
Division 11	130,000
Division 12	130,000
Division 13	130,000
Division 14	130,000
Division 15	130,000
Drone Fleet 1	100,000
Drone Fleet 2	100,000
Drone Fleet 3	100,000
Drone Fleet 4	100,000
Drone Fleet 5	100,000
Drone Fleet 6	100,000
Drone Fleet 7	100,000
Drone Fleet 8	100,000
Drone Fleet 9	100,000
Drone Fleet 10	100,000
Drone Fleet 11	100,000
Drone Fleet 12	100,000
Drone Fleet 13	100,000
Drone Fleet 14	100,000
Drone Fleet 15	100,000
Drone Fleet 16	100,000
Drone Fleet 17	100,000
Drone Fleet 18	100,000
Drone Fleet 19	100,000
Drone Fleet 20	100,000
Exploration Fleet 1	20,000
Exploration Fleet 2	20,000
Home Fleet	25,000
Planetary Forts	1,200
Marine Fleet	25,000
Special Ops Fleet	20,000
Support Fleet	250,000

RDC's	20,000
Grand Total	3,950,000

Admiral Bumelton, 'I think that this summarises our position. Any questions?'

Admiral Gittins, 'Have you come to a conclusion regarding the use of the super-vessels?'

Admiral Bumelton, 'We have concluded that the super-battleship is just for show. It might even be a liability. The fortress could be quite useful as a way of protecting our flanks. Time will tell.'

Admiral Richardson, 'What about Godfire?'

Admiral Bumelton, 'It needs to be fitted on all military vessels. We still need to sort out the munitions issue, and we need to make the equipment smaller and less power-hungry assuming that is possible.'

Admiral Mustard, 'In your opinion, what should we focus on now?'

Admiral Bumelton, 'I would suggest Godfire, drones, and force fields.'

Location: Grand Assembly of the Peoples of the Path
Sequence of Events: 122

Getting approval for jihad was one thing, but getting a jihad organised was another. They needed the support of the Supreme Jihad Master. That was a lot harder than it sounded.

A meeting was organised, and the fee was paid. It took some time to herd the two thousand, five hundred slaves into the vat. Their destiny was to be made into a pickle for the jihad scout fleet.

The First Lord of the Spirit, 'It is an honour allowing us to meet with you, Supreme Jihad Master.'

Supreme Jihad Master, 'I know.'

The First Lord of the Spirit wasn't sure who had seniority during this meeting. Still, he had to be careful, as the Supreme Jihad Master was not showing any signs of inferiority.

The First Lord of the Spirit, 'What is the next stage?'

Supreme Jihad Master, 'Have you paid the fee?'

The First Lord of the Spirit, 'Yes.'

Supreme Jihad Master, 'Yes, what?'

The First Lord of the Spirit, 'Yes, your Supreme Jihad Master. Do you know who I am?'

Supreme Jihad Master, 'One of the lords, there are so many.'

The First Lord of the Spirit was even more confused about seniority. This man was a tradesman whilst he represented God. Nonetheless, he decided to be careful as the Supreme Jihad Master must have connections.

The First Lord of the Spirit, 'So what is next, my Lord?'

Supreme Jihad Master, 'The fee has been paid. The scouting will take place.'

The First Lord of the Spirit, 'Excellent, what happens then, my Lord?'

Supreme Jihad Master, 'If the path is clear, then you die the death of the cockroaches. If you are right, The Hotmans die.'

The First Lord of the Spirit, 'And when do you start, my lord?'

Supreme Jihad Master, 'When the pickling is done.'

The First Lord of the Spirit, 'Excellent, my Lord.'

Location: Admiral Mustard's Office, Planet Napoleon
Sequence of Events: 123

Garth, 'I hear that you are supposed to say good day.'

Admiral Mustard, 'That was to stop people trying to work out what time it was all of the time.'

Garth, 'Well, it's early morning here.'

Admiral Mustard, 'It's late evening here. That's the problem.'

Garth, 'Well, sorry to ring you so late, but I have some news.'

Admiral Mustard, 'Empire news?'

Garth, 'The little rats have just had an assembly meeting. The first one in decades. It looks like they are on the move.'

Admiral Mustard, 'Against us?'

Garth, 'That's my bet, but I can't be sure. But a jihad has been approved because the path is blocked.'

Admiral Mustard, 'What does that mean?'

Garth, 'The first thing they do is send out a scouting party.'

Admiral Mustard, 'Haven't the rodents done enough of that already?'

Garth, 'They have to follow the ways of the Path, so expect some company soon.'

Admiral Mustard, 'Thanks for the warning. How is it going on your end?'

Garth, 'Well, I have to thank you for all of your help. Our planet is looking good, and your ships are a revelation.'

Admiral Mustard, 'That's good.'

Garth, 'And I've also got some dates for those meetings that I promised. They are even more keen to meet now a jihad has been declared.'

Admiral Mustard, 'I will get back to you with confirmations.'

Location: Admiral Mustard's Office, Planet Napoleon
Sequence of Events: 124

Admiral Mustard, 'Update me.'
　　Fleet Operations, 'Yes, Sir:

- The current status is low alert
- Division One is defending Earth
- Divisions Two, Four, Five, Nine and Ten are defending the standard alien entry point
- Divisions Three, Six and Eight are defending Planet Lovelace
- Division Seven is defending Planet Napoleon
- The marines are in quarters
- Special Ops are on two asteroids.'

Admiral Mustard, 'My orders:
- Warn all military forces that an Empire Scouting Force is expected
- Warn the president
- Put all planetary defences on alert.'

Fleet Operations, 'Yes, Sir.'
　　Admiral Mustard, 'Comms, get me Commander Black.'
　　Comms, 'Yes, Sir.'
　　Commander Black, 'Morning, Jack.'
　　Admiral Mustard, 'And a very good morning to you. How are your prisoners?'
　　Commander Black, 'Which ones?'
　　Admiral Mustard, 'The leaders.'
　　Commander Black, 'Now that they are with their troops, they are fine.'
　　Admiral Mustard, 'Have you found out anything?'
　　Commander Black, 'Only that they were sent to take photos and vids. That's all they know.'
　　Admiral Mustard, 'That doesn't help much.'
　　Commander Black, 'There was a very strange incident this morning. One of their troops was slaughtered and eaten.'
　　Admiral Mustard, 'Didn't you try to stop them?'
　　Commander Black, 'Well, to be honest, it was a total surprise, as they

had lots of food. Anyway, he was killed and ripped to pieces before we could act.

We had a chat with them afterwards, and apparently, they have to eat each other to stay healthy. It has been the case for millennia.

And to be fair, the victim didn't seem to mind.'

Admiral Mustard, 'Can you check out the science to see if it stacks up?'

Commander Black, 'Will do.'

Location: On-board Admiral Bumelton's Flagship
Sequence of Events: 125

Admirals Mustard and Bumelton were on their way to meet three different groups at RDC5. It was chosen, as Garth was going to join them. The first meeting was with a representative from another system that was also being attacked by The Empire. The other two sessions later in the day were with free forces, those left behind from previous conquests.

Garth had warned them that they were a strange lot, but no special environmental conditions were needed.

They were late, which Garth said was not unusual. They are not really a species that is interested in time.

Admiral Mustard had seen photos of them, but they were much weirder in real life. They looked a bit like stick insects but with pin cushions for heads. They spend the first twenty or thirty years of their lives as plants, and then they evolve a brain, which effectively is the pin cushion. They speak by rubbing mandibles together. It was lucky that Garth had learnt their language. In fact, the dragons seemed to have the ability to absorb any language, even visual ones.

The Empire had deliberately targeted their young, destroying thousands of hectares of baby minmoses. Their future was in doubt as the forthcoming generations had been terminated. They wanted revenge and were ready to join the fight against The Empire.

Admiral Mustard accepted their offer, and a comms channel was set up. There wasn't much else to discuss, but all help was gratefully received.

Admiral Mustard left Admiral Bumelton to meet the two free forces groups as he had been recalled.

Location: GAD2 Control, Planet Napoleon
Sequence of Events: 126

GAD2, 'Admiral Mustard, small fleets have been appearing all over The Galactium. They don't seem to be aggressive at the moment.

There is another force of about three thousand vessels following a straight path across sector 11-769.'

Admiral Mustard, 'Show me on a map.'

GAD2, 'Yes, Sir.' There were over a thousand sightings.'

Admiral Mustard, 'What's the total number of vessels.'

GAD2, 'We are tracking about sixty-eight thousand, but more are appearing all the time.'

Admiral Mustard, 'What have you done?'

GAD2, 'We have sent drone hunter packs out to every occurrence. We have kept the Fleet back in case there is a more significant incursion.'

Admiral Mustard, 'This looks like their scouting exercise before the big one, except for those three thousand vessels which are following a straight path. What have we done about them?'

GAD2, 'Division Six is trailing them.'

Admiral Mustard, 'That's one of the Lovelace Divisions.'

GAD2, 'Correct. Do you want them recalled?'

Admiral Mustard, 'No, you have done the right thing. There isn't much else that we can do.'

GAD2, 'All planetary defences have been activated. Everyone else is waiting for your command.'

Admiral Mustard, 'Carry on, send me the kill statistics on a regular basis. And can you inform the dragons?'

GAD2, 'Yes, Sir.'

Location: On-Board the Supreme Jihad Master's craft
Sequence of Events: 127

Supreme Jihad Master, 'How many vessels do we have in Hotman space?'

Sergeant at Arms, 'Ninety thousand, seven hundred and sixty-four, my lord.'

Supreme Jihad Master, 'How many have remained undetected?'

Sergeant at Arms, 'Only eleven, my lord.'

Supreme Jihad Master, 'Does that include this ship?'

Sergeant at Arms, 'No, my lord, we are being targeted.'

Supreme Jihad Master, 'Why wasn't I informed.'

Sergeant at Arms, 'I beg your indulgence. I'm hoping that it is on the screen: the big flashing light.'

Supreme Jihad Master, 'Remove me from danger immediately'

They shot off, zigzagging at terrific speed.

Supreme Jihad Master, 'Has that worked?'

Sergeant at Arms, 'No, my eminence.'

Supreme Jihad Master, 'Why not?'

Sergeant at Arms, 'It's faster and more agile than us and is being directed by AI.'

Supreme Jihad Master, 'Are you saying that their craft is better than ours.'

Sergeant at Arms, 'Certainly not, my Lord. They are just faster, more agile, and react quicker because of AI control. And being unmanned, they can carry out manoeuvres and ignore the effects of G-force.'

Supreme Jihad Master, 'You are sailing very close to being a traitor.'

Sergeant at Arms, 'Sorry, my Lord, I was saying that the enemy craft is clearly inferior to us in every way.'

Supreme Jihad Master, 'That's what I thought you said. So, if that is the case, how come we are still being pursued?'

Sergeant at Arms, 'I've recalled vessels to come to our assistance, but they are also being chased by the ineffective enemy craft.'

Supreme Jihad Master, 'Show me the kill statistics.'

Sergeant at Arms, 'Yes, my Lord:

| Enemy Ships Engaged | 500,000 |
| Enemy Ships Destroyed | 11 |

Total Remaining	499,989
Ships of the Path Engaged	90,764
Ships of the Path Destroyed	63,705
Total Remaining	27,059

Supreme Jihad Master, 'Those figures are wrong.'

Sergeant at Arms, 'I agree, my Lord.'

Supreme Jihad Master, 'Change them now.'

Sergeant at Arms, 'I'm sorry, my Lord, but I have no means of changing them.'

Supreme Jihad Master, 'I will not stand for this incompetence.'

The Sergeant at Arms could not see a future, and he slit his own throat. The blood spurted out over the Supreme Jihad Master, but then his days were also numbered as the drones drove home their attack.

From the engagement's point of view, the loss of the Supreme Jihad Master was no great loss, but the loss of the Deputy Supreme Jihad Master was a real loss which meant that The Empire fleet was directionless.

Location: GAD2 Control, Planet Napoleon
Sequence of Events: 128

Admiral Mustard, 'Update me.'
GAD2 Control, 'Yes, Sir. Do you want the statistics?'
Admiral Mustard, 'Yes, please.'
GAD2 Control, 'They are on the screen, Sir:

Galactium Ships	500,000
Galactium Ships Lost	201
Total Remaining	499,799
Empire Ships	90,800
Empire Ships Destroyed	79,768
Total Remaining	10,232

Admiral Mustard, 'Are there still three thousand Empire ships on a straight line?'
GAD2 Control, 'Yes, Sir.'
Admiral Mustard, 'My orders:

- Division Six to destroy the enemy fleet
- Destroy all remaining vessels
- Main Fleet to stand firm.'

Admiral Bumelton, 'Comms, get me Admiral Mustard.'
Comms, 'Yes, Sir.'
Admiral Mustard, 'It's going rather well.'
Admiral Bumelton, 'It is, but I thought that I would let you know that the crews are getting frustrated that they are not seeing any action.'
Admiral Mustard, 'Believe me, their time will come and sooner than they want. Tell them to be patient.'
Admiral Bumelton, 'Yes, Sir. Talk to you later.'
Admiral Mustard, 'Show me the stats.'
GAD2 Control, 'They are on the screen, Sir:

Galactium Ships	500,000
Galactium Ships Lost	326

Total Remaining	499,574
Empire Ships	90,800
Empire Ships Destroyed	86,399
Total Remaining	4,401

Admiral Mustard, 'My orders:

- All forces go in for the kill.'

GAD2 Control, 'Yes, Sir.'

Location: Grand Assembly of the Peoples of the Path
Sequence of Events: 129

The First Lord of the Spirit was waiting for a meeting with the new Supreme Jihad Master. On the recent encounter with the Hotmans, they lost the Supreme Jihad Master, his two deputies and the four in training. Nothing like this had ever happened before.

Supreme Jihad Master, 'Apologies for the delay, but I never expected to be in this position.'

The First Lord of the Spirit, 'What was your path?'

Supreme Jihad Master, 'I was going to be the First Master of the Emperor's Toilet.'

The First Lord of the Spirit, 'A very reasonable position.'

Supreme Jihad Master, 'Indeed, my dear First Lord of the Spirit.'

The First Lord of the Spirit, 'I imagine that it gives you the insight you need for this job.'

Supreme Jihad Master, 'I'm sure that it does, but I'm not sure what a jihad is.'

The First Lord of the Spirit, 'I will assist you.'

Supreme Jihad Master, 'That is very generous of you, my dear First Lord of the Spirit.'

The First Lord of the Spirit, 'Think nothing of it, the Path has cleared the way for you.

We need to send out the biggest fleet we can against the Hotmans. They must be taught a lesson.'

Supreme Jihad Master, 'And we need to do it soon, but how do we make it happen?'

The First Lord of the Spirit, 'You need to raise a jihad order and get it signed by the First Lord of each chapter. So, you only need to get four signatures, as you can have mine now. Once that is done, the fleet admirals have no choice but to act.'

Supreme Jihad Master, 'That can't be too difficult.'

The First Lord of the Spirit, 'It won't be with my help.'

Supreme Jihad Master, 'Thank you, First Lord of the Spirit.'

Location: Terry's Flat
Sequence of Events: 130

Terry, 'I've had some discussions with President Padfield, Admiral Mustard and Thanatos.'

Angelina, 'Have you, Daddy?'

Terry, 'Yes, and they all seem to be under the impression that we should leave the Gods of the Underworld alone.'

Angela, 'But we can't.'

Terry, 'Thanatos said that they are all very dangerous and that they could easily start a plague or a famine, or cause earthquakes, volcanic eruptions or just make people go mad.'

Angelina, 'We know that, Daddy, but we can control them for the sake of "Erin Yes kill mischief".'

Terry, 'What does that mean?'

Angelina, 'The reason we need the Gods of the Underworld.'

Terry, 'Are you sure you can control them?'

Angela, 'Watch this.'

Terry dropped onto all fours and started crawling around the room, saying, 'Give me a bone or I will pee on the carpet.'

He then jumped up and started impersonating Paul McCartney singing 'Yesterday'.

Angelina, 'What did you think?'

AI Central, 'That was a great impression. I've got it all recorded.'

Terry, 'I will believe that you can control them if you can control Thanatos.'

Angela, 'Bring it on.'

Location: GAD2 Conference Centre, Planet Napoleon
Sequence of Events: 131

As they just defeated The Empire again. It had all been too easy. Admiral Mustard was concerned that the Fleet was getting too complacent. The supreme test was still to come. So, he called a meeting of the senior admirals to discuss their upcoming battle plans.

The following were present either physically or remotely:

- Admiral Bumelton
- Admiral Mustard
- Admiral Gittins
- Admiral J Bonner
- Admiral Pearce
- Admiral Richardson
- Admiral Taylor
- Admiral Tersoo
- Admiral Zakotti
- Admiral Wallett
- Admiral Adams
- Admiral Abosa
- Admiral Dobson
- Admiral Quinn
- Admiral Woodward
- Admiral Ying
- Admiral Vanrooyen
- Admiral Pitt
- Commander Goozee
- Commander Salton
- Admiral Mynd
- AI Central
- Guest – Garth
- Guest – Thanatos

Admiral Mustard, 'A warm welcome to our newer members. Could you stand up, please?'

Admirals Quinn, Woodward, Ying, Vanrooyen and Pitt stood up, and the rest clapped. It was a genuine achievement to become a Fleet admiral. There was a lot of pride in the room.

Admiral Mustard, 'I want us to work on a battle plan, and then as a group, we can refine it or develop a new one. These are my thoughts:

Our assets
- Galactium forces – nearly four million vessels
- New vessels in the next few months – three hundred thousand
- Galactium alien forces – twenty to seventy thousand
- Dragon and other free forces – twenty thousand.

Regardless of the breakdown, we are likely to have four and a half million assets. This is a remarkable achievement, but we are probably up against at least double that. Of course, we have been up against odds of twenty and thirty to one before, but we have also had some luck. On at least one occasion, Zeus saved us.

Everyone has told us that we have not been up against their best. To date, we have only encountered The Empire's light forces.

Our technology
- Super-battleships
- Super-fortresses
- Improved stealth systems
- Improved force fields
- Godfire
- Better drone technology
- Deception

Our strategy
- We have home advantage
- Our planets have improved force fields
- They have got to defeat us
- Inside information

Their plan:
- It could be a considerably large fleet or numerous smaller fleets
- To date, they have tended to attack two places at once. However, they

need to draw us into battle first

- It will probably end up as a line battle because of the scale of their fleet

Our response:

- All planets will have to defend themselves
- Planetary forts will be left to defend their home planets
- Planet Napoleon will have its home Fleet
- This will free us from the need to defend
- Our only chance is to be aggressive
- We will have to assume that our losses will be high

Detailed response:

- Generally, our drones will attack at every opportunity. Pods of drones will attack suspected leaders and chatter activity
- Five Divisions under Admiral Bumelton, along with the alien fleets, will go to The Empire home system when The Empire starts the attack. Then they will bombard it
- Nine Divisions will form the line and three Divisions will defend each flank, along with super-battleships and super-fortresses
- We will use deception techniques to make the centre look really strong
- A single reserve Division will also protect the flanks but will only be used if things look bad
- After the bombardment, General Bumelton's forces will return and attack The Empire's forces.

Preparation:

- Special Operations Forces will go to The Empire home system and establish portals to aid the attack
- Special Operations Forces will identify targets in their home system
- Admiral Mynd will start developing deception tools ASAP
- Admiral Zakotti will do everything she can to improve planetary defences
- Special Operations Forces to set up traps
- Marines and the Marine Fleet to assist with planetary defence
- Production and Engineering to provide Fleet repair services

- Medical facilities to be organised
- Load up all our ships with as many munitions as they can store
- Long-range Monitoring Unit to be on highest alert.

OK, that is it. Any questions or observations?'

Admiral Bumelton, 'Splitting our forces could be fatal.'

Admiral Mustard, 'I agree, but my thinking is:

- We need to take the fight to them
- They won't be expecting it
- Depending on what our Special Operations Forces find, we might change our mind
- We need something to distract them and hopefully make them return home
- If they destroy ten divisions, then it is just as likely that they will destroy fifteen.'

Admiral Gittins, 'What if the deception doesn't work?'

Admiral Mustard, 'Then we will have a fragile centre. The Reserve Division will have to move to the centre.'

Admiral Quinn, 'Will we have enough Godfire munitions?'

Admiral Mustard, 'Probably not.'

Admiral Dobson, 'What's the plan if we are defeated?'

Admiral Mustard, 'We need to work on that. We will need an agreed collection point.'

Admiral Woodward, 'What should we do if our munitions run low?'

Admiral Mustard, 'Restock at Planet Napoleon.'

Commander Black, 'What sort of traps are you thinking of?'

Admiral Mustard, 'Force field combinations.'

Admiral Abosa, 'I tend to agree with you regarding the line of battle strategy, but what if they don't play our game?'

Admiral Mustard, 'Then we will have to change our game, but at least we would have planned. I'm happy to work on alternative plans.'

Admiral Gittins, 'Jack, you have a brilliant record in getting these things right.'

Admiral Pearce, 'What are our weaknesses?'

Admiral Mustard. 'The Empire has hardly shown any decent military strategy, but they are going to have numbers. They could simply beat us through attrition.

Our deception might not work. We may run out of munitions. Admiral Bumelton might come up against overwhelming resistance.

Possibly our biggest weakness is going to be overconfidence.'

Thanatos, 'The biggest weakness is the supposition that they will attack in a specific way. Plans to adapt the strategy need to be worked on. If they attack in a different manner, then we should have a revised plan ready.'

Admiral Mustard, 'I agree. Would you be happy to assist with that?'

Thanatos, 'I would be honoured.'

Admiral Mustard, 'Can you all go away and consider this plan. We still need to work on it.'

Location: Terry's Flat
Sequence of Events: 132

Terry, 'So tonight's your chance. Thanatos is coming to dinner.'

Angela, 'Are we invited?'

Terry, 'Of course.'

Angelina, 'That's good. I quite fancy getting into his pants.'

Terry, 'I've been meaning to talk to you about that sort of thing. You can't make love to every man you see.'

Angelina, 'I wouldn't call it making love. It's just a good fuck.'

Terry, 'I wish that you wouldn't use that word.'

Angelina, 'Daddy, you have to accept that I've got a high sex drive. I enjoy sex and can't see any reason why two consenting adults can't partake.'

Terry, 'Technically, of course, you are not an adult.'

Angelina, 'But the rules don't apply as I'm an angel.'

Angela, 'Daddy is right, you know. You are a bit free with that fanny of yours.'

Angelina, 'And you are a bit frigid. When was the last time you got a screw?'

Angela, 'You can be so crude. You have converted an amazing act of love into something dirty.'

Angelina, 'And you have done the opposite, converted a primaeval urge into something aesthetic. Daddy wouldn't have started this conversation if we were boys.'

Daddy, 'That's not true.'

Angelina, 'Do you really believe that? You would be saying something like, "Go on, give her one." The old conventions are still deeply ingrained. And just to spite you all, I have every intention of fucking Thanatos tonight.'

There was a knock on the door, and Thanatos was invited in. He stepped into the hall and started undressing until he was naked.

Terry, 'Why have you stripped off?'

Thanatos, 'I really can't tell you why.'

Then Thanatos started masturbating himself.

Terry, 'Stop that, you are embarrassing the girls.'

Clearly, that wasn't true as both girls were enjoying watching a fine figure of a man with a very impressive erection getting his rocks off. Who would have thought that the God of Death would be giving a pornographic exhibition? It was clear that Thanatos was not far off from coming.

Angelina, 'Do you want me to stop him?'

Terry, 'Yes, and do it now.'

Angelina, 'Before or after he comes?'

Terry, 'Before.'

And Thanatos stopped. He did not know why he was standing in Terry's flat, naked and holding his penis in full view of two angels.

Angela and Angelina couldn't help laughing, as Thanatos had always been a gentleman and somewhat formal in his appearance.

Angelina, 'Thanatos, come this way as I can help you with that.'

It was hard to tell who was screaming the loudest, Angelina or Thanatos. It looked like primaeval lust had prevailed over Disneyesque love-making.

Terry phoned Admiral Mustard and President Padfield to let them know that, in his opinion, his daughters could control the Gods of the Underworld.

Location: Admiral Mustard's Flat, Planet Napoleon
Sequence of Events: 133

Edel, 'It's getting worse.'

Jack, 'What is she saying now?'

Edel, 'It's still "Erin Yes kill mischief." This time, she is saying it in her sleep.'

Jack, 'What I don't understand is that she can hold a pretty good conversation.'

Edel. 'For her age, her language and conversational skills are astounding.'

Jack, 'So why is she speaking gibberish?'

Edel, 'I think she is conversing at an unconscious level, but there is a pattern, or rather a wave, of activity. For example, now she is fairly quiet, almost mumbling. In an hour, she will be highly animated and start shouting. Strangely, it doesn't seem to be affecting her.'

Jack, 'We are back to the old question. Do we seek help?'

Edel, 'I wish I had an answer to that question.'

Jack, 'As she seems OK, shall we just leave it for a few more weeks?'

Edel, 'Do you think we should discuss it with her?'

Jack, 'That's not a bad idea.'

Location: Grand Assembly of the Peoples of the Path
Sequence of Events: 134

Supreme Jihad Master, 'Well, that wasn't too difficult.'

The First Lord of the Spirit, 'I doubt they knew what they were signing.'

Supreme Jihad Master, 'Surely not.'

The First Lord of the Spirit, 'Well, the under-secretary's under-secretary will have slipped the paper into the bundle of papers for signature.

The paper for signature would have gone to the assistant commissioner's assistant for signing, who would then pass it on to the under-secretary's under-secretary for approval. Then it would go to the Clerk of the Realm's clerk for interpretation and then the associate keeper of the roll's second clerk for finalisation.'

Supreme Jihad Master, 'So, it's a pretty slick process then.'

The First Lord of the Spirit wasn't sure if he was joking or not.

The First Lord of the Spirit, 'My first boss had proposed some streamlining, and for his troubles, he was skinned alive and then placed in a vat of acid whilst his wife and children were anted.'

Supreme Jihad Master, 'Anted?'

The First Lord of the Spirit, 'Yes, they are covered in honey and then an ant's nest is placed on top of them. They are then eaten alive over a period of weeks. Death by one hundred thousand ant bites.'

Supreme Jihad Master, 'Why do we organise so many horrible deaths?'

The First Lord of the Spirit, 'I understand that it is motivational.'

Supreme Jihad Master, 'Does this signed document mean that we are ready to go?'

The First Lord of the Spirit, 'Of course not. We have to inform the five fleet admirals and then offer sustenance to the Supreme Fleet Controllers.'

Supreme Jihad Master, 'So who is in charge?'

The First Lord of the Spirit, 'The admirals do the work, but the Supreme Fleet Controllers manage the politics and governmental relationships.'

Supreme Jihad Master, 'What sort of bribe do we need?'

The First Lord of the Spirit, 'Each controller will want at least one thousand bods. At this stage, we won't know if they will want them alive or dead.'

Supreme Jihad Master, 'Bods?'

The First Lord of the Spirit, 'Sorry, I mean bodies.'

Supreme Jihad Master, 'Where do you get them from?'

The First Lord of the Spirit, 'Well, I've used up most of my stocks getting this far. The Chapter has a few spare bodies. We obtain others from the orphanages, prisons, and if necessary, we use press gangs.'

Supreme Jihad Master, 'Well, it is for the common good.'

The First Lord of the Spirit, 'Exactly.'

Location: The President's Office, Planet Napoleon
Sequence of Events: 135

The schedule of meetings with the president had gone to pot for obvious reasons. But Admiral Mustard thought it would be good to get together before the storm.

President Padfield welcomed Admirals Mustard, E Bonner and Bumelton and Henrietta Strong.

President Padfield, 'So, this is the calm before the storm?'

Admiral Mustard, 'I'm afraid so. We know the storm is coming, but we are not sure when it is going to arrive and from what direction it is going to come.'

President Padfield, 'How come you are so sure that it is coming?'

Admiral Mustard, 'Garth has told us that the paperwork is being raised for a jihad.'

President Padfield, 'Are we doomed?'

Admiral Mustard, 'No, but it might be our biggest fight to date. But we do have the biggest Fleet in human history.'

President Padfield, 'How many times have you said that?'

Admiral Mustard, 'It's definitely true this time. We have nearly four million vessels.'

President Padfield, 'Never! You have been busy.'

Admiral Mustard, 'Better force fields, better weapons, better stealth systems. We are ready to take them on.'

President Padfield, 'Better troops?'

Admiral Mustard, 'Not really. We have too many rookies and too many inexperienced admirals.'

President Padfield, 'That's less bluster than usual.'

Admiral Mustard, 'You are right. It could all go horribly wrong.'

President Padfield, 'What's your view, George?'

Admiral Bumelton, 'I can only agree with Jack.'

President Padfield, 'But you have easily beaten the enemy so far.'

Admiral Bumelton, 'Strangely, we would all feel better if we had beaten a tougher foe. The easiness of it has made everyone nervous. The next lot must be considerably better. Otherwise, they couldn't have conquered such an extensive empire.'

President Padfield, 'What about my planets?'

Admiral Mustard, 'We have fitted the strongest force fields we have, and we are leaving the forts in place. Rachel is doing everything she can to improve their protection.'

President Padfield, 'What happens if the Fleet loses?'

Admiral Mustard, 'We have agreed on a meeting point for the surviving vessels. And I hoped that we could discuss possible failure at this meeting.'

President Padfield, 'I guess then it will be every planet for itself?'

Admiral Bumelton, 'A lot would depend on how many surviving vessels there are.'

Admiral Mustard, 'Dave, have you decided what you want to do?'

President Padfield, 'I was planning to stay here.'

Admiral Mustard, 'Well, Planet Napoleon is going to be the meeting point. Should we fight or flee?'

President Padfield, 'I guess that it is too early for the other option?'

Admiral Mustard, 'It is. Fight or flee?'

President Padfield, 'Flee.'

Admiral Mustard, 'So be it.'

President Padfield, 'I understand that the Gods of the Underworld issue has been resolved?'

Admiral Mustard, 'Apparently.'

Henrietta Strong, 'Back to The Empire threat, what do we tell the civilian population?'

Admiral Mustard, 'I would always argue that we should tell them the truth.'

President Padfield, 'I know you would, but you don't have to cope with the aftermath: mob violence, looting, suicide, breakdown of government, etc.'

Admiral Mustard, 'That provides a poor picture of humanity.'

Henrietta Strong, 'A message like that brings out the best and worst in humanity.'

Admiral, 'I'm glad that's your shout.'

Location: Grand Assembly of the Peoples of the Path
Sequence of Events: 136

This was rarely good news. The Archbishop of the Pontification has asked to see the First Lord of the Spirit and the Supreme Jihad Master.

Supreme Jihad Master, 'What do you think it is about?'

The First Lord of the Spirit, 'I guess that it's the jihad, but he has a fearsome reputation.'

Supreme Jihad Master, 'Fearsome?'

The First Lord of the Spirit, 'A sneeze at the wrong time will give you a week on the rack.'

Supreme Jihad Master, 'I've heard of worse.'

The First Lord of the Spirit, 'You usually die from dislocation, and if you don't, they generally ensure that you bleed to death.'

Supreme Jihad Master, 'Do we have to meet him?'

The First Lord of the Spirit, 'If you don't, you might as well put yourself on the rack.'

Supreme Jihad Master, 'I understand.'

They caught a buggy to the archbishop's palace, which was mostly underground. The tunnel down to his domain was lit with burning corpses. The living were queuing up to replace them when the fires dimmed.

The First Lord of the Spirit had travelled a bit and wondered why their race was so viciously brutal. He had always assumed that it was because of their birth rate. A typical brood consisted of fifty plus, and they could successfully mate in four clikons. In one circuit of their star, they could have two hundred and fifty offspring.

The bishops banned all forms of contraception except infanticide. It was totally acceptable to feed your children to the horde, even though they were thrown into the harvesting machines alive. Their flesh was ripped off their bones and fed directly to the waiting crowds. Nothing was wasted; everything was used as a food source. It was a truly disgusting circle of eat and be eaten.

Even their empire was a by-product of their birth rate. They needed space and protein. Their only way out was the path.

The First Lord of the Spirit had often thought that the universe would be a far better place without them, but then he wanted to live.

The Archbishop of the Pontification, 'Come in, honoured guests.'

The First Lord of the Spirit, 'It is us that are honoured, my Holy Master.'

Supreme Jihad Master, 'That is indeed true, Your Holiness.'

The Archbishop of the Pontification, 'Can we ignore all that crap and focus on the issues.'

The First Lord of the Spirit, 'Of course, the issue being the jihad?'

The Archbishop of the Pontification, 'Yes and no. Have you noticed a change in our civilisation if you can call it that?'

The First Lord of the Spirit, 'Yes, I have noticed that there is more aggression and perhaps slightly more resistance to "the will of the people." Am I right?'

The Archbishop of the Pontification, 'You are right, but do you know why?'

The First Lord of the Spirit, 'I wondered if it was evolution.'

The Archbishop of the Pontification, 'No. It's much simpler than that. We have run out of mind control devices.'

The First Lord of the Spirit, 'But that will lead to chaos. We will go back to the times of the Dipbanger.'

The Archbishop of the Pontification, 'Exactly.'

The First Lord of the Spirit, 'So what is the problem?'

The Archbishop of the Pontification, 'We sourced the biological control units from The Brakendeth, and they are no more.'

The First Lord of the Spirit, 'What happened to them?'

The Archbishop of the Pontification, 'They were destroyed by The Hotmans.'

The First Lord of the Spirit, 'The Hotmans defeated The Brakendeth?'

The Archbishop of the Pontification, 'Yes, they did. I bet that puts a different perspective on your little jaunt?'

The First Lord of the Spirit, 'It does rather.'

The Archbishop of the Pontification, 'What have you got to say? You jumped-up, little runt. I could eat you for breakfast.'

Supreme Jihad Master, 'I agree with the First Lord of the Spirit.'

The Archbishop of the Pontification, 'Of course you do. Do you understand what we are talking about?'

Supreme Jihad Master, 'No, Master.'

The Archbishop of the Pontification, 'That is what we are up against.'

The First Lord of the Spirit, 'So without The Brakendeth, who is supplying the control units?'

The Archbishop of the Pontification, 'No one. That is the point. They are desperately needed, or else we are all doomed.'

The First Lord of the Spirit, 'Could we not manufacture them ourselves?'

The Archbishop of the Pontification, 'Yes we could, but we need the basic ingredient: Hotman DNA, and lots of it.'

The First Lord of the Spirit, 'So our little jaunt is now a fight for the survival of our species.'

The Archbishop of the Pontification, 'Exactly. This documentation gives you the clearance to start the jihad immediately. Without you, the path is closed. Open it for us all.'

Location: Grand Assembly of the Peoples of the Path
Sequence of Events: 137

It was amazing just how quick things changed. There was a hive of activity as the five admirals prepared their fleets. The Supreme Jihad Master became an unexpected national celebrity. They were all determined to clear the path.

The general public did not know how critical the mission was. Path clearing was necessary, but the capture of human DNA was paramount to the long-term survival of the species. Four fleets would take on the Hotmans' forces, and the other fleet would secure the DNA.

The four admirals under the direction of the Admiral of the Path would line up and attack in line order. They weren't sure how many vessels would be available, as several other engagements were going on. It would be at least six million vessels, although some were way past their sell-by date. Others were awe-inspiring fighting machines.

The logistics of getting that many vessels together in one place was a nightmare. The loading of munitions and supplies was a massive task, but it had to be done. The Hotmans needed to be taught a lesson.

The 'go date' had been agreed upon, and the five bishops started the blessing process, which cost the lives of nearly a million locals. Blood needed to flow to guarantee success.

Location: Admiral Mustard's Office, Planet Napoleon
Sequence of Events: 138

Garth, 'Good day, Admiral.'

Admiral Mustard, 'How are you?'

Garth, 'I believe that I'm supposed to say "Fine" even if things are not fine.'

Admiral Mustard, 'What's happened?'

Garth, 'We are kitting up. The rats are on the move.'

Admiral Mustard, 'Are you sure?'

Garth, 'I will send you vids. There are between five and six million vessels.'

Admiral Mustard, 'That's more than we are planning for.'

Garth, 'That's likely to increase as they seem to be temporality suspending the local engagements. You are the big bogeyman now.'

Admiral Mustard, 'I better push the panic button and get things ready.'

Garth, 'I will get the free forces organised.'

Admiral Mustard, 'Thanks, Garth, I appreciate and welcome your involvement.'

Garth, 'There is one last thing. Their fleet is divided into two. One fleet has most of the craft. The other fleet, which is about a fifth of the other, seems to have a different destination.'

Admiral Mustard, 'Still us?'

Garth, 'I would say so.'

Admiral Mustard, 'Interesting.'

Garth, 'Good stoking.'

Admiral Mustard, 'And to you, too.'

Location: GAD2 Conference Centre, Planet Napoleon
Sequence of Events: 139

This was going to be the final get-together for a while, or perhaps forever. The following were present either physically or remotely:

- Admiral Bumelton
- Admiral Mustard
- Admiral Gittins
- Admiral J Bonner
- Admiral Pearce
- Admiral Richardson
- Admiral Taylor
- Admiral Tersoo
- Admiral Zakotti
- Admiral Wallett
- Admiral Adams
- Admiral Abosa
- Admiral Dobson
- Admiral Quinn
- Admiral Woodward
- Admiral Ying
- Admiral Vanrooyen
- Admiral Pitt
- Commander Goozee
- Commander Salton
- Admiral Mynd
- AI Central
- Guest – Garth
- Guest – Thanatos
- President Padfield

Admiral Mustard, 'Thank you for coming and thank you for all the hard work you have done. Now is the time.

The current information is as follows:

- The Empire fleet comprises six million plus vessels

- It is likely to increase as they seem to be suspending other engagements
- The Empire has two fleets, with the smaller one having about a million vessels
- They would appear to have two different destinations
- Garth is organising the free forces.

So, in terms of our plan, we need to change it. Admiral Bumelton's Fleet will now address the smaller fleet. Are you OK with that, George?'

Admiral Bumelton, 'Joyful.'

Everyone laughed.

Admiral Mustard, 'Some of us will not meet again, so I want to wish you all good luck. You are the best, the very best. I have every confidence in you and in our ability to win.'

The audience cheered, but there was a mixture of excitement and worry in the room.

Admiral Mustard, 'My orders:

- The Long-Range Monitoring Unit will keep everyone updated
- The order of seniority is as follows:
  o Myself
  o Admiral Bumelton
  o Admiral Gittins
  o Admiral J Bonner
  o Admiral Pearce
  o Then the date of the appointment
- Planet Napoleon is the meeting point for survivors and munitions.'

Fleet Operations, 'Yes, sir.'

Admiral Mustard, 'Go to your post.'

Location: On-board the Admiral of the Path's Flagship
Sequence of Events: 140

The Admiral of the Path didn't really have much of a strategy, as they had always used their numbers as a sledgehammer. He would just attack at their weakest point and then attack and attack and attack.

He considered discussing his plan with the other admirals, but they all knew how they did things. That was the way of the path.

He was somewhat concerned about how many collisions there had been. There had not been a jihad in a thousand Ouses, and the Navy was not used to flying in fleets of this size, but then some collateral damage was to be expected.

The Admiral of the Path suspected that the Hotmans knew that they were coming, as they had been waiting for them on previous occasions. He had planned to send some scouts in advance, but he never got around to it. Anyway, he thought, our forces outnumber them by a considerable factor, so what is the point in being careful?

It took an exceptionally long time to get their vessels through the portal. If he had thought about it, they should have created multiple portals. That mistake will probably cost quite a few lives, but then they had lives to spare.

He wouldn't mind ending the lives of his three exulted guests: The Archbishop of the Pontification, the Supreme Jihad Master, and the First Lord of the Spirit. He realised that there would come a time when he or they would decide each other's fate. He was determined to be the survivor, and history was on his side.

Location: Angel Delight
Sequence of Events: 141

Angels didn't need to sleep, but Angela and Angelina often did, partly because everyone else did, and it was also a chance to dream.

They both woke up at precisely 4.04 a.m. and said together, 'Now is the time.'

They left a brief note for their daddy and teleported to Hades. In fact, they teleported back to Hypnos's cave and outlined their plan. They needed the Erinyes, and they needed them to be operational as soon as possible.

Hypnos, 'What do you know about the Erinyes?'

Angelina, 'The mythology about them is both confusing and conflicting. Female by nature, they could also pose as men. Originally, they were imposing figures: tall, beautiful, winged, extremely capable fighters, highly disciplined, ruthless and cunning.'

Hypnos, 'That's about right, but they eventually changed into wingless demons. They are savage, brutal killing machines. They were often nicknamed "The Furies". They had the "Charm", which they used to impose loyalty until death.

There is no way that you will be able to control them.'

Angela, 'We know that you are wrong. We will be able to control them. If you can do it, we can do it.'

Hypnos, 'What makes you say that?'

Angelina, 'We know.'

Hypnos, 'Let's see you control me.'

Angelina, 'What do you want us to make you do?'

Hypnos, 'Make me laugh. I haven't laughed in years.'

Soon, the sound of unbridled, raucous laughter was filling the cave. Both Angela and Angelina couldn't resist joining in, as his laugh was infectious.

Hypnos was desperately waving his arm, which might have been a signal for them to stop it. So, they stopped it.

Hypnos, 'That was impressive, but hardly a proper test. Now make me walk over that cliff edge.'

Angel, 'Won't you get hurt?'

Hypnos, 'I will take my chances.'

Angelina, 'We won't do it unless you guarantee that you will survive.'

Hypnos, 'If there were no danger, then it would not be a fair test.'

Hypnos couldn't believe it as he walked toward the cliff edge and then walked one step too many. He was so convinced that they couldn't make him do it that he had no backup plan. It could well be his ultimate end.

Fortunately, the girls did have a plan, and Angela swooped down and collected him in her arms. Hypnos couldn't believe how strong she was. He had clearly underestimated their capabilities, which he reflected had happened between males and females throughout history.

Hypnos, 'The Erinyes are yours, but you must realise that they will not be happy bunnies when they wake up. Their anger will be terrifying and awesome.'

Angelina, 'We will see. When can you wake them up?'

Hypnos, 'Tonight, so you better be ready.'

Location: On-board Admiral Mustard's Flagship
Sequence of Events: 142

The time had come. The long wait had ended. For most, it was a relief, tinged with a genuine sense of excitement, except for the old hands who had experienced the downside of war before. Every survivor from a previous battle wondered if it was now their turn.

The drones were already attacking The Empire ships as they emerged from the portal. It was a killing field, but the numbers coming through were more than the drones could target.

Admiral Mustard had his Fleet organised in line of battle order:

- Divisions Seven, Nine and Thirteen were defending the right flank
- Divisions Ten, Twelve, and Fourteen were protecting the left flank
- Divisions Two, Four and Five were defending the centre
- The deception team had added a further six fake Divisions in the centre
- Division Fifteen was acting as a reserve
- The super-battleships and super-fortresses were also guarding the flanks
- One million drones were engaged
- Drone Fleets Eleven, Twelve, and Thirteen were defending the right flank
- Drone Fleets Fourteen, Fifteen, Seventeen and Eighteen were protecting the centre
- Drone Fleets Nineteen, Twenty-nine and Twenty-one were defending the right flank
- Pods of drones were ready to attack 'chatter and leader vessels.'

The game had started, and Admiral Mustard had made the first move with the drone attack.

Some chatter had been detected, and drone pods went on the attack, but The Empire soon stopped their mistake.

The drones were doing an excellent job of stopping The Empire fleet from getting into the formation and their key success was still eliminating new arrivals. However, slowly The Empire was building a protective ring around the portal. Carrying on would cause the loss of too many drones. Admiral Mustard wondered if he should withdraw them.

Location: On-board the Admiral of the Path's Flagship
Sequence of Events: 143

The Admiral of the Path wasn't surprised that the Hotmans were waiting for him. Their pesky drones did quite a bit of damage, but the portal was now protected, and slowly the fleet was getting into position.

The Empire formation consisted of five chapters. Within each chapter, there were simply lines of ships waiting to attack. The Admiral of the Path wanted them to be sub-divided into manageable units so that he could order them forward in some sort of order. Annoyingly, he had to instruct the chapter admirals, and they would then order their underlings.

The scanners indicated that the enemy's strength was in the centre, leaving their flanks relatively weakened, although their fleet was much larger than he expected. He had always preferred to attack the flanks. He was trying to decide whether he should attack both flanks at once or go for one and see how the Hotmans respond.

He decided on a single flank, as the Hotmans had proved quite tricky, although they were up against a professional this time.

The Admiral of the Path, 'Dear Admiral of the Book, it would give me great pleasure if you attacked the right flank of the enemy.'

The Admiral of The Book, 'That seems to be an eminently sensible tactic, my dear Admiral of the Path.'

Location: On-board the Admiral of the Book's Flagship
Sequence of Events: 144

The Admiral of the Book had two hundred squadrons of about six thousand vessels. The Bishop of the Book had instructed him to get a victory, but not to make it look that good for the Admiral of the Path. An outstanding success would give the Chapter of the Path too much power. Everyone knew that this was going to be a problem.

The Admiral of The Book, 'Master of Telephonic Communications, put me through to all squadron leaders.'

The Master of Telephonic Communications, 'Of course, Great Leader.' After a few unns of time, the connections were made.

The Admiral of The Book, 'This is your admiral. Our time has come. The path must be cleared. We have been given the honour of clearing the right flank of the infidels.

But caution must be observed. Our chapter must be protected. So only odd squadrons are to attack the infidels. Even squadrons will appear to join the attack, but they will avoid combat. Is this understood? Failure to obey will be terminal.

Start the attack.'

Location: On-board Admiral Mustard's Flagship
Sequence of Events: 145

Their combat systems showed the movement of about a million vessels from The Empire's centre to their right flank, leaving a yawning gap.

Admiral Mustard, 'My orders:

- Fifty battle-cruisers fitted with Godfire will attack The Empire's portal
- All engaged drones to attack the portal
- Drone Fleets Sixteen, Seventeen and Eighteen to move to the right flank
- Reserve Division to prepare to support the right flank.'

Fleet Operations, 'Yes, Sir.'

Admiral Mustard watched the slow movement of The Empire forces, and then they attacked.

At the same time, all of the engaged drones focused on the portal. Then fifty powerful battle-cruisers from Division Four shot forward. Clearly, The Empire wasn't expecting this attack, as there was little opposition.

The battle-cruisers unleashed an AI-controlled Godfire blast. It was actually fifty blasts, but the power involved caused the portal to collapse, which stopped further Empire ships from arriving.'

Admiral Mustard, 'My orders:

- The drones and battle-cruisers in enemy space will attack the rear of The Empire forces attacking our fight flank.'

Fleet Operations, 'Yes, Sir.'

The Empire fleet did not expect Hotman incursions into their space this early in the battle and either ignored them or decided not to engage. The drones and battle-cruisers were attacking the rear squadrons belonging to the Admiral of the Book.

The Galactium forces couldn't understand why there was no resistance. Most of The Empire squadrons were not returning fire.

Admiral Mustard was going to recall both the drones and the battlecruisers, but they were being phenomenally successful.

The Empire's frontal attack on the right flank was also stalling. The AI-controlled use of drones and Godfire was proving to be a serious barrier, and the attack on their rear was causing confusion.

Admiral Mustard, 'My orders:

- Fleets 4.1 and 4.2 to attack the left flank of the attacking Empire fleet.'

Fleet Operations, 'Yes, Sir.'

Location: On-board the Admiral of the Path's Flagship
Sequence of Events: 146

The Admiral of the Path, 'Master of Operations, update me.'

Master of Operations, 'My Lord, the Hotmans are not following agreed battle protocols.'

The Admiral of the Path, 'I can see that. They attacked while we were still moving our forces. That is clearly against the rules.'

Master of Operations, 'And they have knocked out our portal.'

The Admiral of the Path, 'Well, create another one.'

Master of Operations, 'With huge regret and apologies, we had not foreseen this situation, and it's not my fault, but we can't recreate the portal.'

The Admiral of the Path, 'Why not, you scum?'

Master of Operations, 'The portal generators are on the other side of the portal.'

The Admiral of the Path, 'Well, get them to open a portal.'

Master of Operations, 'My Lord, we have no way of communicating with them.'

The Admiral of the Path, 'Your family will suffer for this.'

Master of Operations, 'It wasn't my job to organise that, my Lord.'

The Admiral of the Path, 'Stop snivelling. Did the entire fleet get through?'

Master of Operations, 'No, my Lord, about seven hundred thousand vessels are trapped in jump-space.'

The Admiral of the Path drew his ceremonial dagger and stuck it hard into the Master of Operation's eye. It was a quick but foolish death, as there wasn't a suitable replacement for him. A poor alternative was soon found.

The Admiral of the Path, 'Junior Operator, continue the update.'

Operator, 'My Lord, it would appear that the Hotmans who attacked the portal then struck the rear of the fleet of the Book doing serious damage. It's not my fault. Please don't kill me, but our fleet did not return fire.

That same fleet is encountering tough resistance from the Hotmans from their biz-bizs and Godfire.'

The Admiral of the Path, 'Are you saying that they have Godfire?'

Master of Operations, 'Yes, Super-Master. That's what destroyed the portal.'

The Admiral of the Path, 'No one told me.'

287

Master of Operations, 'Apologies, my Lord, but it was mentioned in the report.'

The Admiral of the Path drew his ceremonial dagger for the second time and stuck it hard into the operator's eye. The admiral realised that it was a stupid thing to do, but he enjoyed it.

An even poorer replacement was found.

Poorer Replacement, 'Sir, I have no idea what happened next as I don't know how to use the battle logistics system.'

The Admiral of the Path drew his ceremonial dagger for the third time and stuck it hard into the operator's eye. The admiral realised that it was a stupid thing to do and to make it worse, he didn't really enjoy it.

The admiral had no choice but to use the system himself. It was clear that the Fleet of the Book was now being attacked on three sides and that they were at the point of systematic failure. He had the choice of leaving it as it was or ordering a withdrawal. A retreat would have serious morale considerations. What should he do?

Location: On-board Admiral Bumelton's Flagship
Sequence of Events: 147

Admiral Bumelton really wanted 'to march to the sound of the drums,' but he had his orders. He was tasked with defeating The Empire's second fleet, which hadn't yet appeared.

In his mind, he evaluated his assets:

- Divisions One, Three, Six, Eight and Eleven, equating to six hundred and fifty thousand vessels
- Dragon fleet
- Galactium alien fleets
- The Minmoses, or stick insect fleet.

That was rushing towards a million vessels. It was undoubtedly the biggest Fleet he had ever commanded.

He would have liked some more drones. With luck, there should be another delivery from production soon.

Location: On-board Admiral Mustard's Flagship
Sequence of Events: 148

Admiral Mustard, 'Update me.'
Fleet Operations, 'Yes, Sir:

- The drones and Godfire of our forces on the right flank are causing severe damage to The Empire forces
- The drones and battlecruisers attacking them in the rear are causing confusion. However, the battlecruisers are reporting that their stocks of Godfire munitions are running low
- Fleets 4.1 and 4.2 are holding their own, but they are being attacked by force as the enemy fleet tries to escape to the front and rear
- It would appear that their portal is inoperative
- All other forces are operational.'

Admiral Mustard was contemplating his next move. Should he recall the two Fleets and those vessels attacking the rear of the enemy fleet, or should he throw in more resources, as the enemy was clearly on the run?

There was a danger that the retreating forces would decimate his battle-cruisers, but he didn't want to look too cautious. In most battles, morale was often a decisive factor. He had to look strong.

Admiral Mustard, 'My orders:

- Drone Fleet Fifteen will support Fleets 4.1 and 4.2
- Super-battleships on the right flank to attack The Empire fleet but be prepared to retreat on my order.'

Fleet Operations, 'Yes, Sir.'

Admirals Cheung and Colley were very grateful for the drone support, as things were getting rather hot.

The super-battleships shot forward into the alien fleet. Their sheer size was intimidating, which was their primary purpose. They were also very heavily armoured and shielded, and carried the most extensive mix of weapons ever fitted on a Galactium vessel. With their AI-controlled targeting systems, they looked like a box of fireworks that had accidentally caught fire. Their three hundred and sixty degree weapons systems just exploded with raw destructive power. Each of them just cut a wide path through the enemy's resources. It was the final straw. The camel's back was broken, and their fleet was in fall flight.

Location: On-board the Admiral of the Path's Flagship
Sequence of Events: 149

The Admiral of the Path had secured an experienced Master of Operations from another fleet which was timely as the fleet of the Book was in disarray.

The Admiral of the Path, 'The fleet of the Book will retire in good order.'

Master of Operations, 'Yes, my Lord.'

They both knew that this was a rout, but appearances must be maintained.

If the Admiral of the Path had his way, the Admiral of the Book would be publicly tortured and then executed, but it wouldn't be politic. Well, not at the moment.

The Admiral of the Path, 'Master of Operations, please beg the Admiral of the Spirit to defend the retirement of the Book Fleet.'

Master of Operations, 'Yes, my Lord.'

The Admiral of the Path had tried using his weakest fleet. His other fleets ranked in terms of competence were: Holy Relics, Spirit, Pontification and his own fleet, Path. He wanted to hold his back to the end so that his chapter could claim the final victory. The glory of it would be immense.

He decided to send in the second strongest fleet: Pontification. That should weaken them and reduce their future status. He secretly hoped that the Hotmans would give them a good pasting.

The Admiral of the Path, 'Master of Operations, please request that the might of the fleet of the Pontification should eliminate the Hotmans left flank.'

Master of Operations, 'Yes, my Lord, it will be done.'

Location: On-board Admiral Mustard's Flagship
Sequence of Events: 150

Admiral Mustard, 'My orders:

- All forces to return to the formation
- Provide battle statistics.'

Fleet Operations, 'Yes, Sir. The stats are on the screen:

Resource	Total	Current Total
Division 2	130,000	130,000
Division 4	130,000	92,000
Division 5	130,000	130,000
Division 7	130,000	124,000
Division 9	130,000	119,000
Division 10	130,000	130,000
Division 12	130,000	130,000
Division 13	130,000	98,000
Division 14	130,000	130,000
Division 15	130,000	130,000
Drone Fleet 1	100,000	77,000
Drone Fleet 2	100,000	82,000
Drone Fleet 3	100,000	69,000
Drone Fleet 4	100,000	98,000
Drone Fleet 5	100,000	57,000
Drone Fleet 6	100,000	89,000
Drone Fleet 7	100,000	96,000
Drone Fleet 8	100,000	97,000
Drone Fleet 9	100,000	85,000
Drone Fleet 10	100,000	76,000
Drone Fleet 11	100,000	100,000
Drone Fleet 12	100,000	100,000
Drone Fleet 13	100,000	100.000
Drone Fleet 14	100,000	100,000
Drone Fleet 15	100,000	82,000

Drone Fleet 16	100,000	88,000
Drone Fleet 17	100,000	92,000
Drone Fleet 18	100,000	89,000
Drone Fleet 19	100,000	88,000
Drone Fleet 20	100,000	91,000
Grand Total	3,300,000	2,969,000
Total Losses		331,000

Empire fleet (estimates):

Resource	Total	Current Total
Fleet 1	860,000	860,000
Fleet 2	860,000	820,000
Fleet 3	860,000	680,000
Fleet 4	860,000	820,000
Fleet 5	860,000	360,000
Grand Total	4,300,000	3,530,000
Total losses		760,000

Admiral Mustard, 'Update me.'

Fleet Operations, 'Yes, Sir:

- All of our forces are back in position
- The fifty battle-cruisers are being rearmed
- The Drone Fleets are spread as follows: left – five Fleets, Centre – eight Fleets, right – six Fleets
- All super-battleships have returned intact
- It now appears that The Empire is preparing to attack our left flank.'

Admiral Mustard, 'Are they exposing their centre again?'

Fleet Operations, 'No, Sir. It looks like their left-hand fleet is going to attack our left flank.'

Admiral Mustard, 'At least it keeps it tidy.'

Fleet Operations, 'Yes, sir.'

Admiral Mustard, 'My orders:

- The Reserve Division will move to the left flank but will only assist on my orders
- All super-battleships will assemble on the left flank
- Drone Fleets Nineteen, Twenty, Four, Five, Six and Seven will move to the left flank.'

Fleet Operations, 'Yes, Sir.'

Location: On-board the Admiral of the Pontification's Flagship
Sequence of Events: 151

The Admiral of the Pontification, 'Master of Operations, tell me why the fleet of the Book failed.'

Master of Operations, 'Did they fail or did the Hotmans win?'

The Admiral of the Pontification, 'I hope you are not suggesting that the Hotmans won.'

Master of Operations, 'Of course not, my Lord, but the statistics show… '

The Admiral of the Pontification interrupted, 'I don't care what the statistics show, tell me what went wrong.'

Master of Operations, 'Yes, my Lord. Firstly, the fleet of the Book was not fully committed.'

The Admiral of the Pontification, 'How dare you suggest that?'

Master of Operations, 'There were rumours, my Lord, that half of the Book Fleet was ordered not to fight as they didn't want to give the Admiral of the Path too great a victory.'

The Admiral of the Pontification, 'You are dangerously close to talking treason.'

Master of Operations, 'Deep apologies, my Lord.'

The Admiral of the Pontification, 'Let's assume that there may be some truth in what you say. What else did they do wrong?'

Master of Operations, 'They did not react in time to the attack in the rear, and they had no answer to Godfire.'

The Admiral of the Pontification, 'You know that officially they do not have Godfire.'

Master of Operations, 'Deep apologies again, my Lord.'

The Admiral of the Pontification, 'If there was Godfire, how do you counter it?'

Master of Operations, 'Historically, you throw resources at it until their ammunition has run out because base materials are difficult to obtain.'

The Admiral of the Pontification, 'So how would you attack the Hotman scum.'

Master of Operations, 'Have you ever commanded a fleet before, my Lord?'

The Admiral of the Pontification, 'Not exactly.'

Master of Operations, 'Have you ever experienced battle before?'

The Admiral of the Pontification, 'Not exactly.'

Master of Operations, 'Well, our usual tactic is to just charge at the enemy, but the Hotmans will have that covered.'

The Admiral of the Pontification, 'What's the alternative?'

Master of Operations, 'None really, that's all our fleet has ever known?'

The Admiral of the Pontification, 'In that case, let's charge.'

Master of Operations, 'Before we charge, we need to consider the wishes of the bishop.'

The Admiral of the Pontification, 'What do you mean?'

Master of Operations, 'He wants us to bring the fleet home. You need to consider the needs of our chapter.'

The Admiral of the Pontification, 'I see what you are saying. Shall I tell half the fleet not to engage?'

Master of Operations, 'I can't really say, but that seems to be standard procedure.'

The Admiral of The Pontification, 'Master of Telephonic Communications, put me through to all squadron leaders.'

The Master of Telephonic Communications, 'Of course, my master.'

After a few unns of time, the connections were eventually made.'

The Admiral of The Pontification, 'This is your admiral. You saw the great success that the Fleet of the Book had. It's now our time to emulate that success and give the infidels a thorough beating.

The scum that are blocking our path must be eradicated from our path. Their very existence must be purged.

Our chapter insists that half of our fleet attack the scum, and the other half creates a situation when the Hotmans can be outflanked. So, only odd squadrons are to attack the infidels. Even squadrons will start the outflanking manoeuvre.

I order you to start.'

Location: On-board Admiral Mustard's Flagship
Sequence of Events: 152

Fleet Operations, 'Admiral, it looks like the enemy's left-hand fleet is dividing into two. Half is coming straight at us, and the other half are exiting the field.'

Admiral Mustard, 'They are probably planning to outflank us. My orders:

- Reserve Division to defend the extreme left flank
- Super-fortresses on the right flank to join the Reserve Fleet
- Drone Fleets Six and Seven to join the Reserve Fleet
- Divisions Ten, Twelve and Fourteen to use Godfire against the oncoming fleet.'

Fleet Operations, 'Yes, Sir.'

Admiral Mustard realised that this attack was going to be tougher, as there weren't any distractions. Then he had an idea that actually came from the movie, *Zulu*.

Admiral Mustard, 'My orders:

- Fleet Ten will spread out
- Fleet Twelve will position itself directly above Fleet Ten
- Fleet Fourteen will position itself directly above Fleet Twelve
- AI will synchronise a rolling volley of munitions so that there was no break whatsoever.'

Fleet Operations, 'Yes, Sir.'

There was shock all around, as this was certainly not in the textbooks, but the manoeuvre was excellently accomplished.

Location: On-board the Admiral of the Path's Flagship
Sequence of Events: 153

The Admiral of the Path, 'Master of Operations, update me.'

Master of Operations, 'Yes, my Supreme leader. The fleet of the Pontification has divided into two. One half is attacking the Hotman scum, and the other half is going off into space. It is believed that they are attempting to outflank the pig-dogs.'

The Admiral of the Path, 'They were not my orders.'

Master of Operations, 'As you know, my master, you are technically the guest leader of the entire fleet. Each chapter admiral has a level of individual discretion.'

The Admiral of the Path, 'So you are saying that I can't counter-order their action.'

Master of Operations, 'I fear that is the case, my Lordship.'

The Admiral of the Path, 'So the only fleet that I can really trust is mine.'

Master of Operations, 'I hope that is the case, my master.'

Location: Angel Delight
Sequence of Events: 154

Hypnos, 'Are you ready?'

Angelina, 'I guess so.'

Hypnos cast his spell on the three Erinyes. Over the years, there have been many myths and stories about them and their numbers. Some limited the number to three and others to over a hundred. Anyway, the three in Hades were Hezebel, Alecto and Desmonda. They weren't the originals given birth by Nyx, but they would do.

The three Furies woke up, and the cave was filled with the haunting screams of three minor goddesses who either were mad or simply enjoyed screaming.

Angelina soon calmed them down. They were much easier to control than she expected, but then they had been sleeping for a very long time. Perhaps they will be more challenging in the future?

Angela teleported all five of them back to Terry's flat. Terry now had two naked angels, two gorgeous looking Erinyes and one old hag in his lounge. But fortunately, history had given him the ability to cope with the unexpected.

Angelina was congratulated by her 'guide' on a job well done. The time of 'Erin Yes kill mischief' was almost upon us. They were instructed to take the Furies out to the battlefield.

Location: On-Board Admiral Bumelton's Flagship
Sequence of Events: 155

Admiral Bumelton was caught off guard as The Empire portal opened behind them and their ships streamed through. They must have seen The Galactium Fleet, but they totally ignored it.

It appeared that The Empire had five destinations in mind as there were five long lines of identical vessels plus some large industrial containers with mechanical equipment. It was not what Admiral Bumelton expected.

Admiral Bumelton had the classic dilemma of whether to divide his forces or concentrate them, but in reality, he had no choice but to divide. He formed five separate navies with permission to act on their own initiative:

1. Force One – Division One, plus half of the Galactica alien forces
2. Force Two – Division Three, plus the dragons
3. Force Three – Division Six, plus the Minmoses
4. Force Four – Division Eight, plus the free forces
5. Force Five – Division Eleven, plus half of the Galactica alien forces.

Admiral Bumelton, 'Comms, get me Admiral Mustard.'

Comms, 'Yes, Sir.'

Admiral Mustard, 'We are having a bit of fun here. How is it going your end?'

Admiral Bumelton, 'Well, they caught us off guard. Their portal opened way behind us. They could have done a lot of damage, as we would have been totally out of position.

Instead, they exited the portal into five separate columns. We have divided into five Fleets and are going after them.'

Admiral Mustard, 'Any idea where they are going?'

Admiral Bumelton, 'It's too early to guess at this stage. But I would suggest Earth, Lovelace, Dragonia and Napoleon.'

Admiral Mustard, 'You better warn them.'

Admiral Bumelton, 'I will, but they might be coming for you.'

Admiral Mustard, 'I will issue some orders. A little gift for you: three hundred thousand drones are waiting for you at Planet Napoleon.'

Admiral Bumelton, 'I think I'm going to need them.'

Admiral Mustard, 'My orders:

- Activate all planetary defences
- Warn all planetary forts
- Warn The Home Fleet
- Activate all drones at Planet Napoleon and order them to take Admiral Bumelton's orders
- Inform the president.'

Fleet Operations, 'Yes, Sir.'

Location: On-board Admiral Mustard's Flagship
Sequence of Events: 156

They came, and they were met in the same old way. The three-tiered firing strategy proved to be devastating to The Empire forces. The Empire's strategy of trying to exhaust The Galactium munitions and especially their Godfire munitions proved fatal.

The Galactium was finding it harder to target The Empire vessels because of all the debris. There were literally millions of dead rodents and tons of smashed spacecraft. But The Galactium forces just stood their ground.

Admiral Mustard had considered doing something innovative, but what was the point? The 'wall of lead' was doing the job for them. There was, in fact, some lead or rather iron involved from the rail weapons. Apart from Godfire, the weaponry also included proton beams, atomisers, stud guns and nukes. The planet busters were also available if required.

The second force was being tracked, but it seemed to be going nowhere. There was no attempt on their part at a sweeping flank manoeuvre.

Admiral Mustard was ready to launch the battlecruisers and super battleships at the enemy, but all of their forces were retreating. He decided to wait and see what they did next.

Admiral Mustard, 'Give me the stats.'

Fleet Operations, 'Yes, Sir. They are on the screen now:

Resources	Total	Current Total
Division 2	130,000	130,000
Division 4	130,000	92,000
Division 5	130,000	130,000
Division 7	130,000	124,000
Division 9	130,000	119,000
Division 10	130,000	126,000
Division 12	130,000	107,000
Division 13	130,000	98,000
Division 14	130,000	118,000
Division 15	130,000	130,000
Drone Fleet 1	100,000	68,000

Drone Fleet 2	100,000	77,000
Drone Fleet 3	100,000	61,000
Drone Fleet 4	100,000	98,000
Drone Fleet 5	100,000	57,000
Drone Fleet 6	100,000	89,000
Drone Fleet 7	100,000	96,000
Drone Fleet 8	100,000	97,000
Drone Fleet 9	100,000	85,000
Drone Fleet 10	100,000	76,000
Drone Fleet 11	100,000	88,000
Drone Fleet 12	100,000	91,000
Drone Fleet 13	100,000	96,000
Drone Fleet 14	100,000	100,000
Drone Fleet 15	100,000	82,000
Drone Fleet 16	100,000	88,000
Drone Fleet 17	100,000	92,000
Drone Fleet 18	100,000	89,000
Drone Fleet 19	100,000	88,000
Drone Fleet 20	100,000	91,000
Grand Total	3,300,000	2,883,000
Total Losses		417,000

Empire Losses (estimates):

Resource	Total	Current Total
Fleet 1	860,000	610,000
Fleet 2	860,000	820,000
Fleet 3	860,000	680,000
Fleet 4	860,000	820,000
Fleet 5	860,000	360,000
Grand Total	4,300,000	3,530,000
Total losses		1,010,000

Admiral Mustard, 'So they have lost a million plus vessels, but they still outnumber us.'

Fleet Operations, 'Thankfully, our losses are mostly drones.'

Admiral Mustard, 'We have lost twenty per cent of our drone resources. We need them for whatever comes next.'

Fleet Operations, 'I guess that they are going to attack the centre.'

Admiral Mustard, 'Not if our deception is still working. My orders:

- All vessels to return to standard formation
- Rearm if necessary
- Special Ops to install stealthed force fields
- Super-fortresses to take pre-planned positions
- Marine Fleet to defend Planet Napoleon
- Stealthed teams to prepare for an attack.'

Fleet Operations, 'Yes, Sir.'

Location: On-Board Admiral Bumelton's Flagship
Sequence of Events: 157

Admiral Bumelton, 'Comms get me Admiral Mustard.'

Comms, 'Yes, Sir.'

Admiral Mustard, 'We are resting at the moment, waiting for their next encounter. They are hardly what you would call innovative.'

Admiral Bumelton, 'I can't say that I'm that surprised.

We have now projected their destinations, and they are as we suspected: Earth, Napoleon, Lovelace and Dragonia.'

Admiral Mustard, 'What about the fifth destination?'

Admiral Bumelton, 'It seems to go nowhere, but if you project the trajectory for a remarkably long distance, you come to an unpopulated barren planet. At one time, it was supposed to have a cave where the Gods of the Underworld lived.'

Admiral Mustard, 'Well, that is interesting. AI Central, what do you make of that?'

AI Central, 'It seems to tie back to their religion. I also need to tell you that Angela and Angelina have collected the Erinyes from Hades, and they are on their way to the battlefield.'

Admiral Mustard, 'Really?'

AI Central, 'Really.'

Admiral Mustard, 'What are the Erinyes?'

AI Central, 'In Greek mythology, they used to be called The Furies.'

Admiral Mustard, 'Well, they probably can't cause too much trouble. What do you think so far?'

AI Central, 'You are on schedule to lose.'

Admiral Mustard, 'What makes you say that?'

AI Central, 'The two encounters so far are half-hearted affairs. At least half of each fleet were not engaged. I suspect that there were political motivations involved.

They will fix their portal soon, and more resources will arrive. You will have a series of minor victories, but ultimately it is going to be a numbers game, and you will lose.'

Admiral Mustard, 'Thanks for the vote of confidence.'

AI Central, 'It has nothing to do with voting or confidence. It's just pure logic.'

Admiral Bumelton, 'Our electronic friend can be quite encouraging at times.'

Admiral Mustard, 'He's a little shit.'

AI Central, 'I heard that.'

Admiral Bumelton, 'All we can do is carry on. I had a chat with Garth, and he said that there is no point in defending Planet Dragonia. And to be honest, Planet Lovelace is an unpopulated nuclear wasteland.'

Admiral Mustard, 'So that just leaves you Earth and Napoleon.'

Admiral Mustard, 'I plan to send three Fleets to Earth and two to Napoleon.'

Admiral Mustard, 'Go for it.'

Admiral Bumelton, 'My orders:

- Forces One, Two and Three to go to the defence of Earth
- Forces Four and Five to go to the defence of Napoleon.'

Fleet Operations, 'Yes, Sir.'

Location: On-board the Admiral of the Path's Flagship
Sequence of Events: 158

The Admiral of the Path, 'Master of Operations, update me.'

    Master of Operations, 'The fleet of the Pontification has returned.'

    The Admiral of the Path, 'Well, that was mostly a waste of time.'

    Master of Operations, 'We have eliminated four hundred thousand of their vessels.'

    The Admiral of the Path, 'But at what cost?'

    Master of Operations, 'One million and one hundred thousand, Your Almightiness.'

    The Admiral of the Path, 'Are you saying that we have lost over a million vessels?'

    Master of Operations, 'It is the cost of ultimate victory.'

    The Admiral of The Path, 'Master of Telephonic Communications, put me through to the other four admirals.'

    The Master of Telephonic Communications, 'Of course, Great Leader.'

    After quite a few unns of time, the connections were made.

    The Admiral of the Path, 'Fellow exponents of the military arts, so far we have been very successful. We have destroyed four hundred thousand enemy vessels.'

    Everyone on the call knew the facts, but the game had to be played.

    The Admiral of the Book, 'We congratulate you on your resounding success. Can I ask what you plan to do next?'

    The Admiral of the Path, 'Thank you for your commendations which are duly noted and appreciated. As you know, we are a team, and as a team, we must share our plans, and as such, I'm looking for your recommendations.'

    The Admiral of the Holy Relics, 'We do what we have always done. We attack across the entire front.'

    The Admiral of the Spirt, 'Here, here.'

    The Admiral of the Pontification, 'I agree, let's smash them.'

    The Admiral of the Path, 'I understand your sentiment, and that will be done.' He realised that it was the only way he could get a buy-in.

    The Admiral of the Path, 'Thank you, there will be a line of attack in one umms.'

Location: On-board Admiral Mustard's Flagship
Sequence of Events: 159

Admiral Mustard, 'Update me.'
Fleet Operations, 'Yes, Sir:

- All assets are back in position as directed
- Special Ops have installed the stealthed force fields. They are the largest ever constructed by humankind
- Sixteen stealthed attack groups are proceeding towards the enemy, partly to determine if our stealth technology works and to create havoc
- Over a quarter of a million stealthed mines have been laid in fixed zones
- The stealthed super-fortresses will be in place shortly.'

Fleet Operations, 'Admiral, we also need to point out that there is a lot of activity in the enemy lines. If I didn't know better, I would say that their entire line is going to attack.'

Admiral Mustard thought, 'That is the last thing we want.' But it was what he was going to get. Three and a half million Empire ships were on the move.

The first problem that The Empire encountered were the stealthed attack groups which confused their formation preparations. They couldn't return fire, as the risk of hitting their own ships was too high. If Admiral Mustard realised beforehand that the stealth technology worked so well, he would have been much more ambitious.

The attack units were doing a good job, but there weren't enough of them to make a difference. The mass of ships moved inexorably and relentlessly forward until they hit the stealthed force field. It was a car crash of immense proportions, with the arriving vessels crashing into those already pinned against the force field.

If there were sounds in space, it would sound like crashing metal canisters smashing into each other at hyper-speeds. Vast amounts of debris piled up against the wall as more and more vessels joined the disaster.

The stealthed force field had proved to be a brilliant innovation. It had destroyed at least a third of the remaining Empire fleet and caused the rest to retreat.

As they retreated, the stealthed attack groups came into their own. They harried The Empire vessels at every opportunity. They continued this process until they were destroyed or they had to return, as their munitions were low.

Admiral Mustard thought to himself, 'That's one in the eye for AI Central. It was just a pity he didn't have an eye. It looks to be a brilliant victory for us.'

Admiral Mustard, 'Update me.'

Fleet Operations, 'Yes, Sir:

- The Empire forces have been seriously punished and have retreated because of the existence of the stealthed force
- The stealthed super-fortresses are still in place. They have not been utilised
- The attack units have returned.'

Admiral Mustard, 'How did the attack units do?'

Fleet Operations, 'They caused considerable asset destruction, but we incurred fifty per cent losses.'

Admiral Mustard, 'Brave men and women, I salute you.

What are the statistics?'

Fleet Operations, 'On the screen, Sir:

Resources	Total	Current Total
Division 2	130,000	129,000
Division 4	130,000	92,000
Division 5	130,000	129,000
Division 7	130,000	124,000
Division 9	130,000	119,000
Division 10	130,000	126,000
Division 12	130,000	107,000
Division 13	130,000	98,000
Division 14	130,000	118,000
Division 15	130,000	130,000
Drone Fleet 1	100,000	68,000
Drone Fleet 2	100,000	77,000

Drone Fleet 3	100,000	61,000
Drone Fleet 4	100,000	98,000
Drone Fleet 5	100,000	57,000
Drone Fleet 6	100,000	89,000
Drone Fleet 7	100,000	96,000
Drone Fleet 8	100,000	97,000
Drone Fleet 9	100,000	85,000
Drone Fleet 10	100,000	76,000
Drone Fleet 11	100,000	88,000
Drone Fleet 12	100,000	91,000
Drone Fleet 13	100,000	96,000
Drone Fleet 14	100,000	100,000
Drone Fleet 15	100,000	82,000
Drone Fleet 16	100,000	88,000
Drone Fleet 17	100,000	92,000
Drone Fleet 18	100,000	89,000
Drone Fleet 19	100,000	88,000
Drone Fleet 20	100,000	91,000
Grand Total	3,300,000	2,881,000
Total Losses		419,000

Empire Losses (estimates):

Resource	Total	Current Total
Fleet 1	860,000	310,000
Fleet 2	860,000	440,000
Fleet 3	860,000	390,000
Fleet 4	860,000	470,000
Fleet 5	860,000	124,000
Grand Total	4,300,000	1,734,000
Total losses		2,566,000

Admiral Mustard, 'That's amazing. It means that we outnumber them now.'
   Fleet Operations, 'Is it the time to attack them?'

Location: On-board the Admiral of the Path's Flagship
Sequence of Events: 160

The Admiral of the Path, 'No one told us that they had stealth technology.'

The Admiral of the Holy Relics, 'It was in the report.'

The Admiral of the Spirt, 'No one reads those reports.'

The Admiral of the Holy Relics, 'I did. It mentioned their stealth technology, Godfire, super battleships and fortresses and other wonders.'

The Admiral of the Pontification, 'I never saw the report.'

The Admiral of the Holy Relics, 'It was circulated to all of us.'

The Admiral of the Pontification, 'I tell you, I never saw it.'

The Admiral of the Path, 'My fellow military masters, we need to move on. We have now lost two and a half million vessels.'

The Admiral of the Spirt, 'No one cares how many vessels we lose as long as we win.'

The Admiral of the Path, 'Exactly. I'm going to propose that we use the second fleet to attack the rear of our enemy. They won't be expecting that.'

The Admiral of the Holy Relics, 'I'm not sure if I could agree to that.'

The Admiral of the Path, 'Why not?'

The Admiral of the Holy Relics, 'It's not following our orders'

The Admiral of the Path, 'If you return without a win, you are dead. We will all be dead. So go with us, or we will kill you.'

The Admiral of the Holy Relics, 'I understand.'

The Admiral of the Path, 'Are you with us?'

The Admiral of the Holy Relics, 'I have no choice.'

The Admiral of the Path, 'Master of Telephonic Communications, put me through to the five captains attacking their planets.'

The Master of Telephonic Communications, 'Of course, my Supreme Admiral. Should I include the fleet following the Path?'

The Admiral of the Path, 'Absolutely'

After a lot of unns of time, the connections were made.

The Admiral of the Path, 'Fellow member of the fleet, you have done well, and you will be rewarded. Military reasons dictate that your objective must be changed.'

Captain 1342 of the Path, 'Sir, I'm sure that I speak on behalf of the other captains. Our instructions are unambiguous.'

The Admiral of the Path, 'Am I not your admiral?'

Captain 1342 of the Path, 'You are indeed, Sir, and a very exalted admiral.'

The Admiral of the Path, 'So you recognise my authority?'

Captain 1342 of the Path, 'Yes, I do, Sir.'

The Admiral of the Path, 'In that case, you will cease your current task and attack the main Hotman fleet. Co-ordinates will be sent to you. Do you understand?'

Captain 1342 of the Path, 'Yes, Sir.'

Location: On-board Admiral Mustard's Flagship
Sequence of Events: 161

Admiral Mustard was now under a lot of pressure to launch an attack against The Empire's forces. They outnumbered them and clearly had better tactics and technology.

Admiral Mustard was reluctant, as the attacker generally lost more resources than the defender unless the technology was totally disproportionate. He valued every life, and why not just let The Empire come at them in the same old way.

A quick discussion with the other admirals convinced him that he was wrong and that it was the right time to launch an attack.

Admiral Mustard, 'My orders:

- Divisions Ten, Twelve, Two, Four, Seven, Fifteen, and Nine will attack the enemy on my command
- All Drone Fleets except Three, Six, and Nine will attack the enemy on my command
- All super-battleships will join the attack
- All super-fortresses to defend the flanks
- Deactivate battle force fields,'

Fleet Operations, 'Yes, Sir.'

Nearly two million vessels shot forward in their quest to destroy The Empire fleets.

It was probably the worst decision that Admiral Mustard had ever made as more than a million Empire ships attacked them from the rear. Then, to make it worse, The Empire had re-opened the portal, and thousands of battleships were arriving. The Galactium forces were surrounded and being crushed in a classic vice manoeuvre.

Admiral Mustard, 'My orders:

- Divisions Five, Thirteen and Fourteen to join the main Fleet ASAP
- All remaining drones to join the main Fleet ASAP
- Super-fortresses to join the main Fleet ASAP
- Divisions Two, Four, Five, Ten, Twelve, Thirteen, Fourteen and Nineteen to form a circle

- All Drone Fleets to form an outer circle
- Forts and super-fortresses to form a circle between the drones and ships of the line
- Super-battleships to maintain inner-circle position.'

Fleet Operations, 'Yes, sir.'

Admiral Mustard thought to himself, 'Nothing is new. We are now a wagon train in a circle fighting off the Indians. Now he needed to call for help. But would the calvary get here in time?'

Admiral Mustard, 'Comms, get me Admiral Bumelton.'

Comms, 'Yes, Sir.'

Admiral Bumelton, 'You are not going to believe this. We are waiting for the enemy to arrive at Earth and Napoleon, but there is no sign of them.'

Admiral Mustard, 'I know where they are.'

Admiral Bumelton, 'How come?'

Admiral Mustard, 'They are surrounding us. We were just about to attack their main Fleet when almost a million bogies jumped us from behind.'

Admiral Bumelton, 'That's the worst possible time.'

Admiral Mustard, 'We are in a circle been attacked from all directions.'

Admiral Bumelton, 'In a circle?'

Admiral Mustard, 'Yes, I'm playing cowboys and Indians.'

Admiral Bumelton, 'Let's hope that it's not Custer's last stand.'

Admiral Mustard, 'Very droll. So, you need to collect all your forces and rescue us.'

Admiral Bumelton, 'OK, boss, I will see if I can fit that into my busy schedule.'

Admiral Mustard, 'I've had enough of your joviality, now come and rescue us.'

Admiral Bumelton, 'Hold your horses; we are on our way.'

Admiral Bumelton 'My orders:

- All Divisions and Fleets defending Earth and Napoleon will meet at the point agreed with Fleet Operations
- They will then form a single Fleet and rescue Admiral Mustard's task force

314

Location: On-board the Admiral of the Path's Flagship
Sequence of Events: 162

The Admiral of the Path, 'My fellow space commanders, we have got them. We have won.'

The Admiral of the Holy Relics, 'Are you sure?'

The Admiral of the Path, 'Of course. They have lost their ability to manoeuvre, which is fatal for any military force. We can sit outside of their sphere and lob our munitions at them.

Gradually they will be pushed into a smaller and smaller sphere.'

The Admiral of the Holy Relics, 'But they still have powerful weapons that are destroying our vessels.'

The Admiral of the Path, 'That's true, but our losses are being easily replaced by reinforcements. They cannot win.'

The Admiral of the Holy Relics, 'That's a relief.'

The Admiral of the Path, 'All we need now is patience, although there is one possible fly in the ointment.'

The Admiral of the Holy Relics, 'What is that?'

The Admiral of the Path, 'There is another Hotman force that has been established to combat our second fleet. They are probably on their way here to rescue their brothers.'

The Admiral of the Holy Relics, 'Then we need to give them a very hot reception.'

The Admiral of the Path, 'We need to withdraw some of our forces without the Hotheads noticing, and along with the reinforcements, we can ambush the rescuers. They are bound to be in a hurry, and as a consequence, they will lack caution.'

The Admiral of the Holy Relics, 'I will set a trap for you.'

The Admiral of the Path, 'You are a gentleman.'

Location: On-board Admiral Mustard's Flagship
Sequence of Events: 163

Admiral Mustard, 'Update me.'
Fleet Operations, 'Yes, Sir:

- The circle structure is operational, but we are in a somewhat desperate situation. We are losing vessels at a rate of five to one
- The enemy is still receiving reinforcements, making the odds against us even worse
- Admiral Bumelton is only a few hours away
- If he takes any longer, we will need to consider a break-out.'

Admiral Mustard was betting on Admiral Bumelton getting there on time.
Admiral Mustard, 'What are the stats?'
Fleet Operations, 'You won't like them, Sir. They are on the screen:

Resources	Total	Current Total
Division 2	130,000	81,000
Division 4	130,000	62,000
Division 5	130,000	69,000
Division 7	130,000	74,000
Division 9	130,000	59,000
Division 10	130,000	76,000
Division 12	130,000	87,000
Division 13	130,000	56,000
Division 14	130,000	58,000
Division 15	130,000	67,000
Drone Fleet 1	100,000	38,000
Drone Fleet 2	100,000	37,000
Drone Fleet 3	100,000	41,000
Drone Fleet 4	100,000	28,000
Drone Fleet 5	100,000	47,000
Drone Fleet 6	100,000	39,000
Drone Fleet 7	100,000	46,000
Drone Fleet 8	100,000	37,000

Drone Fleet 9	100,000	45,000
Drone Fleet 10	100,000	36,000
Drone Fleet 11	100,000	58,000
Drone Fleet 12	100,000	41,000
Drone Fleet 13	100,000	36,000
Drone Fleet 14	100,000	50,000
Drone Fleet 15	100,000	32,000
Drone Fleet 16	100,000	38,000
Drone Fleet 17	100,000	72,000
Drone Fleet 18	100,000	39,000
Drone Fleet 19	100,000	28,000
Drone Fleet 20	100,000	41,000
Grand Total	3,300,000	1,519,000
Total Losses		1,782,000

Admiral Mustard, 'How did that happen?' He held his head in his hands. 'What's The Empire position?'

Resource	Total	Current Total
Fleet 1	860,000	211,000
Fleet 2	860,000	340,000
Fleet 3	860,000	301,000
Fleet 4	860,000	360,000
Fleet 5	860,000	74,000
Reinforcements		480,000
Second Fleet		1,000,000
Grand Total	4,300,000	2,766,000
Total losses		2,566,000

Fleet Operations, 'The loss figures are correct, but the figures are rather misleading because of the reinforcements and the arrival of their second fleet.'

Location: On-Board Admiral Bumelton's Flagship
Sequence of Events: 164

Admiral Bumelton's Fleet was quite formidable, with over three-quarter of a million vessels. He imagined his Fleet bursting through the enemy encirclement, rescuing his boss, and gaining boasting rights for the rest of his life.

In his effort to achieve maximum speed, the force fields and automatic defence systems had been turned off. Every second was costing lives, but so was his failure to maintain a level of caution.

As his Fleet entered a dwarf star system, they were pounced on. One million and two hundred thousand Empire vessels fired everything they had at the incoming Galactium Fleet.

Admiral Bumelton was killed instantly along with nearly half of the Fleet. A firefight entailed, but The Galactium forces were outgunned. Most of the friendly aliens decided that retreat was the order of the day.

It looked like the cavalry were not going to make it, and perhaps it was Custer's last stand after all.

Location: On-board Admiral Mustard's Flagship
Sequence of Events: 165

Fleet Operations, 'Admiral, I have some bad news.'

Admiral Mustard, 'That's the last thing I need.'

Fleet Operations, 'It would appear that Admiral Bumelton's Fleet has been ambushed and effectively destroyed.'

Admiral Mustard, 'That's not possible.'

Fleet Operations, 'And sadly Admiral Bumelton has been killed.'

Admiral Mustard, 'George can't be dead.'

Fleet Operations, 'The pressure on the circle is getting worse. As they force us to concentrate, it dramatically improves their kill rate.

There have also been several other admirals who have been killed.'

Admiral Mustard, 'Don't tell me, I'm working on a way out.'

Location: On-board Admiral Mustard's Flagship
Sequence of Events: 166

Admiral Mustard, 'AI Central, we need to initiate our emergency time plan.'

AI Central, 'I'm not sure if this is what you would call an acceptable or even a responsible use of TIME. We are guardians and probably should not be using it for our benefit.'

Admiral Mustard, 'Fuck off.'

AI Central, 'OK, at what point do you want to go back to?'

Admiral Mustard, 'To the point where we have just beaten their second attack, and there is pressure on me to go on the offensive. I also need my memories of what happened before.'

AI Central, 'Give me twenty minutes, and you will be back. Good luck this time.'

Fleet Operations, 'Admiral, if we are going to make a break-out, it better be sooner rather than later as the pressure is increasing. It looks like the fleet that defeated Admiral Bumelton is adding their firepower to that already directed at us.'

Admiral Mustard, 'Are reinforcements still coming through?'

Fleet Operations, 'No, they seem to have stopped.'

Admiral Mustard, 'Have we found any way of identifying their leader's vessel?'

Fleet Operations, 'Yes, we think the admirals have those three lights on their old-fashioned tail fins.'

Then there was an almost imperceptible rush of air.

Location: On-board Admiral Mustard's Flagship
Sequence of Events: 167

To his relief, Admiral Mustard was back in time, at just the point he wanted.

His previous self had been under a lot of pressure to go on the offensive from Fleet Operations and his merry band of admirals.

Admiral Mustard, 'Comms, please put me on the public address system.'

Comms, 'Yes, Sir. The system is now yours.'

Admiral Mustard, 'Dear colleagues, old and young, junior and senior, we have performed well, really well. There are those amongst you who would like us to attack but now is not the right time:

- The enemy is far from defeated
- They will get their portal working again, and reinforcements will arrive in great numbers
- Their second fleet could come to the aid of this fleet
- There is no point wasting lives on an attack when we can still let them come at us.

Thank you for all your efforts and good luck to all.'

The crew wondered why the admiral made this speech as it was not his usual style.

Admiral Mustard, 'Is the battle force field still in place?'

Fleet Operations, 'Yes, Sir.'

Admiral Mustard, 'Can we identify the five vessels with the three lights on their old-fashioned tail fins?'

Fleet Operations, 'We will work on it.'

They were wondering if the admiral had gone mad.

Admiral Mustard, 'That is urgent. Please give it the highest priority.'

Fleet Operations, 'Yes, Sir.'

Admiral Mustard, 'Comms, get me Admiral Bumelton.'

Comms, 'Yes, Sir.'

Admiral Bumelton, 'How is it going?'

Admiral Mustard, 'It is so good to hear your voice. Yep, we are in a good position, but I have a lot of information for you. I can't tell you how I got it, but it is correct.

As you know, you projected the trajectories of The Empire fleets as Earth, Napoleon, Dragonia, Lovelace and a barren planet where the Gods of the Underworld are supposed to live.'

Admiral Bumelton, 'That's correct.'

Admiral Mustard, 'You then sent three Fleets to defend Earth and two to defend Napoleon.'

Admiral Bumelton, 'That's also correct.'

Admiral Mustard, 'And again, as you know, The Empire fleets never arrived as they have been re-directed to attack us. You learn this, and you rush to assist us. In your rush, you went for speed, and you turned off the force fields and the automatic defence systems.'

Admiral Bumelton, 'That's not like me.'

Admiral Mustard, 'But you justify it by the precarious position of my Fleet. You are then trapped and destroyed in a dwarf star system.'

Admiral Bumelton, 'OK, assuming that I accept this as being is correct, what do you want me to do?'

Admiral Mustard, 'I've been pondering that. I need you to eliminate as many of their ships as possible, but my inclination is for you to follow them, but at all costs, avoid any traps.

I might need you to join us. We need to keep in close contact.'

Admiral Bumelton, 'I'm yours to command.'

Location: On-board the Admiral of the Path's Flagship
Sequence of Events: 168

The Admiral of the Path, 'No one told us that they had stealth technology.'

The Admiral of the Holy Relics, 'It was in the report.'

The Admiral of the Spirt, 'No one reads those reports.'

The Admiral of the Holy Relics, 'I did. It mentioned their stealth technology, Godfire, super battleships and fortresses and other wonders.'

The Admiral of the Pontification, 'I never saw the report.'

The Admiral of the Holy Relics, 'It was circulated to all of us.'

The Admiral of the Pontification, 'I tell you, I never saw it.'

The Admiral of the Path, 'My fellow military masters, we need to move on. We have now lost two and a half million vessels.'

The Admiral of the Spirt, 'No one cares how many vessels we lose as long as we win.'

The Admiral of the Path, 'Exactly. I'm going to propose that we use the second fleet to attack the rear of our enemy. They won't be expecting that.'

The Admiral of the Holy Relics, 'I'm not sure if I could agree to that.'

The Admiral of the Path, 'Why not?'

The Admiral of the Holy Relics, 'It's not following our orders'

The Admiral of the Path, 'If you return without a win, you are dead. We will all be dead. So go with us, or we will kill you.'

The Admiral of the Holy Relics, 'I understand.'

The Admiral of the Path, 'Are you with us?'

The Admiral of the Holy Relics, 'I have no choice.'

The Admiral of the Path, 'Master of Telephonic Communications, put me through to the five captains attacking their planets.'

The Master of Telephonic Communications, 'Of course, my Supreme Admiral. Should I include the fleet following the Path?'

The Admiral of the Path, 'Absolutely'

After a lot of unns of time, the connections were made.

The Admiral of the Path, 'Fellow members of the Fleet, you have done well, and you will be rewarded. Military reasons dictate that your objective must be changed.'

Captain 1342 of the Path, 'Sir, I'm sure that I speak on behalf of the other captains. Our instructions are unambiguous.'

The Admiral of the Path, 'Am I not your admiral?'

Captain 1342 of the Path, 'You are indeed, Sir, and a very exalted admiral.'

The Admiral of the Path, 'So you recognise my authority?'

Captain 1342 of the Path, 'Yes, I do, Sir.'

The Admiral of the Path, 'In that case, you will cease your current task and attack the main Hotman fleet. Co-ordinates will be sent to you. Do you understand?'

Captain 1342 of the Path, 'Yes, Sir.'

Location: On-board Admiral Mustard's Flagship
Sequence of Events: 169

Admiral Mustard, 'Give me the latest stats.'
    Fleet Operations, 'They are the same as a few minutes ago.'
    Admiral Mustard, 'Give them to me again.'
    Fleet Operations, 'Yes, Sir. They are on the screen now:

Resources	Total	Current Total
Division 2	130,000	129,000
Division 4	130,000	92,000
Division 5	130,000	129,000
Division 7	130,000	124,000
Division 9	130,000	119,000
Division 10	130,000	126,000
Division 12	130,000	107,000
Division 13	130,000	98,000
Division 14	130,000	118,000
Division 15	130,000	130,000
Drone Fleet 1	100,000	68,000
Drone Fleet 2	100,000	77,000
Drone Fleet 3	100,000	61,000
Drone Fleet 4	100,000	98,000
Drone Fleet 5	100,000	57,000
Drone Fleet 6	100,000	89,000
Drone Fleet 7	100,000	96,000
Drone Fleet 8	100,000	97,000
Drone Fleet 9	100,000	85,000
Drone Fleet 10	100,000	76,000
Drone Fleet 11	100,000	88,000
Drone Fleet 12	100,000	91,000
Drone Fleet 13	100,000	96,000
Drone Fleet 14	100,000	100,000
Drone Fleet 15	100,000	82,000
Drone Fleet 16	100,000	88,000
Drone Fleet 17	100,000	92,000
Drone Fleet 18	100,000	89,000

Drone Fleet 19	100,000	88,000
Drone Fleet 20	100,000	91,000
Grand Total	3,300,000	2,881,000
Total Losses		419,000

Empire Losses (estimates):

Resource	Total	Current Total
Fleet 1	860,000	310,000
Fleet 2	860,000	440,000
Fleet 3	860,000	390,000
Fleet 4	860,000	470,000
Fleet 5	860,000	124,000
Grand Total	4,300,000	1,734,000
Total losses		2,566,000

Admiral Mustard was pleased to see that they were as he expected.

Admiral Mustard, 'My orders:

- Divisions Nine and Ten to join Division Five
- All three Divisions will protect the Fleet from an attack in the rear
- Drone Fleets Twelve, Thirteen, Fifteen, Sixteen, Seventeen, Nineteen and Twenty to join the reserve and protect the Fleet from an attack in the rear
- Fifty per cent of all super battleships and super fortresses to protect the rear of the Fleet
- All stealthed fighters to attack the enemy with a special objective of destroying the five ships housing their admirals
- Special Ops to install further stealthed force fields
- Special Ops to destroy the enemy portal if it re-opens
- Stealthed battlecruisers to lie in wait to destroy the enemy portal if it re-opens if instructed to do so by Special Ops
- The drones in Production should be used to defend Earth.'

Fleet Operations, 'Yes, Sir.'

His orders totally mystified them, but time and time again, he had been right, so there was a high level of faith in his orders.

Location: On-board the Admiral of the Path's Flagship
Sequence of Events: 170

The Admiral of the Path had expected the Hotmans to attack. Their leader was either very astute or cowardly, or perhaps both. They now have the numbers and technology, so why didn't they attack. He decided to provoke them, but that force field was still in the way.

He needed to keep the Hotman forces occupied until the second fleet arrived.

While he was wondering what to do, there were a series of explosions throughout The Empire fleet. The Galactium fighters, single-person stealthed, micro-spacecraft, had entered their space, selected their targets, and had destroyed over two hundred vessels, including two of their admirals.

The Master of Telephonic Communications, 'Dear Admiral of the Path, I have to tell you that the Admiral of the Holy Relics and the Admiral of the Spirit have both been assassinated.'

The Admiral of the Path, 'By who?'

The Master of Telephonic Communications, 'By an unknown assailant.'

The Admiral of the Path, 'Come on, two hundred ships have been attacked, so it was clearly the Hotmen, but how are they doing it?'

The Master of Telephonic Communications, 'Dear Admiral of the Path, I suspect that their stealth technology is better than we expected.'

The Admiral of the Path, 'How did they know that those two ships contained admirals? We thought that we had removed all differentiators.'

The Master of Telephonic Communications, 'Dear Supreme Admiral of the Path, I have further bad news. The Admiral of the Book has been killed along with about two hundred other craft.'

The Admiral of the Path, 'Get me transferred to another craft now. immediately.'

The Master of Telephonic Communications, 'Of course, Mighty Leader, it will be done.'

The Admiral of the Path, 'And find out when the portal will be fixed. We need those reinforcements.'

The fighters had to return, as their munitions were exhausted.

Admiral Mustard, 'How did it go?'

327

Commander Hawash, 'We believe that we destroyed four hundred Empire ships.'

Admiral Mustard, 'That has been confirmed. Well done.'

Commander Hawash, 'What's more exciting is that we think we took out three admirals.'

Admiral Mustard, 'Spot on, give your guys a drink on me.'

Commander Hawash, 'Thank you, Admiral.'

Admiral Mustard, 'Have a rest, refuel and re-arm and prepare for a second attack.'

Commander Hawash, 'Yes, Sir.'

The Master of Telephonic Communications, 'Sir, your new craft is ready.'

The Admiral of the Path, 'About time.'

The Master of Telephonic Communications, 'Should I warn the Admiral of the Pontification?'

The Admiral of the Path, 'I don't think that will be necessary.'

The Master of Telephonic Communications, 'My admiral, I've checked on the portal, and it should be operational shortly.'

In all honesty, he had no idea when it would be operational again.

The Admiral of the Path, 'About time. Then he had a flashback where he saw ships pouring through the portal and the enemy scum in some sort of circle. He decided that it had to be a dream.'

The Special Ops team could see that the portal was almost operational, but they waited for the first ship to come through before setting the explosives. They were surprised at how great the big bang was. What they didn't know was that the first ship coming through was a munitions storage ship. Equally, they didn't realise that thousands of the following vessels were destroyed by the domino effect of the explosion.

The stealthed battlecruisers weren't needed, and their commander, Denise Pally, decided to cause some damage on the return trip. In the scheme of things, it wasn't much, but every little bit helps, and they returned safely.

The Master of Telephonic Communications, 'My admiral, I'm pleased to say that the portal was fixed, but then I regret to say that it has been destroyed by unknown assailants.'

The Admiral of the Path, 'Stop calling them unknown assailants. It must have been stealthed Hotmans again.'

The Master of Telephonic Communications, 'Yes, my admiral.'

The Admiral of the Path, 'So we are not going to get any reinforcements. We will have to get this job done ourselves, and we can't operate effectively with The Hotman scum walking freely amongst us.'

The Master of Telephonic Communications, 'What can we do about it, my admiral?'

The Admiral of the Path, 'We need to attack them. Send out ships to find gaps in the force field.'

Location: On-board Admiral Mustard's Flagship
Sequence of Events: 171

Fleet Operations, 'Admiral, we have detected Empire ships scouting the battle force field.'

Admiral Mustard, 'They are obviously looking for gaps. How many gaps are there?'

Fleet Operations, 'There are two major gaps and about a dozen smaller ones.'

Admiral Mustard, 'Can they be turned on and off remotely?'

Fleet Operations, 'I believe so, but I will need to get that confirmed.'

Admiral Mustard, 'Can you find out how much more we could install?'

Fleet Operations, 'Of course, Admiral.'

Admiral Mustard, 'Comms, get me Admiral Bumelton.'

Comms, 'Yes, Sir.'

Admiral Bumelton, 'How is it going?'

Admiral Mustard, 'All good, this end. How are your friends?'

Admiral Bumelton, 'We are still following them with our full Fleet. Some of the alien forces are struggling to keep up.'

Admiral Mustard, 'Does The Empire fleet know that you are following them?'

Admiral Bumelton, 'They must do, but they are not showing any interest.'

Admiral Mustard, 'We had outstanding success with our stealthed force field. The Empire ships just crashed into it, destroying at least fifty per cent of their fleet. I wondered if it is worth trying it again?'

Admiral Bumelton, 'I don't see why not, but you are going to need exact coordinates.'

Admiral Mustard, 'Exactly, can your guys work on that and update our Special Ops guys?'

Admiral Bumelton, 'Of course.'

Admiral Mustard, 'By the way, we have been using stealth fighters against them. If you wanted, you could knock off any stragglers.'

Admiral Bumelton, 'Great idea, that will motivate some of our captains.'

Admiral Mustard, 'Talk to you later.'

Location: Angel Delight
Sequence of Events: 172

Angelina, 'This must be the slowest ship ever in the fucking history of space.'

Angela, 'It's actually quite fast.'

Angelina, 'Why couldn't we just whizzbang there like usual?'

Angela, 'I don't know where "there" is. I need to have an exact reference point to teleport to. We are just going to outer space.'

Angelina, 'Why didn't we pick on a particular ship?'

Angela, 'Because we need our freedom of action. Anyway, how do you think the humans would react if two naked angels, two goddesses and a witch just arrived on their flight deck?'

Angelina, 'I can see where you are coming from now.'

Angela, 'A key question is, what are you going to do when we get there?'

Angelina, 'To be honest, I have no idea, as usual. Somehow, I know what to do when I get there. Anyway, let's focus on getting there.'

Location: On-board Admiral Mustard's Flagship
Sequence of Events: 173

Fleet Operations, 'Admiral, I'm not sure what has happened, but the battle force field is down, and their entire fleet is coming at us.'

Admiral Mustard, 'Are we ready?'

Fleet Operations, 'Yes, sir, although we have less fire-power than usual as a large part of the Fleet is facing in the wrong direction.'

Admiral Mustard, 'Contact Special Ops and find out why the force field went down. Was it something The Empire did?'

Admiral Mustard, 'My orders:

- Prepare to engage the enemy
- Make full use of Godfire
- Stand your ground.'

There wasn't much more he could do in the circumstances.

The advanced units of The Empire fleet were in range, and firing on both sides had begun. Somewhat ironically, The Empire fleet seemed better organised after the removal of three admirals. Life is like that sometimes.

Fleet Operations, 'Admiral, Special Ops said they had overloaded the battle force field system after installing the second one. They want to know which force field they should give preference to.'

Admiral Mustard, 'Tell them that we fucking need the preference now.'

Fleet Operations, 'Yes, Sir.'

Admiral Mustard, 'Then tell Admiral Bumelton that his force field won't be ready in time.'

Fleet Operations, 'Yes, Sir.'

The battle force field proved to be a very effective weapon. Turning it on unexpectedly caused lots of interesting effects. Empire ships were caught halfway through, others exploded on contact, and automated firing systems started shooting at each other.

The Galactium forces were shocked, but they knew what to do. Their training kicked in, and their onslaught on the Empire ships that had got through was devastating. It wasn't long before there were no targets.

Location: On-board the Admiral of the Path's Flagship
Sequence of Events: 174

The Admiral of the Path wasn't sure if the force field tactic was deliberate or just circumstantial. He thought the latter, but he couldn't be sure.

His force wasn't strong enough now to take on the Hotmans. He was going to have to rely on the second fleet, which should be here shortly. Then he thought, 'Why wait for them?'

The Admiral of the Path, 'Master of Telephonic Communications, put me through to each captain.'

Master of Telephonic Communications, 'Of course, Your Excellency.'

The Admiral of the Path, 'Noble captains, we have had tremendous success against the Hotman scum, but now is the time to join our brothers in the second fleet. We will bypass the Hotman force field, join the second fleet and destroy the infidels.'

In his mind, he could hear the cheers of the captains. In reality, the captains were totally demoralised by the ineptitude of their leaders, but they had not been conditioned to question but to follow, and that is precisely what they did.

Location: On-board Admiral Mustard's Flagship
Sequence of Events: 175

Fleet Operations, 'Admiral, things are happening on The Empire front. It looks like they are preparing to leave.'

Admiral Mustard, 'I think you are right. After the last pasting we gave them, they have probably realised that they are not large enough now to take us on.'

Fleet Operations, 'It was a pasting, but there was a fair amount of luck involved.'

Admiral Mustard, 'What did Napoleon say about generals? Something like if it is a toss-up between competence and luck, give me a lucky general every time.

So, the big question is, where are they going?'

Fleet Operations, 'There are probably three options:

1. Going home
2. Attacking our planets
3. Joining their second fleet
Where do you want to put your money?'

Admiral Mustard, 'They can't go home without a victory. They are probably too weak to attack our planets, or they think they are too weak. So, it must be option three.'

Admiral Mustard,' Give me the stats.'

Fleet Operations, 'Yes, Sir. They are on the screen now:

Resources	Total	Current Total
Division 2	130,000	119,000
Division 4	130,000	81,000
Division 5	130,000	129,000
Division 7	130,000	104,000
Division 9	130,000	119,000
Division 10	130,000	126,000
Division 12	130,000	87,000
Division 13	130,000	68,000
Division 14	130,000	88,000
Division 15	130,000	130,000

Drone Fleet 1	100,000	55,000
Drone Fleet 2	100,000	63,000
Drone Fleet 3	100,000	41,000
Drone Fleet 4	100,000	78,000
Drone Fleet 5	100,000	57,000
Drone Fleet 6	100,000	74,000
Drone Fleet 7	100,000	66,000
Drone Fleet 8	100,000	97,000
Drone Fleet 9	100,000	75,000
Drone Fleet 10	100,000	46,000
Drone Fleet 11	100,000	52,000
Drone Fleet 12	100,000	49,000
Drone Fleet 13	100,000	96,000
Drone Fleet 14	100,000	80,000
Drone Fleet 15	100,000	82,000
Drone Fleet 16	100,000	58,000
Drone Fleet 17	100,000	82,000
Drone Fleet 18	100,000	79,000
Drone Fleet 19	100,000	68,000
Drone Fleet 20	100,000	71,000
Grand Total	3,300,000	2,420,000
Total Losses		880,000

Empire Losses (estimates):

Resource	Total	Current Total
Fleet 1	860,000	111,000
Fleet 2	860,000	421,000
Fleet 3	860,000	187,000
Fleet 4	860,000	170,000
Fleet 5	860,000	45,000
Grand Total	4,300,000	934,000
Total losses		3,366,000

Admiral Mustard, 'My orders:

- Special Ops to activate second battle force field ASAP

- All forces to realign formation to meet oncoming second fleet
- Standard defensive formation
- Send out scouts to detect on-coming fleet
- Re-arm, as necessary.'

Fleet Operations, 'Yes, Sir.'

Admiral Mustard, 'Comms get me Admiral Bumelton.'

Comms, 'Yes, Sir.'

Admiral Bumelton, 'We were making good time, but The Empire fleet has slowed down for some reason.'

Admiral Mustard, 'Well, our Empire friends have disappeared. We suspect that they are planning to join the fleet you have been following.'

Admiral Bumelton, 'That explains why they have slowed down.'

Admiral Mustard, 'How many assets have you got?'

Admiral Bumelton, 'With our friends, about nine hundred thousand, perhaps a little more.'

Admiral Mustard, 'I've got two million and four hundred thousand vessels still.'

Admiral Bumelton, 'Wow, that's pretty impressive.'

Admiral Mustard, 'With the two fleets together, The Empire will still have two million vessels. So, what should we do?'

Admiral Bumelton, 'I was wondering if we should still attack their home world, but who knows what we will find there, and you won't have the edge regarding numbers.'

Admiral Mustard, 'I agree. We need to stick together. But the sad thing is that we are going to have two huge navies that are going to pound each other to death.'

Admiral Bumelton, 'I can only agree, but what's the alternative?'

Admiral Mustard, 'And we are up against an enemy who really doesn't care what happens to their crews.'

Admiral Bumelton, 'Well, tactically, we are in an excellent position. They have two million vessels that are going to attack a larger foe. You have the advantage of being larger and being the defender. Then I will be attacking them from the rear. Their fate is sealed.'

Admiral Mustard, 'But we will lose more than a million men and women,'

Admiral Bumelton, 'That, I'm afraid, is war.'

There, in front of Admiral Bumelton's Fleet, was the entire Empire fleet, two million ships against his one million.

Location: On-board the Admiral of the Path's Flagship
Sequence of Events: 176

The Admiral of the Path, 'Kill every one of them, kill the fucking lot. Don't let a single infidel live.'

Admiral Bumelton's Fleet more or less collided with the enemy. Nukes, particle weapons, atomisers, proton beams, everything was thrown at each other. The Empire had the advantage both in numbers and in preparation.

The drones proved their worth, but the rat-finks were exceptionally skilled at close proximity fighting. No mercy was shown on either side. The human forces generally benefitted from better strategy and tactics, but this was primaeval cut and thrust murder.

The Galactium could not use its more potent weapons, as they were likely to hit their own side. The rats had no such qualms and were also quite happy to use ramming techniques.

Admiral Bumelton decided that the best option was to run for it. They needed to run to the safety of their comrades.

Admiral Bumelton, 'My orders:

• All vessels to cease fighting and flee toward Admiral Mustard's Fleet.'

Fleet Operations, 'Yes, Sir,'

It would have been a great strategy if the battle force field was not directly in their path.

It was a disaster equivalent to the one that The Empire had experienced. Ship after ship, battleships, battlecruisers, destroyers, frigates, carriers, forts, and drones created a massive wrecker's yard in outer space. At least half a million naval staff were killed instantly. Those that survived were being picked off by The Empire fleet that had turned to pursue their hated enemy.

The dragon fleet was totally destroyed along with most of the free forces. The Galactium had let them down, big time.

Every Galactium admiral in Admiral Bumelton's Fleet had been killed.

The Admiral of the Path had never been so excited. It found it especially ironic that the Hotman scum had been destroyed by their own technology. What a wonderful day. What glory. He decided that he would roast one of the chambermaids alive for dinner to celebrate. That always cheered him up.

Now all he had to do was kill the rest of those bastards, but he knew that he was on a roll.

Of Admiral Bumelton's Fleet, only thirty-six vessels managed to escape, and they were being pursued.

At least they managed to update Fleet Operations.

Location: On-board Admiral Mustard's Flagship
Sequence of Events: 177

Fleet Operations, 'Admiral, I have some terrible news. Admiral Bumelton's Fleet has been destroyed.'

Admiral Mustard, 'Not again.'

Fleet Operations had no idea what he was talking about.

Admiral Mustard, 'What happened?'

Fleet Operations, 'The entire Fleet crashed into the combined Empire fleet which was waiting for them. There was a considerable amount of close combat fighting, and Admiral Bumelton decided to flee to the safety of our Fleet. Unfortunately, they flew straight into the battle force field.'

Admiral Mustard, 'Had we informed them that the battle force field was activated?'

Fleet Operations, 'No, Sir.'

Admiral Mustard, 'How many survivors?'

Fleet Operations, 'Thirty-two ships, and they are being pursued. I've sent out some forces to bring them home.'

Admiral Mustard, 'What about Admiral Bumelton?'

Fleet Operations, 'I'm sorry to say that every admiral in that Fleet has been killed, Sir.' She said it with tears running down her cheeks.

Admiral Mustard, 'Are our defences ready?'

Fleet Operations, 'Yes, Sir.'

Admiral Mustard, 'AI Central, we need to initiate our emergency time plan again.'

AI Central, 'I said the first time that this was unacceptable behaviour for the custodians of TIME.'

Admiral Mustard, 'And last time I said fuck off, and I'm saying it again.'

AI Central, 'I warn you, there will be consequences.'

Admiral Mustard, 'There are always consequences. Now get the job done.'

AI Central, 'OK, for the second time, what point do you want to go back to?'

Admiral Mustard, 'To the point where Admiral Bumelton is following The Empire's second fleet.'

AI Central, 'OK, give me another twenty minutes, and you will be back. Better luck this time.'

Location: On-board the Admiral of the Path's Flagship
Sequence of Events: 178

The Admiral of the Path, 'Onward, the Gods of the Underworld, are with us. It is our destiny to remove the Hotmans from our universe. The path will not be contaminated.

There is no need to assemble into a formation. We will drive straight into their fleet and eliminate them once and for all.'

Then there was an almost imperceptible rush of air, again.

Location: On-board Admiral Mustard's Flagship
Sequence of Events: 179

Admiral Mustard, 'Comms, get me Admiral Bumelton.'

Comms, 'Yes, sir.'

Admiral Bumelton, 'Hi Jack, we were making good time, but The Empire fleet has slowed down for some reason.'

Admiral Mustard, 'I have some information that I can't share with you at the moment, but it is imperative that you cease chasing The Empire fleet and join us.'

Admiral Bumelton, 'But Jack, we have got them just where we want them. Between us, we can crush them and eliminate our problems in one fell swoop.'

Admiral Mustard, 'My orders:

• Admiral Bumelton and his associated Fleets will cease following the Empire fleet and will join my Fleet immediately.'

Fleet Operations, 'Yes, Sir.'

There was genuine joy when the two fleets met. Fleet Operations had quite a challenge merging them.

Admiral Bumelton, 'So why did you stop me chasing them?'

Admiral Mustard, 'There is a stealthed battle force field directly in their path. I was anxious that you might have hit it.'

Admiral Bumelton, 'But you could have told me to stop and then destroy any of their surviving vessels.'

Admiral Mustard, 'I hadn't thought of that.'

Admiral Bumelton, 'Jack, I've known you long enough to know when you are lying.'

Admiral Mustard, 'I promise that I will tell you the truth, but not now.'

Admiral Bumelton, 'Why not now?'

Admiral Mustard, 'Because you won't like it, and we have still got a major battle to fight.' .

Admiral Bumelton, 'This is not one of your time-travel games.'

Admiral Mustard, 'You are on the right track, but we need to prepare ourselves.'

Location: On-board the Admiral of the Path's Flagship
Sequence of Events: 180

The Admiral of the Path, 'No, it's not possible, not again.'

He couldn't believe that he had fallen into the same trap for the second time. His belief was soon shattered as his brain was smashed against the control unit.

It was hard to believe that one force field could do so much damage and cause the death of so many individuals. Every one of The Empire admirals had been killed, but the ratty underlings knew their duty, and the survivors were preparing to reform so that they could continue the war against the infidels.

They had to carry on because they always won. It was going to be an uphill battle as the numbers were now seriously against them: three million, three hundred vessels against half a million, but victory belonged to the Empire.

Admiral Mustard, 'I can't believe that they are still coming.'

Admiral Bumelton, 'They must know that we will annihilate them.'

Admiral Mustard, 'But then another fleet will arrive, and we will defeat them and then it will continue ad infinitum.'

Admiral Bumelton, 'Basically, you are saying that the only way we can defeat them is species genocide, and I don't think I could live with that.'

Admiral Mustard, 'Perhaps it's just survival of the fittest. Regardless, we need a way of destroying The Empire's control mechanisms. Once that has been achieved, we can defeat them.'

Location: On-board Admiral Mustard's Flagship
Sequence of Events: 181

Fleet Operations, 'Admiral, a solitary Galactium ship has entered our space sending out very powerful energy signals.'

Admiral Mustard, 'What type of energy signal?'

Fleet Operations, 'Our systems can't define it.'

Admiral Mustard, 'Is it dangerous?'

Fleet Operations, 'It doesn't appear to be, but my screen has just been taken over.'

In fact, every display on every ship, both Empire and Galactium, had been taken over, and the following message was displayed:

'Erin Yes kill mischief.'

Then, Angelina spoke on every speaker system they had. 'The Erinyes are going to destroy the implants in the rat brains. The mischief of rats will be free.'

Admiral Mustard, 'What's a mischief?'

Admiral Bumelton, 'It's the collective name for a group of rats.'

Hezebel, Alecto and Desmonda did as they were instructed by Angelina, and every rat-fink in The Empire fleet was suddenly free. Not that they knew how to cope with freedom, but at the very least, the battle was over.

The Erinyes killed the mischief.

Location: On-board Admiral Mustard's Flagship
Sequence of Events: 182

Admiral Mustard and Bumelton sat down with Angelina and Angela. The Erinyes were in the room, but Angelina had put them to sleep. Admiral Bumelton still found it difficult to cope with two naked vaginas just opposite him, but he had a book strategically placed on his lap to avoid any embarrassment.

Angelina, 'Mr Mustard, we need your help.'

Admiral Mustard, 'I got the impression that you can handle most things yourself.'

Angela, 'We need your help to travel through The Empire, freeing all of the societies and even The Empire inhabitants from the control units in their brains.'

Admiral Mustard, 'What help do you need?'

Angela. 'We need transport and protection. We need your doctors to help with psychological problems. We need your bureaucrats to help run their societies. We need your policemen to maintain control.

It's your chance for The Galactium to grow and develop and to establish an intergalactic civilisation based on trust, trade, and peace.

Anyway, you owe it to your daughter.'

Admiral Mustard, 'Why my daughter?'

Angela, 'She is our mistress, the one who has been guiding us.'

Angelina, 'You look surprised.'

Admiral Mustard, 'I'm more than surprised; I'm flabbergasted.'

Angelina, 'You should not be that surprised. You are the son of Zeus.'

Angela, 'What is your answer regarding the requested help?'

Admiral Mustard, 'I will have to discuss this with President Padfield, but I'm sure that the answer will be yes. I need to do it for my daughter.'

Angelina, 'Right answer.'

Admiral Mustard thought to himself, 'It might be the right answer, but what was he going to tell Edel?'

Location: An Anonymous Bar, Somewhere Seedy
Sequence of Events: 183

George, 'I think I'm in love with Angelina.'

Jack, 'I think that it is more likely that you are in love with her pussy.'

George, 'You might be right.'

They ordered their third drink of the night.

Jack, 'Anyway, we saved humanity again.'

George, 'That's our job. And this time, we did it fair and square. We took them on and beat them at their own game.'

Jack, 'You have never liked some of my tactics.'

George, 'You know me. I regard warfare as a bit like boxing. You hit each other until one wins. No clever tricks, no hitting under the belt. You know what I mean?'

Jack, 'I'm more interested in winning.'

George, 'But at what cost. I wouldn't be sitting here today if I thought we used trickery of any sort.'

They ordered their fourth drink.

George, 'Anyway, why did you stop me from destroying the enemy fleet?'

Jack, 'To stop you from being killed for the third time.'

George, 'What do you mean killed?'

Jack, 'Twice I had to roll back time to save you and the fleet.'

George, 'I don't believe you.'

Jack, 'Ask AI Central.'

George, 'So what you are saying is that I've got to pay for all the drinks tonight.'

Jack, 'That's the least you can do.'

They laughed and ordered some more drinks at George's expense.

The End

Other books by Alan Frost:

Admiral Mustard Series
> 1. Beware The Brakendeth
> 2. Beware The Nothemy
> 3. Beware The Humans
> 4. Beware The Future
> 5. Beware The Empire
> 6. Beware The Past

Merlin Series
> 1. The Battles of Malvern
> 2. The Struggles of Malvern

Other
> • Blind to the Consequences